WICKED SOUL

ANCIENT BLOOD: ONE

NORA ASH

ABOUT THE AUTHOR

Nora Ash writes thrilling romance and sexy paranormal fantasy.

Visit her website to learn more about her upcoming books.

WWW.NORA-ASH.COM

ONE

"*Ow*, what's *wrong* with you?" I aimed a futile kick at the burly guy manhandling me out of the back of the white van he'd tossed me in a good twenty minutes earlier.

A smarter girl would probably have been terrified at being kidnapped off the street, but I was mainly just furious.

"Let go of me, you goddamn fanatic!"

Then again, most girls didn't get tossed into the back of cross-riddled vans for their choice in reading material. Somehow, even as the big goon wrenched my bound hands up high behind my back and shoved me through the door of a house somewhere in the bad part of Chicago's suburbs, part of me still thought it was all some horrible joke. Any minute now, an over-excited TV host would jump out with a bunch of cameras and tell me I'd been pranked. *Haha.*

I looked around the inside of the house. There wasn't any light apart from the little that managed to seep in through the dirty windows, but from what I could see of the room we were in, no one had lived here for a very long time. There was no furniture, apart from a broken couch and a tipped-over coffee table in the far corner of the room, and both walls and flooring looked like they were rotting away.

"Time to learn what happens to filthy little vamp sluts," the guy who'd been driving the van sneered as he closed the door behind us.

"Jesus, the state of public education is as bad as the Internet says, huh? I swear to you, reading a paranormal romance novel is not the same as *actually* banging a vampire."

Yup, that was what had gotten me kidnapped

Reading a sexy vampire book at a cafe, minding my own business. I swear, this sort of thing could only happen to me.

"Shut your mouth, bitch," the goon behind me growled, giving me a hard shove that had me stumbling across the floor and face-planting against a heavy, wooden door. "Don't you dare take the Lord's name in vain!"

Okay, so not a game show then. I swallowed a

whimper of pain when he yanked me away from the door by my ponytail so he could unlock and open it.

I was pretty sure, despite the sorry state of American TV these days, that no candid camera would get away with physically abusing its unsuspecting contestants. The acrid taste of true fear burned in my throat when realization of how bad my situation truly was finally set in.

I gritted my teeth against the swell of panic in my chest when the newly opened door revealed a dark, narrow staircase leading down below ground level. I tried to throw myself back and away from the gaping chasm of darkness in front of me, but it was useless. My kidnappers simply gave me a shove between the shoulder blades, and thanks to my bound wrists, I didn't have any means of resisting.

Squealing, I stumbled down the stairs, only narrowly managing to keep on my feet, until I smacked up against another door, this one made of solid metal. Face first. Again.

The goon and his accomplice were right behind me, and a second later, I was shoved through yet another door. Pale light illuminated the walls of a large, concrete room. I stared open-mouthed at the many odd-looking weapons lining the walls—wooden stakes, crossbows, scary-looking knives. And among them, crosses and long metal chains of varying thicknesses. Just what the hell sort of place was this?

"The sun sets in two hours, deadwhore. If I were you, I'd spend that time praying for forgiveness," my kidnapper sneered. He pulled a knife and sliced through the zip-ties binding my wrists, then pointed at the far end of the room. "Get in."

I followed his finger with my eyes and saw a large, metal cage half-hidden behind a pile of junk. *Whoa, whoa, whoa.* Who the fuck had a cage in their basement? Just how many girls did they force into their little rape-cave because of their taste in smutty literature?

My frozen silence was met with a gentle, yet unmistakably threatening poke of a knife's point against the back of my neck.

"*In.*"

Slowly, I forced my feet to move toward the cage where the other guy was holding the cell door open for me. *How fucking gallant.*

I glared at him as he swung the gate shut with a clang, locking it behind me and taking a step back.

"How long do you plan on keeping me in here?" I demanded, feeling oddly relieved to have bars between us. It was an illusion of safety, of course, since they held the keys, but it was enough for me to find some of my anger again. And anger felt a lot better than fear.

"Oh, just for a couple of hours," the driver said, a cruel smirk on his face. "If you get bored, you can always see if you can wake up your new friend."

He nodded at something behind me, and I turned halfway around to see what the hell the crazy old goat was referring to.

And that was when I realized I wasn't alone in the cage.

A dark-haired young man who looked like he was in his early twenties sat cross-legged at the back of the cage on the bare concrete floor. His eyes were closed and he wasn't moving a muscle, a serene look on his face as if he was meditating or something.

Outraged, I spun back around to my kidnappers. "Great, so now you kidnap college kids? What did he do, watch *Van Helsing*? You sick fucks!"

Both men laughed, and I felt like I was missing some twisted joke. "Start begging God for forgiveness. You don't have much time left."

"What the hell is that supposed to mean?" I snapped, but they didn't answer me. Instead they turned around and left the room, the heavy metal door closing behind them. The keys rattled in the lock from the other side, and then I was alone with the meditating college kid.

I cussed and turned around, leaning heavily against the metal bars. What the hell sort of crazy whack jobs kidnapped people off the streets and locked them in their creepy basement?

I looked at the kid—or guy. A possibly twenty-one-year-old would likely take umbrage with being called a kid.

He still hadn't so much as cracked open an eyelid at the commotion of getting a new cellmate.

I pinched my lips in a disapproving frown. Nice to see that *someone* could keep their cool while being locked up by crazies. "Hey, hello?"

Not even a muscle spasm to indicate he'd heard me.

Was he in some sort of trance? Or was he just a complete asshole? I knelt down on the concrete in front of him so my face was less than five inches from his and stared intently at him. "Hello?"

Still no response.

I blew in his face. Perhaps not the most mature thing I could have done, but his complete lack of interest in my existence was just the tipping point. I'd just been kidnapped and manhandled, and he couldn't even take a break from being all hipster-zen? Hello, damsel in distress here!

A groan slipped past his full lips as he opened a single eye to a narrow slit.

"Don't... do that." It was hardly more than a whisper, and his eyelid immediately closed again.

His obvious grogginess scared me. Was he sick? Drugged? Just what on earth had they done to him?

"Are you all right?" My voice pitched shrilly with

worry, all thoughts about my own shitty situation vanishing. When he didn't respond, I slapped him across the face and gently shook his shoulders with both hands to make sure he didn't slip into unconsciousness. "You gotta stay with me, okay?"

Slowly, both his eyelids cracked open this time, revealing nearly black eyes with just a ring of blue, so much were his pupils blown.

"Shh, little one." He slowly lifted a hand from his knee and wrapped it loosely around my right wrist. Gently, he pried my hand off his shoulder before he let go again, his hand falling bonelessly back down in his lap. "Have to sleep... a little longer. Until... sunset."

Bewildered, I moved back a little so I wasn't breathing right in his face, but I stayed in my low crouch so I could study his blank features for clues. His hand had been very cold against my skin, and even though we were in a basement, it worried me. He clearly wasn't feeling well, and just what was everyone's obsession with sunset around here?

His pale face and the fact that he was hardly breathing made me worry he was seriously, fatally ill, and I somehow doubted the creeps who had locked us both in this cage would care to call an ambulance.

I rubbed my face in frustration and tried to recall what I'd learned about caring for possibly-dying people on my one and only first aid course nearly eight years ago. It was then that I realized he wasn't breathing at all.

"Omigoddess!" My pulse sped up to warp-speed as adrenaline kicked in, but it turned out my instincts were on point even if most of my conscious brain was busy freaking out.

With a swifter movement than was usual for me, I tackled my cellmate to the ground and pinched his nose shut before I put my lips on his and blew air into his lungs.

This time, his eyes opened wide as a cough shuddered through his body.

"Oh, thank the stars!" I gasped as I placed a hand on his chest, relieved beyond belief to feel his chest moving again. "You stopped breathing! You..."

But his chest *wasn't* moving.

I glanced from my hand against his completely still torso to his face. His eyes were still open, looking at me as if he couldn't quite comprehend that a stranger had just tried to perform CPR on him.

But he wasn't breathing.

And his heart wasn't beating, either.

It was in that moment that my brain finally decided to arrive at the party.

Sleeps until sundown, cold to the touch, doesn't breathe...

"Motherfucking *fuck!*" I flew backward and scrambled away from him until the bars at the other end of the cage pressed against my back, unable to take my eyes off his still form even as his eyes slid shut again.

Mother above!

I was locked in a cage with a... a *vampire!*

TWO

I'd always known vampires were real, of course.

Everyone did.

After they revealed their existence to humans in '72, everyone had been painfully aware that the undead walked among us.

It was just that I, like most people, had never seen one. And we counted ourselves lucky for it.

I stared at my once-again sleeping cellmate, unable to calm my racing pulse.

Suddenly, my kidnappers' snide remarks made gruesome sense. They'd tossed me in here to feed him. I was a goddamn *snack!*

Mother of all things holy, what was *wrong* with those people? Sure, I'd known they were crazy—kidnapping random people off the street kind of gives off that vibe.

But *this?* Feeding live humans to their... their pet vampire? Who even thought about keeping a pet vampire? *And why were they feeding him humans?*

I desperately searched the cage for something —*anything*—to defend myself, but there was nothing. They'd made sure there was nothing in there but him and me. And two hours until sunset.

I'd like to say that I spent the last two hours of my life MacGyvering a makeshift weapon strong enough to take on a vampire, or even meditating over my life's accomplishments, but I'd be lying.

I spent the entire time pressing my body up against the bars and quivering like a leaf, *I don't want to die!* running on repeat in my panicked brain while I stared at my dark-haired killer-to-be.

It was both the longest and the shortest two hours of my life.

When the vampire's dark eyes opened once again, there was a different sort of awareness in his gaze than when I'd forced him awake earlier in the day. Probably the difference between a vampire before and after dark.

Neat. I get exciting, anthropological knowledge of vampires before I die! I didn't manage to clamp down on the hysterical giggle before it bubbled out between my lips, shattering the silence between us.

The vampire raised a single, dark eyebrow in question.

I made a vague gesture between us, inexplicably compelled to explain my behavior. He was probably more familiar with uncontrollable sobbing. "S-sorry, it's just... Everyone always want to know more about vampires, and here I am, getting some quality one-on-one time. I'll be the envy of the entire Internet!" Another shrill giggle escaped me.

"You're an odd one, aren't you?" His face never changed from the blank expression, but his tone was tinged with curiosity.

I flailed a hand in the empty space between us again, offense taking over my hysteria. "Well, excuse me for not knowing the right etiquette for getting eaten alive. It's not exactly something I do every other Saturday."

He sighed, seemingly losing interest in me as he swiveled around to stare blankly into the room behind the bars without getting up from his seated position. "I'm not going to hurt you."

"Oh." I blinked. "Aren't you hungry?"

The vampire turned his head to give me an incredulous stare.

"I mean, I'm not offering!" I quickly amended. "I'm just pretty sure I've not been tossed in here to be your bridge partner, is all."

He gave a snort of amusement, the faintest hint of a smile touching his lips. "Nevertheless... I will not harm you, little one."

"So... You've eaten recently? Do they toss women in here often then?" *Oh my goddess, why are you still talking? You don't want to know about his diet, for crying out loud! Shut up!*

"They do not." His tone was flat, but he didn't turn back around to stare at the basement again, his eyes taking in my still-quivering form with something akin to curiosity. "You are the first. May I ask why?"

I blinked. "You're asking me why I got kidnapped and used as a vampire snack?"

He gave a single nod, a patient expression on his solemn face.

I opened my mouth to explain how I'd been minding my own business, reading a book, when the oafs took offense to my choice of literature, but managed to stop myself in time. Suddenly, when faced with an *actual* nightwalker, confessing to enjoying the occasional smutty vampire romance seemed more than a little embarrassing.

"Well, why'd they capture *you*?" I asked.

"They don't like vampires," he answered, even though we both knew my question was pretty ridiculous. The stakes on the walls made it obvious they fancied themselves some sort of delusional vampire slayers. I'd heard rumors about people like that—people who took on the night creatures, vigilante-style—but I'd never thought they'd actually ever capture any of them. The people who made YouTube videos about how to *"capture vamps"* tended to look like they'd have trouble putting on pants in the morning.

"But *how?*" I pried, my initial fear of him waning now that it didn't look like I was going to end up as dinner. "Aren't you supposed to be super strong and fast?"

His eyebrow quirked again, and I had the good grace to blush when I realized how rude that must have sounded.

"Sorry. I didn't mean to imply you're a failure of a vampire or anything. Just..." My voice died at his stare. "Sorry."

"You ask a lot of questions for a human who thinks I'm going to eat her," he said.

"Excuse me for trying to make the most of a shitty situation," I snapped in reply.

He softened his tone. "I apologize. I did not mean to offend." Still, a ghost of a smile lurked at the corner of his mouth.

"You're an odd one too," I said, frowning at his youthful face. "You don't want to eat me, and you apologize for offending me. No offense, but you're not at all what I'd imagined vampires to be like."

His expression didn't change, but with another sigh, he turned all the way back around toward me. "Let me guess—you imagined a beast who would break your neck and slake his thirst with your lifeblood?"

I felt another blush heat up my face. "Well, yeah. That or... you know. The *other* kind."

He frowned. "The *other* kind?"

"Er..." Flashes from my book appeared before my mind's eye—the kind containing breathy moans, heaving breasts, and a lot of neck sucking. "Never mind. Look, please don't take this the wrong way—I'm very happy you don't want to eat me and all, but... why not? I've always heard vampires are insatiable. Do I... do I not smell appetizing?"

This time, he laughed. It was deep and rumbly, and surprisingly pleasant to listen to for the few seconds it rang through the basement.

"A doe who worries the lion does not find it appetizing," he murmured, an amused twitch still playing at the corner of his mouth. "That's a first."

"I am not a doe," I huffed, fighting back the warm tinge heating my cheeks. "And I'm not worried. Just... curious. I've got so many questions, and... well, this is sort of a once-in-a-lifetime chance for me."

His blue gaze was fixed on my face, expressionless, and it dawned on me I'd probably committed yet another faux pas.

"Um, I mean... it's only a once-in-a-lifetime chance if you *want* to answer my questions, of course. I can't force you. Uh... I just... you know, want to make the best of a bad situation and... stuff?" I grimaced. "Sorry, there's probably a reason vampires don't do interviews in *People* magazine. You value your privacy—*shrouded in a veil of mystery*, and all that. Forget I asked."

The silence spread between us, seeming so much heavier in the wake of my unhinged babbling.

"You didn't ask," he said at last.

"Huh?"

"You didn't ask me your questions."

"Oh!" I couldn't suppress my wide and immediate grin of elation. "You mean I can...? You don't mind?"

He leaned back a bit, supporting his weight on his hands. "I cannot promise I will answer them, but you may ask—if, in return, you will answer my questions."

I blinked, surprised a nightwalker was even remotely interested in knowing anything about me. I didn't exactly lead the most interesting life. "Yeah, sure. That seems fair." I hesitated, weighing what would be the least offensive question to start off with. I wasn't about to let this once-in-a-lifetime chance slip through my fingers by accidentally offending the stoic young man in front of me.

"All right, so... coffins? Do you all really sleep in them, or...?"

The vampire's sensitive lips twitched, giving his eyes an amused gleam. "It's not overly common, no."

"Oh." Well, there went centuries of vampire myth down the drain. "Where do you sleep, then?"

"I prefer a bed."

I don't know what I'd expected—upside-down in a cave like a bat, maybe. But a *bed?* It sounded so... normal. "I thought you slept in the ground?"

"It happens." Judging from the amused twist of his mouth, my disappointment was visible on my face. "But if we do, it's usually with nothing but the dirt around us. Is it my turn?"

"Sure." I leaned back against the bars of our makeshift prison. "Ask away."

"What's your name?"

A rush of shame stemming back from my Midwestern upbringing spread across my face. How had my first question not been his *name?* He might be a vampire, but that didn't excuse bad manners. I could practically feel Grandma's ruler cracking down across my knuckles in disapproval.

"Liv. Olivia Green," I answered.

"*Liv?*" he asked. Something sparked in his eyes, curiosity perhaps, but it was hard to pinpoint. "Your name is Liv?" The way he pronounced it, it suddenly dawned on me that he had the slightest accent. It was a harder sound, like he was swallowing the *v.*

"It's my nickname," I said with a shrug. "I like it better than Olivia. And, uh, what's your name?"

"Warin," he said, disturbingly blue eyes intent on my face, as if he was trying to see *through* me somehow. "I am known as Warin Waldlitch."

"Oh, you're from abroad?" I latched onto that opening with both hands. Somehow, the idea that vampires immigrated had never crossed my mind. But of course, if they were in America, it stood to reason that at least a few would have made the journey across the Atlantic at some point. "Whereabouts?"

"The northern parts of Europe."

I'd always assumed most Scandinavians were tall and blond, and from the looks of it, Warin was just a few inches above my height and his short hair was even darker than mine. At least he had the blue eyes. "Do you miss it? Your home country?"

"No."

All righty, then. "What about your family?"

"My family?" he looked puzzled, as if it was the strangest thing I could have asked. It wasn't. It really, *really* wasn't. I had about a hundred inappropriate questions burning on the tip of my tongue, from whether he had a favorite "cuisine" to how personal hygiene worked for an undead. But I didn't ask them, partly because that would probably be rude, and partly because I didn't want to cut short the most amazing Q&A session I'd ever have access to.

"Yeah, you know, your parents, siblings, grandparents. Aunts, uncles. Or do you still keep in touch?"

Warin cocked his head, and I got the wild urge for pen and paper so I could draw him. The way the shadows played over his features underlined his inhuman beauty, from the paleness of his skin and hollows of his cheeks, to the strength of his jaw and softness of his lips. I hadn't had much time to appreciate how jaw-droppingly handsome he truly was, what with being locked up by crazies and thinking I was going to get eaten, but as I looked at him now, it dawned on me that he was quite possibly the most beautiful person I'd ever seen. It felt a little strange to think of a man as "beautiful," but for Warin, the word fit perfectly.

"I do not miss them," he said, pulling me out of my contemplations of his face with a start, even though his voice was quiet. "They were a part of another life."

I frowned. "Does that mean vampires have no interest in their former life after they are turned?" It sounded so... harsh.

He considered me for a moment. "That's something I can't answer, Liv. It is not discussed in our society, so I do not know what it's like for other vampires."

I guess it made sense that something like that would be private.

"Why do you have ink smears on your arms?" he asked.

I twisted my arms out in front of me to have a better look. Sure enough, a few high-placed ink smudges had avoided my attention the last time I washed my hands. "Huh. I was doing an ink drawing earlier and apparently didn't notice. I always have random spots and smudges in odd places after doing a drawing or a painting." I popped my finger in my mouth to wet it so I could rub the offending smears off.

"You're an artist?"

I snorted. "A girl can dream! No, it's just a hobby. I work in a shop to pay the bills. Today was *supposed* to be my day off to relax. What about you? Do you have any hobbies?"

The vampire looked a little perplexed, as if he'd never pondered the concept of a hobby before. "I... read a lot, when I have the time. My work keeps me busy for most of my waking hours."

I looked up from my smudges, fascinated. I'd never really thought about vampires holding down jobs. "What do you work with? Ooh, let me guess! Mortician?"

Warin shook his head once, smirking at my enthusiasm.

"Nightclub bouncer?"

Another head shake.

"...Bartender?" I frowned, trying to think of nighttime employment that'd suit the young-looking man in front of me. It was surprisingly hard. "College student who only takes night classes...?"

Warin huffed. I wasn't sure of it was from amusement, or if I was starting to get insulting with my suggestions.

"Okay, fine, I give up. What do you do?"

"Hmm. I suppose humans would call it *law enforcement*," he said after thinking for a moment.

I blinked. Repeatedly. *"Humans* would call it law enforcement? Do you not...? Is there some secret vampire agency we don't know about? Like a..." Excitement bubbled through my veins as I recalled the romance book that'd landed me in here in the first place. "Oh, my goddess, are you a secret vampire agent saving humans from all the terrors we don't know exist? Like... Like an undead superhero?"

This time, there was no mistaking the disdain in Warin's snort, and I deflated a little.

"Vampires are not superheroes, Liv," he said, and the sudden, dark glint in his eyes made something at the base of my skull—some primitive instinct in charge of keeping me alive—wake up with a shudder that traveled the full length of my body. "Never, *ever* make the mistake of thinking we are safe. We are not."

"O-okay," I stuttered, pressing my back up tighter against the bars. "Noted."

"What did you do to make these people lock you in a cage with a vampire?" he asked, and it took me a moment to realize he'd gone back to our Q&A session without missing a beat. As if he hadn't just looked at me all scary-eyed, warning me that vampires were *not our friends*. While apparently not getting the dark irony of me currently being locked in a cage with one—him.

"I read a book they didn't approve of," I said, still too startled to remember why I'd swerved that question before.

"Which book?" he asked with a frown, and I could have bitten my own tongue off.

"Er... just a... book. Fiction." I fidgeted uncomfortably under his scrutinizing gaze.

"What book of fiction would lead them to capture a woman off the street?"

I couldn't tell if he was mystified, or he thought I was lying.

"One about vampires," I begrudgingly admitted.

"You read a fictional tale about vampires, and they thought you a threat?" Warin's frown deepened.

Great. Just great. Why drop an embarrassing subject when we could just keep right on digging?

"It was a romance, okay? A vampire *romance*," I snapped. I normally didn't care what people thought of my trashy novel selection, but then I'd never really had to explain to a vampire that I loved reading about silly human girls falling for a sexy undead.

"Vampire *romance?*" The dark-haired young man arched both eyebrows at my confession. "What is a vampire ro—?" His voice died as he turned his head toward the door. "Someone's coming."

THREE

The vampire gracefully got to his feet faster than my eyes could track.

I got up too, though somewhat less elegantly, and waited with my hands wrapped around the bars. I couldn't hear anything, but my heart thudded unevenly in my chest. If my kidnappers had expected me to be eaten by now, what were they going to do once they saw I was still alive? Even though I was very much hoping for *"give up and let me go,"* it wasn't the option that kept tap dancing before my mind's eye. More like *"knife to the throat,"* or *"burned at the stake."*

There was a clanking of keys on the other side of the heavy metal door, and then the lock clicked open.

The same two men who'd kidnapped me entered the

room. One of them had a mop and a bucket in his hands, the other a large plastic sack. I paled when I realized they'd probably been meant for disposing of my body and wiping up any leftover bodily fluids.

"Well, would you look at that?" Mop Guy said when he caught sight of me by Warin's side. "You're still alive, huh? What's the matter, vamper? She not your type?"

Sack Guy barked a laugh. "Could've sworn I saw him eyeballing a rat the other day. "Oh, well. Guess we should let you use the can, then."

I stared, entirely taken aback by this turn of events. Nothing about these guys had given me the impression that they'd stick to the Geneva Convention, to put it mildly. "Oh, uh..." I didn't like the sly look that passed between them, but I *was* pretty thirsty and could use a trip to the bathroom. Pushing aside my unease, I stepped over to the cage door. "Thanks."

"No problem, darlin'," Mop drawled. He leaned his tools up against the wall and reached into his pocket for the key. "Come on, vamper. Don't let the pretty girl wet herself—at some point you'll get hungry enough, and you're not gonna like her soaked in her own urine, are ya?"

Warin's face remained stoic as he slid his wrists through the bars. I looked on, puzzled, until Sack pulled a long metal chain from the wall and sauntered over to Warin with a mocking smirk.

"There's a good bloodsucker," he jeered while he wrapped the thin chain around Warin's outstretched wrists. "Not so fucking cocky now, are ya? Dumb fuck."

"Cocky" wasn't exactly the word I'd use to describe my vampire companion. He'd remained remarkably placid since waking up with a stranger trying to perform CPR on him mid-nap—even the goon's insults didn't seem to faze him in the slightest. I eyeballed the thin chain around his wrists and wondered why they'd think it offered them any safety if he decided enough was enough. It was wrapped around his wrists multiple times, but so thin I was pretty sure even I'd be able to snap it if I was motivated enough.

"Come on then, girl," Mop said, jingling the keys in the lock before the door slid open. "Let's leave those two to it."

I stepped out of the cage, but hesitated when I saw Sack grab a wooden stake from the wall before he turned back to Warin with a sadistic smile on his bloated face.

"What are you doing? Don't hurt him!"

Both goons turned toward me, incredulous.

"Don't hurt him?" Sack repeated in an imitation of my worried tone. "Don't *hurt* him? Would you listen to the deadwhore!"

"You got any idea how many of our kind he's hurt, you stupid cunt?" Mop growled. "How many *humans* he's sucked dry? You're a fuckin' race traitor. Just wait until he gets hungry enough—we'll see how much sympathy you have left while he's tearing you apart."

"He's just a kid, you sick fucks!" I snarled, giving Mop a shove so I could push past him and wedge myself in front of the tied-up vampire and Sack. *"Don't. Hurt. Him!"* I didn't exactly have a plan for how I was going to keep the two men from hurting him—or me, for that matter—but I hoped my bravado would at least make them reconsider.

"Liv. It's okay. Go."

It was the first Warin had spoken since the men entered the basement, and he sounded so... calm. I glanced at him over my shoulder, unable to comprehend how he could possibly still be so damn *Zen. He* was the one tied up and about to experience torture-by-stake, for fuck's sake!

Piercing blue eyes met mine, and the commandment in them nearly made me lose my balance. Something in that gaze pulled on me, like a vortex. "Go with him."

I blinked, too stunned by the weird sensation of floating as much as his insistence that I leave him to his fate. "I... are you sure?"

"I am. Go."

I shook my head to clear it and turned back to the two goons. Sacks' stake was aimed at my chest now, and I suppressed a shudder. I might not be allergic to wood, as the urban legend suggested vampires were, but I had no doubt I'd take getting stabbed in the heart with a stake about as well as your average movie vampire. Shoulders slumping in defeat, I stepped around Sack's pointed weapon and back to Mop.

He greeted me with a rough shove in my back, making me stumble across the basement toward the door.

"Ungrateful whore," he sneered as he followed me out the basement and up the stairs. "We should'a let you piss yourself."

He led me all the way up to the first floor, which seemed as neglected as the living room, and pushed me into a small bathroom.

"You've got two minutes" he said, shutting the door behind me. Apparently he had enough manners to let me pee without an audience.

A quick look around the moldy bathroom explained why—there was no lock on the door and the small window had been boarded up, allowing only a few cracks of light to enter. There was nowhere for me to escape, and nothing I could use as a weapon.

I did my business as quickly as possible, attempting not to touch any surfaces in the process, and drank from the tap until I was no longer thirsty.

"If you're not out in three seconds, I'm coming in," Mop shouted from the other side of the door.

"Chill, dude. Some of us can't just shake dry," I

snarked before I opened the door and stepped out into the dingy hallway. "Why—" I didn't get to finish my sentence, because just as I exited the bathroom, Mop grabbed a hold of my long ponytail and ripped me off balance.

I squealed and flailed, but before I could right myself, Mop threw me against the wall, smashing my face against the hard surface. When he pressed his heavy body up against mine, pinning me there, sick dread settled in the pit of my stomach.

"There's a good slut," he hissed, and I felt the tip of a knife against my neck.

"You sick son of a bitch! If you try to rape me, I'll rip your fucking balls off!" I tried to stomp at his feet, but he pressed the full length of the blade against my throat before I could get him, and I froze with a curse.

"I wouldn't stick my dick in you if you were the last hole on Earth, *race traitor,*" he rasped. The sickening hardness pressing against the small of my back suggested otherwise, but I wasn't about to goad him.

"Your vampire friend, however... Did you know they like to fuck after they feed? And trust me, we'll get him to feed. We just need to make you a bit more *irresistible,* don't we?" The blade sliced through the skin over my collarbone, sending searing pain through my chest and arm.

I cried out and tried to elbow him in the gut, but he

had me completely immobilized against the wall. He cut me again, a long, languid movement across my shoulder, making me scream once more.

Mop grunted, his excitement at my torture evident against my backside. He reached down between my legs to lift my dress up, and I closed my eyes and tried to think of anything else. How I was going to plunge that blasted knife deep into his gut the second I got the chance played before my mind's eye. I clung to it with all my might.

But instead of ripping my panties off, Mop ran the blade over first my left and then my right inner thigh.

"There we go," he rasped before licking the shell of my ear. I cringed away, and he laughed and finally shifted his weight off me. "All ready for your big date."

I wanted to punch him so bad my fist ached, but all I could do was lean against the wall and draw in shuddering gasps of air to try and control the pain radiating through every cut he'd given me. He'd sliced through both my dress and bra straps, and blood dripped sluggishly from my wounds.

"You sick fuck," I said. It sounded like more of a whimper than the curse I'd wanted it to. "You call the vampire a monster when you're the one abducting and abusing me? You're pathetic."

"Oh, don't you worry—once he gets a look at you, tits out and blood dripping, he's most definitely going to *abuse* you," Mop snarled. He fisted a hand in my hair again and yanked me along, pulling me back toward the stairs.

I stumbled after him, hissing at the pain in my scalp as well as my wounds, as I tried to both keep my dress up and not fall down so I'd get dragged along by my hair.

I made both sets of stairs still on my feet, but when Mop pushed the door to the basement open, he gave me a hard shove between the shoulder blades again, sending me sprawling to the floor.

I landed with a cry, the rough concrete scraping my knees and adding to my injuries.

"Dinner's ready!" Mop sang. "All nice and juicy. Think she looks more appetizing now?"

A deep, inhuman snarl answered him. It sent goosebumps up and down my arms and made every hair on my body stand on end. It was the sound of a predator.

Sick dread filled my veins like icy lead as I turned my head to look in the direction of the sound.

It came from Warin. Only he didn't look like Warin anymore. Instead of the handsome young man who'd seemed so calm and so *human,* a creature taken straight out of a horror movie stood there instead. He still had the same pale features, but his face was twisted in a furious snarl. Long, deadly fangs protruded from below his curled upper lip, gleaming with menace, and his eyes were pure demon black. Dark blood marred his skin and shirt from what looked like multiple stab wounds. He was still restrained by the thin chain, but from the way his muscles bulged, it looked like he was fighting against it with all his might. Like a trapped animal.

"Up you go!" Mop said as he grabbed my ponytail again and lifted me to my feet. "Since you love vampers so much, why don't you go give him a big kiss?"

He dragged me by my hair toward the cage, paying no mind to my desperate attempts at scrambling backward and away from the furious monster.

I tried to bite, kick, and claw at my kidnapper as he unlocked the cage door, but he was much stronger than I. Mop threw me to the floor and I landed, sprawling and scraping my knees once more.

The cage door slammed shut behind me with a metallic clang. Sealing my fate.

I scrambled on my hands and knees to the farthest corner and curled up in a ball so I could keep my dress up and stem the bleeding form the deepest cut along my collarbone at the same time.

"Here ya go, vamper," Sack said. "Perhaps she's more to your liking now."

And then he cut Warin's chain with his hunting knife.

"Hope it was worth being a race traitor, deadwhore," Mop called as they made their way to the basement door. Sack barked a rough laugh before the door shut behind them with a heavy clang.

Leaving me alone in the cage with the furious vampire.

I looked up, only to find him staring down at me, fangs extended and pitch-black eyes glued to the blood seeping between my fingers.

A deep growl emanated from him in unceasing waves.

FOUR

"W-Warin?" I gulped, hoping against hope there was still some shred of humanity I could reach behind those black eyes.

The sound of his name cut his growl short. He stared at me for another second. Then he shook the broken chain off his wrists and forced his gaze away from my blood as he turned his back on me.

"Tie me to the bars." His voice, so silky smooth before, had turned rough and gravelly—as if he were speaking through an animal's jaws. *"Now!"*

I jolted at the sharp crack of his command. "H-how? With *that?*" I eyeballed the flimsy chain on the floor behind him. It'd been pretty pathetic before, and after the goons had taken pliers to it, I wasn't even sure it'd reach around his wrists once.

"It's silver—it'll hold. *Hurry.*"

I wasn't exactly keen on getting closer to him, but I had enough wits about me to realize that I was running on borrowed time. If the silver chain could really hold him, I needed to strap him down with it, stat.

Trembling as much from rampant anxiety as the steady drip of blood from my multiple lacerations, I scrambled across the cage floor to snatch up the broken chain. It felt too light between my fingers as I edged closer to the vampire. But he'd said it would hold, and I had to believe that... because it was pretty obvious it was the only thing that would save me from becoming vampire dinner.

I edged around Warin's shoulder and reached for his wrists he'd already shoved through the bars. When my fingertips skimmed over his hands, a full body shudder went through him, and I jerked my hand away. "S-sorry!"

He didn't reply, and he kept his head turned away while I fumbled with the chain. It was very short, but I managed to get it wrapped around his wrists and tie a tiny knot with the ends. As soon as it was done, I backed several steps away. "There."

Warin's shoulder moved in a deep sigh, and I realized he'd been holding his breath.

"Do vampires need to breathe?" I asked, confused at the memory of his completely still chest when I'd tackled him in an attempt to perform CPR earlier.

He turned his head to give me an incredulous stare over his shoulder.

"Right. Not the time," I muttered. Our little vampire Q&A session was definitely over. Something about fighting off the urge to gorge on my blood probably didn't lend itself to a presentation about vampire do's and don'ts. I giggled, hysteria starting to edge in.

"You're losing too much blood," Warin said. He was probably right—there really wasn't much to laugh about. With a strength of will, I forced myself to pull it together. I had to stem as much of the bleeding as I could—I might not be hemorrhaging, but goddess knew how long we'd be stuck in this cage.

With a determinedly set jaw, I began ripping strips of the bottom of my dress to act as gauze. My muscles burned from the effort, and I pushed back a wave of panic. I must have been bleeding more than I'd thought.

"You'll die if we stay here."

I glared up at him from tying a strip of my ruined dress around my left thigh. "Not fucking helpful, dude! I'm trying to not have a panic attack over here as is."

He muttered a word I didn't grasp. Probably nothing particularly nice.

"Let me drink from you."

My fingers stilled against the cloth scrap. "Um... beg your pardon?" Did he just... suggest I offer up a taste, in the middle of me slowly bleeding to death?

"Your blood. I haven't eaten in weeks—I can't break us out when I am this weak."

I blinked. "You can... break us out? If you have my blood?" My voice was sounding about as skeptical as I felt. About zero percent of me wanted to get close enough to the still feral-looking vampire for him to sink those very sharp fangs into my flesh.

"Yes." He turned around as much as the chain around his wrists allowed and looked me straight in the eyes. "Do you want to die in this basement, Liv?"

"No." It came out as a broken whisper, because I knew he was right. Even if blood loss didn't kill me, our captors would eventually return. My options were pretty much to either trust a vampire, or die.

I drew in a deep breath and walked back toward him, doing my best to keep my legs steady. Once I reached him, I ducked under his left arm so I could lean up against the bars and wedge my body in between him and his tied wrists.

"Don't kill me," I said as I leaned my head back against the bars, offering my neck. It was meant as a playful joke to ease the tension, but it came out as scared as I felt.

Warin didn't answer. His gaze was glued to my bloody shoulder and chest, the darkness in it flaming from within. His fangs seemed to lengthen even further as he curled his lip back and inhaled.

I closed my eyes and clenched my fists, preparing for the pain.

But instead of sharp fangs piercing my skin, cool lips brushed over my chest. And then he *licked* me.

Despite my woozy state, my eyes flew open from sheer shock at the unexpectedly sensual touch of the vampire's tongue flicking up along my collarbone. I stared down at his bent head, the messy, dark brown hair shielding what he was doing from my vision.

When Warin groaned low in his throat, apparently at the taste of my blood, I was suddenly thankful for my miserable state. I was pretty sure it'd be highly inappropriate to *enjoy* getting eaten.

He gave my collarbone and shoulder three long, slow licks before he paused, mouth hovering above my clavicle at the bottom of my first cut. "I need you to move behind me," he rumbled. "Give me a moment. Then untie me."

"Trying to fight off the urge to suck me dry?" I joked shakily.

Judging from the glare he shot me, I wasn't as funny as I thought. Probably because I'd hit the nail on the head.

"Excuse me for trying to lighten the mood," I muttered as I slid out from in front of him to hide behind his back.

He didn't respond, and I focused my attention on not passing out while I waited for his self-control to strengthen.

"Untie me."

At least the vampire *sounded* like he was back in control of himself again. I sent a silent prayer to my goddess and reached around his body to work the knot. It was harder than it'd been to tie it, partly because I couldn't really see what I was doing and partly because my fingers seemed less obedient. The dripping of blood from the wounds on my shoulder and collarbone had slowed down after Warin licked them, but I was still not doing too great. It wouldn't be that much longer until my need for a hospital visit became urgent.

"Look away," I said when my fingertips slipped on the knot for the fifth time. "I need to see what I'm doing."

Warin turned his head to the left, and I slipped out from behind him to his right side and bent over the chain. Now that I could see, it only took me two tries to get it loosened. Two seconds later, I pulled it off him with a triumphant smile. "There. Free vampire!"

The vampire shot me another *"you're either insane or high from blood loss"* look, but instead of commenting, he crouched down—and then punched the floor.

The cement cracked like a broken plate under his knuckles.

I yelped and stumbled back against the bars when the floor shifted under my feet. Warin didn't so much as glance in my direction. Instead, he grabbed a large piece of the broken cement and began digging. It took less than a minute before there was a large hole right up against the front part of the cage, next to the door. Warin tossed the chunk of cement aside and continued with his hands, scooping dirt up into an ever-increasing pile next to me at a pace no human could ever have replicated.

Once it was deep enough, he jumped in with all the grace of a panther and continued clawing at the side of the hole with his fingers. He'd scooped out so much soil only his legs were sticking out by the time I realized exactly what his plan was.

"You're actually... you're digging a tunnel. We're legit going to make our grand escape by *digging* our way out?" My legs wobbled, and I sank to the broken concrete floor with a dizzy giggle. My head felt so woozy, images from old movies featuring files baked into cakes and Wild West cowboys flickered in front of my eyes. Warin didn't answer me, and I decided it was probably a good idea to lay down and rest my eyes.

It felt like a second later when rough hands pulled on my shoulders. I jerked, and then squealed when the same hands dragged me into the hole. Dirt fell into my eyes, and I screwed them shut. The next moment, I was pulled by my shoulders through a claustrophobia-inducing space. Mass pushed in from all sides, and the smell of dirt surrounded me as clumps drizzled onto my face and body. I began to let out another squeal of protest, and promptly got a mouthful of dry soil.

I was pulled up through another hole, hacking and spitting dirt, before the distinct sensation of being lifted up into the air made me realize I was finally free.

Carefully, I cracked my eyes open to squint at the room. We were, indeed, out of the hole again, and judging from my view of Warin's dirt-streaked face, plus the feeling of iron bands around my hamstrings and back, he was holding me, bridal-style.

"I can walk," I croaked, wiping at my mouth with my arm to get the dirt out. Only my arm—and the rest of my body—was also covered in crumbled up soil, so all I managed to do was wedge more of it in between my lips.

The vampire let me slide to my feet, and I noticed the two ragged holes in the floor, one inside the cell and one outside where we now stood. Then my legs gave out and I landed in a graceless heap next to a mound of dirt.

Warin didn't pay my swooning damsel routine any mind. He leapt to the door, kicked it once, and sent it plus the frame flying into the stairwell beyond. Then, in a blink of an eye, he was gone.

That's what I got for being all *"independent female, can walk herself out of the creepy basement."* Gritting my teeth, I got to my knees before my head began to swim. I decided to not brave my feet again and began crawling toward the now very much open door.

I made it to the new hole in the wall and grimaced at the pile of broken metal and wood I'd somehow have to climb over. Then a pair of leather shoes and black-clad legs landed on the rubble right in front of me with a *thud*.

I looked up and saw Warin staring down at me with a blank expression.

"Turns out I can't walk," I said, grimacing at the pangs of pain from the cuts on my thighs. Getting dragged through a hole and then crawling across concrete was apparently too much for my impromptu bandages. "Do you mind giving me a hand before you disappear into the night?"

The vampire jumped down to the bottom of the steps, bent down, and scooped me up as easily as if I'd been a toddler. Then the world blurred with motion, and g-force pressed my body tightly against his for a short second before he stopped.

I blinked the blur from my eyes, slowly recognizing the upstairs living room in the crappy house we'd been imprisoned in. Two motionless bodies lay on the floor. When I looked closer, I recognized the nearest corpse. It was Mop. His head lolled at an unnatural angle, neck broken.

I gulped, but before I could even process the gruesome scene, Warin kicked open the door leading to the outside. Cooling wind brushed aside the warm summer air as he leapt into the night. Broken soundbites and blurry flickers of light passed us by. He was running so fast my eyes couldn't track our surroundings.

I closed them tightly and buried my face in Warin's shirt to avoid throwing up from motion sickness. At least this was faster than an ambulance.

When he finally stopped several minutes later, we were standing in the driveway of a large McMansion, surrounded by impeccably manicured bushes and a trickling fountain. It was such a vastly different neighborhood than any part of Chicago *I'd* ever been to before that I only managed to gape up at the fancy building in confusion. It wasn't until Warin, at a human pace this time, walked up to the front door and rang the bell that the surrealism of it all gave way to more practical concerns.

"I think I need to go to the hospital," I said.

"I'll take care of you," he said, his voice still gruff like it'd been after he was tied up. At least he wasn't staring at the blood soaking my shoulder and chest anymore. "I just need to feed first."

I blanched. "Uh, I don't think I have enough blood left for you to—" My stammered protest died when the door opened, revealing a pretty blonde woman.

"Warin! Thank the stars! We thought you were..." She quieted, her eyes zeroing in on my disheveled form. And then, from behind her pouty, red lips, her fangs lengthened into daggers as her pupils blew wide.

Panic pulled on my hazy mind at coming face to face with another predator when I was already too weak to fight, but Warin simply shouldered past the woman as if she hadn't just gotten a fang boner in the middle of greeting him.

The entry hall was exactly as magnificent as you'd expect from a mansion like this. White marble floors spread out into a wide staircase leading upward, accentuated by black and gold accents around the two open doors on either side.

Movement caught my eye as Warin stopped in the middle of the open room and put me down next to a slim marble pillar. I clutched it tightly to keep on my feet and watched as my savior-slash-potentially-still-murderer turned to the three newcomers spilling out from one of the open doorways.

From behind us, the blonde woman joined them.

"Brother." A tall man with auburn hair and eyes as piercingly blue as Warin's stepped forward, clasping Warin's shoulder. "Have you been hiding in a grave again? You're filthy."

"Aleric," Warin acknowledged the redhead. "It has been so long. What brings you here?"

"Your loyal subjects were certain you'd been kidnapped," Aleric said, his eyes twinkling with mirth. "They requested my aid in retrieving you."

Warin cocked a dark eyebrow and turned to look at the three other people in the hall. He didn't say anything, but his displeasure was nearly palpable, even to me. After a moment, he returned his gaze to Aleric's. "There have been disappearances in my territory. I investigated. I apologize for my subordinates—they should not have disturbed another Ancient unnecessarily. But if you'll excuse me. I will need to feed. We will catch up later."

Aleric's blue gaze flickered to me. "Your snack seems to be leaking."

Warin spared me a single glance. "Bring her to my bedroom."

And then, as if that wasn't the creepiest thing to say, he walked off, leaving me alone with what I was now very sure were four vampires.

They all stared at me, fangs lengthening, as if I were a doe who'd accidentally waltzed right into a lion's den.

Only the rushing in my ears drowned out the steady drip of my blood hitting the marble floor.

FIVE

The blonde who'd opened the door for us took a small step closer to me, her gaze locked on the blood dripping down my thighs past my makeshift bandages.

Holy shit, holy shit, hoooly shit! And I'd thought the night couldn't get any worse after Mop sliced me open and threw me into a cage with a very hungry vampire.

I fidgeted anxiously, doing my best to keep an eye on all of them while still clinging to the column for support. How the hell did you chase off a herd—*pride? Flock?*—of vampires? I was pretty sure lying down and playing dead —the most tempting option right then—wasn't going to do me any favors, and I was fresh out of bear spray.

Mother above, if you get me out of this, I swear I will never read another vampire novel ever again!

"Lay off." The big auburn-haired man—Aleric—

stepped into the center of the semi-circle, shielding me from the other vampires' greedy looks, and placed a heavy hand on my shoulder. It nearly made my knees buckle. "Warin claimed her. Has he been gone so long you'd really sink your teeth into an Ancient's meal?" Then he turned to me. "C'mon, bloodsack."

"I c-can't walk," I stuttered when the pressure on my shoulder indicated he was expecting me to follow along.

He arched a contemptuous eyebrow at me, heaved a deep sigh, and then swung me over his shoulder in one, easy scoop, like I was nothing more than a sack of grain.

I groaned in discomfort, and was thoroughly ignored as the tall vampire *swooshed* up out of the hall and down a wide corridor, faster than a human could have moved by far, but not as swiftly as Warin had run to get us here. He stopped in front of a heavy-looking black door with a keypad attached to the frame. Faster than my eyes could follow, he punched in a code.

The door *beeped* and swung open, allowing the vampire to walk inside in three long strides.

Once in, he unceremoniously dropped me to my feet. "Stay here."

And then I was alone.

I stared at the now closed door, too dazed to fully comprehend what had just happened. Not that it really mattered *how* I'd gotten here, as much as it did that I was locked in a vampire's bedroom, waiting for him to come have dinner.

The thought that I should probably try to call for help briefly flickered and died. The fanatics had taken my cellphone when they kidnapped me, the bedroom door was locked, and I didn't see any phones or computers in the surprisingly modern room. Only two nightstands and the king-sized bed Aleric had dropped me by filled the large space, and the sheets on the bed looked to be simple, light gray cotton. Not blood-red or black silk, like I'd kind of expected thanks to my paranormal romance novels.

Apart from the entrance, there were two more closed doors on either side of the room. I assumed they led to an en-suite and a walk-in closet, respectively, but even if Warin had hidden wooden stakes and PIN-free cell phones, I didn't have the strength to look for either.

I sank down on the bed with a pained groan. There was nothing I could do but hope Warin would remember his promise not to harm me. And that hopefully, he'd bring me to a hospital before it was too late.

I stared miserably at the door while I waited for the man who'd been a stranger to me up until mere hours ago to decide my fate.

I didn't have to wait long.

After only a few minutes, the door swung open and Warin stepped in.

There was something distinctly *lighter* about him than

there'd been since the fanatics tied him up, and when I caught his gaze, I saw his eyes were once again startling blue, rather than pitch black. He'd also retracted his fangs, which did a lot to take the edge off his *"terrifying creature of the night"* vibe.

He didn't say anything as he took in my disheveled form sprawled on his bed.

"I... think I need to go to the hospital," I said, breaking the silence and hopefully reminding him of his promise not to harm me. My voice was about as pitiful as I felt—which was quite a bit. "I'm not doing too good."

Warin shook his head and walked to the bed. "No. I will take care of you. It will be much faster."

"What will be much faster?" I asked. He hadn't brought a First Aid kit with him.

The vampire sank down on the bed next to me and rolled up his left sleeve, displaying a patch of clean, pale skin emblazoned with an intricate tattoo. "Vampire blood has strong healing properties for humans. Come." With a smooth movement, he scooted further back on the bed, spread his legs, and grabbed me by the hips, easily lifting me up and then depositing me between his thighs, my back pressed against his chest.

I squeaked and was admonished with a, *"Shh."*

Warin wound his right arm loosely around my stomach, ensuring I stayed put, and lifted his bare left arm out of my field of vision. I heard a *snick* right by my ear, and then his arm reappeared in front of my lips. Blood bloomed from two puncture wounds on his wrist. "Drink."

What? Ew. Ew, ew, so much ew! Did he really expect me to...?

I stared at his wrist, suddenly overwhelmed with the intimacy of the situation as much as the thought of actually drinking someone else's blood. His strong body was pressed against my back, his legs cushioning mine, and while he might have been fully clothed, I was only in a ruined summer dress. And my tits were out, I suddenly remembered. If I'd had enough blood left in my body, I'd have blushed when the realization hit me that I'd effectively flashed him and every other vampire in the mansion.

I'd forgotten. In the middle of all the horrors, I'd actually forgotten I was half-naked, save a solid smearing of dirt that clung to every inch of me.

"Er... I think I prefer some iodine. Thanks, though."

Warin chuckled softly in my ear. "Drink, Liv. I promise, you will feel much better for it." And then he pressed his bleeding wrist to my lips.

The tang of blood hit my nostrils before my tongue slid out without my consent to lick at the sticky fluid smeared against them.

Sensation exploded across my taste buds, making me gasp into his wrist. More blood dripped into my mouth, and I moaned without meaning to. Oh, goddess, it tasted like... like wild, dark, *fantastic...!*

I clutched onto the vampire's wrist with a strength that surprised even me and deepened my mouth's contact with his skin. Blood, thick and sinfully sweet, dripped past my lips and buzzed on my tongue.

"That's enough," Warin groaned. "If you drink too much, you will become intoxicated."

When I only clung on tighter, he released my waist and gently dislodged me from his wrist. He remained close, though—near enough that I could feel his hard chest press against my back and his even breath against my ear. It didn't feel awkward anymore, though.

"Intoxicated?" My lips prickled pleasantly, and I licked them with a happy hum. My entire body seemed to buzz with a low frequency.

"My blood is very potent," he said. "How do you feel?"

"Amazing." I smiled, completely at peace with the universe and life in general. That was when I realized my wounds no longer ached. I traced the cut on my collarbone with a fingertip and found the flesh welded back together. "Magic?"

"Hmm," he hummed, neither confirming nor denying. His breath blew some of my hair that'd escaped the ponytail during the night's abuse against my cheek. It tickled.

"Warin?"

"Liv?"

"Why do you breathe? You weren't while you were sleeping, so clearly you don't need to."

The vampire made an amused noise. "More questions?"

"Well, yeah, if..." Something dawned on me, and I sobered considerably. "If you don't mind. I know you were, ah, hungry." Would he expect me to return the favor? I rubbed subconsciously at my neck, the small hairs all along my body standing on end. Suddenly, his proximity was less than soothing.

"I ate. We breathe because that's how we scent. Our sense of smell is as important as our eyes and ears." I paled significantly at the casual reference to his meal.

"Oh, you... uh, you *ate* someone? While your brother took me up here?" Flashes of our dead kidnappers played on loop before my mind's eye. I didn't mourn them—the bastards had tried to get me eaten alive, after all. But their lifeless bodies had been a very clear indication that my new vampire buddy wasn't always as pleasant as he seemed now.

"No." Warin moved away from me, swiveling his legs around so he could leave the bed. He stood up and began to fiddle with his sleeve, covering up the tattoo and bite. A quick glance at his face confirmed his fangs were safely hidden away again.

As if he could feel my eyes on his mouth, he gave me a

short look. "I have donor blood in storage." Then, for the briefest moment, his gaze flickered to my chest. "I'll get you a change of clothes. If you wish, you can wash up in the bathroom."

"Oh. *Oh!*" I quickly slapped my hands up to cover my breasts. "Y-yeah, thank you. That'd be great."

My legs were still wobbly as I made my way to the en-suite, but not like before. It felt more like I was walking on clouds rather than having two pieces of boiled noodles attached to my body.

Warin's bathroom was as sparsely decorated as his bedroom, but there was no questioning the luxury of it. Black marble tiled both the walls and the floor, and the shower looked like something straight out of *Millionaire Living*. I gave it a long look—he'd said to wash up, and I'd planned on maybe using the sink, but the sight of the glass-paned shower made me reconsider. It might be a bit odd to shower in a stranger's home, but on the other hand, drinking someone's blood really ought to ease up the rules of etiquette.

Mind made up, I tossed my ruined dress and underwear on the floor and stepped in.

I'd never enjoyed a shower more than I did then. The warm spray rinsed off caked dirt and dried blood, and somehow managed to feel like a massage to boot. I was surprisingly free from any aches and pain, but standing underneath the hot water as brown and red swirls disappeared into the drain below me eased my frazzled mind too. Somehow, I'd made it out of getting kidnapped and fed to a vampire.

I giggled, the sound of it trickling through my throat, seemingly from out of nowhere. And another. I laughed so hard I could barely breathe, until the cramps in my chest turned to sobs. I cried, leaning against the cool tiles of the vampire's bathroom, as I silently thanked my goddess for getting me out of that basement alive. I'd thought I would be raped and murdered more times this evening than anyone should in the full span of a lifetime, and yet I'd made it through my ordeal relatively unscathed.

It took me a few minutes to pull myself together enough to stop crying again. Somewhat shaky, both from the emotional outburst and the lingering effects of Warin's blood, I turned off the tap and promised myself a good, long cry later, in the privacy of my own bathroom. Crying in the shower of the vampire who'd saved my ass seemed somewhat ungrateful—especially since he'd been gracious enough to let me use the facilities first, even though he was also filthy from our great escape.

I used one of the pristine, charcoal towels to dry myself off, luxuriating in the softness of it as I wrapped it around my body. When I wiped the steam off the mirror above the sink to check my reflection, I looked much more human than I'd felt before washing the day's horrors off.

In fact... I squinted at myself. I looked pretty damn

good. No bruises, no scrapes... My green eyes even seemed brighter, and my complexion was flawless.

I pressed my face all the way into the mirror and peered down at my nose. Nope—not so much as a black-head in sight.

"Well, I'll be damned." Was that because of Warin's blood too? Or maybe the dirt underneath the fanatics' house had some form of miracle mud mixed in.

A soft knock on the door made me pull back from staring at my own nose, a sliver of guilt at my vanity making me cringe as I turned. Here I was, taking my sweet time admiring myself, and Warin was probably dying for a shower too.

Or, undying, as it were.

Making absolutely sure the towel was secured over my breasts—because there's only so many times you can flash a dude before it becomes awkward—I cracked the door open and peered out.

Warin stood outside the door, a small pile of fabric in his hands. "If you need a change of clothes," he said, politely pretending like my dress hadn't been dangling around my waist for a good part of the night.

"Thanks." I smiled, thankful my first run-in with a vampire had been with him, rather than one of the ones from the government scare campaigns. Hell, I was pretty sure I'd never met a human man who'd been this polite. "You're a lifesaver."

And then I punched him lightly in the shoulder.

He stared at me for two full seconds, and I stared back, not quite comprehending what I'd just done.

You just bro-punched a vampire in the shoulder is what you did, Liv. A smoking-hot vampire who literally saved your life and fed you his blood as if it was NyQuil.

I grimaced and snatched the clothes out of his hand before he could change his mind about offering me any further assistance, quickly shutting the door behind me with a, "Won't be a minute!"

Only I definitely would be, I realized as I pulled on the clothes he'd brought me.

The shirt—light gray, crisp linen with an Armani tag—wasn't a problem. I sniffed the collar as I buttoned it up, and hummed with pleasure at the smell of the fresh night air. It was much too big on my frame, which wasn't overly surprising as it clearly belonged to Warin. He was only a couple of inches taller than me—maybe six foot or thereabouts—but he was much wider across the shoulders. I rolled up the sleeves to not look like a little girl playing dress-up in her daddy's closet, and turned my attention to the bottoms he'd brought me.

The were a dark charcoal gray, the same shade as the towels, and as immaculately wrinkle-free as the shirt. The only problem was that they were clearly also tailored to Warin, and I only got them to mid-thighs before they got well and truly stuck.

"Sonuvabitch," I muttered, pulling desperately at the waistband. They refused to budge so much as an inch. Goddamn my round hips and inability to stay away from fast food! "Come on!"

"Liv? Is there a problem?" Warin's voice sounded from outside the door.

"Yeah, just..." I sighed, giving up on my fight with the pants. "Do you have some other pants? ...With an elastic waist?"

He was silent for a bit, then said, "I'm afraid not. What size are you? I will send someone to purchase something suitable." His voice came from further away—from inside his walk-in closet, I guessed.

"No, that's not necessary!" I protested, cringing at the thought of the perfectly beautiful—and very well-dressed—vampire who'd opened the door for us having to go to an all-night Wal-Mart just because my ass was too big. "Don't you have a pair of sweatpants? Or even boxers would be fine."

Another moment's pause, followed by a knock on the bathroom door. I cracked it open, ensuring my lower half was hidden behind it, and peered out.

Warin held out a pair of blue silk boxer shorts for me. "If they don't fit, it is no trouble to send for a set of women's clothes."

"They'll fit." If it was the last thing I did, I'd get into them or die trying. Sending vampires to run errands might have been business as usual for him, but I was not about to attract any more attention from the three who'd surrounded me downstairs, fangs out and basically salivating at the thought of full-on *eating* me.

Did vampires salivate?

"Thanks!" I slammed the bathroom door shut and stepped into the boxers, praying they wouldn't rip.

The thick silk fabric was pulled tight over my thighs and rear-end in a way it definitely wasn't meant to, but I managed to squeeze into them without any accidents.

"Oh, thank the goddess," I mumbled as I finally went to leave the bathroom for good. I might not have had much dignity left, but I very much appreciated not having to flash the poor vampire anymore of my lady bits.

Warin was waiting for me on the bed, absentmindedly stroking a hand over one of my now dried-up blood splotches on his sheets.

"Uh, yeah... sorry about your sheets," I said. "I can have them cleaned for you."

He looked up at me, mild surprise at my offer evident on his still-dirty face. "That's not necessary."

"You sure? I kind of wrecked them good." I made a vague gesture at one of the bigger splotches.

"Yes." He touched a cleaner part of the sheets. "Come, please. Sit. I wish to talk with you for a moment."

"Sure." With what he'd done for me this night, he could talk at me as much as he pleased.

I sat down on the bed, careful not to plant his silk boxers in any of the grime. "What's up?"

"In the basement... you stepped in front of the man with the stake. Why?"

I frowned, trying to remember what he was referring to. The entire night was blurring into one long horror story, so it took me a little while to remember what he meant. "Oh. I dunno. Isn't that a pretty normal reaction to seeing someone attempt to torture a person?"

Warin stared at me for a long moment before he softly said, "No, Liv. It's not a normal reaction for a human to try to shield a vampire from harm with her own body."

I shrugged, the unwavering attention from his blue gaze making me fidget on the bed. "I guess I've never liked seeing people pick on someone weak. I didn't really think about it."

Warin blinked three times in rapid succession, then narrowed his eyes at me. "You think I'm incapable of protecting myself?"

Oh, lovely. Had I managed to hurt his male pride?

"I'm sure you're very capable, under normal circumstances. But, I mean, they had you tied up in a cage."

His full lips twitched. "They had us *both* in a cage." He placed a single, cool fingertip underneath my chin. "Never, *ever* put yourself in danger for a vampire again."

I wasn't exactly used to near-strangers touching me like that—and especially not near-strangers with features like Adonis himself, with blazing blue eyes that made made my heart speed up and the rest of the world seem to fade. I blamed my lack of experience with such situations for why it took me nearly five full seconds before I realized I, instead of answering the man, was staring dreamily at Warin with a dumb smile on my face.

"Ugh-um," I coughed as I swiftly pulled back from his light touch, face hot and undoubtedly bright red. "Yeah, I mean, it's not like I've got any set-in-stone *plans* about throwing myself in harm's way, or anything, but I'm pretty sure that in the unlikely event I find myself in a similar situation, I'd do the same again. Sorry."

I don't know why I tacked the "sorry" on—maybe it was because Warin looked absolutely dumbfounded, sensual mouth agape and eyes wide, and I felt kinda guilty about making a man that hot lose his composure.

Apparently unaware of my inappropriate thoughts, Warin wrapped his hand around my jaw, squishing my cheeks and trapping my gaze with his once more. "Liv. I am far stronger than you—far faster, and *far* more durable. You are too fragile to get between a vampire and a wooden stake, and you will *never* again defend one of my kind with your own life. Do you understand?"

It felt as if magnets deep in his sparkling blue eyes pulled on me, making me woozy and my thoughts foggy. I blinked, trying to clear my head before I gently reached up to free my face from his grasp.

"Look, I appreciate the sentiment and all, but let's be honest here. Yeah, I don't have super speed, and while I've never tried, I'm pretty sure I can't kick a door in. *But.* I *can* lift a silver bracelet, and I don't have any wood allergies, so please calm your tits with all your macho bullshit, a'ight?"

Warin stared at me for another drawn-out moment. Then his eyes crinkled at the corners and his deep laughter rumbled through the room.

It was such an unexpected sound from the otherwise stoic vampire, I narrowly caught my rampant hormones before they galloped off on a tangent about his gorgeous face again. He might have been sexy as sin, and I might have felt inexplicably calm in his company, now that I was relatively sure he wasn't gonna eat me, but I *so* wasn't going there.

Plus, at twenty-seven, I was way too old to crush on a guy who'd inevitably get carded every time he went out to a bar—undead or not.

"Can vampires drink alcohol?" I asked, frowning at the idea of Warin in a bar. My paranormal romance novels had plenty of broody nightwalkers hanging out at college bars, sipping whiskey and trawling for dinner.

Warin hummed, but didn't answer. He peered into my eyes, his own alight with curiosity as if he was looking for something—like I was some intricate puzzle, and if he just searched long enough, he'd find the missing piece.

I bit my lip and tried to return his gaze, but my

hormones were harder to control while maintaining eye contact. It didn't take long before I began to fidget on the bed, wishing he'd get bored soon.

"My apologies—you must be tired," Warin said, finally breaking his one-sided staring contest with a soft sigh. "I have a guest room made up, if you would like to sleep here. I'll have someone drive you home when you wake up."

Sleep in a house filled with vampires? Uh, thanks but no thanks.

"I think I'd better get home." I got up from the bed and stretched.

"Of course." He followed me up, but kept a more socially acceptable distance than when he'd stared into my eyes. "I'll have Edward take you."

"Uh, is he... human?" I grimaced. "No offense."

"Yes. You will be in safe hands—I promise."

I smiled at his earnest tone. "Thank you, Warin—for everything." I flashed him a grin. "And for not eating me."

"Meeting you was a pleasure, Liv." He took my hand between both of his, squeezing it briefly before he released his grip and walked to the door, opening it. "Be safe."

SIX

THREE MONTHS LATER

"The thing about witches is that there're so many colors in the world. What's so great about black? Black candles, black clothes, black nail polish... black, black, black! How about you try summoning spirits with a nice pink candle? Might attract a less sour disposition!"

I snorted into my rum and Coke at my colleague's animated rant across the table from me. The four of us—me, Skye, Raven, and our boss, Dennis—had captured a booth in one of the more popular *alternative* bars for our delayed annual "company party." It was supposed to have been on Halloween, but working in a popular New Age shop meant October had been too busy.

Instead, Dennis had taken his three employees out the first Friday of November, and we were definitely on our way to becoming well and truly sloshed—which was typically when the bitching about our somewhat eccentric clientele began. I'd only been with *Dark Dreams* for about four months, but it was my favorite job by far, in large part due to my colleagues. They were the closest thing I'd had to friends in a very long time.

"Aw, come on, Skye—if it wasn't for moody teenagers and their love of all things black, Dennis wouldn't have been able to mark up the last shipment of altar cloth, and then we'd have had to pay for our own drinks tonight. We're practically drinking the tears of rebellious teenagers." I grinned at the blonde. "Very thematic."

She stuck her tongue out at me before downing the last of her vodka-Redbull. "I don't remember you being this cheerful about it when he had us drape the entire window display in the stuff. Go on—why don't you tell Dennis how his Samhain display wrecked your day?"

I sighed dramatically and began my—if I may say so myself—hilarious parody of the customer who'd come by the shop looking like she'd stepped straight out of a *Harry Potter* novel, claiming the altar cloth spread decoratively across the window display ruined her ability to see the future from her apartment a couple of floors up.

It was only when Skye and Raven both uttered a weird sort of *whimper*—some five minutes of animated storytelling later—that I realized I'd lost two thirds of my captive audience. They were both staring at something—

or, judging by the glazed look on both women, some*one*—behind me and Dennis.

"That's just great. Way to make a girl feel important," I huffed as I turned around to check out what'd made their ovaries start tangoing on the table. "What are you—?"

My irritated question died in a surprised croak of recognition as I spotted the object of their attention.

Blazing blue eyes met mine as the young man who'd just entered the bar looked up. His dark brown hair was tousled from the cold November weather, and his gray woolen coat did nothing to hide the wide set of his shoulders or trim waistline.

Soft lips, dark eyebrows, and high cheekbones completed his perfect physique—this time without so much as a speck of dirt to hide how drop-dead gorgeous he was. Pun intended.

"Warin!" My face cracked into a huge smile at the sight of the vampire I'd met over the summer.

Perhaps if I hadn't been two hairs past tipsy, I would have remembered the many disturbing sex dreams I'd had of him since we parted ways. Instead I scrambled up from the booth to throw myself across the bar and around his neck as if he was my long-lost brother. Sadly for me, it was only when I collided with his solid chest that a vivid memory of waking up with a soaked pillow between my legs the day after we'd said goodbye came back in ultra-sharp high-definition.

"I, uh... hey!" I fought back a hefty blush and detached myself from my one-sided hug—he'd stopped dead the moment my arms went around his neck—and gave him what I hoped was a slightly less insane smile. "I did *not* expect to see you again—especially not here, of all places." I looked at the drunk, black-clad bar patrons with a raised eyebrow.

"No?" he asked, and even though his velvety voice was soft, it carried easily over the music and loud chatter.

"Well, I didn't exactly take you for the type to trawl bars for—" I was about to say *"women,"* but then realized what, exactly, a vampire was likely looking for in a crowded bar filled with drunk humans.

Sex probably wasn't it.

"Uh," I said, smart as ever. "Company."

The corner of his full lips curled up in the faintest echo of a smile at my lame ending.

"So... you pub-crawl, huh?" I said, looking around at the drunk people, arms crossed. I caught Raven and Skye making wild gestures of encouragement out the corner of my eye and hurriedly refocused on Warin.

Warin's lips hiked up a bit higher. "I wouldn't go that far. And yourself? Are you here with friends?"

It was such a normal question to ask, it took me a

moment to remember my already lacking social etiquette. "Oh, yes. Work night out. You should join us."

His gaze flickered over my shoulder to where I'd left my colleagues. "I don't wish to interrupt your night."

"Nonsense, you won't." I flashed him a happy smile, feeling a lot less awkward now that I was no longer plastered across his chest. "Besides, Skye and Raven are dying to meet you. Just don't eat any of them. Even though they'd probably let you." I grabbed his arm and began to pull him toward our table.

"Guys, this is Warin—Warin, this is Skye, Dennis and Raven," I said as we arrived at the booth. I let go of Warin's arm to let him slide in next to Dennis, but I needn't have bothered.

"Oh, wow, it's *so* good to meet one of Liv's friends!" Skye chirped as she shot out of her seat and pulled the vampire into a hug, one that had her ample chest smooshed up against him tight enough for her bra to nearly lose its grip on her breasts. Warin froze at the unexpected touch, every muscle in his body tensing even harder than when I'd force-hugged him, but Skye didn't seem to notice.

"Come, sit!" she said, beaming smile still in place. She practically pushed him into the bench next to Raven and hurriedly scooted in after, effectively trapping him between them both.

Raven mouthed an enthusiastic *"thank you"* at me

before she focused her attention on the newcomer too. Her top wasn't as low cut as Skye's, but when she purred, "Yes, what a *pleasure,*" at the vampire, an impressive amount of her tits suddenly appeared right underneath his nose.

I rolled my eyes so hard they nearly got lost in the back of my skull. "Smooth, girls."

Dennis managed a decent attempt at disguising his laugh in his pint of beer.

"So, Warin... How do you know Liv?" he asked once he'd downed a swig. "You one of her friends from back in Denver?"

"No, we only met recently," I quickly stepped in. I hadn't told any of them about my little kidnapping adventure, partly because it seemed somehow inappropriate to answer, *"So, what did you do on your day off?"* with *"Was kidnapped and stabbed by fanatics, but oh, I made a vampire friend!"*—and partly because I wasn't exactly keen on getting linked back to the two dead men Warin had left behind when we made our escape. "We met at, uh, a book club a little while ago."

"Oh, you like to read? Who's your favorite author?" Raven lit up, and I recalled her grumbling about how hard it was to find a well-read man the last time she came into work after a disappointing date.

"I've enjoyed many over the years. Kierkegaard is always thought-provoking, but I often find myself revisiting Dante," Warin said, as if throwing that level of literary references on the table was no big deal. "Do you have favorite authors?" He directed the question to the table at large, but Raven was not about to let his attention waver. She looked like Christmas had come early as she casually let a finger travel up the back of Warin's hand to regain his focus.

It didn't surprise me when Warin froze at the uninvited touch this time—but Raven's wide eyes as she quickly snapped her finger away did. *Huh.*

I shrugged it off, assuming she was just sober enough to catch social cues somewhat better than both Skye and I.

"What about favorite movies?" I asked, not feeling a need to divulge how much further down the social capital ladder my taste in books hung out.

"Movies? Didn't you two meet at a book club? I'd have thought you'd be all about discussing Tolstoy and Dostoevsky," Dennis teased.

I narrowed my eyes at him, all too aware he'd caught me hanging out in the back room with a wide variety of smutty romance novels over the months I'd worked for him, and a distinct lack of Russian philosophers. But two could play this game. "Sure, who wouldn't be—especially five rum and Cokes in. Tell me, Dennis, darling, if you were stranded on a desert island, which highbrow book would *you* pick over a cell phone with an Internet connection?"

My boss laughed and held up both hands in defeat. "All right, point well made. So, movies, then?"

FOR THE NEXT couple of hours, Warin fielded less-than-subtle flirting from Skye like a pro, intermixed with general banter and drunken human humor. But I guess he was a pro—at blending in with humans, that is. When he hadn't been locked up and starved for goddess knew how long, at least.

I was pretty amazed with his transformation from when I'd first met him—especially when he not so much as glanced at Skye's cleavage or neck. I recalled the darkness in his eyes when he'd stared at my bleeding collarbone and suppressed a shudder. Vampires were clearly better company when they'd been fed.

Skye, however, was less than impressed with his lack of interest in her booby offerings. When Warin ignored her batting eyelashes for probably the tenth time since his arrival at our booth, she'd clearly had enough of playing it subtle and deemed it time for a more direct approach. I was pretty sure, judging from Warin's involuntary jerk, that when she reached under the table, she wasn't grabbing at his leg.

"How about we all take it to a nightclub? I want to dance! Don't you feel like a bit of *grinding*, Warin?" She shot the vampire at flirtatious smile.

"Actually, I'm beat," I said, stretching for emphasis. "I should head on home. Warin, would you walk me, please? You never know what lurks out there." I winked at the vampire and got a soft chuckle in return.

"Of course." He very firmly moved Skye's hand—which was, indeed, placed on his crotch, I noted as I got to my feet—and made to stand up.

"See you later, guys," I said as Skye blew a raspberry at me behind Warin's back.

We exited the bar and weaved our way past clusters of drunk people on the pavement. I led the vampire about a block away before I turned to him with a teasing smile.

"All right, the girls aren't following, so you should be safe. You don't actually have to walk me all the way home—it's pretty far."

"I would nevertheless like to," he said

"Okay, then, but don't complain if you get tired," I teased as we began walking.

His hoarse laughter made my already present smile bigger. There was something about the sound of his mild amusement that warmed me from the inside out, almost as effectively as the several rum and Cokes I presently had in my system.

"You've seen firsthand how much stronger vampires are, and yet you worry a walk will make me tired? You are a funny human."

I snorted. "Sorry, didn't mean to put your entire race in a bad light with my concern for your comfort.

"Hardly. I find you rather intriguing."

The way he said it so absolutely casually, as if it was a perfectly normal thing to say to a girl, made my already alcohol-fueled hormones spike.

Way too young, Liv. And *a vampire,* I mentally scolded my ovaries. Not that he seemed to be really flirting. He was casually strolling next to me with both hands in the pockets of his wool coat without so much as looking at me.

Yeah, I so wasn't going there. A shudder rose up through my spine at the thought of mixing the kind of bedroom antics vampires were infamous for with what my lady bits currently seemed focused on. I was way too vanilla to ever want to try out blood play, that's for damn sure.

"Are you cold?" my vampire companion asked at my shiver.

"Yeah," I said. It *was* fucking freezing, and I hadn't wrapped up as thoroughly as I should have when I got dressed for the night out. Foolishly, I'd chosen vanity over a healthy respect for Chicago's November temperatures once the sun set.

He didn't so much as stop as he swiftly unbuttoned his coat and draped it over my shoulders.

"*Oh.* You don't have to—I don't want you to get cold..."

My voice died when he shot me an incredulous look, eyebrow raised. "Yeah, okay... vampires don't feel the cold, do they?"

"No," he said, an amused twitch to his lips at my belated light bulb-moment.

"Well... thank you," I said, clutching it closer around me. The same scent—of crisp night air and a hint of earthy notes—as I'd noticed when he'd lent me his shirt months earlier wrapped around me. Flashes of some of the more X-rated dreams I'd been plagued with after we parted helpfully arrived in the forefront of my mind, making my face heat up. Apparently, the smell of him was enough to reactivate whatever had triggered them to begin with.

"Warin.... You know, when you, ah, fed me your blood...?" I asked, doing my best to keep my tone neutral.

"Hmm?"

"Are there... sometimes, uh, *side-effects?*"

The way he stole a glance at me from below his dark eyelashes made me suspect he was fully aware of what I was referring to.

"There can be some, yes. Which ones depends on the donor and receivers," he non-answered. "Are you still feeling any... effects?"

I shook my head with vigor, silently thanking the goddess I hadn't run into him while the dreams were still at their height. "Nope, damn shame too."

His eyebrows shot up in surprise. "Oh?"

I gave him a teasing smile. "Yeah, my skin was flawless for *weeks*. You have no idea how many girls would kill for never having to reach for their foundation again."

Warin chuckled at my theatrics.

"Seriously, you should bottle that stuff. You'd make a killing in the beauty industry." I wasn't serious at all.

However, Warin's good-humored smile withered, dark severity taking its place as he grabbed my shoulder lightly, making me stop. "Liv, you can never tell anyone about taking vampire blood, or its effects. Do you understand? *Never*."

"Yeah, just joking." I gave him a reassuring smile. "Don't worry, I'm not about to repay you for saving my life with running my mouth about the healing properties of your blood. Don't wanna think about what the pharmaceutical industry would do with *that* information."

"There've been rumors circulating since the Night of Revelations. I am not worried about some foolish human attempting to extract blood from a vampire—but if an undead hears you speaking of such matters, they *will* end your life."

"Oh." I blinked, some of my pleasant buzz disappearing in the face of his seriousness. "Okay, got it. Any other warnings you wanna share? Or has the government got it covered with their anti-vamp campaigns?"

Warin snorted derisively. "They know very little of

value." He released my shoulder and began walking again. I fell in beside him.

"So? Do you have any good tips? Just in case the next vampire I get locked in a cage with isn't as friendly?"

He chuckled mirthlessly. "I've not seen many humans capable of coming out on top from an encounter with a vampire. But we do have some vulnerabilities."

"Like silver?" I asked, thinking back to the thin chain the fanatics had tied Warin with. "As far as I know, that's never been in any of the campaigns. I can't believe those lunatics were better prepared than the Nightwalker Department. Will wearing a silver necklace protect me?"

"No. Nothing will protect you from a vampire, Liv. Your best defense is to avoid us at all costs."

"Says the vampire currently walking me home in the middle of the night," I said with a cheeky grin. "Just what any girl wants to hear."

His laugh sounded more genuine this time. "You're amusing when you're intoxicated."

"*Psh.*" Eloquent as always. "What about you? Do vampires not get drunk? I saw you finish several glasses."

"You saw nothing but a well-practiced trick," he said with a casual shrug. "We can't ingest alcohol or other food substances. Most of my kind learn sleight of hand if they wish to blend in with humans."

"Huh," I said, feeling extra bad that he'd had to sit through getting mauled by my female colleagues while stone-cold sober. "Guess that's handy—don't know many other bars that'd let a kid drink."

"Excuse me?"

I grimaced. "Sorry, I mean *'young men under twenty-one.'*" A moment's clarity made me stop and squint at him. "Wait..." I mentally facepalmed. He was a goddamn *vampire. Well-fucking-done, Liv.* I wanted to excuse my idiocy with how drunk I was, but the truth was that I'd assumed he was very young since we met.

"You're older than you look."

His sculpted lips quivered once. "I am."

I blew a raspberry, displacing my bangs with the gust of air before I resumed walking so I didn't have to see the gleam of amusement over my idiocy in his blue gaze. "Well, don't I feel like a tit. In my defense, it's really hard to relate to. Do you just... freeze in time? Face-wise, I mean?"

"Something like that." He was smirking, but at least he wasn't rubbing my nose in it. "We have another way of estimating age than by appearances."

"Length of fangs?" I suggested with a grin.

His laughter rumbled in the cool air around us. "Charisma."

"Hmm..." I turned my head to look at him through narrowed eyes, trying to sense anything about his charisma that would help me put an age on him. "Thirty... two?"

"No."

I looked at him expectantly, waiting for him to reveal the real number.

"C'mon, how old are you?" I finally moaned when he failed to bite.

A downright wicked smirk spread across his lips. "Older than you, little one."

I made a crude noise, which brought back his laughter. "And how old am I, then, oh wise one?"

"Twenty-seven," he said without missing a beat.

Huh. "That's cheating, you know."

"Would you like me to guess again with a blindfold over my eyes this time?"

He was mocking me. The infuriatingly smug vampire by my side was full-on *mocking* me for my lack of age-guessing superpowers.

"Yeah, well, I can drink alcohol. And eat chocolate ice cream, so there," I huffed.

Warin crinkled his nose as if that wasn't something to envy. *Psh!*

"I'd die without Ben & Jerry's chocolate fudge brownie—it's nothing to turn your nose up at," I proclaimed with a dramatic flourish of my hand.

His blue eyes sparkled mischievously. "I'm already dead."

"I'm really not sure that argument can win this discussion," I said, voice tart.

Warin chuckled. "You truly are a strange human, aren't you?"

"How rude," I hummed. "You know, you told me the same thing when I was locked up in a cage and certain you'd eat me too. It's not saying anything great about your character, you know."

"That's true." He sent me a gentle smile.

Something down low in my abdomen melted in response.

"Warin...?"

"Liv?"

"Are you *really* older than me?"

"Is it important?" He sounded infuriatingly unconcerned.

Only if I don't stop having perverted thoughts about you.

Which I was. As much as I wanted to give in to my booze-addled hormones, I so wasn't going there. And who's to even say he was interested anyway? He hadn't so much as glanced at Skye's or Raven's cleavage, and I didn't have nearly as much to offer in that department.

Maybe he was gay.

The silence stretched between us as we walked side by side along the pavement. The streets became quieter and quieter as we left Chicago's busier areas, only the odd car passing us by. With anyone else I'd known as briefly as I had Warin, I would have felt compelled to fill the silence with smalltalk, but not with him. It was a comfortable silence, the kind I'd always imagined you could only get with friends you'd known for years.

He was the one to break it some minutes later.

"Were you raised in Denver? Your friends mentioned it."

"Yes. Got out of there as soon as I could, though."

He must have caught on that I didn't want to talk about my hometown, because he changed the subject without prying further. "Have you been in Chicago long?"

"No, just about four months. I move a lot. You?"

"I've been here a while."

"You don't sound too happy about it," I noted. "Do vampires not get to travel much?"

"Some do. I have... obligations that keep me here."

"Secret vampire business?" I guessed from his cagey answer.

He chuckled. "You could call it that."

I sighed as as I came to a stop, looking up toward the complex where my rental condo was located. It was a two-hour walk from the bar by *Dark Dreams*, but it felt like it'd only been twenty minutes.

Warin stopped too, eying the building behind me. "This is your home?"

"Yes. Well, the condo over there." I nodded toward the ground floor apartment furthest to the left of the building. I bit my lip as I looked at the vampire in front of me, and realized I didn't want it to be the last time I saw him.

"Will you model for me?" I blurted.

"Pardon?" His eyebrows raised half an inch.

"I want to draw you. Your portrait," I hastily explained, not wanting him to think I was a complete pervert. "Nothing, uh, nude or anything."

He considered me for a moment. "Could we continue talking while you did this?"

I lit up, warmth blooming in my stomach that he'd apparently also enjoyed our chat on the walk back. "Yes, of course. As long as you sit somewhat still. Uh... when do you have time?"

His eyebrows furrowed as he pulled out a smartphone from his pocket and tapped on the display a few times. "I have a couple hours free after sundown on Monday. How long would you need for this drawing?"

"Oh, we can stop and pick up as many times as needed," I beamed. My answer was purposely noncommittal—I was planning on getting as much pencil time out of his face as possible. And as many facts about vampires as I could too.

"I will stop by after sunset on Monday," he confirmed.

I nodded and took his coat off, handing it back to him. "Thanks for walking me home."

"It is not safe for a human to walk the streets alone at night," he said. "You should always remember this."

"Yeah, yeah." I rolled my eyes at him as I turned toward my door. "No walking home alone, no getting between vampires and stakes. For someone who's *supposed* to be part of what goes bump in the night, you're pretty tightly laced, Warin."

The vampire's chuckle followed me as I walked into my apartment building.

I saw him through the window in my living room before I turned the light on, waiting.

My front door slammed shut behind me, the noise making me jolt—I hadn't meant to kick it closed with as much force as my drunken foot had apparently managed —and when I looked back out on the street, Warin was gone.

Such a gentleman.

SEVEN

"Raven says your hot friend is a vampire. Is that true?"

I blinked at Skye's excited face as I paused mid-unwrapping my wooly scarf from around my neck. It was eight thirty on Monday morning, and my brain had yet to wake up. That's why I only managed an unconvincing, "Uh, what?" at my colleague's unexpected question.

"Oh, my stars!" she gasped, mouth dropping open even as her eyes sparkled with elation. "He *is!*" She pulled the scarf from my frozen hands, spinning me half a round before lifting my hair out of the way to scan my neck. "Did he bite you? Did it feel good?"

"What? No, of course he didn't! And he isn't a..." My denial died on my lips at Skye's raised eyebrow. Sighing, I shrugged out of my coat. "Fine. How did Raven know?"

"He had cold hands and is pale as a ghost. And she

said she tried to feel for his pulse and couldn't find one. She was a bit worried about you, but he seemed so nice."

I rolled my eyes as we walked out of the staff room to the front of *Dark Dreams* to set up the cash register. That explained the many text messages I'd woken up to Saturday, about 'checking in' on me. "She *checked his pulse?*"

"Well, you know..." Skye made a flapping motion with one hand. "It's one of her *things,* isn't it?"

"Uh-huh," I agreed, because anything else would have been rude. Raven did tarot cards and palm readings for customers every Thursday, and claimed she had prophetic dreams. And it wasn't necessarily that I didn't believe her —I did have a stack of spiritual books at home, after all—it was just that her abilities always happened to pop up whenever they would get her the most attention. And she *did* dye her hair black and insist on being called Raven.

Of course, this time she'd been pretty spot on.

"Did you sleep with him?"

I shot Skye an exasperated look. "No! It's not like that."

"So you're not seeing him again?"

"Well..."

"Oh, you are!" Skye leaned over the counter, shoving a couple of crystal skulls aside to level me with her blue eyes. "Tell me *everything.*"

I'd never really had proper girlfriends. School had been difficult, and I'd been branded the odd one out early on. And since I'd left Denver, I'd never stuck around anywhere long enough to make real friendships. As a result, gossiping about a man was kinda unfamiliar territory for me. Especially when that man was a vampire with completely platonic interests in me.

"I just find him really interesting. It's a friendship—I've never really seen blood donation as a sexy thing, if you know what I mean."

"Uh-huh. Nothing sexy about a hot man sucking on your neck." Skye's voice was dry as tinder. "How did you meet him? And don't tell me that book club story again, I ain't buying what you're selling, girl." She wagged a finger at me.

I sighed. "Fine. We both got kidnapped by some crazy fanatics. They tried to feed me to him, but he politely refrained. And then proceeded to save my ass. And before you ask—all I was doing was reading a vampire romance."

Skye gaped at me, some of the excitement replaced by horror. "You were *kidnapped?* And you didn't think to tell us? Fuck, Liv, did you go to the police?"

I grimaced. "Of course I didn't. Best-case scenario, they would have hounded me for information about Warin, and I didn't particularly want to sell him down the river after he saved my life. Not to mention that worst-case scenario, they'd have taken me as a vampire sympathizer and held me for the more unpleasant kind of questioning. Which, by the way, is why I'd really appreciate if this whole vampire discussion doesn't get any further, okay?"

"But what about the people who kidnapped you? What if they find you again?" Bless her, she really did look genuinely worried for me. A small twang of warmth in the pit of my stomach made me reach out and pat her hand— I'd enjoyed working for Dennis more than I'd enjoyed any of my other retail jobs before, and it was in large part thanks to how sweet everyone was. The thought that if I stayed around this time, perhaps they'd turn into friends one day flitted through my mind as I took in Skye's worried frown.

"You don't have to worry. They won't find me. It's... been taken care of."

"But—" Skye's protest died at my grim look. "*Oh.*"

I forced my lips into a smile. Time to change the subject. As much as I understood her interest in learning more about Warin—hell, I'd bombarded him with questions about his kind myself the moment I realized he wasn't going to eat me—no one would benefit from dwelling on what exactly had happened to our kidnappers. The less you know, and such. "So how about you? Are you seeing anyone?"

IT WASN'T until I was standing in the supermarket on my way home from work that same afternoon that I realized I had no idea what to serve a vampire guest.

The thought of not putting up at least a small spread for a visitor just seemed all kinds of wrong, but as I frantically spun around myself in the aisles hosting corn chips and salsa dips, it dawned on me that Warin would be pretty fucking difficult to cater for.

I couldn't even open a bottle of wine. Or, well, *I could*, but it'd be entirely for my benefit.

It was only when I'd spun around myself for the third time that I spotted the sign for the butcher's at the far end of the aisle—and an idea finally took form. Clutching my chips-and-dip filled basket, I hurried to the counter.

"Hi, can I have..." How much did a vampire even eat? "Four pints of pigs' blood, please?" I shot the older man behind the counter a beaming smile, hoping I wasn't giving off any *"creepy cultist"* vibes.

"Oh, how refreshing. It's so rare to see the younger generations make some of the good old-fashioned dishes from scratch. Blood sausage, is it, dear?" he asked.

"Uh-huh, grandma's recipe. She'd roll over in her grave if I ever so much as thought to buy it factory-made," I lied. My grandmother was unfortunately still very much alive, and the only thing she'd ever taught me was how to hold back tears to avoid getting a whooping for *"being a big baby."*

Not that that kind of edifying family tales were likely to put my new blood-pusher at ease.

I waited for the butcher to shuffle to the back to get my goods with some impatience—I only had a couple of hours before sunset, and I still had to clean my apartment and ideally transform my work-worn self into something less undead-looking. Of *The Walking Dead*-variety. Warin pulled off the whole *undead*-thing pretty well.

I didn't manage to stop a loud giggle-snort at my own wit from escaping my throat, making the other patrons in the vicinity turn to look.

The kind butcher chose that moment to reappear from the back, four pint bottles filled with dark-red, viscous liquid. "Your pigs' blood," he said with gusto. Out the corner of my eye, I saw a mother pull her child closer.

"Thanks. Can't wait to make that *blood sausage*," I said loudly, snatching the bottles from him two at a time to put into my basket.

The mom only gave me a pinched frown before she walked away, child in tow, and the old lady by the deli-counter didn't look convinced, either.

Great.

I was so gonna bitch Dennis out for making us wear black clothes to work.

·   ·   ·

I DROVE HOME in my ancient Ford Fiesta, shoved the bottles into the fridge, and began *Project Oh-Shit-I-Didn't-Clean-Over-The-Weekend-Like-I-Meant-To* with only about an hour left until sundown. In my usual, well-organized fashion, I was only just done with the impressive pile of dishes on my kitchen counter when my door buzzer went off.

I looked up, noticed it was pitch-black outside, and muttered a curse. I'd decluttered most of the living room and dining room—and by "decluttered," I mean I'd shoved everything into my bedroom—and managed to run a brush through my hair and change out of my goth work ensemble, but the space certainly didn't represent anything from a *Better Living* magazine.

Or an immaculately kept vampire mansion, for that matter.

I pushed aside the sudden rush of insecurity over the difference between my home and Warin's. If we could be friends cross-species, a class difference really shouldn't be the dealbreaker.

Wiping my hands on my butt—like a lady—I walked over to my door phone and picked it up. "Yeah?"

"It's Warin. We have an appointment."

I couldn't hold back a grin at his formal tone. "Sure do. Hang on, I'll buzz ya in."

I pressed the buzzer and heard the street door opened

and shut, followed by a knock on my front door less than two seconds later.

I pulled it open, and my face split into an automatic smile at the sight of him. "Hey! So glad you could make it."

"Hello, Liv," he said politely. He looked so *proper* as he stood at my doorstep, gray woolen coat buttoned up and both hands folded in front of him, it made a nervous giggle bubble out of my chest.

I mentally facepalmed myself and waved him in as I turned to get the blood out. "I've been looking forward to this—it's rare I get to do live model drawings. "

Warin didn't answer, and when I turned back toward him halfway to the fridge, he was still standing in the door opening.

"I cannot enter without a spoken invitation," he said softly.

"Oh. *Oh!*" I blinked, entirely taken aback by the unexpectedness of his request. "Uh, come on in, Warin."

"Thank you." His voice was still soft as he stepped over the threshold and closed the door.

I bit the inside of my cheek as I watched him shrug out of his coat and hang it on the coat hanger I'd put up next to the door. Something not remotely connected to his magnetic blue eyes made a shiver travel up the length of my spine at the realization that I'd invited an undead creature into my home. Not that I hadn't known what he was when I asked him to come by, but... there was just something deeply unsettling about that very real reminder that he was something other than human.

"You are fearful," he said as he turned toward me. His face was blank, but his eyes seemed... saddened.

"What? No." I waved him off and resumed my previous smile. "It's just kind of odd, ya know?"

"I can detect fear quite easily," he said, touching his nose with a finger. "There is no need to lie, Liv. I can leave if you are uncomfortable."

He could *smell* me? Well, that was just all sorts of disconcerting. I sighed. "All right, it's kind of... a *tiny* bit terrifying that you have to be invited into my home, like in one of those awful scary stories. But I'm not scared of *you*—you could have eaten me like, a million times by now, if that was your grand plan. *And!*" I skipped to the fridge and swung it open. "You seriously can't leave now—do you have *any* idea how awkward it is to buy blood at a butcher's? I don't think anyone but the butcher himself bought that I was gonna make blood sausage. Pretty sure everyone else thought I had some sort of Satanic ritual planned."

I pulled out one of the pint bottles of pigs' blood and held it out toward him as a peace offering.

He stared at it for a long moment before he lifted his gaze to mine. "It was very kind of you to go out of your way for me. You needn't have gone through embarrassment for my sake."

My shoulders slumped. "Don't tell me you ate already. I have four pints of this stuff." His cheeks *did* look slightly flushed.

"I would never turn down your kind gesture," he said, offering me a faint smile. "Thank you. I will have a glass."

I beamed, relieved I hadn't committed some form of vampire *faux pas*. "Make yourself comfortable, I'll be right over," I told him, gesturing to the sofa.

I turned to my small kitchen and busied myself pouring the blood into a glass. It smelled pretty horrid, and it took everything I had not to gag. I was going to pour myself a glass of wine, but after getting the stench of pigs' blood in my nostrils, I couldn't face drinking any sort of red liquid. Instead, I got myself a drink of Mountain Dew, grabbed both glasses, and turned toward the sofa.

But Warin wasn't sitting down. Instead, he was standing in front one of my paintings of a sunrise, seemingly absorbed.

"I did that one this summer, shortly after coming to Chicago," I said as I put the glasses down. It was odd, having someone look so intensely at my art. It made me feel a bit shy—I rarely had people over, so it wasn't a common occurrence. My paintings had always been just for me, since I was a kid needing somewhere beautiful to escape to.

"You have a lot of talent," he said, not taking his eyes off the sunset. "Do you exhibit?"

"Ha, I wish," I snorted, flopping down of the couch. With a finger, I pushed Warin's glass of blood farther toward the other end of the coffee table. "I doubt anyone would offer up their gallery for an amateur. But thank you for the praise."

"I would," he said, finally turning away from the painting. "Do you have other pieces?"

"Yeah, tons." I smiled, flattered by his obvious enjoyment of my art. As much as my inner critic claimed he was just being polite, I could see the sincerity in his eyes. "Most are in boxes in my bedroom, though."

"I would like to see them sometime. If you don't mind?" He walked across to the sofa and finally sat down, eying the glass of blood.

"Of course." I reached for my drawing pad and pencil I'd strategically laid out on the coffee table in preparation for his arrival. Or hadn't tidied up in my frantic rush to make my apartment look somewhat inhabitable, more like, but whatever.

"But it'll have to wait. I've been so looking forward to this. You have really beautiful features."

"Thank you," he said after a moment's hesitation, giving me a glance out the corner of his eye, and it wasn't until then that I realized I'd called him beautiful. The young man on my couch whom I'd had more than one perverted dream about. Of course he would think I was flirting.

"Uh, I mean—you've got the face of any artist's dream. Your cheekbones and jawline are very... structured," I finished lamely, realizing I wasn't making things any better. Judging from Warin's arrow-straight posture and lack of eye contact, I'd managed to make him feel about as awkward as I did.

Great. Just great.

"Uh, so just relax and have a drink, and I'll get started. I need to find your lines, so I don't need you to sit super still just yet," I said, thankful he at least couldn't see my mortified blush while refusing to look at me.

I began drawing in the angles of his high cheekbones, and Warin reached for his glass and sank a bit further back into the couch. He looked like he was trying to appear relaxed, but his back was still obviously tensed.

"You don't spend a lot of time around humans, do you?" I guessed. He looked completely out of place in my small home, and not only because of his immaculately pressed charcoal pants and soft cashmere sweater.

"Not socially," he admitted, the corner of his mouth quirking up in just a ghost of a smile as he finally looked toward me.

"More for food, huh?" I asked as I quickly captured the small tilt of his lips. "I guess that's not what most people would call a social affair, even if it involves dinner."

He was polite enough to smile at my terrible joke.

"I only spend time with humans for business affairs. I haven't fed from a human in... years. Apart from you." His gaze brushed over my collarbone, and I subconsciously brought a hand to where he'd licked my blood off all those months ago.

"Huh. Then what do you eat?" I asked, forcing the echo of his tongue lapping against my skin firmly from my mind. "Animal blood?"

"Sometimes. Mostly donor blood."

"Do people often guess what you are? Like, do your business associates know they're dealing with a vampire?" I asked as I began sketching in his eyebrows. The shadows of his refined Cupid's bow and the angle of his jaw were begging for a charcoal drawing, but I always liked to start out in pencil until I was familiar with the subject. Especially with a live model.

"Not often, no. And when they do, it's easy to Compel them to forget." His fingers tightened around the stem of the glass for a moment before he brought it to his lips.

I opened my mouth to ask what on Earth he meant by *"Compel them to forget,"* but before I could, Warin's features contorted in revulsion and he harked and spat the deep red liquid back into the glass.

"Jesus fuck, are you all right?" I tossed my paper and

pencil aside and rushed to his side to slap his back as he heaved.

The vampire made a groaning sort of noise in response. His coughing fit lasted for nearly a minute before it finally seemed to ease. Whatever blood remained in his mouth he wiped on his arm, seemingly not caring about the expensive cashmere sweater.

"What *was* that? Do you need some water?" I asked, already halfway up to get him a glass of water before he stopped me.

"No." He muttered something that sounded an awful lot like a curse. "I'm fine."

"You don't *look* fine," I said. It was true—he looked if possible even paler than normal, with a slightly green tinge. "What the hell happened?"

Warin touched the glass with a single finger, pushing it farther away. "It's dead blood."

"Uh..." I frowned, looking at the glass. "Isn't all blood...?"

"We cannot drink corpse blood. If the blood is drained after the last heartbeat, it is poisonous to vampires."

"Oh, my goddess! I am so, so sorry!" I slapped a hand up to cover my mouth, feeling about as horrible as one should when nearly poisoning their unsuspecting guest. Martha Stewart would certainly never give me any sorts of rewards, that's for certain. "I had no idea."

"Where did you get this blood?" he asked, a speculative frown on his still slightly ill-looking face.

"The local supermarket's butcher. Why, is it uncommon for it to be, uh, from a dead animal?"

"Yes." He rubbed his face with his blood-free hand. "Butchers always sell fresh blood."

My eyes widened. "You think... you think someone deliberately swapped it with dead blood? To target vampires? Who would even know to do that?"

"That's what I've been trying to figure out for months. There have been... concerning events. I was close to unraveling their network this summer, but they have been laying low since August." He gave the glass another disgusted look. "They could certainly be organized enough to target blood distribution, and the victims would rarely be high ranking enough for anyone to notice."

"Oh, wow, I forgot you said you were in vampire law enforcement." I stared at him with renewed appreciation. Then something he'd said dawned on me, and my stomach dropped: since August.

"Is that why you were in that basement? Did I ruin some undercover mission, or something like that?"

The first smile since what I'd undoubtedly be referring to as *"the blood incident"* for years to come touched his lips. "Something like that."

"Oh, fuck. I'm sorry."

He snorted. "You're *sorry* you got kidnapped and

offered as food for me? You are an odd one.”

“Yeah, well,” I huffed, not entirely sure how to take his continued insistence that I was a weird human. “I’m gonna help you get to the bottom of the blood thing. It’s the least I can do for nearly poisoning you.”

The wry smile on his face disappeared in the blink of an eye. “You will do no such thing.”

“Beg your pardon?”

He frowned at me. “I believe I’ve made it perfectly clear that I do not wish for you to get in between vampires and those who seek to harm us.”

I rolled my eyes. “And you always get your way, do you? Whoever they are, they thought it was perfectly acceptable to feed me to a vampire, remember? I think I have a right to get as involved as I want. Which isn’t much, by the way. But I could just go to the butcher’s during daytime and ask casually about the blood. Probably less suspicious than if a ghostly guy shows up and starts chatting to them about their suppliers, eh?”

Warin’s frown deepened. “Liv, I am serious. You are not to get involved. Do you understand?”

Well, wasn’t he Mr. Domineering? Get a little corpse blood in him and the polite young man I’d let into my home earlier in the evening turned all patronizing. I rolled my eyes and grabbed my drawing kit again.

“Right, whatever. So what does it mean to Compel someone?”

If he was suspicious of my quick capitulation, he didn't show it. "It's a hypnosis, of a sort."

"And you use it to make people forget what you are?" I asked, arching my eyebrows at him. That sounded pretty fucking creepy. "What else can you do with it?"

His looked down, and I resumed my drawing to capture the way his dark eyelashes shadowed his cheekbones. "We can capture the mind of any human. Make them do whatever we ask. How long it lasts depends on the strength of the vampire and the will of the human."

"That..." My pencil came to a halt as I stared at him. "I'm sorry, are you telling me you can... *mindfuck* people?"

"Yes. If humans truly understood what we were, what we can do, it wouldn't be our physical strength you feared." He looked up at me then, capturing my gaze with the magnetic pull of his. "Would it?"

"I..." I frowned, unable to ignore the icy tendril traveling up my spine when I remembered all the little things he'd told me about his kind. Things most humans didn't know—shouldn't know. "Are you going to Compel *me* to forget?"

"No." He didn't move his gaze from mine. "I can't. You're the only human who's ever been able to resist my Compulsion."

"Oh, that's... Wait, you *tried?*" Mild outrage made me scowl at him.

"Of course I did. You know about our weakness for silver, you know the location of my home, benefits of ingesting vampire blood..."

"Pure safety procedure?" I asked, still feeling kinda miffed about his apparent attempt to mindfuck me without my consent.

"Yes. And that's why you can never tell anyone what you know. Other vampires are unlikely to let you wander around with so much information and a free mind." He finally released my gaze, settling back into the couch as if the matter was fully discussed.

But I only had more questions.

"But why? Why can't you Compel me? I'm as ordinary as ordinary can be," I said, frowning at the vampire.

"There is nothing ordinary about you, Liv," he said softly, flicking those long eyelashes up to look at me once more with the most intense stare I'd ever received in my life. "I do not know why you can resist my Compulsion, but I know you are far from ordinary. I've known it since we first met."

Predictably, the deepest blush of my lifetime heated up my entire face, until I was pretty sure I was glowing like a lighthouse. Before I could think of a joking deflection, a sharp shrill cut through my living room.

I jolted, dropping my pencil in my lap.

Warin slid his hand into his pants pocket and withdrew his fancy smartphone. Faster than my eye could follow, he'd lifted it to his ear. "Yes? Yes. I'm on my way." He hung up without another word.

"Running late?" I asked, glancing at my own phone. To my surprise, it had been four hours since he'd arrived. *Huh.*

"Yes. My apologies—I will have to leave now." He got to his feet, but turned toward me before he'd gotten more than a few steps toward the door. "Would it be acceptable if I come back another night?"

I smiled—I'd been low-key worried he wouldn't want to repeat the evening after the blood incident. "Yes, you have to. I'm nowhere near done with my drawings. I have time tomorrow night, if you do?"

He frowned, regret flickering across his pale features. "It would be hard to fit it in tomorrow night."

I reached out my hand. "Give me your phone."

He obeyed, eyebrows raised in question.

I quickly typed in my number and gave it back to him. "There. Give me a call when you have time, and we'll figure something out."

Warin nodded. "I will. Thank you for tonight, Liv."

I grimaced and got up to see him out. "Yeah, sorry again about almost poisoning you. I promise, I'm done attempting to play *Better Housekeeping* hostess. You'll have to bring your own dinner next time."

I didn't miss the look of brief relief on the vampire's face as he turned to leave.

EIGHT

I drove back to the supermarket after work the next day.

The same old man who'd served me the previous day was minding the butcher's counter again. He lit up in a smile of recognition when I stopped in front of him, shopping basket over one arm.

"Ah, how was the sausage-making, dear?"

"Not good, I'm afraid." I leaned on the counter and gave a dramatic sigh. "It tasted off. I was wondering if there might have been something off with the blood? Grandma always made it with very fresh ingredients, and this was just not up to par."

"Oh dear, that's a shame. I can assure you there's nothing wrong with the blood, but..." He looked thoughtful for a moment. "I suppose it's possible our new suppliers treat it slightly different before they package it for shipping."

"Oh, you have a new supplier?" I perked up. "Could I get the name and address for them? To give them customer feedback, I mean."

The butcher hesitated for a moment, but then nodded. "Yes, I suppose that would be all right. You're certainly no vampire."

I snorted. "No, can't say that I am. What, are the undead trying to infiltrate pig's blood suppliers?"

"You would be surprised," he said, face grave. Leaning over the counter, he whispered, "I've had five colleagues across the city have their storerooms raided just this past month. The only thing missing was blood. Now, I might not know much about the undead plague, but I do know the city hasn't been overrun by thieving sausage makers."

"Oh, goodness me," I said, not having problems getting my face to display a sufficient amount of shock at this news. Why on Earth were vampires raiding butchers? Chicago's murder rate certainly hadn't dropped, and vampires certainly were accountable for a percentage of it. Maybe they were like Warin and didn't drink directly from humans? If someone had truly contaminated the animal blood supply, they were targeting peaceful vampires, rather than the ones who hunted humans. That seemed... unusually cruel. And counterintuitive.

The butcher nodding knowingly at my shocked

expression. "Mmhm. Those filthy monsters are every-where. The general population likes to try and forget they exist, but they're out there. Just waiting for a moment's inattentiveness to pounce."

Waiting to pounce on a butcher's supply of pig's blood so they could eat without hurting humans, it seemed. I nodded empathetically nonetheless.

"Let me get you that address for your letter," he said, nodding as if he saw in me a *Friend of the Cause*. "It ain't right that we can't make a good blood sausage because of those monsters."

I GOT HOME in time to call Bolton & Son, the slaughterhouse supplying my local supermarket, before they closed. Much to my surprise, the address was in the southwestern part of the city—I'd definitely thought it would be located somewhere in the countryside, but apparently not.

"*Mjello?*" I rough voice greeted me, on the second ring.

"Hi, is this Bolton & Son? The slaughterhouse?"

"*Affirmative,*" the man on the other end said. "*What can I do you for, lady?*"

"I wanted to talk to someone about the recent changes to the blood you supply. I was making my grandma's old recipe for blood sausage, and the taste was off. When I talked to my local butcher, he said the change might come from their new supplier—which would be you. To stop vampires, or something like that?" I was pretty impressed with how much I managed to sound like someone who didn't live off microwave meals and takeout.

There was silence on the other end of the line for a little while. *"Well, yes, we have implemented some changes. They were never intended to harm good people like yourself, just looking to make some home-cooked food. Tell you what, why don't you come by the office? I'd love to have you sit down with some of the people in charge of this change—they might listen to a consumer more than they do us. We have a few of the old school butchers here who ain't too keen on messing with the food, if you know what I mean. How about noon tomorrow?"*

"Er..." I blinked. I hadn't exactly been planning to make an excursion out of this, but on the other hand... if I did go, I'd get to snoop around more. So long as I could continue faking a keen interest in the proper preparation of blood sausage, it was undoubtedly a one-time chance at getting closer to the core of whatever network had deemed me expendable enough to kidnap this summer.

"How about Friday around noon? I'm off work then," I suggested cheerfully.

"It's a date. Just ask for Billy when you arrive," he said.

"All right, see you then, Billy!" I hung up, feeling mightily proud of my sleuthing skills.

WHEN FRIDAY ROLLED AROUND, I drove my beat-up Fiesta to the address given to me by my supermarket butcher. The slaughterhouse was located at the edge of an industrial estate, surrounded by busy roads, and the stench rolling out from its open gates when I pulled up spoke its clear language that I'd gotten to the right place.

I parked up by what looked like the office-part of the building and got out, shielding my nose with one hand. It wasn't so much the smell of animals—I'd spent some time in the countryside before—but the overwhelming smell of... death. It was the only description I had for the pungent stench that hung over the building.

Before I could start walking to the nearest steel staircase leading up to a door I assumed hosted the office, that same door swung open and a portly man in a vest and with face stubbles squinted out into the dull November light.

"Hi! I'm Olivia Green—here to meet Billy. We spoke on the phone earlier this week," I said, lowering my hand from my nose to not be rude. The slaughterhouse's smell immediately overwhelmed my senses once more, and I forced myself not to gag.

The guy cracked a lopsided smile. "Ah, yes, the sausage specialist. Come on up, sugar. We're all ready for you."

The way he said it made something at the back of my brain perk up, a small bolt of adrenaline sparking in my blood. I hadn't been too worried about my amateur spying, because there was no way in hell they'd ever be able to guess my ulterior motives. I'd even made sure to come during daytime hours, to ensure they didn't mistake me for a vampire. But now, as Billy the butcher waved me up the stairs and into the gaping maw of the slaughterhouse, I suddenly found it hard to make my feet move up the steps.

Why? Why were my fight or flight instincts on high alert, just from one sentence from this guy?

I hesitated, reconsidering whether this was such a good idea and if perhaps I should just hightail it out of there, when the middle-aged man let his eyes roam over my winter coat-covered body, his smile turning distinctly lecherous.

Ah. And there was the reason for my reluctance to get any closer.

Sausage specialist, my ass.

I pushed my uncomfortableness aside and ascended the stairs with a forced smile. I wasn't going to back down from investigating this slaughterhouse and the people behind it just because its entry was guarded by a horny dude with wandering eyes and a creepy vibe.

"Great, can't wait. So, who am I meeting?" I asked as he stepped just enough aside that I had to brush past him to get in. Yup, he was a full-on creep. No wonder my immediate instincts had been to turn tail and run.

"Just Elliot from, ah, PR," Billy said as he led me down a short corridor that looked like it could use a renovation. The beige paint was peeling off parts of the walls, and the linoleum floor was worn with brown patches from old spillage that hadn't been cleaned up in time. And over it all the smell of death still hung like a depressing cloud, even if it was milder than outside.

"You have a PR department?" I asked, not managing to banish the surprise from my voice as he opened a door into what turned out to be a small office in as desperate need of TLC as the hallway. The beige paint on the walls was the same, but the floor had been upgraded to a worn, orangey-brown carpet. A desk overflowing with paperwork took up about a third of the room, and three chairs had been squeezed into the remaining space. In one of them sat a lanky, black-haired man who looked to be about thirty.

"Yeah, 'course," Billy said. "After that incident with the lamb, we had to. Nobody was in the mood for mutton for weeks. This is Elliot—our PR guy. Elliot, this is Olivia Green—the girl who called about our blood supply."

I wasn't even close to asking about what *"lamb inci-dent"* had made Chicago stop buying lamb chops for two weeks, so instead I put on my best *dim homemaker* smile and stretched out my hand toward the guy who'd won *"slaughterhouse PR dude"* in the job lottery. "Pleased to meet ya!"

"I'll leave you two to it, then," Billy said, giving me another once-over before he shut the door behind me, leaving me alone in the small office with Elliot.

"Likewise." Elliot gave me a thin smile and reached for my hand for a brief handshake. His hand fell cool and clammy against mine, with no strength. A bit like I imag-ined holding a lukewarm dead fish would be like.

I masked my grimace with another smile.

"So, you make blood sausages?" he said as he motioned for me to take the chair next to his.

I obeyed. "Yeah. Grandma's recipe."

"And this is the first time you notice any difference?"

"Yes, well it's the first time I've made it since moving to Chicago. It was such a disappointment," I said, faking a saddened frown. *"Disappointment"* wouldn't quite be the term I'd have used to describe Warin's violent retching.

"Uh-huh, I can imagine. Naturally, we feel terrible if our new blood procedures have had an impact on your grandma's recipe. I know my own nan would never forgive if one of her recipes went haywire." He gave me a sympa-thetic smile that somehow didn't reach his eyes. Not that I was surprised a PR guy had to fake sympathy for my equally fake sausage story. I probably wouldn't have had a whole lot of empathy left over for picky consumers if my job consisted of making a slaughterhouse appealing to the masses.

"Say, why don't you take a look at some of the formulas involved in our new process?" he asked.

I blinked. "Er... I doubt I'd understand much."

"Let's have a look at them, anyway. I'd like for you to see what we're doing that's different. I find that understanding a problem always helps when trying to find a solution."

I highly doubted any formulas would help the whole "corpse blood" situation, but I nodded nonetheless. "Sure, I guess it couldn't hurt."

Elliot reached into the briefcase by his feet and pulled out a thick piece of parchment. "Here you go," he said, holding it underneath my nose.

I took it from him and scanned the page. Chemistry had never been my strong suit, so most of the scribbled formulas on the side just looked like mishmash to me. But one of them made me blink. It was located at the dead center of the page, and looked more like some of the amulets we sold at *Dark Dreams* than it did a chemistry formula. When I blinked, it began to glow with a sickly green light.

I nearly dropped it. "Who—what's that?" I asked,

snapping my head to the side to see if Elliot saw what I did."

"Keep looking at the page, Olivia," he said, and this time there was a weird sort of command to his voice. It made my neck turn without my conscious will, so I was once again staring at the oddly glowing circle.

"Who is your master?" Elliot's voice seemed to come from *inside* my head. I shook it, certain I'd heard wrong, and felt... *something* tighten around my mind. Almost like an iron blanket clamping down around my own will.

"W-what?" I asked, blinking rapidly to regain my focus. I struggled against the iron band that seemed to fog up my brain.

"Who sent you here today?"

"No one," I croaked. "I'm not with PETA, if that's what you think. I just..." The words seemed hard to get out. I put the page in my lap and rubbed at my eyes. The instant I no longer looked at the paper, the fog began to clear. "I really am just here because... because I wanted to know if there was a way of getting uncontaminated blood for my sausages."

He didn't reply for a long moment, so I turned my head to look at him. "Is... everything all right?"

He looked startled, his pale green eyes wider than they'd been when he handed me the page, dark eyebrows drawn into a frown.

Then he slowly nodded. "Of course. I understand."

Abruptly, he got to his feet. "Come. I would like to show you where we harvest the blood, to explain the process and why it's necessary."

"Uh..." I really didn't want to. I had no idea what had just happened, if a migraine was coming on or what, but something about the change in Elliot's demeanor put me on edge. He looked guarded, despite his clearly fake smile. Withdrawn. And that same something that had niggled at me at Billy's first words to me was very much present again.

Once might have been nothing more than an instinctive reaction to a lecherous old man, but twice within the span of fifteen minutes? No. It was time for me to leave.

"I really appreciate it, but I need to get going. I think I'm feeling a migraine coming on, and my husband will be expecting me home soon." I was pretty sure my smile looked as fake as his as I got to my feet.

"Oh, it will only take a minute," Elliot said. He put his hand lightly on my arm, and despite my coat being between his fingers and my skin, every hair on my body stood on end in response. Something similar to the fog from before edged in at my consciousness, but this time my mind remained clear as the sensation of iron locked around it. "I insist."

I briefly considered shoving him out of the way and running for the door, but pushed the urge aside. As much as I didn't want to be here, they weren't gonna up and murder me. For all they knew, I did have a husband waiting for me at home, with knowledge of exactly where I'd gone.

And really, straight-up killing a complaining customer was going a bit far, even for these two creeps.

That same something that'd niggled at the back of my skull about danger seemed to agree—the safest option here was to not let on that I thought something was off.

Still with absolutely no idea why my instincts were going haywire, I nodded at Elliot. "All right then, if it's only for a minute."

He moved his hand from my arm, giving me another thin smile as he herded me out the door. "Excellent. Come this way."

We walked down the hallway and through two sets of doors before Elliot stopped me by a white room. "We'll need hygiene covers before we go any further," he said.

"Uh-huh," I agreed, wanting to just get this over with as quickly as humanly possible. My nerves were so frayed, I kept jumping every time I caught a flicker from the fluo-rescent lights above us out of the corner of my eyes. And what had I gotten out of my little excursion? Nothing, except a nervous twitch.

So much for moonlighting as an amateur sleuth.

Once suited up in white plastic covering from head to toe, we continued through a set of double doors followed by a thick plastic fringe.

Once through, the temperature immediately dropped. I'd had to leave my coat behind in the room with the hygiene covers, and the sudden change made me shiver. But the second my eyes adjusted to the much sharper light within the warehouse we now stood in, all thoughts of being cold faded to the background at the sudden lurch of horror.

Bloody carcass after bloody carcass hung on meathooks as far my startled gaze could see, and at the far end a couple of men dressed in white were sawing up body parts with huge, noisy power-tools.

It wasn't that I was unfamiliar with what went on in a slaughterhouse, but one thing was to have a theoretical idea where your burger came from—it was something else entirely to step into the set for a slasher movie, with the stench of freshly slaughtered animals assaulting your nostrils.

"It's this way," Elliot said as he began walking down a path lined by rows of animal carcasses.

I did my best to keep my eyes on his back as I followed him, thankful I'd caught an early lunch before coming here. I was pretty sure I wouldn't be able to eat for a while after this visit.

Elliot led me around a corner and into another section of the warehouse, and I'm not too proud to admit I nearly fainted at the sight that met us there.

This section also had dead animals on hooks, but they

were in various states of getting skinned and, as it turned out, bled.

Elliot stopped us in front of a lamb that hung upside down above a bucket, blood dripping from its slit throat and into the pool of red liquid in the container.

"I'm sure you're aware that, when we get a call about someone complaining about the freshness of our blood supply, we get a bit antsy these days," Elliot said as he looked emotionlessly at the hapless animal in front of us. "Let me demonstrate what we are doing, and explain why."

He pointed at the dead lamb. "Previously, due to religious sensitivities and improved texture of the meat, we would take a bolt gun to the forehead of each animal before we slit their throat and let them bleed to death. The bolt gun technically left them brain dead, but their hearts still beat. These days, we kill the animal dead before we drain their blood, and the reason is quite simple: vampires can sustain themselves on animal blood —but only fresh animal blood taken while the heart still beats. When we found this out, we changed our procedure, so we would no longer be feeding the filthy monsters."

I stared at the dead lamb, trying to gather my thoughts enough to get through this without raising his suspicion of me further than it was becoming obvious it already was. "But... won't that just... make them attack humans more?

And what about the religious people? And my sausage? It seems to me you're punishing your human customers and potentially making the streets even more unsafe in one swoop."

Elliot snorted. "The vampires who break into butcher shops to steal their blood supply are weak. Desperate. They won't survive long with their supply cut off. Any vampire who would have a chance at going undetected while preying on humans would never stoop so low as to feed on animal blood—least of all pre-bottled. No, our new policy ensures the monsters don't grow stronger and increase their numbers—and I'm afraid both religion and grandma's recipe has to take a secondary seat to the protection of human life. I'm sure you agree?"

"Uh... huh," I mumbled, as images of Warin's reaction to my dinner offering flashed before my mind's eye. By supplying butchers with dead blood, they weren't just starving vampires unwilling or unable to feed on humans... they were actively killing them.

"Now, seeing as this is in the middle of the day, I am comforted in the fact that you are no vampire," Elliot said. When I lifted my gaze to his, he gave me that same thin smile as before. "But I know there are certain... sympathizers out there. Servants to the undead. You seem like a smart girl, Olivia. Can I count on your support for Bolton & Son's new policy? You do wish to make the streets safer, don't you?"

NINE

A large raven sat on the roof of my car when I stumbled out the office door, more than keen on putting as much distance between myself and the House of Horrors and its creepy PR agent some minutes later.

"I would get the hell out of here, if I were you," I muttered at the bird, and shuddered at the memory of the dead lamb and all the other carcasses I'd gotten way too close a look at today.

It cawed at me and flapped its wings, lazily flying up to sit on the side of the gate leading in.

"Smart bird," I said as I quickly climbed into my Fiesta and shoved the key into the ignition.

I drove out the gate, only breathing in a deep sigh of relief once I could no longer see the industrial estate in my rearview mirror. I could, however, see the raven following me, and managed a small smile. Seemed it'd taken my warning to heart.

I SPENT the rest of the afternoon in a jittery mess, and when my phone went off just after five, displaying an unknown number, I hesitated to answer.

You think you're being phone stalked by slaughterhouse employees now, Liv? I snarked at myself before I pushed the answer button. Worst-case scenario, it'd be a determined telemarketer. And best-case scenario...

"*Liv?*" The voice on the other end was deep and smooth and automatically made my lips curl up into a smile. "*It's Warin. I'm calling to hear if you have time to see me this evening?*"

"Of course," I answered, hastily casting a glance around my once-again messy living room.

"*Good. I shall be there in fifteen minutes.*" He didn't wait for my confirmation before he hung up.

Well, shit. I glanced down at my attire—I'd changed into my most comfortable pajamas and a pair of fluffy pink socks once I got in this afternoon—and mentally calculated what needed a last-ditch effort the most, me or the living room.

. . .

I ENDED up deciding on the room, so when the buzzer by my door sounded fifteen minutes later, I'd just finished the pile of dishes by the sink. I hurried over to buzz Warin in.

I unlocked my front door just as there was a light knock. Vamp speed was so handy for getting around quickly.

"Hey, you," I said when I opened the door.

"Liv," he said, nodding in greeting.

I stepped aside, and he walked in without needing an invitation this time. I couldn't help but smile when his eyes seemed immediately drawn by my painting of the sunset again.

Something about his presence in my small home seemed to ease all the tension that'd accumulated in my shoulders after the day's excursion, his aura of calm projecting out in almost tangible waves.

"Oh! Wait here a sec, while I still remember it this time!" I hurried into my bedroom and grabbed the small pile of neatly folded clothes I'd borrowed from him in August.

"I've got the clothes you lent me this summer," I said when I re-entered the living room.

"Oh. Thank you." Warin turned from his study of the sunset, mild surprise clear on his face, and I realized he'd forgotten about the shirt and boxers completely. I supposed someone who lived in a mansion the size of

Warin's home wouldn't care much about a couple of items of clothing, even if they were expensive pieces. I was pretty sure the cost of the shirt alone would have paid a month's rent for me.

He accepted the items from me with a polite smile.

And then he bent his head to sniff them.

I froze, insulted. "I *have* washed them."

He raised his head to shoot me a quizzical look, potentially at my frosty tone. "They smell of you."

"They're clean. But I can have them dry-cleaned for you, if you prefer." I folded my arms across my chest, lips pinched in what was undoubtedly a decent imitation of my grandmother.

Warin blinked a single time as he took in my displeased expression, and then comprehension seemed to dawn across his beautiful features.

"Oh, I am sorry, Liv. It was not... That they smell of you is not a negative observation. I am truly sorry... I forgot humans don't..."

"Sniff things?" My tone was still a tad curt, but it seemed he'd just had a "vampire moment." I was pretty sure I'd done a lot of things that would be considered a *faux pas* in his eyes too. "Is it kind of like when dogs say hello to each other?"

Judging from his expression, I'd just committed one.

"I suppose you could compare the two," he replied

carefully as he placed the folded clothes on the coffee table. "Do you wish to continue drawing tonight?"

"Definitely." I motioned for him to sit on the couch in the same spot he had last time, a genuine smile creeping back across my lips. I'd been looking forward to this all week. "Did you bring some blood for dinner? Want a glass?"

"I ate before I left," he said. "It's easier to be around you when..."

"When you're not hungry?" I said with an easy grin as I plopped down on the sofa next to him and grabbed my drawing kit off the coffee table. "Does that mean I smell like dinner, then?"

His head snapped in my direction, blue eyes staring at me with incredulity.

"I mean, since you said the clothes smell like me," I said, nodding at the small pile of fabric on the table. "Is hanging out with me a bit like chatting to a hamburger?"

I was perhaps entirely too calm about comparing myself to a hamburger around a vampire, but despite having seen Warin's hunger up close and personal before, I couldn't bring myself to fear him. Something about his aura felt too calm, too *safe* to allow my brain to see him as a threat.

Warin shook his head at me. "I... don't think it's comparable."

I raised my eyebrows encouragingly

He sighed, perhaps not entirely keen on discussing his eating habits with one of his main food groups, but humored me nonetheless. "There are many nuances to a human's scent. Only a part of it is the blood."

"So what do I smell like?" I asked, intrigued.

I only got an arched eyebrow in response.

"Right," I mumbled. Maybe there were lines you shouldn't cross with your vampire buddy, after all.

I began to sketch out Warin's face again, but despite his hesitance at discussing his food, I was still curious. "So... remember when you told me you mainly drink donor blood?" I asked.

"Yes?"

"How come? Is it more hygienic, or...? And where do you get it from? Hospitals?" I knew there'd been a major clamp-down on blood security across the country. Once humans had realized that vampires could and would steal their blood supplies, they'd been vamp-proofed. I wasn't entirely sure what that entailed, but the spokesperson for the Department of Defense had seemed quite confident when he was interviewed about it.

"We Compel humans to donate. They believe they have given blood to the medical industry." He sighed. "And I primarily feed this way to avoid... certain side effects of live feeding. This way, the human will go about their business with minimal interference."

I really wanted to know what *side effects* he meant,

but something in his tone kept me from asking. He'd been very patient with being carpet-bombed for information so far, and I didn't want to push it too much. Who knew how much pestering he could take before he decided not to come back for another visit?

"So you're kind of a vegetarian, in vampire terms?" I said, giving him a wry smile. "Or a free-range farmer?"

"You are remarkably calm, discussing such things with a vampire," Warin noted, both eyebrows raised.

I shrugged. "I know you won't hurt me. You kind of had the chance plenty of times already, you know? And it's fascinating to learn more about your kind—it's not exactly something you can just Wikipedia."

He shook his head at me. "My kind is not fascinating, Liv. We're dangerous."

I shrugged as I drew the frown of his brows. "So are lions, crocodiles... sharks. Doesn't mean they aren't fascinating."

"You're—"

"An odd human?" I interrupted him with a grin. "So you keep saying. But you're the one who's patiently answering all my dumb questions. And letting humans donate blood rather than drink from them. I dare say, you're an odd vampire too."

He chuckled, a rumbling sound that vibrated through the room and seemed to warm the air and even my skin. "Perhaps that's why I enjoy your company so much."

"Yeah," I said, unable to hide my happy smile as the warmth in my skin sank in deeper.

We sat in pleasant silence for a little while as I sketched the vampire on my couch, until the quietude was interrupted by a demanding growl from my stomach.

Warin shot my midsection a look. "Have you not eaten?"

I grimaced. "No." I hadn't been able to eat since the slaughterhouse.

"I don't mind if you eat while I visit," he said. "You should not go hungry for too long—humans need regular feedings, correct?"

I snorted at his phrasing. "No, I'm good. Don't think I'll be eating anything but veggies anytime soon, anyway." I glanced at him and sighed. I'd been dragging my feed at bringing up what I'd spent my day doing, because judging from how stern he'd been about his whole *"thou shall not investigate the local butcher"* thing, I was reasonably certain he wouldn't much appreciate me going to the slaughterhouse. But, I'd gone there to help with his investigation, so keeping what little I'd learned from him wouldn't get me anywhere.

"Uh, so... remember the whole blood incident?"

He arched his eyebrows in question. "I do." There was just the slightest note of warning in his tone.

"Yeah, so... I went and talked to my butcher, who confirmed that their supplier uses a different technique to harvest the blood now, due to vampires breaking into several butcher shops lately."

"After I *specifically* told you not to get involved?" There was no mistaking the clipped disapproval in his voice this time.

"Yeah, well, free will and all." I gave him a half-smile that ended more in a grimace at the sight of his narrowed eyes. Okay, so I wasn't *afraid* of him, as such, but he could still project and awfully effective *"don't mess with me, human"* aura when he wanted to.

"Anyway, the butcher gave me the number for their supplier, and today I went to speak with the people at the slaughterhouse," I continued.

"You did *what?*" he growled. "Liv, do you not understand how dangerous this is? If you are suspected of being a vampire sympathizer, they will target you. Does your life mean that little to you? You experienced firsthand how easy it is for these people to hurt anyone they suspect of being on our side."

"I didn't think there'd be any harm in it. Though the PR dude made it quite clear that they definitely are using dead blood to weed out what he believes to be the weaker vampires."

Warin muttered what sounded distinctly like a curse, even if I didn't catch the words. "You do realize that this is exactly the same information I have managed to procure?

There was zero reason for you to risk your life in interacting with them."

My shoulders slumped. "Oh. How...? I mean, you can't exactly go there during the day, and they are quite on edge about vampires coming around."

He arched an eyebrow at me. "I tracked down one of their employees at his local bar and Compelled him."

"Oh." Well, way to deflate the importance a girl's detective-skills. "Did he say anything about any chemical they'd added? The PR guy made me look at all these formulas, but to be honest, I didn't understand any of them. And he didn't explain further."

Warin frowned. "There's no chemical added. There doesn't need to be." He was silent for a bit before his eyes widened ever so slightly. "Liv, what did these formulas look like?"

"I dunno, chemistry-like. Apart from one of them—it was pretty odd. Like a circle with squiggles. Why?"

This time, I was certain he spat out a curse. He got to his feet, agitation suddenly rolling off him in waves. It was such a vast difference to his usually so calm aura, unease penetrated my brain and sank into my gut.

"Warin? What is it?"

"And this circle—did it glow?" he asked, not bothering to answer my question. "Did you feel anything? A headache? Confusion?"

My eyes widened. "How did you know that?"

His angry snarl made me jolt, my pencil clattering noisily to the floor as I lost my grip on it.

"Witches!" he hissed. "Of course. I should have known."

"Wha— *witches?*" I blinked up at the agitated vampire as he began to pace back and force in my small living room. "I'm sorry, did I hear you right? *Witches?*"

"Yes," he said, still pacing. "I've clearly been too lenient for too long."

"I'm... sorry, do you mind catching me up?" I looked at him, both eyebrows arched as high as they would go. "And can we maybe start with '*witches are* real'?"

"Of course they are real." He stopped long enough to give me an incredulous look. "You thought vampires were the only kind of monsters to walk the Earth?"

I blinked. "Uh... kind of, yes. Er... and *monsters?* Isn't that going a bit far, for humans with magic? Or is there something I don't know here?"

He gave me a long look that made me think there was *a lot* I didn't know, but instead of elaborating, he resumed his pacing, muttering to himself.

"So... do you mind telling me what it was about that formula that made you jump to the conclusion that honest-to-god witches are behind this blood contamina-tion thing?" I asked.

Warin waved a hand, still deep in his own thoughts. "The circle—you described a sigil. He made you look at a sigil. I assume since you're not dead, it didn't reveal anything about your connection to me."

He stopped then, a flicker of regret crossing his features as he looked at me. "I should not have come here. I've drawn you into the middle of supernatural business. And I've put you in danger."

"What? No." I got to my feet. "You haven't done anything. If that PR guy really was a witch, he clearly didn't think I was a threat. Calm your tits, everything's okay."

"Everything's *not* okay, Liv. If witches are involved with this, I am putting your life in danger just by being around you. I should—"

He didn't get to finish before I'd taken two steps toward him and put my hand across his mouth. I hadn't really thought my move through, so when he stared down at me—probably from sheer shock that I'd dared silence him so rudely—it took me a second to remember what I meant to say. It resulted in a couple of seconds awkward silence while we stared at each other.

"Er... what I wanted to say was—don't even think about saying you shouldn't be here, okay? I know we don't know each other all that well, but I am not about to stop getting to know you just because some witches, of all things, have a grudge against vampires. I... I don't have a lot of friends, and I'm not about to lose one over something this stupid." I slowly lowered my hand, aware of the heat in my cheeks as he stared at me. "Sorry about touching you—I know you don't like that very much."

He looked silently at me for a moment longer. Then, slowly, he lifted his hand to place it on my shoulder, not taking his gaze off mine. It was still dark, pulling me into its shadowed depths. "I don't mind when you touch me. I am... just unaccustomed to such gestures."

"Oh. All right." Despite his cool temperature, my skin felt warm underneath my shirt where his hand rested.

"I do not have many friends, either, Liv," he said, softly this time. "But I would be a poor one if I let my selfish desire for your company jeopardize your safety."

I narrowed my eyes at him. "Okay, then. How about this: If you do cut and run because of this, I promise you I most definitely *will* search out these witches and figure out a way to stop them. On my own."

His eyes widened for a moment, then narrowed to mirror mine. "Are you attempting to *blackmail* me?"

"Little bit." I shot him a sweet smile. "So, which is it? Are you leaving to ensure witches won't catch on to our connection, and thereby guaranteeing I go seek them out... *or* will you stay, and in return, I promise I won't get involved with any 'supernatural business'? S'long as *'supernatural business'* doesn't try to kidnap me and throw me in a cage again, of course."

Warin glared at me for a moment longer. Then his shoulders slumped in defeat. "I'm starting to think maybe you're foolish, rather than odd," he muttered as he walked back to the couch to sit down.

"It's highly likely," I said cheerfully as I sat down too, once more picking up pencil and paper. "Thank you for staying."

"Don't thank me," he said, staring gloomily straight ahead. "If I could Compel you to forget me, I would."

"Well, that's not very nice," I chided.

"It would be kinder. You have no idea what you're getting yourself into."

"Then tell me," I suggested. "All I know about witches is what I see at work, and to be honest, they don't seem all that intimidating."

Warin froze, his head snapping in my direction. "*What?*"

"Uh... what?" I blinked, entirely taken aback by the sudden reappearance at his obvious anger. It rolled off him in waves, and this time I seemed to be in the direct line of fire.

"You work with *witches?*" he growled. "When were you going to tell me?"

"I... just did? What the hell, Warin? They're just your garden variety tarot readers and black candle aficionados. They're harmless people. Could you please stop staring at me like that? It's pretty goddamn scary." I pushed myself back against the armrest, silently reminding myself that the angry vampire in my living room was of the vegetarian variety.

"There is no such thing as a harmless witch," he spat, the anger still plain on his face, but at least he'd calmed down with the growling.

I snorted, feeling mildly better now the snarly sound was out of his voice again. "You clearly haven't been to *Dark Dreams* before. Pretty sure our clientele is just hippies, pagans, and general weirdos."

"You work at *Dark Dreams?*" Warin narrowed his eyes again.

"Yeah? What, is that extra offensive?"

He shook his head at me, as if I were a particularly slow child. "You sell magic supplies."

"In my defense, there's a pretty awesome range of herbal teas there as well." My attempt at lightening the mood didn't change his tense expression, and I sighed. "All right, obviously I'm not getting what the big whoop is. Could you please tell me why you're so worked up about the prospect of me selling a candle to an actual witch?"

He sighed too, running a hand through his dark, tousled hair. "Witches have always been our enemies, as far back as anyone can remember. They seek to destroy us, and due to their powers, they are a far greater threat than any regular human. Some who master necromancy have even been known to possess our bodies."

For someone who was still wrapping her head around the fact that magic was apparently real, the idea of *necromancy* made me shudder. "Does that mean zombies are real too?"

"Yes," he said. "But witches who are strong enough to control the dead are thankfully rare."

"Well, that's a relief." I frowned as I took in what he'd told me. "Okay, I guess I can see why you'd be a bit antsy around witches, but... no offense or anything, I don't see how they're all evil because they've got beef with vampires. So do humans; we just lack the skills to actually win, most of the time. And not all humans are evil, so I doubt all witches are. Just like not all vampires want to tear the throat out of any human they pass by." I gave him a gentle smile, but he just sighed and shook his head.

"You cannot understand the darkness of the supernatural because your humanity is so pure." When he looked at me this time, there was no anger left on his pale features. Only gentle regret. "I fear if I do not separate our connection soon, your innocence will be tainted, Liv."

I did my best to fight back the blush at the images his talk of *"tainted innocence"* brought to the forefront of my mind. Forcing a smile, I said, "Maybe my *humanity* will taint your gloom. Have you thought about that? You might end up all happy, losing your broodiness, and then what will all the other vampires think? It'd be a scandal!"

The rumble of Warin's laugh sent warmth radiating from my chest into my arms and down my torso. When I looked at him, he was watching me with a mix of amusement and wonder that had my blush returning despite my best efforts to keep it at bay.

"You are truly a unique soul."

I grimaced, trying to take the edge off the flutter in my belly at his words. "You mean *special*,' don't you? Just trying to be nice about it."

He just smiled softly, not confirming one way or the other. Then, the curve of his lips hiked up higher and he cocked his head as he looked at me. "There's something... I would like you to experience with me. Are you afraid of heights?"

TEN

"Heights?" I asked, frowning at the change of subject. "Not particularly. Why?"

"I'd like to take you flying with me," he said.

I blinked, quickly pushing away the barrage of *Fifty Shades* scenes involving fancy helicopter rides followed by some light spanking that filled my brain. "Uh, now?"

"Yes. If that's all right with you?"

"Yes, of course it is!" I shot him a wide grin and got to my feet faster than I'd moved all day. "You didn't really expect me to be all *'let me just check my calendar,'* did you?"

Warin chuckled at my obvious eagerness and stood up too, albeit at a much more dignified pace. "Dress warm. I don't want you to freeze."

I sprinted into my bedroom, pulled out a thick

sweater, and was back in the living room in three seconds flat. Once I'd donned my winter coat, scarf, gloves, and wooly hat, I turned back to Warin. "Good enough? I feel like a kid experiencing her first snow, here."

"I think so." He held out an arm, indicating my front door. "Shall we?"

I led the way outside and stopped on the sidewalk in front of my building. "Are we taking your car, or mine?"

Warin shook his head. "Neither," he said as he stepped onto the road, clearly expecting me to follow.

I did, frowning in confusion—which turned to downright incredulity when he continued into the alleyway meant for garbage bins on the other side. My dreams of romantic helicopter trips to Seattle withered and died. "Er, Warin...?"

"Come," he called from the depths.

Maybe I should have been hesitant of following a vampire into an abandoned alley at night, but my curiosity was much too strong for such contemplations.

I found him at the very end of the alley, squashed between two apartment buildings. "Now what?" I asked.

He shot me a downright mischievous grin, making him look like the young man his face would have me believe he truly was, turned his back, and crouched down. "Climb up."

I blinked. "Excuse me? You want me to *piggyback* you? Why...?"

Warin looked at me over his shoulder, eyes sparkling in the low light making its way into the darkened alleyway. "You said you wanted to fly. So jump on."

It took me a full second before what he was saying finally set in. "Shut up! You can *fly*? No way! You're bullshitting me!"

"I promise you I'm not."

"*What?* What! How is that even possible? No, that's... Oh my goddess, Warin, how have you never *told* me?" I was aware my voice was reaching notes only dogs could hear, but I couldn't contain my disbelief at this new development. Super speed, sure, I'd heard of vampires being ridiculously fast. But *flying?*

"It never came up," he said, the grin still on his face. Judging from his expression, he was enjoying my frazzled meltdown of excitement. "Have you changed your mind about flying with me?"

"Fuck, no!" I hurried to his side before *he* changed his mind and placed my hands on his shoulders to easier crouch down on his back. He didn't make a sound when I accidentally placed my knee on his spine, but I still grimaced. "Sorry. Tell me if I'm too heavy."

Warin snorted, and I had the good grace to blush.

"Right, yes, vampire strength. Sorry."

"Put your arms around my neck," he said, and I did as instructed. No sooner had I linked my arms around him than he straightened up.

I squealed at the sudden shift, but Warin locked his arms around my thighs, ensuring I stayed put. It was like being encased in granite.

"Ready?" he asked.

"Oh, goddess, yes!"

Warin chuckled at my obvious excitement and set off.

We rose faster than I had anticipated, and I screamed and clung to his neck with all my might as the g-force pushed at me and the wind whipped at my face.

The pressure stopped as soon as it started, and I gasped in a breath of air as I stared over Warin's shoulder down on the rooftops far below. Red and white lights from the city's many cars coiled in the distance.

"Holy shit, Warin, you can *fly!*" I gasped from where I was pressed flush against his strong body. "Oh, goddess, we're *flying!*"

"Would you like to go farther?" he asked.

"I want to go as far as you'll take me," I said, and I meant it.

Warin shot forward instead of up this time, like an arrow from a bowstring toward the center of town. The cold air whipped against us, bringing with it scents of the night I'd never smelled so clearly before.

"Fuck, fuck, fuck, fuuuuuuuuuck!" I chanted as the vampire looped a few times and then suddenly dove straight down, landing smoothly on top of a skyscraper.

Apparently we'd arrived at our destination.

It took me a little while to release Warin's neck from my death grip, and I had to lean on his shoulder for support while my jellied legs solidified again.

"So, what did you think?" A small smile tugged at his lips.

"It was fantastic!" I managed to gasp. "Best experience of my life, hands down."

"I'm glad." His smile softened as he turned away to look across the city. "I like to come up here, when I have time."

"I can see why," I said, plopping down on the roof. Warin followed my example with far more grace.

I let my upper body fall back so I could starfish and looked up at the night sky. It was too cloudy for stargazing, but the sensation of having nothing but the celestial concave above us was amazing.

"If I could fly, I'd never stop," I breathed happily, and turned my head so I could look up at him. He was leaning back, weight supported on one hand as he looked down at me.

"Can all vampires fly?"

"If they live long enough," he said.

"Wow, talk about perks." I shot him a teasing grin. "You wouldn't be taking applications for new vampires, would you?"

"I will never Embrace you, Liv. I could never taint you with this curse." The smile was gone from his face, grim seriousness replacing it. "There is no *perk* great enough to twist every beautiful thing you are into a monster of the night. Do not even joke of such matters."

"You're not a monster, Warin," I said. "Is that truly how you see yourself?

"You have no idea what I am, little one. What I used to be. And you would not recognize a monster if it bit your leg." He turned his gaze from my face to the sky. "You are far too innocent for your own good."

"And *you* are too melodramatic for your own good," I sighed. "Why do you keep trying to scare me off with these grand claims about how terrible you are? I know I've only known you a very short time, but I've never met anyone with as much kindness in their heart as you. You saved my life, Warin. You took me *flying*, for fuck's sake. And you keep coming back to see me, yet you tell me you're this awful monster. Why do you want me to fear you, when we both obviously like hanging out together?"

"I enjoy speaking with you... very much," he said. "But I know you're unaware of what you're getting into, and I... feel guilt."

I rolled over onto my side and propped myself up on an elbow. "So tell me."

"I am a killer." His voice was quiet. "I have many, many lives on my conscience. And there was a time when I... enjoyed inflicting violence and pain on others."

It was a little hard to relate to, especially when I knew

the vampire by my side drank blood from donor bags these days.

"A part of me is still that monster. It is in my nature, even when I suppress it." His eyes flickered to me for a brief moment. "When I was starving in that cage and I smelled your blood... I nearly gave in."

"But you didn't," I reminded him. "A monster would have taken my life without a second thought. Instead, you saved me from my own kind."

Warin only sighed and lay flat on his back so he could stare up at the sky.

"What changed?" I asked. "When did you stop killing?"

A spasm pulled on his sculpted lips. "I haven't stopped. You saw the bodies of our captors. I would still kill without remorse today, if..." He glanced at me, growing quiet without finishing the sentence.

"But why did you decide to only drink from donor bags? To not hurt people who didn't deserve it?" I wanted so much to understand the man by my side. He was an enigma to me, but it wasn't the mystery he presented that drew me in like a moth to a flame. It was that deep, intense *something* that pulsed off him in slow waves. Like a near-tangible loneliness that resonated so deep in my very soul I couldn't put words to the connection I felt to him.

"I don't know," he said. "I don't... I remember being so

vicious—lost to the bloodlust. When I rose at night, the only thing that drove me was my need to sate my hunger. To inflict my power on those I deemed weaker than myself. But then... it just... vanished. One night it was there, and then it was gone. And I understood... I *felt* the pain I'd inflicted on others. Here." He rested a hand on his chest and sighed.

"You learned empathy," I said softly.

"I suppose I did. But it doesn't erase what I've done. It doesn't change what I am."

"It doesn't need to." I sat up and wrapped my arms around my legs as I watched the solemn vampire by my side. "Yes, you may have done horrible things in your past, but that doesn't mean you can't be a good person today. If you have really done what you say you have, that just makes it so much more important that you spend the rest of your time on this planet making amends."

Warin rolled over onto his side to better look at me. "You believe a monster can make amends?"

"I do. There has to be a balance, you know? In the universe. If you take a life, you must save one too." I gave him a small smile. "So you're already on your way, after saving my ass."

"Hmm," he hummed, the expression on his pale face mildly intrigued. "I've never thought about it in those terms."

"That's what I'm here for," I assured him, offering him

a cheeky grin to lighten the mood. "To point out the brighter side, so you don't get lost in all that broody smolder."

Warin laughed, a rumbling sound from deep in his chest that made my stomach feel light with happiness. "Do you know that your name means 'life' in my native language? I find it very apt."

"Olivia?"

"No. *Liv*." The way he pronounced it made it sound so exotic, like a sensual caress. He sighed and rolled over again, getting to his feet in a graceful move. "I should take you home. I am late for a meeting... again. I seem to forget the time when we speak."

THAT NIGHT, I dreamt about flying among the stars on a ball of golden light.

ELEVEN

Surprisingly, the first time I realized that there were distinct downsides to having a vampire friend had nothing to do with witches.

I stuck to my end of mine and Warin's bargain and kept my nose out of any and all blood investigations, though I found my job had gotten a new edge to it. Every time someone came in to buy anything from tarot cards to one of our very delicious herbal teas, I found myself staring at them in an attempt to work out if they were an actual witch or not. The fact that I had no clue what to look for didn't help matters.

. . .

THREE NIGHTS after Warin's last visit, he called me again to see if I had time to meet. And, too excited to pause to think, I happily agreed.

It was undoubtedly pretty pathetic, but after our few interactions and how little we truly knew each other, he already felt like the best friend I'd ever had.

He knocked on my front door not twenty minutes after sundown, and I opened it with a cheerful, "Hey!"

Only instead of responding, Warin grabbed me by the shoulders with his cold, strong hands, eyes scanning me with clear worry. "Liv, are you hurt?"

"What? No, I'm fine?" I squawked, alarm rising in my throat at his obvious concern. "Warin, what's—?"

Without warning, his nostrils flared wide and his body went rigid as his gaze locked on my abdomen, pupils blown.

I squeaked, the sudden change in his demeanor sending flashes of the time I'd been bleeding in the cage in that creepy basement to the forefront of my mind. But before I managed to do anything else, he'd released me, the air around us *swooshing*. When I turned with a blink, he stood at the other end of my living room, clearly holding his breath.

"I'm very sorry," he blurted before I could open my mouth to ask what the hell was going on. "It... caught me by surprise."

"What caught you by surprise? Warin, what the hell

—?" I blinked when his gaze flickered down to the level of my crotch, then swiftly up again. He might not have been capable of blushing, but he managed to look mortified nonetheless.

"*Oh!*" And just like that, it dawned on me that inviting your vampire buddy over when you're on your period was probably not the best idea in the world.

I slapped both hands up to cover my face, too embarrassed to look at the poor vampire still holding his breath.

"I'm sorry. I didn't think," I said, still hiding behind my hands.

"No, I should have..." He didn't finish the sentence, but the discomfort in his voice was unmistakable.

Pulling on every ounce of willpower I possessed, I lowered my hands. "You gonna be okay?"

Warin nodded once without looking at me.

THE NEXT HOUR was fantastically awkward.

Warin sat pressed as far back into the couch as he could get, looking like the epitome of the word "tense."

I tried to pretend like nothing was amiss, but it was pretty damn hard to keep a conversation going when one party refused to breathe, let alone answer with anything longer than one-syllable.

One hour after he'd arrived, after I'd given up trying to get a conversation started and we'd sat in silence for a good fifteen minutes, Warin made up some excuse about work and left as swiftly as he could without actually running for the door.

AFTER A WEEK OF COMPLETE SILENCE, it was pretty obvious that Warin wasn't planning on calling me again. I wasn't entirely sure why it was such a big deal, embarrassing as it was that he could *smell* what was going on in my downstairs department, but it was pretty damn hurtful that I'd apparently been tossed to the side. Again.

For the first while, I'd try to tell myself he was probably just busy. But on the eighth day after *"the second blood incident,"* after I'd had to cover two full shifts because Skye was sick, forgotten my wallet so I hadn't eaten all day, and my beloved Fiesta then refused to start... I'd officially had enough. Of everything.

Thanks to my lack of wallet, I had to walk all the way home on already tired and sore feet. It was dark, and it was freezing cold. I was in no mood for bullshit, and so more than an hour's walking later, when I'd made it out of the busy center and into the blessedly quiet park running along a small river not too far from my home—I called Warin.

Because apparently, a certain vampire had been absent from health class the day they went over the female body and its grosser functions, and he was about to get *schooled*. Thankfully for both os us, only the raven lazily circling above my head would get to overhear me explaining basic female biology.

Warin picked up on the first ring.

"Liv, are you in trouble?" he greeted me.

Okay, so it was the first time *I'd* called *him*, but his assumption that I had to be stuck in another *damsel-in-distress* situation didn't do much to ease my irritation.

"No, I'm not in trouble," I snapped. "And just for the record, I'm perfectly capable of taking care of myself, thanks. I was just calling to see if the fact that I'm a woman means you're now too freaked out to see me again."

"Oh."

Fabulous response.

"Because I can't exactly help that, you know," I continued, letting my irritation have free rein. "I had no idea it would be such a huge deal—I'm not exactly down with how human-vampire friendships are supposed to be handled around that time of the month, but I would have thought *you* would be. I mean, I can't be the first human female you've been around since you got your fangs."

His sighed deeply into the phone, and I could practically hear him pinching the bridge of his nose. *"Yes, I should have been prepared, and I apologi—"*

His voice died when a coyote howled in the bushes not too far off the dirt path I was walking along.

"*You're* outside? *After dark?*"

The urgency in his tone made me frown.

"Yes, I'm walking. My car broke down and I didn't have money on me for the bus. Now, could we get back to why you've been avoiding me, please?"

"*This is not the time!*" he snapped. "*You need to listen to me—*" His voice died as another coyote howled, this time much closer.

"*Liv, run!*"

I blinked. "What?"

"*You're being stalked—I need you to get to the nearest house* now." I could hear from the background noises on his end that he was moving now. Fast.

My steps faltered as I looked around the dark woodland, trying to spot what the hell had him so worked up. The path was quiet, save the rustling from the bushes where the coyotes were hanging out. Even the raven was nowhere to be seen.

"There's no one here but me and some coyotes. Warin, what—?"

"*They're not coyotes! Run!*" His voice was a growl this time, and it made my heart race with fear and my feet pick up speed even if I didn't know what I was supposedly running from.

"What do you mean 'not coyotes'?" I insisted as I jogged along the path.

A crash of snapping branches only a few yards away made me jerk my head around, even as I continued running. Bright yellow eyes emerged from the bushes, but they were much too high up to belong to a coyote.

Wolf.

A growl rumbled from the creature, a threatening sound that made every hair on my body stand on end. It was answered with a howl from the other side of the path—from the bushes right by my side.

I squeaked as pure terror finally set in—and I sprinted as fast as I could down the path.

More growls sounded from behind me, as well as breaking foliage, but I didn't stop to look this time. I ran as fast as I could toward the exit of the park, but even as I did, I knew it was too far away.

And suddenly, two huge wolves with bright yellow eyes broke out from the underbrush ahead of me, blocking the path. Heads lowered and canines exposed, they snarled.

I halted as my terror pounded in my veins, and lifted the phone I still clung on to like a lifeline to my ear. "W-Warin..."

"I'm coming."

Something large and heavy hit me full-force in the back, and I fell forward with a grunt as the air got knocked out of my lungs. I hit the ground with a smack, sending my phone clattering out of reach.

Strong jaws locked around my arms, my hair, and the back of my coat, pulling at me so hard the pain lanced through my body. I wheezed and fought for breath, kicking uselessly at my furry attackers while they dragged me off the path and into the bushes.

Fractured twigs and branches tore at my clothes and face, brambles ripping at my skin, but the wolves paid no attention to my cries of pain. My scalp burned from where one of them had dragged me by the hair, and I was pretty sure the one pulling me by my right arm had punctured the skin.

Once we were deep in the bushes, they finally released me.

I scrambled to get up, but didn't make it further than my knees before a hard push at my back sent me back down on all fours. They clearly didn't want me standing.

I cowered on the ground as I stared wildly at my attackers.

There were five of them, the biggest wolves I'd ever seen, more the size of ponies than canines.

I'm going to get savaged to death by mutant wolves. What an undignified end for a city girl.

Cracking sounded behind me, but not like branches. It was deeper, louder, and followed by the sound of something *tearing*. I spun around, still huddled on the ground—and nearly threw up at the sight that met me.

One of the wolves was... was *breaking* in front of me. It was the only word I could think of to describe what was happening to the creature. Its muzzle was peeling back, skin splitting apart to reveal raw flesh and carnivore teeth. It howled as its body split, contorting beyond its original scope. The flesh along its sides was tearing, too, reshaping itself around broken bones that seemed to fuse again in a new order. Fresh skin spread over bare muscle, until finally, a naked man crouched next to the remaining wolves, his sides heaving.

"A-are you... okay?"

I don't know why I asked him that—maybe my freaked-out mind thought he'd been *inside* the wolf, like goddamn Little Red Riding Hood. Maybe it was just relief over seeing another human being, hope that there would be a way out of this madness. But when he lifted his head, those same yellow eyes stared back at me, and I realized with a sick sense of dread that he wasn't going to help me.

No one was.

"Deadwhore," he snarled.

"Really? You're... you're what, some sort of a *werewolf*, and you're *still* a goddamn evangelical fanatic?" It wasn't that I wasn't still about to wet my pants from fear, but the unexpected insult from something that was clearly not even entirely human surprised me enough that a small measure of indignity rose in my gut amidst all the terror. I clung on to it with both hands.

"You are accused of conspiring with vampires against your brothers and sisters. How do you plead?"

I blinked. "Uh... what? Is this... is this a fucking *trial?* You've *got* to be kidding me!"

He lowered his head, his lips peeling back in a warning snarl. Despite his human mouth, his canines were still eerily elongated. *"How do you plead?"*

"Not guilty!" I snapped.

"Liar," he hissed. "We've seen you with the dead thing. We saw you at the slaughterhouse. You are a betrayer. And we sentence you to death."

My eyes widened at his last word, my precarious grasp on my indignation slipping as pure terror took hold once more.

Death.

They were truly going to kill me.

The wolves behind me howled and snarled, and I spun around to face them. Not that it mattered. They all leapt as one, heavy bodies knocking me down as jaws filled with sharp teeth snapped and tore. I fell to the ground, instinctively curling in on myself to protect my throat. Not that they needed to pierce my throat to kill me.

They ripped into my limbs, pulling at me from all sides.

They're going to tear me to pieces.

It wouldn't be an easy death—it wouldn't be quick.

Out of nowhere, anger welled up from somewhere so deep I'd never known it existed. These strangers, these *monsters,* would rip me to shreds without a second's hesitation because I'd befriended the wrong man. Like the fanatics who'd kidnapped me had tossed me into Warin's cage for reading the wrong book.

Like my family had torn me apart since I was a kid for simply being *wrong.*

The injustice of it all, the absolute fury, burned through my veins. My life—they were trying to take *my life*, and here I was, curled into a ball, sobbing and pleading for mercy.

No more!

That simple thought flamed deep in my mind—and it was as if it lit a fuse.

Fire exploded behind my eyes, raw energy crackling down my arms and *out*.

Bright green light burst out of my palms, sending a shockwave through the small clearing. The wolves flew backward several feet, landing on the ground with pained *yips*.

My breath came in short heaves as I stared at my outstretched hands until I thought my eyes were going to fall out. My palms still tingled, as if I'd held onto an electric fence.

What...?

I didn't have time to wonder what the hell had just happened any further. Furious snarls rippled all around me as the wolves got to their feet once more. And then they pounced.

Teeth snapped shut around my shoulder, buried into my side through my coat, and I had enough presence of mind to know that this was it when a *thud* sounded next to me—and suddenly there was no longer a wolf biting into my shoulder.

A pained *yip*, and the jaws locked on my side and limbs released as well. Growls, snarls, the crunching of bones and tearing of flesh filled the clearing, followed by more pained yips and howls.

Still very much in fight-or-flight mode, I kicked against the ground, forcing my aching body up. That was when I saw him.

Warin was in the clearing with me, fangs bared and blood dripping from his lips. By his feet, two broken bodies lay crumpled. It took me a little while to realize that their heads were no longer attached to their bodies.

The three remaining wolves were spread out, crouched and ready to pounce on the lone vampire, but he didn't give them the chance.

Moving swifter than I could follow, he tore through

the clearing. The wolves spun, but it was too late. One of them fell to the ground, followed by a wet *clonk* as his now human head landed nearby. His vertebrae was sticking out of where his head had been attached only moments prior, shining white against the dark blood.

It took less than half a minute before the two remaining wolves lay motionless as well.

An eerie silence fell over the clearing as Warin stared down at me, eyes wild and fangs gleaming in the faint moonlight that made it through to the forest floor.

It lasted for maybe three long seconds—until I lost the final shred of control over my convulsing stomach and had to roll onto my knees to throw up.

"Liv?"

The soothing voice was accompanied by a cool hand stroking gently against the small of my back. It was only when I felt his touch on my skin I realized my coat and top had been torn so badly they no longer covered me.

"Liv, I need you to breathe for me." Warin rubbed his hand soothingly against my skin, avoiding the many scrapes and cuts. "I need to you calm down so I can feed you my blood."

I shook my head vigorously in between sobbing and retching up bile. I knew he was trying to help, but just the thought of ingesting blood while still being surrounded by broken and bleeding body parts was more than I could stomach.

"No blood," I managed in between dry heaves.

Warin didn't respond, but he moved his hand from my back to my forehead, and I pressed gratefully against it, relishing in his cool touch. Slowly, my breathing became less labored, and my stomach's convulsions eased.

Once I was breathing normally again, Warin scooped me up into his arms and cradled me against his chest.

Safe.

"I need to heal you," my savior said, voice gentle but firm.

I looked up into his face, touched by the obvious concern I saw there. He'd retracted his fangs while I'd been vomiting, leaving only a faint blood smear as evidence of the monster he'd unleashed to save me.

"I'm... I'm not that badly hurt. You came in time." It was the truth. I was covered in what felt like a hundred scrapes and bruises, and my shoulder and side hurt from where the wolves had clamped down, but it could have been so much worse. Certainly nothing that required ingesting vampire blood. "And... and if you try to make me drink blood, I think I'll throw up again," I said, my stomach twinging in warning just at the thought.

The vampire frowned, letting his eyes roam over my face and body as if to confirm my claim. Lips pinched, he nodded once. "As you wish. I will attend to your wounds later."

Without losing his grip on me, he fished out his phone

from his pocket, pressed a couple of buttons and raised it to his ear. "Carina? Send a cleanup crew to McMahon Woods. Bring iron. Five skinwalkers—one's still alive." He hung up without saying goodbye.

One is still alive? I was hesitant to look back at the carnage, but his words made me overcome my squeamishness.

Sure enough, one of the last two men was faintly twitching on the ground. His body was badly broken, far beyond what any normal human could have hoped to survive, but when Warin walked around the front of him, I saw his eyes were half-open.

Warin turned halfway to let me slide to the ground, ensuring I could stand before he released his grip on me. "Stay behind me," he murmured.

I was only too happy to obey. The wolf might be on the ground, but I didn't know how long he'd stay there.

Warin put his foot on the man's—the skinwalker's—broken neck. The skinwalker gurgled in pain, but snapped his eyes open to look up. The moment he did, Warin asked, "Why did you attack the human?"

"Deadwhore," he groaned. "Traitor."

"Who sent you?"

The skinwalker groaned unintelligibly.

"*Who?*" Warin snapped, and even from my spot behind him, I could sense the darkness welling up around him, demanding obedience. He was Compelling him, I realized.

The skinwalker only gargled in response.

"Maybe you need to give him air," I suggested, casting a worried look at Warin's shoe planted firmly against the other man's windpipe.

Warin growled, but eased his weight off the skinwalker's throat just a bit. *"Tell. Me. Who!"* The air of command around him was so strong, it seemed to wrap around every part of the small clearing, making even my knees buckle from the raw *power* of his Compulsion.

The skinwalker gaped, but still no words came up. Then he convulsed once, twice—and fell limply back down, staring blindly up into the night. Blood trickled in a fine stream from both his nostrils.

Warin stepped off his neck and turned to me, a dark look on his face.

"W-what the hell just happened?" I stuttered. "Did you... did you kill him with your... *mind?*"

"No. He was either bewitched not to speak of who sent him, or..." His face darkened further.

"Or?" I prompted.

"Or he was Compelled by another vampire."

TWELVE

"Another *vampire?*" I asked, not entirely sure I was following. "I don't understand. First it was witches, then these... these skinwalkers, and now you're saying it might be another *vampire?* Is this still related to the slaughterhouse and the blood contamination? Why would another vampire wish to harm your kind? Or attack *me,* for that matter?"

Warin shook his head. "I don't know. But I've never seen a spell like that before. It looked... too much vampire Compulsion." Then he looked at me, his expression softening. "We need to get you home, Liv."

I nodded, too wobbly to argue. As much as I wanted to make sense of what'd just happened to me, what I needed most right about then was to get away from the stench of dead in the small clearing where I'd nearly lost my life. I took Warin's offered hand and clutched his neck when he lifted me into his arms once more.

The trees and bushes blurred past us, only to be replaced with roads and houses, and soon he stopped in front of my apartment block.

That was when I realized I'd dropped my keys, along with my bag, during the attack.

"Oh, shit. Warin, we've got to go back—I don't have my keys, or—" I quieted when he pulled a key out of his pocket, shoved it into the lock, and let us into the stairway.

"I picked your key up from the clearing," he said easily as he *swooshed* us up the stairs and let us into my condo.

"Oh. Thank you," I said, wishing he'd also picked up my beloved leather bag, but not being enough of an ungrateful brat to mention it.

He didn't answer as he carried me to the couch and gently lowered me onto the soft cushions. Then he fished out his phone from his pocket and typed on the keypad so quickly my eyes could hardly follow the movements of his fingers. Finally, he returned his attention to me. His gaze swept over my disheveled figure, the same worried frown he'd looked at me with in the clearing marring his pale features. "Will you still not accept my blood? It would heal your injuries."

I grimaced. "I know. And thanks for offering, but..." An unpleasant flash of the vertebrae sticking out of the neck hole of one of the wolf-men made my stomach threaten to roil again. "I think I'm on iodine and Band-Aids today. Would you mind getting the First Aid kit, please? It's in the bathroom cupboard above the sink."

He shook his head and sat down next to me. "That won't be necessary. Take off your top."

I hesitated for a second, my general anxiety over nearly getting eaten alive soothed enough by his presence and the comfort of my own home that modesty managed to rear its head. But it was ridiculous, of course—my clothes were already shredded so badly I was flashing all kinds of skin, and it wasn't as if he hadn't seen plenty more of me the time he saved me from the creepy basement.

Moving slowly, because everything hurt, I shrugged out of the leftovers of my winter coat and pulled my almost equally demolished top over my head, discarding both items on the floor. At least my bra had remained intact during this week's near-death experience.

Warin's fangs descended with a *snick* that made me jolt a little. "Sit still—it won't hurt," he murmured. And then he flicked his tongue out, catching it on one pointy tip.

I frowned as blood dripped from his tongue, but the next second, Warin bent over my shoulder and put his lips on my skin, and my thoughts got well and truly side-tracked.

I stared wide-eyed at the vampire's bent head as he let his tongue swipe up along the deep bite on my shoulder, and then—ever-so-gently—brushed across the wound itself.

If someone had asked me what it'd feel like to have a fresh wound licked clean, I'd have guessed something in the region of *"painful and unhygienic."* The truth was something else entirely.

Heat bloomed from Warin's cool lips against my skin and spread down across my chest and up my neck, until I felt like my entire body would have to be the same color as my Aunt Edna's favorite pants.

Seemingly oblivious to my full-body blush, Warin continued lapping at my shoulder, making small noises of pleasure—presumably at the taste of my blood— that did nothing to keep my thoughts purely medical.

But to my surprise, it did help. When he moved his head from my shoulders down my arm to care for the scrapes and wounds there, my shoulder no longer stung like it had before. Sure, it felt like there would still be a massive bruise come the morning, but when I twisted my neck to catch a glimpse of the it, my skin was healed.

"How does your blood do this?" I asked, partly in an attempt at distracting myself from the sensation of his tongue dancing up along the inside of my arm. "When you think about vampires, you don't really think 'magical First Aid kit,' you know?"

If Warin heard me, he didn't respond.

All righty, then—awkward silence it is.

I leaned back on the couch and did my best not to think sexy thoughts as my strictly platonic vampire friend licked my entire torso. It was a feat that proved increasingly difficult as he moved first to my chest and then down my stomach, crouching between my legs.

When he got to my navel, I was squeezing a throw pillow so hard my knuckles turned white, chanting *"he's your friend, he's your friend, he's your goddamn friend"* in my head while desperately begging my heated body to focus on the not insignificant pain still radiating through it.

"I need you to turn over," Warin said, lips still hovering over my navel. His voice seemed oddly husky, but it was hard to tell with the way my blood was rushing in my ears.

"Huh-m?" I croaked.

"I need to get to the wounds on your back." He pulled his head back a little, but I purposefully avoided catching his gaze.

"Oh. Right, yeah…" Awkwardly, I shifted on the couch to lay on my stomach, my aching muscles and remaining wounds sending shocks of pain through my body strong enough to dull the inappropriate fantasies running rampant in my mind.

Warin took care of the deep wounds on my side and

back, and I managed to keep my thoughts somewhat appropriate until he said, "I will need to look at your legs as well," and proceeded to reach around me to undo my pants, then carefully pull them over my hips and down my legs.

To my great relief, I didn't have any wounds in need of his healing blood too high up on my thighs, and it didn't take long before he pulled back from me, wiping his mouth with one hand.

"How did I taste?" I blurted, mainly to avoid the awkwardness of prolonged silence after having just been licked from head to toe.

He blinked. "You wish to know if I enjoyed the taste of your blood?"

"Well... yeah. Sorry, is it off-putting having your dinner quiz you on your meal?" I grimaced. "I'm not entirely sure what's appropriate after-licking conversation, here."

Warin's rumbling laugh was unexpected, but welcome. He got to his feet and shook his head, the echo of a smile playing on his lips. "You are a peculiar human, Liv."

I sighed. "So you keep saying."

The silence spread between us, long enough for the darkness of my attack to set in—along with the realization that I was only in my bra and panties at the moment.

Wordlessly, I padded into my bedroom to get my

bathrobe. When I returned to the living room, Warin stood in front of the windows, hands clasped behind his back as he stared into the darkness.

"Warin, we need to talk," I said.

He turned toward me, eyebrows raised in question.

I waved a hand as I slumped into the sofa again. "What were those things that attacked me? Werewolves? And why is this happening? I know you know more than you've told me. And I know you're probably just trying to shield me, but... this is the second time I've nearly been killed by whoever's out to get the vampires in this city. I think I have a right to know."

He sighed, turning back to stare out the window. "We've been at war for a very long time. Witches and vampires—until one party exterminates the other, there will never be true peace. Since the Night of Revelations, when vampires became known to the human race, we have managed to keep a precarious truce, of sorts.

"For a long time, I assumed the disappearances in my territory were linked to the human fanatics, that they had finally grown clever enough to organize into splinter groups. But your encounter at the slaughterhouse suggests otherwise. I have tried to track down the witch you met there, but he may as well not exist. Until tonight, they have covered their tracks perfectly. Almost too perfectly.

"We have a long and bloody history with witches, and they have undoubtedly learned much about us—but not this much. Not how to counter our Compulsion, not how to avoid detection. I didn't realize, until tonight... until that skinwalker... that there may be one of my kind involved. But why—and who—I do not know. And I do not know why they are targeting you this aggressively. Five skinwalkers in their shifted forms, so close to human dwellings... they risked exposure to get to you.

"Why they believe my human companion is so valuable, I am uncertain... but they will not get another chance, I promise you that." His voice gained a low, dangerous edge, though he didn't so much as turn to look at me. "I have been passive for too long. Awaited their next move. No more."

I chewed on my bottom lip as I thought through what he'd said. I looked down at my hands and felt the echo of the green light rushing down my arms and bursting out of my palms.

The skinwalkers had called me a traitor.

"Are they... are they witches, these skinwalkers? Or something else?"

"Both," he said. "They were witches who traded their souls to gain the power of shapeshifting. They are dark creatures, and very strong."

"Not as strong as you," I said, remembering how he'd butchered them within minutes.

Warin didn't answer, and I went back to staring at my hands. On one hand, he was the only supernatural being I knew, but on the other... He'd made it plenty clear what he thought of witches.

Not that I was suddenly a *witch* or anything.

Right?

But what in the goddess' name *was* that light? I knew it'd come from within me—felt it too keenly in the very core of my being to deny it.

Nothing like that had ever happened before, that's for sure.

Except...

Except once. I stared blindly at my shaking hands as long-suppressed memories flashed through my brain.

There'd been one time I'd been as certain I was going to die from a violent assault as I had been tonight. I wasn't sure exactly what had happened; I'd been too scared and too young to retain the details. But I remembered a bright green light.

Saving me.

Was I a witch?

Was that why the skinwalkers called me a traitor?

Why the witch at the slaughterhouse warned me to stay away from Warin?

"This... war, between you and the witches... what's it about?"

"Survival," he said, eyes still trained on the darkened windows. "One cannot live while the other still walks the earth. They wish to rid the world of our darkness, and their power makes them dangerous to us in a way humans are not. And my kind..."

"Let me guess—you're not keen on being hunted?" I said with a grimace. It was the same struggle humans had been dealing with since vampires revealed their existence. The knowledge that there were people out there who could—and would—kill you was distinctly uncomfortable.

"No. We will kill witches strong enough to pose a threat. Though it would seem I've been too lenient these past few decades. I've allowed them their gatherings, their shops... and it would seem magic has festered and grown in my city while I've shut myself away, stubbornly thinking there was some way... that if we showed a willingness to coexist, there could be some semblance of peace." His voice darkened, sending tendrils of ice up my spine. "I've been a fool. And you almost paid the price for my idiocy."

I stared at his back, forcing down the panic churning in my gut. "But, uh, I'm sure there are *good* witches too, right?"

"No," he said. "There are weak witches who do not pose a threat. But weakness is not the same as being *good*. I will not forget this again."

I swallowed thickly and clenched my shaking hands in my lap. "Warin, I—"

He turned his head, his gaze locking on something outside. "Carina is here."

"Huh?" I frowned as he walked to my front door and opened it as he pressed the buzzer. A few seconds later, the air outside my front door *swooshed*, and a gorgeous blonde woman wearing a pants suit and black pumps suddenly stood in my doorway.

"My lord," she said. "The bodies have been disposed of, as you asked."

"Thank you," Warin said, turning to me. "Liv, this is my second-in-command, Carina. Please invite her in."

I got up, staring at the blonde as I walked to his side. "Fuck, no."

Warin blinked, possibly in surprise at my less than hospitable greeting.

"Apologies, my lord," the blonde said, biting back a smile at the dark-haired vampire's expression. "The last time your human saw me, I—"

"She was definitely going to *eat* me," I interrupted with an indignant huff. "If that tall guy, your brother, hadn't told her and the others to stuff it, you'd have come back to my dried- out husk in your hallway."

Warin snapped his head back to Carina, eyebrows raised.

"I wouldn't have, actually... She was bleeding everywhere, and her arrival was a surprise," the blonde woman said meekly. "I'm sorry for my unfortunate reaction at the time, my lord. You know I would never touch your property."

This time, I was the one to blink. "His *property?*"

Warin turned to me. He put a gentle hand on my shoulder, capturing my attention fully. The magnetic pull from his blue gaze calmed some of my ire. "I promise you, Liv, Carina will never hurt you. She is my most trusted servant. Please, invite her in. There is much I need to do before the night's over, and we need her help. This has gone too far for me to handle alone—I am not willing to risk your life again."

Well, when he put it like that... I fought back the heat rising from my chest to my cheeks at the velvet steel in his voice, then turned to the door. *"Fine.* Come on in."

The blonde vampire nodded and stepped over the threshold. "Thank you," she said softly.

Warin moved his hand from my shoulder, and I felt the loss more keenly than I had any business doing. It was as if he'd been transferring his strength to me during that brief touch, and now I was somehow struggling to find the energy to even stay upright.

"I will be back tomorrow evening," Warin said, pulling my attention from the loss of his touch with a snap. "Carina will remain here until sunup, and then my day helper will stay with you until I return."

"What?" I blinked rapidly three times in a row. "You're *leaving?*"

"I need to attend to... some business." He reached out again, a bit hesitantly, and touched my cheek with a featherlight brush of his fingertips. "Don't worry—you are safe with Carina."

I frowned. "Look, I appreciate the rescue tonight, but this is ridiculous. We both know you're going to look into the witches who attacked me—I'm coming with. Our deal was that I'd keep my nose clean so long as I didn't get dragged in again—and I dare say getting nearly eaten by five werewolves or skinwalkers, or whatever, classifies as 'getting dragged in.' You can't just—"

"I can," he interrupted me, his voice still soft, but with a core of steel. "And I am. Now, I must go. I will return tomorrow evening."

And with that, he was out the door before I could so much as sputter a protest at the complete shut-down, leaving me alone with the the blonde vampire.

"Well, isn't that just great?" I huffed at the now empty doorway. I slammed the door shut and turned to my unwanted house guest.

Carina was watching me with a small smile playing on her perfectly shaped lips. "You'll have to excuse the lord. He's in a bad mood.

"*He's* in a bad mood? *I'm* the one who nearly got eaten." I folded my arms across my midriff, shielding some of my very comfortable, very hideous bathrobe from the beautiful woman in front of me. She looked absolutely immaculate, not a hair out of place. I hadn't felt self-conscious about my looks around Warin, but in Carina's company, it was hard not to feel like a troll.

"Skinwalkers attacked his human—it's a grave insult," she said, the smile slipping off her face as she looked around my small apartment. "Would you mind if I checked the security of your home?"

I shrugged, still feeling pretty miffed that Warin had stranded me with this stranger. But I guessed she was better than being alone, if I was now a witch-slash-skin-walker target... so long as she kept her fangs to herself. "Sure, I guess. You're the babysitter, after all."

While Carina wandered around my apartment, I set about fixing myself a sandwich. Unwanted house guest aside, I hadn't eaten all day and I was starving. Something about being dragged through the bushes and attacked by wolfmen really did give a girl an appetite.

Carina came out from my bedroom as I sat down by the breakfast bar with my tuna sandwich. "Your security is lacking," she said as she sat down next to me. "Has the Lord not had any protective measures installed?"

"Uh, no. That would be wildly overstepping—and my lack of alarm system isn't really Warin's problem. Also, *the Lord*? Really? Please tell me he doesn't make all his employees call him that." I frowned when the uninvited thought of what it might mean if Carina actually *was* the only one to call him that sprung to the forefront of my mind.

Oh, goddess, don't let this be some weird sex thing.

I wasn't prepared for the hot stab of jealousy *that* thought produced.

"The lord rarely demands, but yes... all his subjects call him this." Carina regarded me with some contemplation. "He hasn't told you who he is, has he? *What* he is?"

I frowned. "Yeah, he's... some kind of vampire cop, right?"

Carina blinked. "He is the Night Lord of Chicago. He rules the city and its surrounding territories."

I stared at her for a second. Then a laugh bubbled out of my throat. "Get the fuck out of town, no he is not! *Night Lord?* What, so he's the vampire king of Illinois?"

She nodded, her face as serious as ever.

My laugh died as I stared at her. "You're fucking with me."

"You and the Lord—you are lovers?" she asked.

I nearly choked on my tuna sandwich at the change of subject. "What? No! We're just friends."

"Hmm." She watched me, the doubt clear as daylight on her pretty face. "Is that so?"

"Yeah." My face flushed hotly up under her scrutiny. "He's great and all, but it's not like that. We just talk a lot." A twinge of something unpleasant in my gut made me ask, "Why? You're not... Are you his girlfriend, or something?"

Carina's laugh pealed through the room, light and

beautiful. "No. I am merely curious. He has been... different, these past few weeks. I suspect you are the cause."

"Oh." My face heated by several degrees, and I returned my focus to my sandwich so I didn't have to look at the blonde's knowing smile. "Well, we're just friends."

Carina chuckled, and I got the distinct impression her amusement was due to my uncomfortable squirming. "How very... unusual." Her tone made it quite clear she thought I was a big, fat liar.

Just fabulous.

I wolfed down the rest of my sandwich as fast as I could without choking and decided to go straight to bed. I was tired and aching all over, and I so wasn't in the mood for any more awkward conversation about my relationship with Warin.

THIRTEEN

I was still a little sore when my alarm woke me up just after dawn the next morning.

It wasn't too bad, though. I took stock of my bruised body as I lay in bed, trying to find the will to push the covers aside and get up. My muscles ached, and I was pretty sure I had a couple of nasty bruises, but it could have been so much worse.

I shuddered at the memory of knowing I was going to die, and I spared Warin a grateful thought. As irritating as it was that he'd just up and left me with a glorified babysitter while he went off to play lonesome hero, it was nice to know that I didn't have to face potential skin-walkers on my own.

Even if I'd never had to entertain the idea of men who turned into freaking *wolves* intent on shredding me like a brisket before I met Warin. No one gave two fucks who I was before him.

Skinwalkers. Christ on a cracker.

I lifted my hands up above my head and stared intently at them in the faint filtering through my curtains. Maybe I'd imagined that green light?

But no. Even now, I could still recall the rush of energy from the deepest part of my being as it burst out of me. It had definitely happened.

I clenched my hands into fists before retracting them underneath my warm duvet. I'd been very close to telling him, before Carina showed up. But... in the clear light of day, perhaps it was for the best that I hadn't. As much as I didn't want to play damsel in distress here, it was pretty obvious I was all kinds of fucked if Warin decided he wanted nothing more to do with me.

A mild shiver traveled down my back when I recalled what he'd said about not being *lenient* with witches anymore. But this was Warin... there was no way he'd actually hurt me, even if he found out that I *might-possibly-maybe* be some kind of a witch.

And who knew if it was even magic that'd burst out of me? There was every chance this was something else entirely. I mean, you'd think you'd grow up knowing if you were some kind of dark creature... right?

Could have been alien possession, for all I knew.

Deciding against traveling further down that particular road, I finally kicked my duvet off and crawled out of bed. It was my turn for the morning shift at *Dark Dreams,* and as much as a New Age shop might be the only job that would potentially accept *"attacked by werewolves"* as a reasonable excuse not to show up for work, I needed to go in.

Since my vampire buddy was off playing Lone Ranger, it was clear I had to take matters into my own hands if I wanted to be in the loop of who was gunning for my life this time around. And the only non-vampire, non-creepy-slaughterhouse lead I had? Witch Supply Central, aka my workplace.

Most of them might just be New Agers, or emo teens, but if Warin's reaction to my workplace was anything to go by, I might be able to get a hold of *someone* who could get me in touch with Chicago's witchy underground.

I WAS SO preoccupied with my plotting that it wasn't until I stepped out of the street door to my apartment block—Thermo in hand and gaze locked on my small, battered Fiesta as I huddled against the cold—that I noticed the huge man standing in front of my building.

"Ma'am," he said when I shot him a cautious glance out the corner of my eye. He was standing with his hands clasped behind the small of his back, like a soldier at attention, and his winter clothes did nothing to hide his bulky form. He had to be at least seven feet tall and built like an ox. Definitely not the kind of guy you'd forget—which meant he wasn't usually hanging around my apartment block.

"Uh, hi," I muttered, and scurried toward where my car was supposed to be be. Only the spot where I normally parked was empty.

It was only then I remembered my Fiesta was still in the parking lot by my work.

"Sonuvabitch!" I growled. I was *so* not in the mood for public transport.

"Is there a problem, ma'am?"

The unexpected voice coming from right behind my left shoulder made me jerk and spin around, heart pounding and keys clenched between my fingers as a weapon.

The huge man had apparently followed me, and either he was a fucking level 10 ninja, or I'd been too decaffeinated to hear a seven-foot mountain walking behind me.

"Jesus tap dancing Christ, if you don't back the fuck up, I'll scream!" I shrieked.

He blinked, surprise clear on his wide face. "Aren't you Olivia Green, ma'am?"

"What's it to you, creeper?" I kept my fist raised, even though his surprise calmed my pulse down a little—the skinwalkers last night hadn't checked my name before they pounced.

"Mr. Waldlitch sent me. I am to escort you for the day."

"Who?" I blinked. "Warin?" He *had* said something about sending a *"day man"* to look after me once the sun rose.

The giant of a man nodded. "Affirmative, ma'am. If you need to leave your residence, I will drive you."

I arched an eyebrow at him. "Yeeeah... I'm gonna need some form of proof you aren't a crazy fanatic, or a crazy witch, or a crazy man-wolf, before I get into a car with you. Otherwise, I hope you like the bus."

"Mr. Waldlitch said, should you request proof of my employment with him, to tell you that your blood tastes like 'life.' And to emphasize that he will be most displeased with you if you attempt to resist my protection." Not a tremor on the big guy's face betrayed if telling random women what his boss thought of their blood was out of the ordinary for him—but I flushed predictably.

It seemed like such an... intimate thing to share with a stranger—that Warin had drank my blood. But I guess to him it was just a meal.

Then I realized he'd answered my question from last night, even if in a roundabout way, and the heat in my cheeks intensified.

Life.

I wasn't entirely sure, but it sounded like flattery. Especially coming from an undead.

"Ma'am?" my new bodyguard said, lifting his eyebrows. "Do you need to leave the premises?"

"Yes, I have to get to work." I looked up at him with a small sigh. At least Warin's overprotectiveness meant I didn't have to get the bus.

The giant held out a hand toward a black pickup truck parked off to the side. "This way, ma'am."

"You can just call me Liv," I said as I walked to the truck. "And unless you want to be called 'Big Guy' for the rest of the day, maybe tell me your name, too?"

"Name's Roy, m—Liv."

I smiled at him. "Nice to meet you, Roy. Now let's get going—I'm late."

THANKS TO ROY'S not-entirely-legal driving, I made it to work just in time.

Raven was already there with the till prepared when I walked in, bodyguard in tow.

She stared up at the giant of a man, but he only nodded at her as he went straight for the back room, presumably to check the security of the shop.

"Liv, who the hell is that?" my colleague whispered. "He looks like he's part mountain! What's he doing here?"

I sighed. "It's... kind of hard to explain."

"Try."

I bit my lip as I considered my options. On one hand, she worked at a New Age store and called herself Raven... and if I wanted to get in touch with witches, she might be a good place to start. But on the other hand, I didn't particularly want to be force-committed to a psychiatric ward, either.

"Remember my friend from the bar?"

Her lips pinched as if she'd tasted something foul. "The vampire."

"Apparently someone took offense to us hanging out, and... uh... I have *witches* on my ass, can you believe it? So Warin... had a friend keep an eye on me today." I flapped a hand in what I hoped portrayed a decent *who-would-have-thunk-it* manner.

She sighed and shook her head, following Roy with her eyes as he returned from the back of the store to take up guard by the door. "Yeah, well, that's what happens when you hang out with *vampires*, Liv."

So apparently the idea that actual witches, magic and all, were real, wasn't news to Raven.

"I don't see why," I bristled. "He's a nice guy—it's not his fault he's dead. He doesn't even drink blood from living humans, you know. Just donor blood." Wow, there was a sentence I'd never imagined speaking out loud before. "And I don't see why *I* am getting attacked on my way home from work just because I have a vampire friend."

Raven frowned. "Attacked? You were attacked?"

"Yeah. Big wolf-men. Warin called them skinwalkers." I shuddered at the memory of my near-death experience. "Look, I know you're obviously not fond of vampires, but you seem to know about witches, and I... I don't know who else to ask. I can't exactly go to the police. Do you know of anyone I can talk to?"

She grimaced. "I don't hang around *skinwalkers*. My coven is not into all the dark shit."

"Oh, wow, *you're* a witch?" I blurted. "You've been keeping that quiet!"

She glared at me as Roy glanced in our direction. "Ixnay on the witch accusations while your boyfriend's lackey is around, please. Do you know what vampires do to us?"

I opened my mouth to tell her Warin would never hurt her... but then I remembered what *Mr. Night Lord* had said about no longer being gentle on witches in "his" city.

"He's not my boyfriend," I ended up muttering. "Raven, can you help me? I'm severely out of my depth here, and I don't know what to do. Please."

She sighed, casting another glance at Roy. "Yes, fine, of course I'll help you. Just... you can't trust him, Liv. The vampire. They're not like us. They're dangerous. Scheming. Underhanded."

I pushed down the burst of irritation at her warning—I knew it was coming from a good place. If I hadn't met Warin, I probably would also have been very worried for a colleague who hung around with the undead. "Warin's saved my life more than once now. I understand there's some beef between vampires and witches, and I'm not gonna make you hang out with him or anything—but he's not like all the scare campaigns about vampires."

Raven didn't look particularly happy at my defense of a vampire, but she didn't argue, either. "I'll talk to the High Priestess. Fair warning—I'll have to tell her about your friend, and she might not be very accommodating. Are you gonna be safe until tomorrow?"

I eyeballed Roy. "Yeah, I... think so. Thank you, Raven. Truly. I owe you."

She smiled weakly. "I know what it's like when you realize what's out there... I'd be a bad friend if I didn't try to help."

I HADN'T THOUGHT of any of my *Dark Dreams* colleagues as friends before, mainly because I didn't really do friends. Sure, I was *friendly* with most people I met, and happy to grab a drink after work if asked, but... I hadn't called anyone my friend since I was a kid.

Except for Warin.

I moved around so much these days, it was hard to develop any true bonds. I'd been in Chicago longer than I'd stayed most places since I left home at eighteen.

I stared out the window at the passing traffic as Roy navigated his big truck through the busy streets. I'd moved for much less than crazy witches with a vendetta before—and the smart thing would undoubtedly be to just get out of Chicago and start over somewhere else. I'd done it many times before. So why did the thought of doing so now, when my life was literally on the line, fill me with dread?

Because of Warin.

Because I'd let myself get attached. *Real fucking smart, Liv.*

Adding more friends into the mix... it was only going to make it all the harder to do the smart thing and leave.

Fuck.

The dread in my gut mixed with a clenching sensation of panic, and I breathed deeply to get it under control before I alerted Roy to my internal meltdown.

Having friends was healthy. Maybe less so when friends were the reason you stuck around in a dangerous situation rather than get the hell out of Dodge, but still...

It'd been so long since I had anyone I could count on. Who counted on me.

Despite the swirl of panic in my gut... it felt good.

And it wasn't like I was just going to leave Warin in the middle of a crisis. I might have been a coward when it came to friendships, but I wasn't an asshole.

I leaned back in the passenger seat, mind made up. I wasn't leaving until I'd helped Warin. He'd done so much for me; it was only fair I stuck around to see him through this. Despite being out of practice with the whole friend-thing, I knew you didn't turn your back on one in his time of need.

Definitely didn't have anything to do with how sick the thought of leaving him behind made me.

ROY STAYED outside my apartment block like a hulking sentinel in his leather coat—which had to have been made with skin from an entire cow. I wasn't exactly used to having a bodyguard hanging around, but as the sun began to set and the temperatures plummeted, I started to feel bad. It had to be pretty damn boring to hang around outside a building for hours. Boring, and cold.

So, coffee in hand and bundled up in multiple sweaters, I walked out there, ready to be a less shitty host.

"Hey," I said as he turned to give me a questioning look. "Coffee?"

"You should be inside," he said, voice gruff, but he accepted the cup from me. It practically disappeared in his large hand.

"Probably," I agreed mildly as I perched on the brick banister leading to the front door of my building. "So, have you known Warin long?"

"Few years."

Yeah, Roy wasn't exactly the chatty type. But, during my day in his mostly quiet company, I'd felt pretty at ease around him. He gave off a weirdly calming vibe. Perhaps it was just due to his size and the pretty solid knowledge that no one was getting past his bulk—but whatever it was, I found I liked his company.

Even if he was basically my glorified babysitter.

"I haven't known him long at all. I sorta met him by accident this summer, and then we ran into each other again recently," I said, attempting to get a conversation going with a bit of smalltalk.

A *swish* from the sky followed by a *thunk* from the street interrupted me—and had Roy straightening up, alert.

"Hey," I greeted the vampire who'd just landed on my road, offering him a smile as if I had friends dropping from the sky on the regular.

"You should be inside," Warin said, face blank and voice dark.

I sighed. "Well, hello to you too." I slid off the banister and gave a half-wave in Roy's direction. "Bye, Roy. See you around."

The large man grunted in response, and I went back inside.

Warin followed shortly after, his dark look still firmly in place.

Tonight was going to be just lovely, I could tell.

"Find out anything good?" I asked as I sunk into my usual spot on the couch and pulled my drawing kit off the coffee table.

Warin sat down in his spot on the other end, leaned forward with his elbows resting on his knees. He sighed softly, making me swap out my pencil. A man that broody needed to be drawn with the rich contrast of charcoal.

"Nothing *good*. I... have to call for a meeting. For the rulers of my kind. What's going on in Chicago can have very serious consequences beyond my borders. The witches moving against us, contaminating animal blood... Who knows when they'll turn their attention to the hospitals' supplies."

"You don't look excited," I said. "Is it not a happy family reunion when the other vamp royalties come to town?"

He glanced at me. "Carina told you what I am."

It wasn't a question, but I nodded nonetheless. "Night Lord of Chicago. Very fancy."

A ghost of a smile haunted his lips. "I am glad you are not... intimidated."

I shrugged. "It's not really my world. To me, you're just... Warin. My friend. Doesn't really matter to our friendship if you're a big vampire boss or not, does it?"

"Not in the slightest." He smiled a short while longer before he sighed and turned to stare straight ahead once more. "There is another matter I need to see the other Lords about. You remember the skinwalker who couldn't speak?"

I shuddered at the memory. "Yeah?"

"If he was under vampire Compulsion, the vampire who Compelled him would have to be... very strong."

I perked up, my fingers pausing from drawing the angle of his jaw. "You're thinking royalty-strong?"

"Yes."

"So... What? You're thinking you can suss out who might be behind it if you get everyone under the same roof?"

He nodded. "Perhaps. But it will be... tricky. And... then there is the thing with us... with our friendship."

"Which *thing*?" Something in his tone made my fingers twitch around the charcoal with an unpleasant sense of foreboding.

He hesitated for a moment. "It is... very clear you have

become a target due to our relations, despite my efforts to be discreet when visiting you."

"Way to make a girl feel like a dirty secret," I muttered.

He ignored me. "I would like you to accompany me to the meeting with the other Lords."

I blinked. "Uh... sorry, are you asking me to waltz into the middle of a vampire gathering? 'Cause I gotta tell ya, the last time you brought me into a crowd of your kind, I nearly ended up on the menu."

"Regrettably, Liv, I'm not *asking*." Despite Warin's still-quiet voice, his tone was like velvet-wrapped granite. "It is the only way I can restore a measure of safety to your life, and so you will go. And I will claim you, among my equals, as my... special companion. As such, you will be untouchable to them. And even other supernaturals will think twice before harming you."

A hot flush of anger made my blood boil alongside a trickle of desire his no-nonsense attitude shot through my abdomen. *Damnit,* now was so not the time to picture him brandishing a leather belt in one hand!

"Excuse the fuck out of me?" I snapped, opting to lean into the anger and avoid the disturbing images my hormones were conjuring. "Since when did our friendship turn into you bossing me around?"

"I am truly sorry, Liv," he said, and he sounded it too. "I am sorry I pulled you into my world. I thought I was careful, but I was only selfish. I should have kept walking when I saw you in that bar, but I..." Warin looked down, his voice faltering for a moment. When he looked back up, there was steel in his eyes. "But regrets are useless now. *I* am the cause of your current predicament, therefore *I* am responsible for your continued safety. You will accompany me to this meeting, and you will allow me to ensure your continued safety until the threat has been eliminated. What you wish to do thereafter... will be your decision. I will not make any further demands of you. But this, Liv... this will happen."

If he hadn't sounded so anguished, I'd have kicked him straight out of my home. But as I glared daggers at Warin, the regret on his marble features took the edge off my anger.

Drawing in a deep breath through my nose, I reined in my hostility. "What do you think *'claiming'* me will do to these witches? I mean, if they try to kill me just because they've seen us hang out together, wouldn't putting attention on our friendship just make things worse?"

"There are... certain procedures in my world," he said, and the hesitance in his voice made it clear he was anything but comfortable with the topic. "Certain rules every supernatural being will adhere to, if they do not wish to suffer... serious consequences. I am the vampire Lord of this territory. Should anyone harm my claimed companion, I would be honorbound to hunt them and their kin to extinction. Even witches would be hesitant to touch you, once you are truly mine."

I bit my lip as I looked at Warin's perfect profile, trying to fight back the roil of conflicting emotions in my gut.

Normally, this would have been simple. I'd picked up and moved for a lot less in the past. I never stayed long enough anywhere to form lasting bonds with anyone. The smart thing—and what the panicked clenching in my gut told me was the only rational choice—would be to tell him thanks, but no thanks on his "special companion" offer. And skip town.

Let's stay in touch. I'll email.

But...

If that was really what I wanted, then why hadn't I done so already? Why had I gone to visit the slaughter-house? Gotten myself tangled up further in crazy-ass supernatural mysteries?

The answer was glaringly obvious... and currently sitting on my couch with a faraway expression of gloom painted across his features.

I'd never felt so... *connected* to another being as I did to Warin. Maybe it would have been easier to shrug it off if it was just sexual attraction, but it wasn't. Not even close. Sure, he was smoking hot, and if things had been different I'd have happily dragged him to bed for a few rounds of commitment-free sex. I had eyes.

And ovaries.

Only I knew, without a shadow of a doubt, that the moment I fucked my vampire friend, things would be completely and irrevocably changed between us.

And I'd lose him.

Like I would if I high-tailed it out of Chicago with a big "no-thank-you" to dealing with any more of this mess.

That's why I stayed, I realized.

For reasons I didn't understand, reasons that made no sense, this man—this *nightwalker*—I'd known so shortly meant more to me than the very real threat to my life.

More than the panic in my gut at the realization that I'd let someone all the way in.

"Okay. I'll go with you to the meeting," I said, clearing my throat at the tremor in my voice. "If it means we can keep being friends, I'll go."

Warin nodded, and his shoulders dropped a fraction of an inch. "Thank you." His voice was soft.

FOURTEEN

I woke up the next morning with the unmistakable woolly sensation of having gone to bed without brushing my teeth. I rolled over with a groan and realized I was still wearing my clothes from last night, apart from socks—and that I didn't have any memory of going to bed. The last thing I remembered was sitting in silence while drawing Warin, neither of us being in much mood for talking... and then my eyelids feeling very heavy.

Had he carried me to bed?

I grabbed my phone to check the time—half past nine, but luckily I had a late shift—and saw one unread text. When I swiped my thumb over it, Warin's name flashed up.

Roy is in front of your building. He will stay with you until I return tonight.

Yup. He'd put me to bed and gotten me a babysitter. I probably should have been annoyed—or at the very least embarrassed, because judging from the way my hair stuck to my cheek, I'd been drooling in my sleep—but I couldn't help a smile from hiking up one corner of my mouth. For something as serious-sounding as a vampire Lord, he still bothered with as small a thing as removing his zonked-out human buddy's socks before tucking her in. It was kind of adorable.

AN HOUR LATER, I walked out the door with two coffee mugs in hand.

Roy accepted my offering with a short nod of gratitude. "Going out?"

"Yup, back to work. You my ride again?"

He nodded again and held out an arm toward where his truck was parked. "Your car is currently at the mechanic's, but as long as Mr. Waldlitch has me watching you, I'll drive you anywhere you need to go."

I blinked. I'd been too out of it to remember my broken-down car, what with the skinwalker attack and everything that'd come with it, and I most certainly hadn't had the presence of mind to call a mechanic. "Did Warin call a mechanic for me?"

"Yes, ma'am. He asked me to take care of it."

"Huh, that was really nice of him. And of you. How much was it? We might have to go to the bank on the way." I looked over my shoulder at the big guy as he shepherded me to his truck, trying not to cringe at the thought of how barren my bank account was. I didn't really have a choice on whether or not I should get my car fixed.

Roy gave me a weird look as he waited for me to climb in so he could shut the door. "It's been taken care of. Mr. Waldlitch paid in full."

I frowned at him as he walked around the front of the truck to get into the driver's seat. "Yeah, but I still have to pay him back."

He blinked, opened his mouth as if he was gonna say something, but then thought better of it.

"What?" I asked as he turned his focus to the car, twisting the key and undoing the handbrake.

"It kinda defeats the purpose, doesn't it?" he said, voice gruff and eyes never leaving the road. "Paying for your own shit."

"What do you mean?" I asked, not following at all.

"Nothing. Forget it," he said, and from the tense set of his jaw, I could tell he was regretting this entire conversation.

"Nuh-uh," I said, arching an eyebrow. "You clearly wanted to say something, so go on. Unless of course you want to play my bodyguard while I discuss every gross biological detail of being a woman with my coworkers today. Your choice, buddy."

Roy nearly managed to hide his grimace. "Fine. Girls who aren't mindfucked out of their skull usually hang around rich vampers for the perks. Such as having their master pick up the bill for cars, rent, shiny shit." He waved the hand not currently on the steering wheel in a dismissive gesture. "You seem to still have some willpower left—"

"So you assumed I was, what? A deadwhore banging the first vampire she meets in return for car service?" I interrupted him, outrage heating my cheeks. "For your information, Warin isn't my freakin' *master*. We're *friends*. He doesn't pay for me, and I don't offer him a vein when he's hungry. Or anything else, for that matter."

A flash of Roy's message from Warin when I asked him to prove who he was made me cringe. He'd said my blood tasted like life, and clearly Roy knew about that.

"Except that one time," I muttered, some of the wind fizzing out of my indignation.

"It's not my place to judge," he said. "I was just surprised. Sorry."

I sighed, slumping back in the passenger seat. "It's fine. I guess it's not every day you're called in to guard your boss' friend from crazy witch-wolves."

Roy snorted. "No, ma'am."

I glanced at him out the corner of my eye. "What do you normally do? For Warin?"

He shrugged, not taking his eyes off the road. "Daytime errands. Anything he needs taken care of while the sun's up. Most vamps got someone like me."

"How does one fall into a job like that?" I asked, curious how other humans stumbled into the supernatural world. Besides as a snack.

Another shrug. "Make a couple poor fucking life choices. I owe him—he suggested this arrangement to work off my debt. Guess it could be worse. The vamper he bought my debt from was a nasty piece of work."

I frowned as I considered this sliver of insight into Warin's life. His *"vampire life,"* as I was starting to distinguish it. When he was with me, it wasn't like I forgot what he was—the whole taking me out flying thing, or licking me down after ripping furry wolfmen apart, didn't really leave much room for forgetting—but it just didn't matter. At all. Didn't matter he was a blood-drinking undead who apparently bought men's debts and lorded over the city's nightwalker population. And it didn't matter that I was a serious fuckup with rampant commitment issues and more skeletons in my closet than most morticians.

When it was just the two of us, my past didn't matter, and his undead-ness didn't, either.

I had a sneaking suspicion that was why he liked spending time with me, too.

"What's he like? To work for?" I asked, unable to rein in my curiosity.

Roy glanced at me out the corner of his eyes, and I held up a hand. "Not spying for him or anything—I'm just really curious. I haven't really seen that part of his world yet."

"Yet?" he asked, arching an eyebrow. "D'you plan to?"

I grimaced. "Well, no. I'd rather not. But apparently there's a *thing*, and I have to go because murderous skin-walkers and whatnot."

Roy sighed. "I guess Mr. Waldlitch's all right, for a vamper. Even provides dental and a pension fund. To be honest, I hardly ever see him. Up until he disappeared last summer, he stayed in his house most of the time, s'far as I know. And then you showed up." He glanced at me again. "S'cuse me for saying, but you seem too smart to get mixed up with the undead."

I shrugged. "Thanks? I'm not *'getting mixed up with the undead,'* though. I'm just... hanging out with one."

Roy shook his head, still keeping his eyes on the road, but he didn't say anything.

I opened my mouth to ask him what he'd meant, but just then he swung the truck into the parking lot by my work, and I decided against it. Whatever his thoughts on girls who hung out with vampires, it didn't matter to my friendship with Warin.

I did appreciate his concern, though. The instances of

anyone caring about me had been few and far between for as far back as I could remember. Roy might not have said it in as many words, but I got the sense he worried for me and my involvement with his boss. Sad as it was, it made warmth bloom in my chest from sheer gratitude.

RAVEN WAS ALREADY THERE when I walked into the shop, Roy in tow, and so were a couple customers.

"Hey," I said as I slipped behind the till. Behind me, Roy took up guard by the door, eying the two customers with suspicion. I grimaced, hoping he wouldn't scare anyone away. Dennis was a pretty relaxed boss, but I doubted he'd look too favorably on my continued employment if my bodyguard scared away his source of income.

"Liv." Raven nodded at me, then glanced at Roy from beneath her eyelashes—ensuring he wasn't looking in our direction. "I've talked with my High Priestess. She's agreed to meet with you. But, uh... there's a catch."

"A catch?" I arched an eyebrow at my colleague. "What sort of catch?"

"She wants to meet with you *and* the vampire. But only if you agree to, uh, have a spell placed on you. To ensure the safety of the coven."

Something about the way she said "spell" made me narrow my eyes. "A spell?"

"It's more of a curse," she muttered.

"A *curse?!*" My outrage made the two customers and Roy look in our direction. I turned closer to Raven and lowered my voice, despite my temper. *"Seriously?* How's that any better than dealing with skinwalkers on my lonesome?"

"It's not like they show in the movies, Liv," she sighed, though she at least had the decency to look somewhat guilty. "You won't get hurt, as long as the vampire doesn't harm our coven. I'm sorry, but it's a non-negotiable. If you knew what his kind has done to us over the years, you'd understand why we need a safety precaution. We'd put it on him, but..."

"But?" I asked, arms folded across my chest.

"He'd never allow it."

"That's real nice," I grumbled, but I guess I saw their point. Warin's opinion on witches made it pretty clear he wasn't about to offer some rando coven the chance to curse him. "What sort of curse?"

"It, uh... you won't feel a thing as long as he doesn't try to hurt any of us," Raven said, avoiding my stare.

"And if he did?"

She grimaced. "You'd suffer. A lot. Look, I know it's not exactly an ideal situation, but it's really important, Liv. Those skinwalkers aren't just causing trouble for you —if they get the vamps riled up enough, they're going to exterminate all of us. We need a way to communicate with them, and... Well, you're kind of the only one any of us knows who's on friendly terms with one of them. We can help you, but we need your help in return.

"Can you do it? Get your vampire to meet with us?"

I sighed and gnawed on my lip as I considered. On one hand, Warin had been very clear on his dislike of witches. But on the other... if Raven's coven could help us both with the skinwalker situation, maybe they'd also provide a lead as to the whole dead blood-situation.The vampires and witches could avoid a war, and I'd get to live. Win-win.

So long as I was okay with having a curse placed on me.

"Okay. I'll do it. And then I'll talk to Warin." I side-eyed Roy's large frame. He was keeping an eye on the two customers browsing the shop, as well as the exit. "But, er, I'm not sure the big guy's gonna be too happy about it. When exactly are we doing this curse? I don't get much babysitter-free time at the moment."

Raven shot the burly giant a glance. "It shouldn't take long. Just play along, okay? I'll keep him occupied."

She stretched to look past the woman browsing our crystal selection, catching the eye of the redhead flipping through a thick book on herbs. "Joana will do the spell."

"Joana?" I whispered as the redheaded customer began to make her way toward us, book in hand.

"My High Priestess," Raven explained, nodding toward the woman. "She's the only one in the coven strong enough for something like that. She came in in case you agreed—the sooner we get this done, the better."

"Yeah, I guess that makes sense," I said, trying to ignore the cold shiver from the base of my spine. I'd kind of hoped to have a little while to come to terms with the fact that I was gonna get a freakin' curse placed on me.

"It's gonna be okay, Liv." Raven gave my arm a small squeeze. "Joana wants to help you, I promise."

"Hi, can I get some help with this book?" The redheaded woman stopped in front of the cash register and held out the book on herbs.

"Sure! What do you want to discuss?" Raven put on an exaggerated smile as she looked at the woman. It might have been because I was feeling on edge myself, but it was hard not to cringe at the sudden change to bubbly service agent in the black-haired girl by my side. Roy was staring at us, and I wondered if Raven's poor acting skills were bad enough to have him alerted.

"Oh, it's a matter best discussed privately," the redhead said. "Would that be possible?"

"Yes, ma'am, Liv here will be happy to take you to one of the back rooms. Isn't that right, Liv?" Raven turned to me, fake smile still plastered on her face.

"Oh, uh, yes, of course. Come with me..." I glanced at Roy again. He was frowning. When I motioned for the redhead to come with me, he moved from the door toward us in long strides.

"Uh... just go on ahead without me, I'll be just a second. It's the first door on the right behind the curtain," I said to my customer as Roy appeared by my side, his bulk cutting off most of my view of the store.

"You ain't going anywhere I can't see you," he said, voice gruff as he stared after the redhead.

"Don't be absurd, it's not like you came along every time I needed a pee yesterday," I said. "And this is a girly matter, if you catch my drift. I can't have you hulking over me while I have a period talk with a customer."

Roy's frown deepened. "I can't have you alone with a stranger. Mr. Waldlitch would have my hide."

"Oh, she's not a stranger—she comes in several times a week. She's perfectly harmless," I assured him, patting his arm with what I hoped was a gentle smile. "I wouldn't do anything to get either of us in trouble with Warin."

The giant looked more than reluctant as he shot another look at the beaded curtain the redhead had just disappeared through, but when he glanced down at me again he sighed in defeat. "Fine. You've got ten minutes before I come looking for you, got it? And if you need me, scream."

"I can do that," I assured him. "Thanks, Roy."

In my defense, I did feel pretty shitty about lying to the guy I'd only just been all warm and fuzzy about showing concern for my well-being, but I silently promised myself I'd make sure Warin took any and all anger out on me, not my bodyguard.

"OLIVIA? I'M JOANA." The redheaded woman had been waiting for me in the small staff break room, perched on the table. She got up and stretched a hand out in greeting, her long skirt flowing gracefully with the movement.

"Just Liv," I said, awkwardly shaking her hand. It felt weird, but what did I know about proper etiquette when meeting a witch to have a curse placed on you?

"Liv, then." She offered me a smile, and I was surprised by how friendly she looked. Again, the whole witch-and-curse thing was hard to reconcile with the sweet-looking middle-aged woman in front of me. She looked like your typical Earth hippie, with long, hennaed hair, a flowy maxi-skirt, and sun-lines on her thin face.

"You're brave for accepting our terms. And Raven tells me you're new to the supernatural world?"

I bobbed my head in agreement. "Always known about the vampires, of course, but witches and werewolves? That was a surprise." Understatement of the year.

"We don't call them werewolves, my dear. They're skinwalkers. Foul creatures," she said, and I was kinda pleased by the grimace she pulled. At least I wasn't the only one who couldn't think about them without discomfort.

"Whatever they are, they nearly killed me," I said. "And if there are more, I want them stopped. So if you really need to curse me, we should probably get moving. My, er, *friend* gave me ten minutes before he'll come looking, and he's not going to be pleased if he catches us mid-curse."

"The giant-blood?" Joana asked. "I take it he works for your vampire?"

"He's really nice, but it's kind of his job to make sure I don't get myself into trouble. And, uh... I think this classifies as trouble." I made a vague gesture between us.

"Yes, of course." She reached into her shoulder bag and pulled a half-liter plastic bottle out. It had a small bit of red, viscous liquid in the bottom. She handed it to me, catching my gaze with hers. "The Coven of the Moon thanks you for your sacrifice, Liv. What you are doing today will save many lives."

I eyeballed the liquid. "What... is that?"

"Blood from every member of the coven," she said, as if it was a completely normal thing to haul around in your handbag. "You will need to drink it."

"Ew, what? No!" I thrust the bottle back at her, but she didn't take it. "That's wildly unhygienic! Ever heard of hepatitis?!"

"You won't get sick, I promise." She put a hand on my arm and looked at me, the expression in her eyes urgent and sincere. "The blood is cleansed by magic. This is the only way of completing the spell—you have to take their life essence inside you to protect them. Please, child. We need your help. And you ours."

I guessed once you agreed to getting cursed, there was no need for catching to be at the top of your worry-list. Grimacing, I unscrewed the cap and raised the bottle to my lips. "I just... drink it?"

Joana nodded. "Make sure you get all of it."

Here goes nothing. I took a deep breath and tilted the bottle upside-down.

The blood of Joana's coven tasted nothing like the sweet, wild, powerful flavor of Warin's. It was slightly sour and tasted overwhelmingly of iron tablets.

I gagged as I forced myself to keep the bottle to my lips so every last drop of the sluggishly dripping fluid landed on my tongue. When it was finally empty, I tossed it to the floor and pressed my hand to my mouth in an effort to not hurl all over the staff room.

"Good," Joana said. And then she clasped her hands to my upper arms with surprising strength, her eyes lighting up with a bright green and one hundred percent unnatural light.

I croaked and tried to jerk away from sheer surprise, but she clung on.

"Be one of us, Liv. Feel for us. Bleed for us. *Die* for us. By the dark goddess, by the power of the blood—take our pain, be our shield against the night. My will be done!"

The oddest sensation of power crackled through my veins as Joana spoke, almost electric in nature. It felt oddly like it had when the green light had shot from me to push away the skinwalkers, but different. Foreign—like an outside force pressing itself through my blood.

Something inside me rose up, like a tidal wave of responding power, as if my body tried to defend itself against the invading magic, but it was too late.

I felt the foreign magic take hold—and then nothing.

Joana let go of my arms with a deep breath. "It's done."

I blinked and stared at my hands, halfway expecting them to glow with the strange green light, but there was not a single sign that a witch had cursed me. "I don't feel any different."

"You won't, so long as your vampire behaves himself." She looked at me, head tilted. "Do you know you have the Gift?"

"The Gift?"

"You have magic, girl. You're one of us." Joana reached out and grabbed my hand between hers. "Did you know?"

I bit my lip. "I, uh... had an *incident* the other day. But I didn't... I mean, it wasn't like a spell or anything. I'm not even sure—"

The redhead shook her head, silencing me. "You're a

witch, Liv, and deep down you must know. We all do, even if we don't know *what* it is."

I wanted to argue, but I couldn't. Not after having felt that powerful green light the other night.

Magic. I had magic.

A week ago my only impressive skill was my extraordinary ability to find *the* bitchiest reality show, no matter when I flicked on the TV.

"Does your vampire know?"

I shook my head. "I don't think he'd be thrilled."

"No." Joana hesitated before she gave my hands a squeeze and let go. "He mustn't find out, Liv. Your life would be in danger. He might act your friend now, you might think you understand him, but... trust me. You don't. And he isn't. Whatever his reason for protecting you now, if he knew you were one of us..."

She paused, letting an ominous silence hang between us. I wanted to deny her suggestion that Warin would ever hurt me. He'd saved my ass twice now, and I trusted him in a way that went beyond even that. It was almost as if part of my mind... *recognized* him somehow.

I'd never felt as safe as I did when I was around him.

And yet...

"I won't tell him," I said softly.

"Good." Joana nodded. "If I were you... I'd try to suppress your power, at least for now. Magic can be volatile and unreliable when a witch first starts out—you don't want it to accidentally burst out when you're around the dead man. Once you part ways, seek me out and I will put you on the path. As a thank-you for what you have done today. But not before."

Wait on delving deeper into my suddenly-appearing magical power? Yeah, that sounded pretty all right. One supernatural disaster was enough to focus on at a time, and at the moment, the skinwalkers kinda had priority.

"Yeah, sounds good. But, uh... one question." I drew in a deep breath, steeling myself. "How does one become a witch? Where does the magic come from? Is it hereditary? Like, were one of my parents...?"

Joana shook her head. "No, it's nothing like that. It's tied to the soul, not the blood. Your parents can be the dullest accountants west of the river, but you could still catch the spark. And even then, you could live your whole life with no sign of it. Maybe a few moments of deja vu, a dream of future events now and then, a strong sixth sense, but no real magic."

"But why me?" I hadn't meant to ask, but the denial that it could be hereditary made the question burst past my lips before I could stop it. I'd hoped...

But of course that was just a silly child's dream. Any little girl who'd been abandoned by her father would wish there was a reason, or at least some mystical tie that would one day lead her to him.

My mom always said my dad walked out on us

because he didn't want to be a father anymore. Hoping he was a great witch hiding from evil vampires was probably too much to hope for, when Mom's explanation was the far likelier.

"Your path is going to be long, Liv. And maybe you'll find the answer to that question one day—but not yet. We have to focus on the skinwalkers, and on forging an alliance with the vampires, and you're our only link. We can't risk that. Not now." The redhead gave me a sympathetic look.

"So hang tight until war's no longer about to break out before I go on any spiritual navel-gazing journeys?" I grimaced. "Gotcha. Don't worry, I'll get Warin to meet with you. As much as he might dislike witches, I'm sure he'd rather focus on getting rid of the skinwalkers in his territory."

A small gasp escaped Joana's lips and she stared at me, eyes wide. "Warin? Warin Waldlitch? The Night Lord?"

"Uh, yeah. Is that a problem?" I hadn't really realized Warin's fancy vampire title might bleed into my day-to-day life, and seeing the complete shock on Joana's face at the sound of his name was unexpected. But then again, I guess getting cursed by a witch wasn't really day-to-day for me, either.

"No, that's—" She blinked again, appearing to shake herself out of it. "That is potentially fantastic. Please bring the Night Lord to *Isla* tomorrow night. We will talk more."

I watched Joana leave the staff room, hoping this meeting was going to go as both she and I hoped. Because if not... there was still plenty time for me to regret this curse. I patted my chest where I'd last felt the swell of magic from within, hoping Warin would see it for the opportunity it was.

FIFTEEN

"What exactly do you mean, you *'met with a High Priestess'?"*

Oh, boy. The dangerous quality to Warin's voice and his narrowed eyes as he glared at me from across the sofa made me fidget in my seat. So far my *"he'll totally see this as the greatest idea since bagged blood"* idea wasn't in line with reality. He'd been in my apartment for a grand total of five minutes before I'd mentioned my meeting with Joana—leaving out the curse aspect as a fun surprise for later—and I was already starting to regret it.

"Calm down, okay? It was the logical thing to do. The witches—at least this coven—want to get rid of the skin-walkers too. We can work with them. They'll have valuable insight we couldn't get without them."

"There are ways of getting information out of an

enemy without aligning yourself with them! Have I not made myself clear, Liv? They are dangerous! You are not to be around them, let alone make deals with them!" Warin's nostrils flared, and for a moment he looked more predator than human, eyes dark and upper lip curled in a snarl.

Unfortunately for him, even in the face of this much anger, I wasn't afraid of him. I was, however, getting mightily pissed off at being bossed around.

"Stop talking to me like I'm your goddamn property!" I got up from the couch, rounding on him. "I see and speak to exactly who I want, and you need to stop treating me like I'm some idiot who needs to be protected from her own stupidity! We need the witches on our side, and if you weren't so goddamn prejudiced, you'd see it too. You want to avoid a war? This is the way we do it."

Warin stared at me. Then, slowly, like a stalking panther, he got to his feet and walked the two steps to stand in front of me. *Power*, the full extent of his presence, wrapped around me in a dark caress that should have been intimidating, but it just made the blood in my abdomen pulse harder.

Dammit. Down, girl, down!

"You will let me protect you. You will not question my will on matters concerning your safety, and you will stay away from these witches. *Understood?*"

Warin's voice was a low growl, gravel wrapped in silk,

and it sent a shiver down my spine as my nipples tightened to aching points underneath my shirt, and my mind hazed while uninvited images of what it'd be like if he spoke to me like that under different circumstances flashed through my brain.

Oh, holy wow, why was it so fucking hot when he went all bossy vampire on me!? I shook my head to clear it from the hormonal fog and crossed my arms over my chest, partly to close myself off and partly to hide my traitorous nipples.

"Nope, that's not how this is going to go down. I don't know how things are between vampire friends, but you don't get to roll up into my apartment and boss me around, dude. Now, I appreciate that you're just trying to protect me, and I am grateful for that. Truly. But I get a say in this too, and that say is that these witches will help us. So I need you—" I unwrapped one arm to poke him in the chest, "—to pull yourself together. Just because *some* witches are apparently murderous bastards, it doesn't mean they're all bad. Like not all vampires are bad. And this High Priestess is a really good person, I promise. So, you and I are going to calm down, and tomorrow we're going to meet her and her coven so we can get to the bottom of who's trying to murder me and poison the blood supply. Okay?"

Warin blinked, his eyes wider than before, as if he couldn't quite believe I'd told him *"no."* But then again, a fancy vampire Lord probably wasn't used to having people disagree with his decrees.

"It's for the best, Warin," I continued, gentling my tone. "Deep down, you know it."

He drew in a deep, unnecessary breath, and finally nodded. "Fine. For you, I will meet with this priestess. But I must warn you, Liv. I am doing this only out of respect for you. Any hint of deceit, and this will not end well for them. Are you prepared for that?"

I nodded, deciding against telling him about the curse. The way his eyes were still dark with anger, I didn't think it'd make things go any smoother if he realized what kind of precaution Joana had put in place. "Just... no bloodshed. Please."

Warin reached out and briefly touched his hand to my cheek. "I will strive to avoid it. I am so sorry that you have been pulled into this world."

I smiled and patted his hand before I sat back down on the couch, curling my legs up under me. "Sometimes we don't really get a choice in what life throws our way. And if I had to choose between this and never meeting you... I'd choose this every time. Now please, come. Sit down so I can draw you."

I HAD TO GOOGLE *ISLA*, and when a hip-looking nightclub in downtown Chicago popped up on my screen, shoot a text to confirm the location with Raven.

I'd never really considered nightclubs to be the place supernatural beings went to discuss business, but according to Raven, it was the right place. And, according to her, the dress-code was black eyeliner, bare skin, and sweat.

So the next night, while I waited for Warin to pick me up, I spent hours in front of the mirror, attempting to get my very laid-back self back into the shape of a girl who was used to wearing makeup and doing her hair. Before Warin, I spent most evenings on the couch watching reality TV under a blanket, just living life to its fullest. These days, the TV had been swapped out for a handsome vampire, but still... I had to rummage in my closet for a good ten minutes before I managed to pull out a black spaghetti-strapped dress from behind the mountain of t-shirts, sweaters and jeans.

When Warin finally pressed the buzzer to my door phone shortly before nine, I'd managed to press myself into an old push-up bra that had my breasts threatening to spill out over the low neckline of my—as it turned out, once I'd screwed myself into it—rather skanky dress. My hair was up in a Dutch braid I'd spent forty solid minutes watching YouTube tutorials to get right, I had a liberal helping of black eyeliner smeared around my eyes, and I held onto my third glass of pre-*meeting-witches-who-have-a-curse-on-me* wine as I swung the door open and greeted the vampire with a wide smile.

"Hello, handsome!" I said—and immediately regretted it when his eyebrows crept up half an inch at the sight of me. "Er, I mean... c'mon in."

Silently, he stepped over the threshold, not moving his gaze from me.

"I just need to finish up," I said, making flapping motions toward the sofa. "Make yourself comfortable."

It's a testament to Warin's patience that I didn't hear him so much as clear his throat while I applied the last of my mascara, fussed with my hair, and spent five full minutes bouncing in the bathroom to ensure my boobs wouldn't escape.

When I returned to the living room, now with an empty wine glass, I found him by my bookshelf, leafing through one of my spiritual books.

"Well look who's being all open minded," I teased as I set the empty glass down on the kitchen counter and grabbed my black clutch. "Looking for tips for the meeting?"

He didn't answer—just put the book down and stared intently at me.

"What? Is my foundation caked?" I rubbed self-consciously at my cheek.

"I asked a few of my Guard to join us, just in case the witches are plotting a trap."

I blinked, confused at the subject change. "I mean, as long as they don't start snacking on anyone, I'm sure that's fine. They can hardly expect you to show up with just a tipsy human as backup."

He hummed, full lips flattening to a tight line.

"*What?*"

"You need to stay close," he said, giving me one lingering look before he moved toward the door. He waited for me there, one hand resting on the handle.

I shot him a confused look as I joined him. "Why?"

"You look like vampire bait, little one," he said as he opened the door for me, a ghost of a smile easing the stern look on his pale face. "And I won't be the only night-walker present."

"*Oooh!*" I laughed, delighted that he was feeling playful despite the meeting awaiting us both. As much as I was a homebody, the wine and skanky dress had gotten me in the mood for a night out, and if things went well, I was so planning on having a dance or two with my vampire buddy. Which would be much easier if he was in a good mood. "Well, thanks... I think?"

"Oh, it *was* a compliment," he said, giving me a good once-over that made heat rise from the tips of my toes all the way to the roots of my hair.

I slapped his arm for good measure. "Be careful with those—I'm a *very* friendly drunk!"

***

I RECOGNIZED Carina the second we entered *Isla*. The beautiful blonde was casually leaning against the bar, eyes scanning the many drunk and dancing humans. She was in a tight black dress that displayed her long legs, but despite the wispy material, hers didn't make her look even the slightest bit skanky. She was all cool elegance and impeccable beauty, and I did my best not to hate her as I waved hello.

She nodded at me, all grace and manners, eyes flicking from my neck to my cleavage, down to Warin's hand resting lightly against my lower back as he led me through the throng of people. When she looked back up at me, a small smile pulled her painted lips up at the corners.

I flushed at what she was obviously thinking. *Vampire bait, indeed.* I wasn't entirely sure why she was so convinced her boss and I were getting it on, but it was somewhat harder to ignore when I wasn't wrapped up in thick sweaters and old t-shirts so unattractive they might as well have *"closed for business"* printed across the front. I hadn't really thought much about my appearance when I hung out with Warin—it was just him and me, after all, and I wasn't trying to get into his pants. However, Carina's knowing smirk made his teasing compliment flash through my brain again.

He liked how I looked tonight.

And I liked that he liked it.

"I'm going to need a drink," I mumbled, banking on Warin's vampire hearing picking it up over the throb of music as I shimmied toward the bar. Since I was mostly here as sacrificial lamb anyway, there was no reason not to drown in alcohol my blooming realization that I was eventually going to fuck up our friendship with ridiculous *feelings*.

"Jack Daniels & Coke," I told the bartender as I fished through my purse for cash. "Double."

A cool touch against my fingers made me still and look up. Warin appeared by my side, sliding a black Amex across the bar. "Keep a tab open for the young lady," he said to the man behind the bar.

"No, it's all right—" Another touch, this time to my bare shoulder, made me quiet down. Despite his chilly body temperature, heat bloomed from where he'd brushed his fingertips against me. *Damn.*

"You're here because of me. Anything you need is on me. If the initial proceedings go well, I expect I will be tied up with details for some time. Carina has been instructed to watch over you, so once an initial understanding is reached, you can feel free to enjoy the facilities."

I only hesitated for a moment, because manners, but modesty be damned—*Isla* was an expensive club. "Thank you." And before I could stop myself, I continued, "S'long as you know it takes more than a couple drinks before I offer up a vein!"

It was *meant* as a joke, but Warin's gaze flickered to my throat for just the briefest of seconds, and instead of feeling the appropriate horror at what he was clearly picturing... my abdomen kind of *melted* in response.

"Oh, goddess." I groaned at the unmistakable sensation of my panties soaking through as a blush to rival the bright neon sign above the bar swept up to cover my chest, neck and face. Without looking back at Warin, I grabbed my Jack and Coke and downed a hearty gulp.

The knowledge that my otherwise tame vampire buddy, who swore he never ate from anything but donor bags, clearly wasn't a complete stranger to imagining his fangs in my throat *should* have filled me with either indignation and/or terror. I mean, it was one thing having him lick me down after my skinwalker attack stirred all sorts of inappropriate thoughts in my depraved mind—after all, he *was* very handsome, and he *had* been licking me from head to toe. But needing a panty change at the thought of having him *bite* me? Puncturing my skin and sucking blood from my veins?

Clearly, it'd been too long since I last got laid, because

no sane woman should say anything but "fuck no" with an extra helping of "nope!" to that.

I glanced at Warin out the corner of my eye, but thankfully, he was too busy staring across the crowd to pay attention to my quiet meltdown.

"We've been summoned," he murmured next to me, his mouth close enough to my ear that I could hear him over the music.

I looked up and spotted Raven, wearing a black leather corset and matching mini-skirt. She stood next to a door half-ajar by the side of the bar, staring at us.

I sighed and downed the rest of my drink in two long gulps. The bartender slid another across the bar for me before I could even ask. I nodded at him and turned to Warin, fresh drink in hand. "Let's go stop a war."

SIXTEEN

Raven stayed silent as she led us through a narrow corridor with red walls lined with black and peeling doors. It wasn't quite wide enough to allow us to walk side by side, so Warin walked ahead of me, and I got the distinct impression it was to shield me from any surprise attacks.

It was kinda cute, even if it was also kinda ridiculous—if these particular witches had wanted me dead, all it would have taken was for Raven to slip something in my tea at work.

Finally, toward the back of the building, Raven stopped and knocked on a door that looked like all the others. A confirming murmur from inside, and the door creaked open. Raven stepped back to allow us in, hands clasped behind her back. She looked at Warin with obvious distaste as we passed her.

Inside, Joana sat by an oval table, and next to her was a man who looked to be in his early thirties, despite a receding hairline. He had a round face, and the hostility on it looked severely out of place.

"Lord Warin," Joana said. She nodded at Warin, an aura of serenity around her. Despite the respectful greeting, she didn't get up.

"Priestess Joana," he said, tone clipped but equally calm.

"This is my First Disciple, Kevin. He is here as my witness." She indicated the man by her side with a gesture underlined by the soft rattle of her many beaded bracelets. "And I brought young Raven to keep your human company, should the proceedings go well and a need for longer discussion arise."

"Three witches present? Not the best start to negotiations for peace." Warin narrowed his eyes at the Priestess. "I must warn you, witch. If I so much as smell a spark of magic, you will not like the consequences."

Joana glanced at me, and I shook my head the slightest bit, hoping she'd pick up on the fact that I hadn't told him about her curse—and that mentioning it right now would be a terrible idea.

Thankfully, she seemed to catch on.

"As long as you and the dead ones you brought to our domain this evening behave, you have nothing to fear from our magic, vampire." She gestured toward the opposite side of the table. "Please, sit. Both of you."

So she knew about Carina and the Guard Warin had mentioned bringing. I wondered if learning to spot a vampire in a crowded room was part of witch training—Raven had also clocked on to Warin's lack of a pulse the first time they met.

I followed Warin around to the other side of the table and sat at his side.

"Liv tells me she was attacked by skinwalkers not far from her home," Joana began. "Before we begin, I must assure you that no one from my coven had anything to do with that."

"If I thought you did, we would be having a different kind of conversation," Warin said, voice cold and even.

I bumped his shin with my shoe underneath, trying to get him to lay off with the threats, but he ignored me.

"Be that as it may," Joana continued, "Skinwalkers so close to our coven is not something we are happy about, either. They have a history of savaging witches to sire offspring. So, it seems we have a common enemy at hand. What I offer is help locating the skinwalker nest in Chicago, in return for your blood oath that no other witch in the city will be harmed."

Warin arched an eyebrow. "You will not receive a drop of my blood. If your help in locating the skinwalkers proves valuable, you have my word any witch who stays out of my business will not be hunted within the city limits."

"The word of a dead man," Kevin spat. "What are we doing here, Joana? This *thing* is not our ally, and no amount of wishing will make it so."

The redhead put a soothing hand on her First Disciple's shoulder without taking her eyes off Warin. "Settle yourself, Kevin. Times change, and we must adapt with them. This particular vampire has not harmed any of our coven, and we must give him a fair chance to prove himself."

Warin remained quiet as he stared at the two witches on the other side of the table.

"Look, you all have to compromise if you want this to work," I interrupted, growing tired of the tension in the room. "Everyone here wants the skinwalkers dead. No one wants an all-out witch-vampire war. So make it work. You," I pointed at the two older witches with a finger from the the hand currently holding my glass, "have to remember that as little as you trust the vampires, as little do they trust you. You don't get to make grand demands about needing proof of trust without offering some up yourself. What will you do to ensure *he* can trust *you*?"

Kevin sputtered, indignation clear across his round face. "How *he* can trust *us*? Young lady, do you have the faintest idea what these... these *creatures* can do?"

I arched an eyebrow at him. "Some. I do know they

don't go around cursing people. As long as I've known this man, he hasn't once tried to harm me. In fact, he's saved my ass more than once. *Your* kind, however... your kind has threatened and assaulted me. So let's try starting these negotiations again, shall we? And let's all attempt to remember that the other party is going out of their way to make this work."

Kevin opened his mouth, the red splotches of blooming anger on his cheeks indicating whatever he was planning to say wasn't going to help matters any. But Joana lifted her hand, silencing him before he could speak. "The girl is right." She drew in a deep breath. "We have a long history of mistrust between us, vampire, and I acknowledge that it will be difficult for you as well as us to put this aside. But, if Liv will put her word in alongside yours, we will forego the demand of a blood oath. As a sign of good faith."

"Sure, of course I will," I said, glancing at Warin to make sure he didn't take offense. His blank expression gave nothing away. At least he didn't realize it didn't make a difference one way or the other, since I was pretty sure I didn't want to find out what happened if the curse was unleashed. "I wouldn't be here if I didn't trust Warin implicitly." Or, ya know, if crazy skinwalker-witches weren't gunning for me.

Joana nodded, though the wariness in her eyes didn't diminish. "Do we have an agreement, vampire?"

Warin nodded once. "We do." He glanced at me. "Thank you for your aid, Liv. I believe, if the Priestess agrees, the rest of this meeting will be best conducted with minimal participation."

"Time for me to shoo," I agreed, feeling slightly guilty at the rush of relief. As much as I wanted to be kept in the loop, the tension in the room was killing my buzz. If Warin wanted to hammer out the details of their truce alone, it was a-okay with me. "See you in a bit."

I got up, grabbed the remainder of my drink and motioned for Raven to come with me with a finger. "Let's leave the important people to their talk."

She snorted, but after a quick look at Joana followed me out the door. We'd only made it a few yards down the corridor before the door opened again and Kevin—looking sullen as all hell—stepped out too.

"No extra seat at the grown-up table, huh?" I asked him, and received an elbow to the ribs from Raven as a thank-you.

Kevin huffed and strode down the hallway toward the nightclub. We heard the sound of pulsing music and loud chatter followed by a slam of the door closing shortly after.

"He's not a people-person, is he?" I asked my friend as I rubbed at my ribs.

"You don't even know the half of it," Raven sighed. "He didn't even want us to help you, let alone meet with the vampire. Don't get me wrong, it's not like I'm keen, either, but I get that it's the smartest move for us. Kevin... not so much."

"Well, hopefully he'll be more cheerful about it once Warin's gotten rid of the skinwalkers for all of us." I gulped down the final bit of my drink and wiped my mouth with the back of my arm, like a lady. "Come on— there's nothing we can do one way or the other, so I say for us lowly minions, it's dancy time!"

Raven laughed as she followed me into the club. "You're awfully relaxed for someone who's got skin-walkers on her ass, Liv."

I shrugged as I shimmied through the throng of people to the bar for another drink. The barman spotted me instantly and had my Jack and Coke ready by the time I made it to the bar. "I know it's probably weird to you, but I trust Warin with everything I am. Now that we have you guys on our side, I know I'll be safe."

"I hope you're right—if there is a skinwalker pack in Chicago, it's gonna be all *'hide yo kids, hide yo wives'* up in here until they're dealt with. Did you know they rape witches to force-reincarnate souls in their wombs?" She shuddered and grabbed the beer the barman slid her way with a, "Thanks, Fred." Apparently, it wasn't the first time *Isla* played host to this coven.

I grimaced. "I'm sorry—*force-reincarnate?* You can... *force* someone to reincarnate?"

"Well, *I* can't. It takes some seriously pitch-black

magic to do the kind of shit the skinwalkers do. To even be able to take on another form, they have to kill first. And in pretty fucking gruesome ways." Raven shuddered again before she put the beer bottle to her lips and downed it in four long gulps. "I'll spare you the details, but I can tell you I haven't been able to look at dogs or birds the same since I found out. Now, come on—finish up your drink. You said you wanted to dance, didn't you?"

IT DIDN'T TAKE us long to get caught up in the music and atmosphere of the club, and—in my case—forget all about the tense meeting in the backroom. I tended to spend most of my nights home on the couch, so when I finally went out to dance, I wasn't about to let an impending supernatural war kill my buzz.

Which was probably why when Raven twirled me a bit too hard and I went stumbling into a tall man next to us, I only managed a giggled, "Oops!"

"Oops, indeed." The auburn-haired stranger grasped me lightly by the elbows to break my fall. The coldness of his fingers against my skin made me look up—and up—until my eyes connected with his. They were bright blue and adorning a face so ruthlessly handsome I'd only ever seen one man more gorgeous in my life—Warin.

"Does your daddy know you're giving every man in a

one-mile radius a hard-on while he's off attending to business?" His deep voice was practically a purr.

Maybe I should have been disturbed by the crudeness of his taunt, but a shock of recognition sparked through my drunk brain before I could. "You're his brother!" I chirped, a wide smile pulling on my lips as I looked up at the vampire who'd ensured Warin's other vampire friends didn't turn me into dinner in his foyer. "Aleric, right?"

"Indeed," he said, releasing my left shoulder so he could nudge my chin up with his finger. "I see he's let you keep your memories, little mouse. And if his second-in-command is to be believed, you're also responsible for this little witchy meeting tonight? I find that... ever so curious."

"Oh?" was my intelligent response. I couldn't quite grasp what he was fishing for, but the predatory spark at the back of his eyes made some faraway fight-or-flight instincts rise through my drunken haze.

"My brother's not the type to let a pretty little mortal get herself all tangled up in his business." Aleric snuck an arm around me as he dipped his head low, letting his cool lips brush over the shell of my ear. "I hear he spends most of his nights with you. And I can't help but wonder... what's so special about you, little mouse, to have enthralled an Ancient so?"

Goosebumps broke out across my body at the feel of

his cold breath brushing against my skin. "Nothing," I croaked.

"No?" he hummed. "No delicious magic in your blood to keep him coming back for more? Are you perhaps my dear brother's dirty little secret? Is that why he's been so reluctant to leash you with a claim? Are you a *witch*, little mouse?"

Despite my drunken state, his question made a nervous bolt of energy shoot through my veins. I gulped and pulled back, trying to break the hold of his arm against my back. I might as well have tried to shift a mountain. "No, I am not a witch. I didn't even know they were real until a week ago. And if you don't get your hands off me *right now*, I'm going to scream 'vampire.'"

Aleric's mouth hiked up at the corner, displaying a gleaming white fang. It wasn't elongated, but it looked wickedly sharp. "Well, well, don't you have a pair of brass balls, little human." His gaze flashed above my head for a second before he released his grip on my waist. "How *delightful.*"

I stumbled one step backward and away from the tall vampire, only to feel another steel band close around my midriff and pull me back against a solid form.

"Aleric. You come early, brother." Despite the noise and music in the club, I recognized Warin's voice effortlessly. Without thinking, I relaxed in his grasp as the sensation of complete safety set in. My drunken brain stopped attempting to shoot danger signals through the fog, and I happily pushed back into my vampire's chest, reveling in the softness of his cashmere sweater and the hardness of his body underneath it. *Well, mm.*

"You call, I don't delay. You know this, my blood." The look on the auburn-haired vampire's face was so different now—filled with reverence, not a hint of a threat left behind. "I hoped we could talk about your, ah, *situation* before the others arrive."

"I will be home before dawn. Bring Carina and the Guard with you and wait for me there. We will speak more then."

I smiled at the obvious dismissal in Warin's voice, but Aleric's gaze remained impassive as he let it slide over me, hovering by my neck and cleavage for a moment before he returned his focus to his brother. "As you wish. Do enjoy your snack—you look like you need it."

Warin didn't respond, and Aleric nodded at him before he took off, leaving us on the crowded dance floor.

Warin kept his grip on me, his strong arm still holding me so deliciously tight against his body. It was such a protective gesture, and maybe I should have wondered what about his brother's appearance had him acting like that given how we usually didn't touch much. But instead, I let his strength and the sensation of his body behind me penetrate deep into my blood, let myself get lost in the familiarity of his touch despite being surrounded by strangers. It felt so... intimate. Perhaps because I knew, in the depths of my soul, that Warin never let anyone close. His solitude was an invisible wall, surrounding and protecting him from ever truly knowing someone. But he knew *me*. He touched *me*. Held me.

Slowly, for every night we sat in my living room and talked about everything and nothing, he had let me in just a little further.

Like I had him.

Right then, as we stood together surrounded by loud music and drunk people who would never understand how profoundly *right* his arm around me felt, I knew I wanted to be like this always.

That it was how I was meant to be—safe in Warin's embrace. Shielded from the world and all its horrors.

Maybe if I hadn't been drunk, I would have handled that moment's clarity with grace, or dignity. Or both.

Unfortunately for me, I chose neither.

With a happy hum I looked over my shoulder so I could nuzzle my face against his, before I lazily threw an arm back to hook it around his neck.

"Your brother thinks you drink my blood," I murmured as I bent my knees a little so I could sway my hips to the music. Pressed up against him as I was, I could feel the fabric of his pants and the hardness of his flesh against my backside, and a hot thrill rushed through my veins. With a flick of my hair I arched my neck back, provokingly displaying my neck to him. "Have I been a bad friend by not offering?"

Warin went rigid behind me, his arm around my waist constricting even tighter. "Liv..."

I laughed, delighted by the slightly tortured note to his voice. "Told you I was a friendly drunk."

"I remember." It was a mix between a laugh and a growl against my ear, and it made my skin break out into goosebumps.

I twisted around in his arm that was still wound around my midsection so I could face him. "Hello you," I teased, noticing the darkness of his eyes and deciding to see if I could push him a little further. Because Drunk Liv is a apparently a moron.

I gave him a saucy wink and tipped my head back, arching until my hips pressed into his as I slid my hands over his soft, gray, V-necked shirt, relishing in the feel of his hard muscles underneath it.

He shot out the hand that wasn't holding my drunk form up and grabbed me by the back of my neck, pulling me back up with a jerk. Growling low, he pressed my ear close to his mouth. "You are drunk." There was a clear, dark warning in his voice.

It should probably have scared me.

But it didn't.

And I leaned in and bit down on his shoulder. Hard.

A hiss erupted from him, and both the arm around my

waist and the hand on my neck pulled me harder against him for a second, making my entire, drunken body shiver with delicious want. It wasn't just his muscles that were hard now.

Purring like a cat in heat, I opened my mouth to nibble at the place where his neck met his shoulder, but he caught my neck before I could, pulling me back. "Stop that. *Right* now."

I pulled my head away, feeling entirely too pleased with the roughness in the vampire's voice—until my eyes met his. They were pitch-black.

Oh. Maybe I'd gone a step too far? A small part of my intoxicated brain felt a flutter of fear just as he grabbed my arm and dragged me through the crowd, up to the bar.

"Settle my bill," he snarled at the barman.

The man jumped a little, probably also freaked out by the predatory sound, and disappeared to fetch Warin's card with swifter-than-average speed.

"Liv, are you all right?" A warm hand landed on my shoulder, and I turned toward its owner with a start. Dennis, my boss from *Dark Dreams*.

"Dennis!" I broke out in a grin at his unexpected appearance. "I had no idea you went to fancy nightclubs!"

Dennis didn't return my smile, his face tight as he glared over my shoulder. At Warin, I realized. The absurdity of my very human boss glaring down a nightwalker finally made his question click. He thought I was in trouble.

"Yeah, yes, I'm fine. Good, really." I beamed even brighter at him to ensure he knew I was being honest. And I was. The fact that Warin had remembered something so earthly as paying for my multitude of drinks meant he was in full control, despite his growling response to my teasing.

I gave his hand a small squeeze. "You remember Dennis, right Warin?"

Warin just stared him down, not bothering to respond. Dennis lifted his chin ever so slightly, a silent challenge.

Men.

I could have kissed the bartender when he pushed Warin's card at him, interrupting the staring contest.

"Come." Warin's voice was still rough as he tugged on my hand, turning his back on Dennis without another look. "We need to get you home."

I stumbled after him as he maneuvered us through the crowd faster than my drunk legs could manage with any form of grace. Only when we were out in the cold and so far down the street the music from Isla could no long be heard in the night did he slow down and release his grip on me.

"Jeez, that was *so* rude," I scolded, even if I couldn't hold back a giggle at the grouchy look on Warin's face. It looked downright adorable, and I leaned in to pinch his cheek. I managed to trip over my own feet and halfway fall against him in the process. "You're really cute when you're sulking, Mr. Vampire, but you should be nicer to my friends. Dennis hasn't done anything to you."

Warin lifted me back onto my feet, keeping a grip on my elbow to help me stay balanced. "He wants to fuck you. The night I met you at the bar, he was planning to take advantage of you."

I snorted at that absolutely ridiculous statement. "Dennis? Don't be ridiculous! He's completely harmless and *so* nice. It's not everyone would hire a stray alley cat like me, and he did, no questions asked."

Warin only breathed in deeply and began to walk toward where he'd parked his car without responding.

"So... we're done dancing, then?" I sighed as I stumbled along beside him, thankful for the support of his grip.

It wasn't meant to be a taunt, but it nevertheless earned me a dark glare. "Yes."

"Bore," I said, blowing a raspberry in his general direction. "I love dancing. *Oooh,* I know what we should do! You should fly me up to the highest skyscraper in Chicago and dance with me! It'll be like we are dancing among the stars!"

Cool fingers ghosted against my cheek in a light caress. "If there is anyone I could dance among the stars with, Liv, it'd be you."

"Is that a yes?" My own voice came out as a hoarse whisper as a familiar, electric heat radiated through me from his cool touch.

But when I turned my head to look at him, there was only regret in his eyes, and not an ounce of the dark heat from before.

"No, little one. There'll be no more dancing for you and me. Not tonight, nor any of the nights to come." He gently touched his thumb to my lower lip before he removed his fingers from my face, leaving me feeling hollow. "Come. You need to sleep, and I need to speak with my brother."

SEVENTEEN

When I woke up the next afternoon, it was to the sensation of something having crawled down my throat to die, and a hangover that made me wish for death.

Groaning, I rolled over onto my side and grasped for the glass of water on my nightstand.

Warin had put it there after he halfway carried me in the door, I vaguely recalled, while I'd been fighting to get out of my dress and into my PJs in the bathroom, singing one of the songs from the club at the top of my lungs.

And that's when the rest of the night came back to me, in way too crystal clear high-definition.

I choked on the water as an involuntary whimper made it past my lips at the recollection of rubbing myself all over Warin. When the memory of biting his shoulder caught up with me, I crawled back underneath the duvet, wishing a black hole would open up underneath me.

Why? *Why,* did I do that?

The answer was glaringly obvious, and did nothing to ease my flaming humiliation.

I wanted Warin. And not as a friend.

He was a vampire, and it wasn't possible—and even if it were, just the thought of opening myself up to him like that... of being vulnerable with the one person I trusted so completely... it made my skin crawl with fear. I recalled the moment in his arms the night before, when I'd realized how right it felt, how I was *supposed* to be in his embrace, safe from all the horrors of the world... And the thought of losing that because I couldn't keep my pants on filled me with more dread than I knew how to deal with.

Thankfully, he had turned my less-than-subtle offer down.

I knew what he'd meant when he'd told me we wouldn't be dancing among the stars together. He'd said what Sober Liv already knew, but Drunk Liv apparently didn't care about.

We would never be more than friends.

Groaning, with humiliation and irrational sorrow alike, I finally managed to shove my duvet aside so I could crawl out. There was no reason to be sad—I should have been thankful he'd stopped me from making the worst mistake of my life. There was, however, every reason to be filled to the brim with self-hatred, so at least I had that part down.

I finished my glass of water and staggered to the shower, hoping the spray would wash away my shame. And my hangover too, while it was at it.

It didn't. Though to be fair, there's probably only so much you can expect out of a shower when it comes to fixing your bad decisions.

I got into a fresh pair of PJs, because today was so not going to be a grown-up clothes sorta day, and went to hunt down my phone. I'd kind of left Raven behind without a second thought last night, and while I didn't have a lot of experience with having friends, I knew that was a pretty shitty thing to do.

My phone was on my kitchen counter where I'd thrown it after coming in last night, and the display showed a missed call. From my mother.

This day just kept getting better and better.

Ignoring the little unanswered call icon in the top corner of the display, I quickly typed out a text to Raven, apologizing for leaving without saying anything and asking if she made it home all right. Then I went hunting through my cupboards, only to find them emptier than a vampire's grave.

Who went for a night out without first stocking up on hangover food? This idiot, apparently.

A beep from my phone broke my contemplations on

whether I could afford to order takeaway or not. It was a reply from Raven.

No worries. Ran into Dennis. Hey, I always wondered - does the D stay cold, or does friction heat things up?

Followed by an eggplant and winky-face emoji.

LOVELY. But for someone with her ingrained vampire hate, maybe Raven giving me shit for the way I threw myself at Warin last night was actually a positive thing.

Nothing happened. Yeah, I saw Dennis briefly too. I didn't realize he was the clubbing type tbh. Glad you got home OK!

HER RESPONSE WAS ALMOST IMMEDIATE. It was an eggplant emoji followed by a sad smiley.

Two seconds later, another text beeped in:

Most witches go to Isla. He comes there regularly enough.

I BLINKED. I hadn't realized Dennis was a witch. I told her as much, and asked if he was part of her coven too.

Really? He owns a New Age shop called Dark Dreams. *I thought it was obvious ;) Not from our coven though. Dunno which one he belongs to, he's kinda secretive about it.*

WELL, huh. Apparently everyone and their uncle was a witch these days. Before I could ask her if Skye was in on the supernatural bandwagon too, my phone buzzed to life in my palm, making me grimace with the sharp sound of the factory setting ringtone. I really should change that.

When I saw the name of the caller, I grimaced again. It would seem Mom wasn't gonna let me ghost her today.

With a heavy sigh, I answered.

"Olivia, did you just get out of bed?"

"Hi, Mom. How are you?"

"You know only bums and drug addicts sleep until the afternoon." The sharpness of her voice more than indicated her continued belief that I was most definitely in the former of those two categories. Not that that was anything new.

I glanced at the clock—four thirty. "I went out last night... and I didn't *just* get up."

"Oh, God forbid! Are you an alcoholic now?"

"No, Mom. It was just a nice night out with some friends," I sighed, dragging myself over to my couch so I could at least be comfortable while I got nagged. "How're things with you and Randy, anyway?"

Randy, her boyfriend of nearly a year, was her favorite subject and the easiest way to get her off my ass, and as per usual, my mom happily switched gears without another thought of her alcoholic bum of a daughter's life.

I halfway listened while she talked and talked, about everything from every excruciating detail about every load of laundry she'd done in the two months since we spoke last, as well as which neighbors she was currently feuding with. The Delawares, turned out to be the answer to the last one, due to their dogs barking in the mornings.

I put *The Bachelor* on—muted with subtitles—settled in for the long haul.

WHEN MY DOOR buzzer went off some three hours later, I was still on the phone with her.

"Mom, hang on a moment, someone's at the door," I tried interrupting her steady stream of words as I got up from the couch. She ignored me and continued talking about the new dance class her and her boyfriend attended every Thursday.

I rolled my eyes and trudged over to open the door, phone still pressed against one ear. Expecting Roy to pop in for a cup of coffee or to borrow the toilet, I pressed the button and opened my front door, while still mm-hmming into the phone.

Only the man on the other side of the door wasn't my giant bodyguard. It was Warin—with a pizza box tucked under one arm.

I stared at him with a rising sense of panic and mortification, frantically debating if I could just slam the door in his face and maybe he'd go away so I didn't have to deal with the shame of it all. However, before I could get my numbed brain to react, Warin said, "Good evening, Liv," which finally made my mother stop mid-talk.

"Was that a man?"

Great.

"Yeah, that was Warin." Defeated, I stepped out of the doorway so he could get in.

"Did he spend the night?" my mother gasped in horror.

Doing my best not to groan, I pinched the bridge of my nose and nudged the door closed with my hip. "No, Mom. He *just* knocked on the door—remember when I said 'just a moment, someone's at the door'..."

"Olivia Teresa Green! Do not take that tone with me! Who is this man who thinks it is appropriate to visit a young woman this late on a Saturday evening?"

This late being seven thirty.

I quietly counted down from ten. "Warin's my friend. We met a few weeks ago."

"Yes, thank you, I am aware what sort of 'friend' you're talking about!" she snapped.

Somehow, I doubted it.

"Mom... was there a reason you called?" I glanced at the pizza box Warin had set down on my kitchen counter. A promising scent of melted cheese emanated from it. "I'm starving, and the food is getting cold."

"Aunt Edna is having a big family Thanksgiving meal this year, but because Aunt Gretchen is on call until late afternoon, we're doing a dinner. I'm counting on you this year, Olivia—I've already told the family you're coming."

I made the mistake of groaning out loud.

"Olivia, you haven't been home for Thanksgiving for three years! It's important *that you come this year—Grandma has some news..."* I instantly felt ashamed over the rush of happiness that went through me when the thought that the news might be that she was suffering from some fatal illness popped into my head. *"... and it has started to get noted that you've not been back in Denver in ages."* She paused briefly. *"Shall I tell Edna that you'll be coming on your own? Again? Or is there a gentleman you would like to bring? You know, your cousin Kathy has just gotten engaged, and to such a handsome young man."*

It is incredible what motherly pressure and years of growing up in a toxic environment can do to your sense of rationality.

"No, I'll bring someone," I heard myself say.

"Oh, good. I shall see you on the twenty-third. Seven p.m. sharp—don't be late. Bye now!"

I stared at my phone after she'd hung up. How did she do that? How did she wrap me around her little finger from a thousand goddamn miles away?

"Your mother?"

Warin's soft voice made me cringe, the frustration with myself for falling for my mother's manipulation taking a backseat to my more immediate mortification.

Groaning, I hid my face behind my phone-free hand. "Please, just don't say anything, okay? I was really, *really* drunk last night, and I am sorry for being... ya know—"

Horny as fuck. "—out of line. I get handsy when I drink too much, and you got caught in the crossfire. So would you please, *please* do me a tremendous favor and pretend like it never happened? 'Cause if you don't, I think I have to murder you and bury your corpse out back, and then I'll undoubtedly get myself arrested and it would just be a whole nightmare, okay?"

Warin's chuckle made me glance up from my hand.

"As you wish." He held up a hand in mock surrender. "I wouldn't want you to get arrested."

I exhaled, grateful he was a much better person than me, and then shifted my attention to the pizza box. "So...?"

"I thought you might be hungry. I'm told humans enjoy this kind of meal after consuming alcohol the previous night." The look on his face said he found the idea revolting, but I could have kissed him regardless. I didn't, though, because after last night, I wasn't gonna risk him getting the wrong idea.

"Fuck yes, you're the absolute best! Thank you, thank you, thank you!" I dove for the box, and practically drooled at the sight of the beautiful deep-pan Hawaiian pizza inside. No idea how he got lucky enough to guess my favorite toppings, not that I cared. Right then, all I wanted was to stuff my mouth with delicious pineappley goodness. "You better look away—this is gonna get gross."

I grabbed the first slice with my hands, not bothering

with such banalities as a plate, or even sitting down. Moaning with food-pleasure I shoved slice after slice in, leaning over the kitchen counter like a feral dog.

It wasn't until I was in the process of licking my fingers after having devoured the final slice of pizza that I realized that Warin—the giant asshole—was leaning against the kitchen sink, watching me like I was some kind of zoo attraction. His expression was a mix between surprise and amusement.

"Not cool," I snapped, though I couldn't muster up the level of anger such betrayal really required. He *had* brought my hungover ass pizza after I'd all but molested him the night before.

"I've seen newborn vampires with less ferocious hunger," he said, that teasing smile still dancing at the corner of his lips. "Do you feel better now?"

I snorted and patted my new food-baby. "Yeah. Just need to lie down for a bit."

I disappeared into the bedroom to get my duvet. When I returned, dragging it along after me, Warin was already sitting on the couch watching the same channel I'd had on while talking to my mom.

I flopped down next to him and, not waiting for him to approve, placed my feet in his lap and swung the duvet over me. "Just unmute it and change the channel if you want. I'm too tired to do anything meaningful."

Warin didn't touch the remote. He just leaned back

and, after a moment's hesitation, rested a hand on top of my duvet-covered feet. "What did your mother want?"

"To guilt-trip me, mostly. And force-invite me to fly home for Thanksgiving." Why, oh, why hadn't I come up with a quick lie about having to work? I'd have to dig into my savings to afford the last-minute flight and motel booking, and for what? The privilege of playing the family scapegoat for a night?

The vampire watched me closely, the blank expression on his face somewhat guarded. "And you will be bringing a... guest?"

I groaned involuntarily. "No! I don't know why I said that! Or yes, I *do* know why I said that—it's because I'm weak and still let myself get manipulated by those horrible, cold, unreasonable..." There just wasn't a strong enough finish for that sentence, so I just flailed a hand for emphasis.

"You have a strained relationship with your family?" he asked, voice soft.

I buried my face in my hands and pushed all the *issues* from my upbringing down, as I'd made a habit of doing since I left my mother's house at the age of eighteen. "I'd really rather not to talk about it right now, okay?"

"As you wish." He gently patted my foot and leaned back against the couch. A tension I hadn't noticed before seemed to ease out of his shoulders as he let his gaze flicker to the muted TV.

It was in that moment, while I looked at the man whose arms I'd felt so safe in last night, that an idea struck like lightning from a clear sky.

"So, er... Warin?"

"Hmm?" His gaze slid back to me.

"What are *you* doing for Thanksgiving...?"

If he knew where I was going with this, he pretended not to. "I usually don't celebrate human holidays."

"...Warin?"

"Yes?"

"Do you remember that horrible vampire party you're going to make me go to tomorrow?"

The corner of his mouth twitched in response to my pleading tone. "I do."

I narrowed my eyes a little, trying to imagine him in a turkey sweater, but the image just wouldn't form. "Is there any possible situation where you would maybe consider...?"

"Consider what, Liv?"

I drew in a deep breath. "Would you go with me to Denver to this Thanksgiving dinner?"

His eyes locked in mine. "There are one or two scenarios where that could happen. But are you certain that you would want that?"

I thought of my family's general ignorance toward everyone who wasn't like them. About how I'd always been so different to them, an outsider, even if we shared DNA. And I thought about having calm, strong Warin by my side through what was bound to be a nightmarish experience. "I am absolutely certain. But..." I sighed. Full disclosure needed. "I have to tell you that it probably won't be a pleasant experience. They are not... very nice people."

Warin watched me with his head cocked for a little while, then nodded. "Very well. In return for your participation and compliance with the meeting I am making you join me for, I shall book plane tickets to Denver when I get home tonight."

I sighed in relief and leaned back in the couch. "A million times thank you. You really are the best thing that's ever happened to me."

"As you are for me," he said quietly.

A blush spread across my body alongside a warm feeling of happiness. I still had no idea why he chose to spend just a little bit of his immortal life with me, but one thing was for sure: every fiber of my being was thankful for it.

"We also need to talk about the meeting with Joana," I said, changing the subject before my stupid heart got any grand ideas. Clearly the little fucker couldn't be trusted. "Do they have information on how to find the skinwalkers?"

"They do." Warin sighed, clearly unhappy. "But I

wish you would let me handle this, Liv. I don't want you further involved."

"Do we really have to do this again? You know I'm not going to accept it. And, if you recall, the only reason you had that meeting with Joana and her merry band of witches was because of *me*. I know I'm not part of your supernatural club, but as long as this involves me, you're going to keep me in the loop. Got it?"

"Got it," he sighed. "The High Priestess has given us the location of one of their main cells, but she also confirmed my suspicions that they have a vampire patron. She couldn't tell me who, or why, but whoever it is, he or she has fed the skinwalkers their blood. They are much, much stronger than regular skinwalkers, and even my Guard and I will have to be cautious when we attack. But I can't move on them before we have discovered who this patron is. If we take down the skinwalkers without unveiling who's behind them, they'll slip between my fingers. And that... that I can't let happen. Whoever they are, they'll be very, *very* sorry they picked Chicago for their schemes."

The look on Warin's marble features was so grim any sane person would have recoiled from the sheer threat emanating off him. I, however, just shot him a half-smile before I nuzzled deeper into the couch. "You gonna go all Night Lord on their asses, huh?"

He snorted, the seriousness on his handsome features

cracking for a small smile. "I'll do much worse than that to anyone who thinks they can hurt you on my watch, little one. Much, much worse."

WE SPENT the rest of the night watching Vampire Diaries, occasionally interrupted by Warin's contemptuous snorts, and at some point I fell asleep with my feet in the vampire's lap. I half-woke by the sensation of floating, and tiredly cracked an eye open just as I was put down on my bed.

"Hmm?" I groaned.

"Dawn is almost here," Warin said softly above me. "I'll send a car to pick you up at six." The press of my duvet being wrapped around me made me contentedly sigh before I went back to sleep.

EIGHTEEN

It was once again pretty late when I woke up, and I had a groggy thought that keeping vampire hours probably wasn't the best thing for my circadian rhythm as I stumbled to the bathroom to pee. Should probably start supplementing with some vitamin D or something, since I wasn't seeing much of the sun these days, save when driving in for a shift for work.

I spent some extra time in the bathroom, remembering I had to get ready for Warin's fancy-pants party tonight. He hadn't gone into much detail about what was expected of me, but judging from his manor-like house, it'd probably be prudent to at least shower. And maybe even do my hair.

. . .

IT WAS five before I walked out of the bathroom with my hair in rollers and a fluffy bathrobe wrapped around me. I wasn't entirely sure how getting attacked by evil shapeshifting witches meant I was now the sort of person who got made up to go out twice in one week, but even if I would have preferred to spend the evening on the couch... it felt kinda good to primp. It made me feel pretty. And feminine.

A flicker of Warin's expression as he'd looked me up and down in my skimpy dress the other night had a flush of shame heat my cheeks. Yeah, okay, so the main reason I now liked hanging out in front of the mirror like a teenage girl with a crush was that I'd liked how he'd looked at me. I seriously needed to pull myself together, or the next time I got drunk around the poor guy would likely be the last time I'd see him. He'd been very clear on the no nookie policy.

No sooner had the thought 'nookie policy' flashed through my brain before my gaze landed on a big, white box on my kitchen counter. The pizza box, however, was nowhere in sight. Apparently Warin had made a trade on his way out this morning.

Curious, I slid up the counter so I could inspect the box closer. It was clearly made from high-quality cardboard, and though I didn't recognize the logo stamped in gold across the lid, it only emphasized the impression that whatever was inside was hella expensive. Only one way to find out!

I couldn't help the small gasp at the revelation of a the pile of exquisite, ruby-red fabric once I lifted the lid. Pure silk, no doubt. A small, white card lay on top of the pile, with my name scrawled across it in a slanted handwriting.

Liv,

Please remember, whatever I ask of you this evening I ask only so I can keep you safe.
Warin.

I ARCHED an eyebrow at the cryptic message, but put it aside to focus on the red dress. No doubt he was aware I didn't own anything remotely this fancy, and didn't want to cause offense.

Though, to be fair, it's kinda hard to cause offense when you give a girl a dress this exquisite.

Unable to rein in my glee any longer, I picked the magnificent piece of clothing out of the box. It was a full ball gown, with a fitted top delicately adorned with beads and a long, flowing skirt. But before I could get too swept away in the beauty of it, my eyes fell on what had been hiding in the box underneath the dress.

A skin-colored strapless bra.

Now, how Warin knew I didn't own a strapless bra I had no idea, but my eyebrow crept up again at its appearance. One thing was getting an amazing silk dress to go to the ball in. There was a certain *Cinderella* quality any woman would find hard to resist.

But a plain bra?

Maybe if it'd been a sexy little number I'd have been all kinds of giddy at the thought of Warin picking out lingerie for me, but this bra was unquestionably of the sturdy, practical variety.

Careful not to crease the dress, I placed it over the counter and picked up the offensive bra. It was even my size.

How the hell did he know what size bra I wore?

ROY WAS on guard duty as per usual when I let myself out some forty-five minutes later, a mug of coffee in one hand and my elbows tight against my sides in order to keep my new dress up.

"Hey," I greeted him when he turned around to see what I wanted. "Trade you a coffee for a zip-up?"

"Sure. S'cold as a vamp's tit out here today," he said. Then, giving me a quick glance, he added, "S'cuse me."

"Ha, got a lot of experience with vampire tits?" I teased as I placed his coffee on the brick banister and turned my back so he could get to my zipper.

Roy made a noncommittal noise that made me laugh as his rough fingers brushed up the length of my spine, pulling the zipper with it. "Never mind," I said. "I probably don't want to know."

"So, what do you think? Warin went shopping." I spun back around and held out my arms despite the cold making me want to huddle up, modeling the dress.

The giant gave me a short nod before he wrapped his hand around his mug and took a sip at the still steaming liquid. "S'ok. Your hair's weird."

I let my arms fall back down to my sides, somewhat deflated. "Well, way to build up a girl's confidence there, buddy. My hair's still in curlers, I'm not going like this."

"Sorry," he rumbled.

"What's the matter?" I sighed, folding my arms across my chest, partly to preserve body heat and partly to achieve a stern *"don't you mess with me, young man"* expression even my grandma would have been proud of.

"Nothin'," he said, dodging my eye contact like a guilty child.

"Yeah, that's obviously bullshit. What's going on, Roy?"

The giant sighed and finally looked up at me, reluctance plain on his broad face. "You shouldn't do this. You need to stay away from whatever the fuck he's got you doing, girl."

I blinked, more than a little surprised at that turn of the conversation. "What do you mean? Why?"

"I've seen this shit more times than I'd like to count. I thought maybe you were right and he's your friend, with how he's kept you away from the nest. But now he's got you dressing up like all the other pretty little girls who end up dead when they get tangled up in vamp society."

"Roy, it's not like that—" I tried, touched beyond words for the obvious care the giant of a man had for me that he risked speaking up about his boss like that. Even if it was misplaced.

But Roy just held up a hand, silencing me. "Yeah, I know, *it's for your own protection.* He might even mean that—who the fuck knows with them? But if you get in any deeper, you're gonna be another dead body I'll have to dig a grave for. Another unsolved disappearance. And you're too fucking sweet to end up like that, Liv. You're too smart. I'm telling you, whatever he's planning for tonight, it's not a place for humans."

I drew in a deep breath and walked down a couple steps so I could reach out and touch his arm. "Roy... I can't tell you how much it means to me that you're saying this. I don't... there's never been a lot of people who looked out for me, and I... Thank you. From the bottom of my heart, thank you. But I can't stay away. It's not just because it's for my own protection—it's also because *he* needs me there."

"Has he ever told you what he used to be like?" Roy's voice was surprisingly gentle for his size. "About his reputation?"

I frowned. "What do you mean?"

"A long time ago, before you and me were born, he was someone else. *Something* else. He may seem domesticated now, he may appear as your friend, but he was a monster. Even other bloodsuckers fear him." Roy shook his head and rubbed at the back of his neck with his free hand. "Shit, I know you ain't gonna listen to me. Maybe you just gotta see for yourself. Just... keep your eyes open, 'kay?"

"I will. Thank you. Truly." I gave his arm a small squeeze.

He shrugged. "Don't worry 'bout it. Just hate shovelin' dirt over a pretty face."

"We really need to work on your compliments, Roy." I grinned, trying to lighten the mood. "Can't call me pretty unless you're imagining me six feet under."

He rumbled a good-natured chuckle. "Ex-wife said the same. Not the dead thing. Just the compliment thing."

Before I could tell him I was glad he didn't talk about burying all the girls he came across, the roar of an engine further down the road pulled both out attentions.

"Get inside," Roy said gruffly, shoving me back up the

step with a hand as he squared up against the silver Porsche that came barreling down the street. I didn't miss how the other went to the back of his jeans, hiking up in his leather coat enough that I saw a flash of a gun.

"Ugh, I doubt skinwalkers are gonna come kidnap me in a Porsche," I bitched, even as I continued up the steps.

The Porsche stopped right in front of Roy with screeching brakes, followed by a slam of the driver's side door.

I blinked at the tall, suit-clad man that stepped around the front of the car, shoulder-length auburn hair combed back and styled to perfection.

Aleric.

"What the hell are *you* doing here?" I blurted.

"Picking you up." His cool eyes slid over me and stopped at my curlers. "Fix your hair and let's go." Clearly expecting his orders to be obeyed, he turned his focus to Roy. "So you're on guard duty for my brother these days, giant-blood? What a pity."

"S'no worse than being his errand boy," Roy shot back. From his tone to his stiff stance, it was quite obvious he'd met Aleric before—and that he wasn't a fan. After my run-in with him at *Isla*, I shared Roy's opinion.

Aleric's blue eyes flashed with a cool spark, his full lips pinching with just the faintest smile. "I see Warin's lax with the whip. You weren't as mouthy when Lizanne had you."

I decided not to stick around to listen to them bicker. The less Roy had to deal with Warin's prick of a brother, the better. It was really the least I could do for the many hours he'd spent freezing his ass off in front of my apartment building.

It didn't take long to pull my curlers out and finger-comb my now wavy hair to ensure the curls sat just right. A quick dose of hairspray later, I grabbed my black clutch housing my cell phone, emergency cash, lipstick, and keys and rushed out the door to save Roy from my newly appointed chauffeur.

It looked like I was just in time. When I stepped out of the door, I was greeted by the sight of Roy standing with both fists clenched, glare leveled at the vampire. Aleric was casually leaning against the Porsche, both hands in his suit pockets, but from the calculating look in his eyes and the cruel hint of a smirk on his lips, I could tell he'd been needling my bodyguard.

Pretty brave, if you asked me. Aleric might have been a vampire and all, but even though he was very tall and obviously well-built underneath his expensive suit, Roy had at least half a foot and a good hundred pounds on him.

"All right, I'm ready. Let's go," I said as I walked down the stairs and patted Roy's arm. "Thanks again. Go home and get warm—I'll undoubtedly see you tomorrow, yeah?"

Roy rumbled a gruff agreement, not taking his narrowed eyes off Aleric.

"Great, get your ass in the car, snack," Aleric said, apparently not the least bothered by Roy's death-glare.

"I think I preferred 'mouse,'" I said as I opened the car door and slipped into the passenger seat. The buttery leather embraced me in just the right way, and I allowed myself a moment to enjoy the luxury of it all. If only my family could see me now, dressed in the finest silk and sitting in a car that cost more than my mom's and aunts' houses combined.

But then again, the whole vampire thing would probably put a dampener on their rampant envy.

Aleric slid into the driver's seat and set the car in gear, pulling out from the curb so fast I was thrown back in the seat from sheer g-force.

"Holy crap, some of us are still alive here!" I yelped as I grabbed for my seatbelt.

Aleric snorted. "So driving scares you, but walking into a vampire nest teaming with Ancients? That's fine?"

"*Your* driving scares me. There's a difference," I snipped. "Why are you my chauffeur, anyway? Why couldn't Roy drive me? No offense, but he's about a thousand times nicer to be around."

The vampire's lips pulled up in a small smile. "I volunteered. You see, I think it's about time I get to know my brother's new pet, before he shows you off to the rest of them." He turned his head halfway, letting those disturbingly icy eyes rest on me. The predatory gleam in them made a cold shiver make its way down my spine.

I pushed the primitive note of fear down and rolled my eyes demonstratively. "Why, because you think I'm a witch? What's the theory then, have I've enthralled your brother with my magic devil vagina?"

Another amused snort. "You're funnier than the last one, I'll give you that."

I frowned, not prepared for the stab of jealousy behind my ribs from his blasé comment. "Which 'last one'?"

"I've talked to Warin about you. He's my blood-brother, he hides nothing from me. Imagine my surprise when he told me, in complete seriousness, that he not only spends his nights with a pitiful human... but he's also *not* fucking you. What I would *love* to know is what you do to keep his attention so thoroughly, without even so much as spreading your thighs."

"Why didn't you just ask him, if he really tells you everything?" I asked, arching an eyebrow at the auburn-haired vampire's profile.

"See, that's the curious part. I don't think even *he* knows."

"Maybe that's because there's no mystery here," I said. "We like spending time together, that's it. No great conspiracy, no magic. I'm sure if you weren't a massive prick, people might like hanging out with you too."

"Cute." Aleric smiled that creepy, cold smile of his as he leveled me with a stare that had my pulse pick up speed. "But then let me leave you with this small... let's call it *warning*: If I get a whiff of the faintest drop of magic from you... if I hear even a *rumor* that you are working with whoever is trying to cause trouble in his territory... you will wish Warin let those skinwalkers eat you alive."

NINETEEN

The rest of the car ride to Warin's house was pretty damn quiet.

Aleric seemed content now that he'd said what he wanted, and I was trying to pretend like I wasn't struggling to keep my sandwich down. I hadn't really worried about Warin's rude brother before, despite his abrasive manners. As scary as he was, I knew Warin would never have let him around me if he was a danger in any way... but that was before his little warning.

I had no doubt he meant every word.

Nor that, should he ever find out the truth about the dormant magic inside of me, not even Warin would be able to protect me from him. If he'd even want to.

"Since Warin insists on keeping your mind free, I suppose I better explain that even though you *can* deny his requests tonight, you would be wise not to," my chauffeur finally said, breaking the silence. The houses in the neighborhood we were traveling through were beginning to look mighty grand, and I guessed we were nearing Warin's place. I hadn't been there since that night in August, and I hadn't exactly had the presence of mind to look out for road names then.

"Is it frowned upon if a lowly human tells a lordly vampire 'no,' then?" I arched an eyebrow at Aleric's profile, but he wasn't looking at me.

"It's more than frowned upon. Let's just say that it would be very, ah, *unfortunate* for both of you, should some of his guests realize what kind of lip he allows from you. So if you could be less... irritating, that would be great."

"Less irritating. Got it," I snarked. "If you keep your distance, it'll probably help."

Aleric turned off into a grand-looking driveway then, and I vaguely recalled the manicured hedges. A multitude of fancy cars were parked along it, and at the end Warin's manor sprawled. Torches flamed on each side of the grand entrance, the double doors flung open in invitation. I got a glimpse of several well-dressed people making their way toward the house as Aleric parked the Porsche, and felt a stab of gratitude for the dress Warin had provided me. I sure didn't have anything in my closet that wouldn't have made me feel like an impoverished gatecrasher tonight.

"It's not a joking matter," Aleric said, his hand shifting from the gear shift to my arm. "They cannot know you have free will. Whatever else your sordid little relationship with my brother is, for tonight, you will sit by his feet like a faithful dog, you will smile prettily and you will not utter the word 'no.' Have I made myself clear?"

"Jeez, yes, calm the fuck down," I said, trying—and failing—to shake his cool hand off my arm. In contrast to Warin's touches, it didn't make me feel warm in the slightest. "I'll be a mindless doll. I just don't get why you're making such a big deal out of it, if Warin never bothered? Is it perchance possible that you're being a tad overzealous?"

"Just do what you've been told, Snack," he said, voice low. Then, finally, he released his grip on my arm and turned to look over his shoulder. "Stay in the car until I come get you."

Realizing for the first time that we weren't alone in the car, I jolted and twisted around so fast my neck cracked. A pretty blonde, blue-eyed girl with long false lashes and a vacant smile sat in the backseat. She didn't so much as blink in my direction as I stared at her, mouth agape.

"Jesus tap dancing Christ! Did not realize you were here! Sorry! Hi, I'm Liv." I awkwardly reached a hand toward her. The girl didn't even acknowledge my existence.

"Don't bother. She's Compelled," Aleric said as he slid out of the car.

"Oh." I stared at the girl, remembering what Warin had explained vampires could do to the human mind. But one thing was to hear about how his kind could mindfuck people—it was something else entirely to sit in the car with a human who looked like nothing more than a ventriloquist's dummy.

Goosebumps crawled down my arms and up my legs, and I hurriedly unbuckled my seatbelt and climbed out, leaving Aleric's companion behind. Was that how most humans in contact with a vampire ended up? No wonder Roy wasn't keen on me going to this shindig.

I wanted to rip into Aleric for keeping the poor girl as a mindless pet, but I had his warning in fresh recollection—he expected me to behave like I'd been Compelled too, and there were more than a few vampires around us now, all making their way to the house. So instead, I quietly seethed by his side as he offered me his arm and led me into the mansion.

The last time I'd been to Warin's house, I'd felt like I'd been surrounded by vampires the second I stepped inside. This time, however... there had to be maybe two hundred people present.

"How many Night Lords do you guys have?" I whispered at Aleric as he led me through the foyer.

"Worldwide, I'm not sure anyone has an exact

number. Only thirty-six are here tonight. The rest are favored human pets and court members." He nodded at a couple pale-looking women who watched us pass with no hint of emotion in their cold eyes. "But please do keep any further questions until the end of the show. It's time for you to be a good little pet. Not to mention quiet."

We walked into a large living space sparsely furnished in a hideously modern style. Toward the far end, on a white armchair in neo-modern Scandinavian design, Warin sat with a blank expression on his face, one ankle resting on his knee. He looked like a bored king on his throne, except for the ultramodern surroundings.

Aleric marched me straight across the floor toward him.

"My blood," Aleric greeted, voice formal. "I bring your pet, as requested."

"Thank you, brother," Warin said flatly. They both ignored my grimace at being called "pet," but Warin raised a hand toward me, palm up.

Hesitating for just a beat, I awkwardly put my hand in his. "Hey. Nice party."

Judging from Aleric's huff, he'd been quite serious about the "quiet" part of my role.

Warin offered me just the briefest tilts of his lips, proving that there at least was some part of him left behind the stoic wall. With a smooth movement, he drew my hand to his mouth, brushing a kiss to the back of it that sent an unexpected thrill through my arm. "A vision of beauty, as always."

"Thank you. You scrub up pretty well too." I let my gaze slide over him, quietly wondering how he could look so immaculate in the dark gray suit at the same time as seeming completely casual. But then again, Warin was always well-dressed.

"Sit with me, my dove," he said.

"Um..." I cleared my throat, trying not to blush at the term of endearment. From the grand total of two comments he'd spoken to me so far, I was getting the impression he had his formal hat on tonight. It wasn't like he was normally the most chill dude, and I glanced at his lap, trying to determine if he meant he wanted me to sit *on* him.

"The floor, Snack," Aleric murmured, discreetly kneeing me in the hamstring to push me in the right direction. Only then did I spot the pillow by one of the chair legs.

"Oh." *Oh.* He'd been literal when he talked about me sitting by Warin's feet like a dog. Grimacing at the idea of subjecting my amazing dress to the floor I stepped up next to Warin's chair and, with the support of his grasp on my hand, sat down as gracefully as I could manage. Which wasn't particularly graceful at all.

Only when I'd gotten into a somewhat comfortable

kneeling position on the pillow did Warin release my hand.

Aleric, apparently happy he'd fulfilled his delivery obligations, nodded at his brother and walked off, leaving us behind.

I glanced up at Warin, unsure of what I was supposed to do now, but he didn't so much as spare me a glance. He just sat there, looking as bored as before as he stared out over the slowly filling room.

Well, this looked like it was going to be a fun-filled night. I heaved a sigh and tried my best to mimic the empty doll-like expression on Aleric's pet's face. At least my guilt over making Warin go to Denver to visit my family with me was sharply declining.

We sat in complete silence for a good twenty minutes before a small group of people—vampires, judging by their pale skin—approached us.

"Lord Warin," the woman said, inclining her head an inch while the two men behind her bowed deep.

"Lady Lizanne," Warin greeted. "Elliot. And... your new Son, if I'm not mistaken?" His blue eyes swept to one of the male vampires—a tall, blonde young man.

"Yes, this is Peter, the newest addition to my blood-line." Lizanne made a motion for Peter to step forward. She looked like a proud mother—but when he moved closer to Warin and she let a hand slide down the small of his back and over his ass, I instantly regretted the comparison. Clearly, vampire families had different moral codes than humans.

Warin nodded. "Congratulations, Lizanne."

"And you, Warin? Still childless?" The female vampire let her gaze slide over me. "Or are you perhaps reconsidering, after all these years? This is the first time you have claimed a pet, if I'm not mistaken."

"There is a world of difference between a pet and a Child," Warin said, his dismissive tone making me bite back a small bloom of hurt. It wasn't like *I* wanted to be Warin's creepy vampire-daughter, either. "As I'm sure you are well-aware."

"Of course. Nothing good ever comes from forcing a bond with a Child who isn't worthy of the Embrace." The woman looked back to Warin. "But to get onto more urgent matters... I have instructed my Guard to look into any irregularities with the blood supply, as well as increasing surveillance of any suspected witch activities."

"But nothing's been reported to you? No increase in disappearances?" Warin asked.

"Nothing. But I will continue my investigations. As unfortunate as the occurrences in Chicago are, I appreciate your warning and your diligence on the matter—no one wants these occurrences to spread across territories."

"We will see," Warin said. "I thank you for your participation in this matter."

Apparently it was a dismissal, because the lady

inclined her head at him again and led her two sons away without another word. And then a new, small group of vampires stepped up to Warin's makeshift throne.

While at first I was fascinated watching the vampires interact, it quickly became incredibly boring. A few made enquiries about my presence—enough to make it obvious that the vampire elite were surprised to see Warin with a companion—but no one ever spoke directly to me. And the line of questioning always led to the same results: no one had heard anything, no one knew anything, and everyone would do their utmost to look for similar cases in their own territories.

By the time a black-haired man with golden eyes stepped up, the first vampire without an entourage, my knees were aching and I'd just about murder for a pee and a glass of water.

"Lord Warin," he said like all the others had, but something in his voice made me look up at him. There was just the faintest hint of a purr in it, like a satiated panther. He was beautiful, with his high cheekbones and sensuous lips, but that wasn't what kept my attention— they were all beautiful. Cold, but beautiful. No, it was the sheer *power* radiating off him in nearly tangible waves. Every hair on my body stood on end when his gaze briefly flickered down to me. "Miss Green."

"H-hi," I croaked, taken by surprise by finally being acknowledged.

His lips curved in a devious little smile. "You should let your pet drink something. Humans require constant hydration, or they simply... wither and die. Like delicate orchids. Isn't that right, my lovely?" Though he was speaking to Warin, he didn't take his disturbing eyes off me.

"I was not expecting you, Lord Zet. London is far away, and my notification was only sent out to the North American Lords and Ladies," Warin said, ignoring his comment about me.

The black-haired vampire's gaze finally moved from me back to Warin. I heaved a sigh of relief. "I go by Zeth these days. It's so much easier to conduct oneself with a modern name—you should consider it, Lord Warin. And I am here simply because I was looking after some business in the West when I got wind of your call. I figured I best stop by—you know how fast trouble travels these days. Blasted internet."

"I take it you are unaware of any similar occurrences in London and the rest of the islands?" Warin asked.

"That would be correct, young Lord. But then again, nothing happens in London without my knowledge. You new continent Lords have some years to go before you will have established a similar rapport, so as long as I am here, my power is at your disposal, should you require any help with these pesky witches in your territory." He nodded at Warin with a small smirk and then walked off, not waiting to be dismissed like the other Lords and Ladies had.

I looked up at Warin, catching his eye for the first time during his talks with the other vampires, and mouthed *"wow"* at him. Lord Zeth was one cocky bastard, that was for sure. I might not have been tuned in to vampire etiquette, but it didn't take an expert to realize he'd snubbed Warin pretty hard.

"You may go to the kitchen for water, my dove," he said, neither his face or voice betraying if he shared my thoughts on the golden-eyed vampire. "It's just past the foyer and down the hall."

"Great, I'm a bit parched. And, um, where's the bathroom?"

"At the northern end of the house. Continue past the kitchen, take two lefts and a right, and it's at the end of the hall." Warin held out his hand again, and when I took it, helped me to stand.

I wasn't exactly sure which direction was north, having not been in a house that required navigation via cardinal directions before, but I figured I'd locate the kitchen first and take it from there.

No one paid me much mind as I made my way through the foyer and down the hall, and I noticed that the further I made it from the main room where Warin held court, the fewer vampires were around. When I finally found the kitchen, there wasn't a single undead in sight.

Which was probably natural enough, I mused as I walked into the large, but somewhat barren room. Vampires wouldn't need a fridge for their dietary needs—at least not if they liked their dinner fresh. I eyeballed the large two-door fridge and wondered if it'd be filled with donor blood. Not that I was curious enough to check.

There were a few humans in the room, all with completely blank expressions as they went about sipping water and nibbling on the spread of finger-food that'd been put out for the humans. The realization that Warin, despite having me sit at his feet like a pet while he played lord of the manor, had cared enough about the human companions to ensure they were well-fed, eased some of the discomfort I'd harbored since entering his house. Even if he was forced to act cold and uncaring like his peers, he was still the thoughtful man I'd gotten to know these past few weeks.

"Nice spread," I commented to the room in general as I grabbed a couple toothpicks with cheese and olives. "Who knew blood drinkers knew how to pick out a good caterer, eh?"

Eerie silence met me. When I glanced up, the five other humans in the room weren't even looking at me.

"So creepy," I muttered. It was a bit like being the only living person in a wax museum.

Wanting to get out of there as quickly as possible, I downed a pint of water in a few gulps and brought the cheese sticks with me to snack on while I went to hunt down the bathroom.

It took me so long to find the damn thing, with plenty of wrong turns along the way, and it soon became quite clear that the kitchen wasn't the only room vampires never needed to use. I made it in time, even if my quick drink of water hadn't slowed my urgency any.

I took a few moments in front of the mirror once I'd done my business to splash water in my face and reapply lipstick. I wasn't exactly in any hurry to get back to being bored out of my skull by Warin's feet, and since the bathroom was nice and quiet and void of brainwashed humans, I decided Warin wouldn't miss me for a bit longer.

I WAS three levels deep in Candy Crush when I heard a murmur of voices on the other side of the door. I swear, I didn't *mean* to spy, but the excitement of finally meeting other humans still capable of thinking an independent thought made me close down my game and listen more intently to the conversation.

Only it wasn't humans.

"—*what you're playing at, but you have no business here, Zeth.*" It was Aleric's voice—clipped and agitated.

"*Since when do you presume to know my business, young one?*" Zeth drawled. "*Your brother invited the Ancients on the continent to come tonight. I'm an Ancient, and I just happened to be on the continent. So I came. You should be pleased—did I not offer you invaluable assistance during the Civil War? Maybe young Warin would appreciate my help with this matter as well.*"

"*Stay away from him, Zeth,*" Aleric growled. "*Our deal was that you'd never get involved with him again, in any way.*"

"*Watch your tone, child.*" Zeth's voice was still calm, but even through the door I could pick up the warning note in it.

"*I don't care how old you are. I swear, if you—*" Aleric's growl was interrupted when my phone slipped from my hands to the floor with a loud clatter, the battery separating from the case and sliding to the other side of the room.

Oh... fuck.

TWENTY

Aleric pushed open the door. He heaved a sigh at the sight of me perched next to the sink. "And just what are you doing here, Snack?"

"Playing Candy Crush," I admitted.

"Miss Green." Zeth's soft voice floated in through the now open door. He walked through, making Aleric step inside as well. When the door shut behind them, I had to fight to keep my heart at an even pace. I was trapped in the bathroom with two vampires I'd been eavesdropping on, and no way of getting a hold of Warin for a rescue. Not good. So not good.

The black-haired vampire walked over to me, placing a cool hand under my chin to tip my head up so he could catch my gaze. "Did you hear any of our conversation?"

Something in his golden eyes pulled unpleasantly at

me, making me woozy. I shook my head to clear it. "N-no. I was just playing on my phone."

"Is that so?" he asked, holding my gaze as if he was searching for something.

"Yup. Why, should I have?" I asked, hoping playing dumb would be the fastest way out of here.

"Stop messing with the human, Zeth," Aleric sighed. "She's harmless, I promise."

"Is she now?" Zeth asked, still staring into my eyes. "It's just a coincidence she's the only un-Compelled human present, hmm?"

"She's Compelled—he just prefers her with enough brainpower left to keep her mouthy. No idea why, but he's always had odd tastes. I personally like my toys silent and obedient." Aleric strolled over to the sink and placed a single, cool finger on my cheek, forcing my gaze from Zeth's. "You're a very naughty pet, hiding from your master. Don't think I won't tattle on you, missy. You'll be in ever so much trouble if you don't get back to Warin. *Now.*"

I wasn't sure why Aleric, who'd made no bones about not being my biggest fan so far, was lying to Zeth about my free will, but I wasn't about to ignore his obvious warning: I needed to get out of there and back to Warin's protection before the other vampire realized I wasn't Compelled.

"Okay." I made to jump down from the counter, but

Zeth's hand on my shoulder stopped me before I could.

"Wait just a second, my lovely." He turned to Aleric. "Have you considered the possibility he might keep her free because he *can't* Compel her?"

Aleric snorted. "You're being paranoid. Believe me, it's not the same girl."

"What makes you so certain? Have you looked at her eyes? They're the exact same shade of green, if I recall correctly. And, if rumor is to be believed, she's his first pet since *her*." Zeth returned his focus to me. "Do you have your free will intact, my lovely?"

"I'm certain because *I've* Compelled her," Aleric interrupted. "Warin invited me to share her the night of my arrival." He gave me a lecherous wink. "She rather enjoyed the double cunt-fuck after a quick mindbend, didn't you, Snack?"

"Y-yeah. It was... yeah." It took all I had not to glare at him for making me agree to something that dirty. Aleric might have looked like a Greek god, but I'd much rather have staked the fucker than get naked with him.

Zeth arched an eyebrow at Aleric. "Or maybe she just wanted to fuck you both. Are you—"

"Odin's beard! You don't think I've checked the blood-bag? I didn't think I'd need to remind you who of us would me more screwed if Thea popped back up again! You've held it over my head enough for eight hundred fucking years." Aleric grabbed my free shoulder and yanked, making me stumble to the floor despite Zeth's grab. I only narrowly avoided face-planting on the tiles. "Now, unless you want to explain to Warin why we kept his pet away from him, I suggest we send her back so the evening meal can begin."

Zeth sighed, gesturing toward the door. "I suppose. But you can't deny, those eyes..."

"Yeah, it's creepy, but it's not like he'd realize, is it? Maybe it's just his fucking type. You, Snack, look at me," Aleric snapped. I didn't dare resist, so I let him capture my gaze.

"Do not tell anyone of what you've heard here tonight. Not Warin—not anyone. I would hate for something *unfortunate* to become of you. Now, run along and find your master. It's dinnertime." He stared at me for a few seconds, letting me digest the absolute seriousness in his face, before he spun me around and smacked my ass. "Scoot!"

MY MIND WAS STILL in wild disarray when I reentered the living room, my heart hammering. None of what had happened made any sense to me, except the ironclad knowledge that for whatever reason, Aleric had saved me from Zeth. I didn't know why the other Ancient cared so much about whether or not I was Compelled, but it seemed to be about more than just whether or not I'd divulge vampire secrets to the world at large. More... personal, somehow.

Warin was still on his throne, the blank look of regal boredom on his face. I was more than happy to kneel down next to his legs this time, his calm aura enveloping me like a blanket the moment I was by his side.

I was more than ready for a few hours of boredom, but as soon as I'd settled down, the atmosphere in the room changed noticeably. The gathered vampires all looked toward Warin and me, and this time, I noticed several more humans in the room than I had before. There seemed to be a sort of anticipation building among the vampires, like wolves before feeding time.

No sooner did that comparison strike me than I remembered Aleric's words—*"It's dinnertime."*

Oh... goddess, no. Surely, they wouldn't... Surely Warin didn't expect me to... The short note that'd accompanied my dress flashed before my mind's eye, and the blood drained from my face.

Yeah. Yeah, those could most definitely have been the words of a man who knew he'd have to put his teeth in my neck, but didn't want me freaking out about it before it was too late to back out.

"Come to me, little one," he said, breaking off my spiraling thoughts. I twisted to grab his offered hand, because I couldn't exactly throw a fit in front of the watching vampires, and got to my feet. I did manage to throw him a pretty convincing death glare as I straightened up.

Warin ignored it and motioned for me to straddle him. I arched an eyebrow at him, but he simply looked at me with calm expectancy.

Alrighty then, if he really wanted this to get as awkward as it could...

I lifted my skirts enough that I could climb onto the armchair, a knee on each side of his thighs. His strong hands went to my hips, steadying me as I lowered myself onto his lap.

His muscles were strong, his clothes shielding me from his cool flesh. When I looked up, doing my best to force down the blush trying to take over my entire body at the intimate positioning, I captured his gaze—and the knowledge that a few hundred people were watching us faded to the background.

Warin's blue eyes were wholly focused on me, and his expression was no longer cold and distant. There was so much gratitude, so much regret... so much of *everything* in their blazing depths that it nearly stole my breath away. He was still silent, but in that moment, we didn't need words. His gaze was begging me for my consent. To remember my trust in him.

Swallowing hard, I nodded once. My anger was gone, and in its place was only a low-set fizzle of nerves.

Warin's sigh of relief was almost imperceivable. He slid his hands up along my waist, letting one brush my curls off my left shoulder. Exposing my neck.

I drew in a deep breath and closed my eyes tightly, waiting for the inevitable.

"Look at me, Liv," he said.

I obeyed, unable to resist the gentleness of his voice, and was once again captured in his blazing gaze.

Warin leaned his head back a little and opened his mouth. A sharp *snick* made me gasp, and I bit my lip hard at the sight of his sharp fangs. There was no denying what he was now. A creature of the night, made to kill.

And yet... he was still *Warin*.

His hand by my neck rubbed soothing circles over the tendons there, making my skin sing with an odd sort of anticipation. Not so much fear for the pain, but... something else.

When Warin wrapped his free arm tighter around me and pulled me close to his chest, I realized what that something else was.

There was no holding back the blush that set in when the crisp scent of night air and musk that was so uniquely *Warin* hit my nostrils. Yeah, there was no mystery to why I was suddenly feeling all kinds of *excited* about what was going on.

Dammit, Liv, control your ovaries! This is not a sexy moment!

Warin moved his hand from my neck for a moment, undoing the top two buttons of his shirt.

Not. A. Sexy. Moment. Nope, nope, nope.

"Bite me," he rumbled in my ear.

"What?" I croaked, sure I'd heard him wrong. I mean, wasn't it supposed to be the other way around, or had there been some sort of a misunderstanding along the way here?

"My shoulder," he said, and I could have sworn I heard just the huskiest of notes to his voice this time. "Bite it. Hard."

Okay, then.

Hesitating, I leaned in as close as I could get, desperately trying not to think about how I was smushing my breasts against his chest, and put my mouth on his shoulder. *Here goes nothing.*

Warin groaned when I bit down, and I immediately pulled back. He closed his hand around my neck, forcing me down again. *"Harder,"* he commanded.

I obeyed, biting down hard with my blunt human teeth. Warin groaned again, but this time there was no mistaking it for pain. Apparently I wasn't the only one getting some pretty inappropriate enjoyment out of this.

That knowledge should have made me feel awkward as fuck again, but... it didn't.

"Harder, Liv," Warin whispered hoarsely, keeping his

hand locked around the back of my neck. "Make me bleed."

I didn't hesitate this time. I bit his shoulder as hard as I could, spurred on by Warin's hitching breath and his tight grip on my body. And then my mouth filled with hot, sweet, liquid, and suddenly Warin wasn't the only one moaning. A flash of recognition sparked at the back of my brain as I latched onto the wound and sucked hard, knowing with every fiber of my being that I needed his blood. Needed it to mix with mine, to erase every worry, every painful memory until there was nothing left of me except the purest bliss.

There was a sting at the side of my neck, but I barely registered it while I drank deeply of Warin's blood. I whimpered in protest when, much too soon, Warin detached me from his shoulder. It took me several deep breaths before I came back from orbit, but when I did, my senses were flooded with an entirely different sort of pleasure.

Warin was sucking at my neck, his soft lips raising goosebumps down my arm. Occasionally he would lap his tongue over my throat, and the sensation went straight to my clit. We were both rocking, slow and in rhythm, as if moving together to music no one else could hear. There was an unmistakable hardness nestled right at my crotch, pressing firmly against my panties, and I had the wild thought that if I reached between us and undid his pants now, he wouldn't stop me.

"*Warin,*" I groaned, clutching at his bloodstained shirt.

He pulled back at the sound of his name, separating the delicious contact of his mouth against my throat, and I instantly regretted the loss.

"Warin," I whispered again as we stared at each other. His pupils were blown, coloring his irises pure black, and blood dripped from his still-extended fangs. *My* blood.

"I'm sorry," he whispered, and I frowned. No, that was all wrong—why was he apologizing? I didn't want that. I wanted—

Deep grunts sounded from close behind us, pulling me out of the sensation of drowning in Warin's magnetic gaze. Shattering the illusion that we were the only ones left in all the world.

I turned my head to see where the noises were coming from—and froze as I took in the scene that'd unfolded in the room while I'd been preoccupied.

"*Vampire orgy*" was the only description that came to mind as I stared until I thought my eyes would roll straight out of my skull. Everywhere, vampires were sucking on moaning humans, fangs buried in throats, thighs, wrists... the floor was pooling with crimson, and in the middle of the blood, several dozen clusters of bodies writhed together in unmistakable rhythm. Hard slaps of flesh against flesh filled the room, mixing in the cacophony of broken human moans.

"Oh, dear goddess," I whispered as the horror of the scene penetrated through the shock.

"Come, Liv." Warin lifted me off his lap and got to his feet. When I didn't move, he closed his hand around mine and more or less dragged me with him.

"No, Warin, they're—"

"*Come,*" he said, tone sharp enough to pull me out of it.

I slapped my free hand across my mouth to stifle the sobs that threatened to escape my painfully tight throat and let him lead me out of the room to the foyer, up the stairs and down a long, winding corridor.

Only then did he release my hand, wrapping his fingers gently around my cheek instead. "Breathe, Liv."

"How can you be so calm?" I hurled at him, even as his cool touch to my cheek eased the tight sobs making me shudder violently. "Those humans have no way to consent to this! They can't—they're living dolls, and your fucking guests are *raping* them! In the middle of the room, as if they have every right! How can you allow this! Goddess, what's *wrong* with you?!"

"Listen to me, Liv." Warin's voice was low and urgent, but it kept me from falling over the edge of hysteria. "I know it's wrong. I know. But there is nothing I can do."

"I thought you were the fucking Night Lord! Why can't you stop them? This is your house!"

"It's not that simple. It never is. This... these feeding frenzies. They happen when we are gathered. If this was not a gathering of Lords, I could have... my power might have been enough to stop them. But not now. If I tried to intervene, it would come to a fight. And I would lose."

"So... you just want me to, what? Accept it? Pretend it isn't happening?" I sniffed.

"It's the only thing you can do, little one," he said, and in his eyes I saw his regret. "The only solace I can offer is that no one will die tonight. That was in my power to stipulate, and I did so."

I stared up at him through the tears and knew he was right. It wasn't even like I could call the police. Without waiting for permission, I pressed my face against Warin's chest and closed my eyes, letting his calming presence slow down my breathing.

Haltingly, he wrapped his arms around me, holding me so wonderfully close.

It was so easy to relax in his embrace—as if everything was just a little bit less terrible as long as he held me. For every slow breath laced with the scent of Warin's crisp scent I sucked in through my nose, I regained some of my composure until I could finally think clearly again.

"I'm sorry," I murmured into his shirt. "I've gotten so

used to you. I'd forgotten... Isn't that crazy? I'd forgotten why we fear vampires. I just... it was a shock."

"I'm sorry I didn't warn you," he said. "I didn't want to scare you away—it was too important that they saw you take my blood."

I shook my head, effectively rubbing my runny nose and undoubtedly smeared mascara on his shirt. "I totally would have chickened out if you'd described it. If it's really so important for them to see us... then it's all right."

"It is," he said softly. "You're protected from other vampires now. The skinwalkers might not respect the bond, but whoever their master is will be forced to. Our laws are few, but unbreakable without attracting severe punishment."

"I don't like your world very much," I murmured.

"I don't, either," he sighed.

"I don't understand... why the rape? I thought it was dinner, but everyone... It clearly wasn't just about the blood." I frowned into Warin's shirt at the memory of the many rocking bodies and moans.

Warin cleared his throat, and I felt his arms stiffen ever so slightly around me. "It's part of the bloodlust, for many of us. The need to copulate is tied to the need to feed."

And that's when I remembered the hardness that'd pressed against my panties while I'd been straddling him. Goddess, how close had we been to joining the bloody orgy in that room? I sure hadn't been thinking about stopping, until I saw the carnage behind us.

"Oh. Uh." I awkwardly released my grip on his shirt, the sudden onset of flaming hot embarrassment making his embrace anything but comforting. He released me so swiftly I was sure he was feeling the awkwardness as keenly as I was, but he had the benefit of not lighting up like a tomato.

"I want you to sleep here tonight. It's the most secure room in the house." He indicated the door we'd stopped by, and a flash of recognition made me frown.

"It's your room... right?"

"I'll be sleeping elsewhere," he said so quickly I could only assume he thought I expected him to suggest we continue what we'd started downstairs. "And I would prefer if you stay the day in my house. I will take you home tomorrow night once I rise, and we can talk more then."

"Yeah, sure. Uh, I just didn't pack any overnight stuff."

"The bathroom should have everything you'll need, and there is a set of clothes laid out on the bed for you for tomorrow." Warin took a step back from me, putting more space between us and the awkward energy left behind once the subject of blood-fueled vampire urges came up. With a swift movement, he brought his thumb up to his mouth. When he removed it again, crimson blood pooled on the pad of it, though I hadn't seen his fangs lengthening. He reached out and smeared the blood over my throat. Healing his bite marks, I realized. "I have to finish the meeting."

"All right..." I grimaced and made a vague flapping motion toward the stairs. "You do that. I'll be up here, trying not to vomit over your guests' table manners."

ONE THING WARIN hadn't supplied me with, amidst the absolute flood of luxurious body lotions, silk bathrobes, Egyptian cotton towels and high-end clothes left in his room for me, was a vibrator.

I woke up from a long night of uneasy dreams drenched in sweat and so fucking horny I wanted to die. My entire body was *throbbing* with need, and all I could think about was the way Warin's cock had felt as it strained against his pants last night.

Fucking hell. I'd forgotten this little side-effect of drinking vampire blood.

SOME FOUR HOURS LATER, I sat curled in a sofa in a small study I'd found downstairs, munching on a huge bowl of cereal and nursing my still-cramping right hand.

I'd eventually managed to get my rampant hormones under control enough that I could drag myself to a cold shower, and then downstairs to refuel. I'd been hungry enough to brave the fridge, and it turned out that amidst a stock of plastic-wrapped donor blood was a decent supply of unopened human food. He'd really thought of everything. Except warning me I'd be having a sleepover, of course.

"Hello! You must be Liv."

I nearly jumped out of my skin at the unexpected, chipper voice that broke through my cereal-crunching.

"Jesus fuck!" I squeaked as I spun around. Aleric's blonde pet stood in the doorway with a plate of leftover finger-foods and a bright smile.

"Did I startle you? Sorry." She walked through and plopped down the other side of the couch I was sitting on. "I'm Diva."

"Hi..." I said. "You don't remember me from last night, then?"

"Oh, we met already? Sorry, Al must've Compelled me. I never remember a thing when we've been around other vamps."

I blinked at her nonchalance. "And... you don't mind?"

"God, no. Ugh, they're always so boring when they're together. So long as he doesn't erase the sex!" She winked at me and stuffed a cocktail sausage in her mouth. "Gosh darn it, I'm hungry. He must've drank more of my blood than normal."

It took me several moments to align Diva's cheerful disposition with the mindless dolls and bloody orgy I'd witnessed last night. "I'm sorry, you... you're the first other human companion I've met. I have so many questions."

"Shoot!" She gave me a brilliant smile. "Al's your master's brother, so that practically makes us sisters. Al said you're very new to this whole thing."

"Uh-huh. Sure. So, how long have you and *Al* been together?"

"A few months, I think," she said after a moment's pause. "I think he was fucking me and Compelling me to forget for a little while before he decided to make me his companion. That's the most annoying thing—when they Compel you, but don't 'fess up to it. Just, *hello dude,* at least own your shit, know what I mean?"

"Yeah, that's..." I blinked down at my now soggy cereal. Diva was not at all what I'd expected, after meeting her while Compelled. "So you don't mind the whole vampire thing?"

She stared at me wide-eyed, then broke out into a laugh. "No, don't be crazy! That's the best part. I mean, the sex alone... isn't that why *you're* with... is it Warin?"

"No, we're just, uh, friends. No benefits."

"Uh-huh, *sure,*" she said. "If you're his companion, he's fed you his blood, right?"

"Yeah?"

Diva snorted. "Girl, you and I both know there's nothing *platonic* about a blood-bond. God, the attraction alone!"

I frowned. "What do you mean?"

She blinked at me, for the first time looking truly shocked. "You mean you don't know? Well, shit."

"Know *what?*" I insisted. An uncomfortable sense of foreboding was growing in the pit of my stomach.

"If he hasn't told you, I really shouldn't..." She hesitated, a small frown marring her pretty face. "But it's not right that he's keeping you in the dark. Oh, shoot! Fine. As soon as you drink their blood, they can feel you."

"*Feel* me?" I asked, eyebrows raising high on my forehead.

"Yeah, you know... where you are. He'll be able to track you. It's a stalker's wet dream, I tell you. And they get crazy possessive. If he's anything like Al, he's got a key to your apartment and several pairs of your dirty panties in his drawer. And forget about sleeping with other men, *whew!* Not that I'd have the stamina, but once I met Al, all my male friends just sorta... stopped coming around. Or he'd tell me they'd been saying nasty stuff about me, so I'd scream at them over the phone and they'd think I was crazy and drop me. It took me a little while to catch on. He's such a naughty boy."

"That's... sociopathic," I said, but Diva only smiled.

"I think it's kinda cute," she said with a shrug. "They can't love, so this is kind of the next best thing, you know?"

"They can't love?" I repeated, mind still reeling at the level of fuckery Warin's brother had put this girl through.

"Nope, he told me. I asked him if he loved me once. He said he couldn't, but if he could... I'd be it." She beamed at me for a moment before her smile fell. "Sorry, I didn't mean to gush. You must be a bit shaken up, if this is the first you learn of your master's tendencies."

"Warin would never—" My voice died as her words finally sank in. One by one, flashes of interactions I'd had with my vampire friend played before my mind's eye. From the bra in exactly my size I'd found with the dress yesterday, to the time I was attacked by skinwalkers and he'd not only found me before it was too late, but later... when I'd dropped my key and he'd just happened to pick it up...

No, this was *Warin.* Warin, who I trusted more than I'd ever trusted anyone in my entire life. Warin, who'd protected me from day one.

Warin, who'd fed me his blood instead of taking me to the hospital like I'd asked the very first night we met.

I SPENT the remaining time before the sun set pacing back and forward in the foyer, trying to walk the icy numbness in my chest away.

Diva had fluttered nervously around me for a little bit, but once dusk began to fall, she apparently decided to be as far away from the incoming fallout as possible and vanished back to her room.

"Liv."

I looked up at the sound of my name and saw Warin at the top of the stairs. He was fixing a shirt sleeve, but stopped when he saw the look on my face. "What's happened?" The air around him swooshed, and he was at the bottom of the stairs in the blink of an eye, walking toward me with a worried frown. In my periphery, I saw Aleric, Carina, and another vampire I couldn't name make their way down the stairs at a more leisurely pace.

I held up a single finger, stopping him in his tracks. "Don't."

His frown deepened. "Is this about last night?"

"I just want you to answer me one thing. Just one, honest answer. Okay?"

"Always," he responded softly.

"When we met again in the bar. Was it by happenstance?"

"Liv—"

"Was it?" I interrupted him, my voice sounding weirdly high-pitched, even to my own ears.

A pained flicker crossed over Warin's face before his expression stilled into a blank mask. "No."

I'd raised my arm before I even realized—but when I brought my hand forward and slapped him across the face as hard as I possibly could, it was with every intent I possessed.

"I don't *ever* want to see you again," I hissed at the still stone-faced vampire. And then I turned around on my heel and walked out of his house and out of his life.

TWENTY-ONE

I couldn't remember ever have been so angry.

I 'd trusted him, in ways I'd never trusted another person before. With everything I was—with my *life*. And he'd... From the very beginning, he'd lied and manipulated me.

Behind the fury, sorrow and sense of loss built every step as I stomped down the road leading away from Warin's house. But for now, I could keep it at bay by focusing on my anger—and I relished it, because I knew the second I didn't have it to cling to anymore, there'd be nothing to stop the despair from closing over my head like the deepest, darkest sea.

But as furious as I was with him, I was even more so with myself—for being so fucking naïve. For letting myself get manipulated by a creature who had told me time and time again what he was. I'd been too blinded by the magnetic resonance between us to realize it'd been make-believe—parlor tricks from a man who wouldn't hesitate to bend my will to his. Goddess, he'd even admitted it, hadn't he? That he'd tried to Compel my memory of our first meeting.

I'd lived my entire life with the unwavering knowledge that I should never trust anyone to have my best interests at heart, and what had I done? I'd dropped my shields at the first run-in with a man who seemed to truly, deeply care.

Key word being "seemed."

Goddess, I was such a fucking idiot.

A swoosh sounded from behind me, and suddenly Warin stood on the road a few yards in front of me.

"Did you not hear me say that I don't ever want to see you again?" I snarled before I took a step to the side so I could get around him.

He mirrored my movement, blocking my way again. "Loud and clear."

"Then maybe you should fuck off!" I stepped to the other side, and he followed me again. Fine! I stomped straight ahead, fully determined to push him aside with my shoulder.

Unfortunately, the result was pretty much the same as what I imagine trying to bully a three-ton rock off the road would have been. I smacked into his shoulder with mine, and was bounced backward with the force of my own momentum.

Warin caught me lightly by the elbow until I regained my balance, but was smart enough to let go immediately after that.

"Liv, listen to me—"

"*No!* You do not get to speak!" I was aware I was screaming, but I didn't care. "I know what you did, you sociopathic prick! I *trusted* you, and you— you manipulated me! You made me drink your blood, Warin. Your *blood*. You could have taken me to the hospital. You could have *not* made me drink it again yesterday, without so much as telling me what I was doing!"

"I know," he whispered. "I know why you're angry. I understand."

"That's fantastic for you," I hissed. "Then kindly get the fuck out of my way!"

"I can't. I can't let you leave like this. The skinwalkers—"

"*Fuck* the skinwalkers!" I snapped. "And *fuck* you!"

"*Liv!*" It was the first time he'd raised his voice at me, and the sheer surprise of having the power of his full authority aimed at me made me take a step backward. "I *understand* you're angry, but I am *not* letting you walk into the night with skinwalkers on the prowl. Do not make this worse by forcing me to restrain you."

I narrowed my eyes at him. "If you put your hands on me right now, I swear..."

"I won't. But I cannot let you leave."

"I'm not going back in there," I said, indicating the direction of his house with a nod of my head. "I'm not going anywhere with you ever again."

"Liv..." There was so much pain in his darkened eyes that it pierced through my anger and stabbed deep into the cesspit of agony behind my ribs. I only managed a broken sob in response this time.

"I am... I am so sorry. I... I know I have no excuse, but I..." Warin trailed off, shaking his head.

"Why? Just tell me why?" I sobbed.

"Because I knew I needed to see you again," he whispered. "You were... I'd given up on everything. I didn't want anything from this world anymore, and then... there you were. This... this burning fire of pure *life*, thrown into my arms when there was nothing left for me. In my entire life, I have never met anyone like you. Being near you— even in that cell... it was like feeling my heart beating again. You don't know how long I've been numb. How many *centuries*, Liv. I couldn't let you walk out of my life again."

I had expected that he'd try to convince me that it wasn't that bad or that I was overreacting. I hadn't expected this.

When I saw the raw anguish deepen in his gaze, something in my heart twisted in response.

"I regretted it that same night. I was so ashamed of what I'd done. You are the only one, save my blood brother, who has ever put themselves in harm's way for me, and I repaid you by deceiving you. That's why I didn't seek you out for the first few months. I told myself it was enough that I knew you were out there, alive. But..." He looked away, as if the shame became too much to bear while still keeping eye contact. "When I felt our connection start to fade, I knew I had to see you again. Just one more time."

"And then I asked you to come back," I said quietly as I wiped at my cheeks. The tears were still falling in a steady stream.

"I promise you... I swear by everything sacred in this damned world, I have not used the blood bond to manipulate you. I wanted to know you for who you truly are. I wanted a friend. For the first time in my life, I wanted a true friend who was not tied to me by this curse in some way. And I wanted you to know me." He grimaced. "I guess now you do."

I hated the fact that my heart ached for him so bad it was hard to breathe. That through my own pain, I did truly see him. Perhaps clearly, for the first time. Not as the mysterious man who was always so in control, and not as the dangerous vampire who'd manipulated me—but as the only creature as lonely, as broken as I was.

"Did you make a copy of my house key?" I asked quietly.

"Yes."

"Why?"

Warin breathed deeply and looked back up at me. "Because I wanted to be close to you, and what I am... I have to fight against it with you. I am... built to *take*. Possess. I made the copy of your key to appease the monster."

"That's what Diva said," I whispered. I dug my fingernails into the palms of my hands. "Have you ever been in my home without my knowledge or consent?"

"No. Never." The absolute sincerity in his gaze broke the final barrier of icy wrath I'd been clinging to.

I hid my face in my hands and finally gave in to the sorrow. It wasn't a pretty, lady-like cry. It was full, deep, body-rocking sobs from the very pit of my belly. I cried so hard I had to gasp for breath.

Strong arms closed around me, hesitantly, to give me the chance to pull away, but I didn't have the strength. Crying like I hadn't cried since I was a child, I let the man who'd hurt me deeper than anyone else comfort me with his presence.

I don't know how long he held me in his arms as we stood in the middle of the street in his quiet, upper class neighborhood, but it felt like hours before my sobs finally quieted and, like the quiet after a storm, allowed a deep peace to settle within.

"I'm not okay with this," I mumbled into his shirt. "What you did is not okay."

"I know," he whispered.

"How are we supposed to be friends when... when there is *this* between us? When you broke my trust, because of... because of what you are?"

"I don't know."

I snorted, a helpless little sound that only reminded me of how fucking lonely I'd been before Warin came into my life. I hadn't even realized, before he'd been there to ease it in a way I hadn't known possible.

"Why the fuck didn't you just ask for my phone number?" I grumbled.

Warin barked a laugh, and for a brief moment his arms constricted tighter around me. "Liv... I will do anything you ask to make this right. Anything. Tell me, and I will do it. I understand that I have no right to ask anything of you, but I am. Please—don't give up on us."

I finally lifted my head and looked up at him—and knew that not only didn't I want to lose him. I couldn't.

"Take me to the skyscraper again," I whispered.

Warin's arms tightened around me again, lifting me. I wrapped my arms around his neck and my legs around his waist.

"Don't let go," I said.

"Never," he promised.

The air whipped against my face as he took to the sky, the wind drying my tears with its icy caress. I didn't watch the city disappear underneath us this time—I just buried my face in Warin's shoulder and wished I'd known him when he was still human.

When he landed on the roof, he sank down to his knees so I could sit on his lap in an imitation of the way I'd been straddling him last night. Only this time, there wasn't any sexual undertones—just a bone-deep urge to know he needed me as much as I needed him—needed me enough to follow through on his promise that he'd do anything to make this right.

A gentle touch against my cheek made me open my eyes and move my head back from his shoulder.

"I am so sorry I hurt you, Liv." It was a gentle, intimate whisper.

I drew in a deep breath. "You said you'd given up on everything when we first met. What did you mean?"

"I..." Warin hesitated, and I stared into his darkened eyes.

"You promised my anything to make this right. I want to know something about you no one else does. I want to know this."

He sighed deeply. "I was planning to meet my Final

death, once I'd gotten to the bottom of the disappearances. It was my last obligation."

"Warin," I whispered, reaching for him without thought.

"It's not... It would not have been a tragedy. It would have been my long overdue penance. And a relief. I have been numb for more than eight hundred years. At first, I stayed for Aleric. I knew he would have been torn apart by my absence. Then it was my obligation to my territory. Chicago was on the brink of a power vacuum when I was given reign here. But Aleric has his own territory now, his own responsibilities, and Carina would have been able to manage the city until a worthy Ancient could take over. I thought I was finally done with this life." He smiled at me, a gentle expression. "But then you showed up."

"What is this? This connection between us?" I asked, because there was no use pretending anymore. We both knew it was there, even if I couldn't fathom why.

"I'm not sure." He reached up and stroked a hand through my hair. "But if I believed in a god, I'd think you an angel of mercy sent to save me from my own darkness."

I snorted at the ridiculousness of that notion. "Good thing you don't, then, because I would have been the *worst* guardian angel ever."

The corner of his mouth quirked up at my comment. "Maybe I can be your guardian angel instead. If you'll let me."

"How about we say we're just friends?" I offered.

"That would make me very happy."

We sat in silence for a little while, and I rested my head back against his shoulder and let the night embrace us both.

"Warin?" I finally said.

"Yes?" he asked. From the distant note in his voice, I guessed his thoughts had been wandering.

"You can't ever give up on life. Even un-life, as it may be in your case. You're still alive because you still have life left to live. I believe with everything that I am that we do not get to make the choice for when we're done. There is no easy way out. We'll just have to live it all over again— all the pain, the suffering, and grow stronger until we can overcome it."

"You believe in reincarnation?" he asked.

"I do. And I believe in *you*. Please, Warin. Promise me, no matter what happens... don't end your life. Not before it's time."

He reached up and stroked a hand across my cheek in a gentle caress. "I can promise that I will always be there for you, as your friend, for as long as you need me."

I frowned. "But I won't always be here. I'll grow old, and I'll die."

"You don't have to worry for me, little one. I will finish whatever Fate has planned for me. Meeting you showed me that even after more than a thousand years, I don't know what will come next."

I guessed that was as much as I could ask for, though I wished he'd been more definitive on the whole "no suicide ever" thing. "Are you really more than a thousand years old?"

"About twelve hundred, give or take."

"That's..." I snorted, the vastness of his lifespan stretching too far for me to fully comprehend. To have been alive for more than a millennium... "I thought you were a kid when I saw you in that cage. Not even old enough to buy a drink legally."

He chuckled, the rumble of it vibrating through his chest to mine. "I think I was around nineteen, maybe twenty, when I died."

I sighed and patted his shoulder. "The next time you call me 'little one,' I'm gonna start calling you grandpa."

"I'd prefer if you didn't."

I smirked into his shoulder. "See it as part of your penance for blood-stalking me."

We sat in silence a while longer, until a thought began to niggle at me. Something about that number he'd mentioned before—eight hundred years. "Warin... do you know someone called Thea? Or have you ever?"

"No. Why?"

"Nothing. It was just a thought." I straightened up

and looked out across the city lights stretching out far below. "Oh, and Warin? One final thing..."

"Yes?"

"I'm not paying you back for the plane tickets to Denver on Thursday. This whole penance thing is going to take a while."

TWENTY-TWO

I flew to Denver alone in the early afternoon on the twenty-third of November, the day of Thanksgiving. Warin had informed me he'd fly by himself the previous night, and as much as I loved flying with him, a nearly three hours spent shivering on Warin's back wasn't nearly as attractive as the first-class ticket he'd bought me.

I arrived not too long after sunset, and found a chauffeur waiting for me with a cardboard sign at the airport.

He turned out to be driving a limo.

Warin was certainly going all-out in trying to make up. As I leaned back and sipped a glass of champagne, I couldn't deny it was pretty nice that he tried this hard. I was already grateful that I didn't have to dip into my savings for the flight and hotel room, but this—this was above and beyond.

The driver took me to a fancy-as-fuck hotel twenty minutes from the airport, and I blinked as he opened the door for me, my weekend bag in hand.

"Wow, you sure we're in the right place?"

"I'm sure, Miss Green. Mr. Waldlitch ask me to relay that the bill will be fully taken care of, and to order from room service as you please. He will be here at six thirty to pick you up."

I didn't even care that the chauffeur probably thought I was some sort of kept woman. Even the anxiety that had been brewing in my gut all day at the prospect of seeing my family seemed easier to deal with as I checked into the most luxurious hotel suite I'd ever stepped foot in and gave into my very own *Pretty Woman* fantasy.

"YOU LOOK VERY BEAUTIFUL."

I smiled at Warin as he stood in the hotel foyer, hands clasped at the wrists while he waited for me. I wasn't in anything nearly as fancy as the silky extravagance he'd bought for me for his vampire meeting. The gray long-sleeved dress, woolen tights, and knee-high boots I was wearing were my own, but they *were* the very best my closet had to offer. I'd spent a long time agonizing over picking out an outfit that my family wouldn't criticize, on styling my hair in a way I knew my mother wouldn't complain about, and applying exactly the right amount of makeup to not be pulled aside for being a slob, nor gossiped about for being a whore. The look of sincere admiration on Warin's face as he looked me up and down went a long way to calm my anxiety that I might have gotten it wrong.

"Thank you. And... thank you for all this." I motioned at the hotel foyer. "So much. You didn't have to... I know I said it was penance, but this is..."

"It's nothing but a small gesture." He waved me off, offering me his arm. "I'm staying with Aleric, but I figured you might want a little break from, ah, my kind."

"I didn't know he lived in Denver," I said.

"He's the Night Lord of the city and its surrounding territories," Warin explained.

"Oh, maybe that explains his haughty attitude." I grimaced. "I don't think he likes me very much."

"My brother can be very... protective," he said as he led me outside.

I stared at the fire-engine-red Ferrari we stopped in front of. "*Wow.* That's... not what I thought your taste was like."

A wry smile pulled on his lips as he opened the passenger side door for me. "It's Aleric's. This was the most modest of his collection."

"Oh, well that makes so much sense," I muttered as I

slid in. So much for keeping a low profile during the visit with my family.

THE KNOWLEDGE that we were approaching my childhood neighborhood and a reunion with my extended family seemed to drain the energy out of me for every mile we came closer. When we finally pulled up in front of my aunt's house, I knew I would never be able to get through the evening without Warin by my side.

Warin parked the flashy car, and I drew in a deep breath, trying to steady my nerves.

"You're frightened," he said softly.

Smoothing my hands over my dress to stop the slight tremble in them, I turned to him with an attempt at a smile. It failed pretty miserably. "My family is sorta my kryptonite."

"Do you wish to leave?"

"No, I... it'd just be worse if I stayed away. Just... please promise me you won't leave my side," I begged.

Cool fingers touched my chin, gently turning my face to his. "I'll stay by you. I promise."

I took another deep breath and managed a slightly more sincere smile this time. "Thank you."

The door opened before we made it all the way up there, revealing Edna's thin form. "Olivia, darling, how good of you to find time to visit your family! And you must be the young man Lily talked about. Will, right?"

"Warin," I automatically corrected.

"Come on in—you're the last ones to arrive," Aunt Edna didn't acknowledge the correction as she swept us inside.

Everyone was there. All the aunts, cousins, uncles, my grandparents, and of course my mother, her boyfriend, and my little sister. They were all staring when we came in—at Warin, at his flawless features and his casual, but expensive-looking clothes—and I knew that they were trying to figure out what on Earth he was doing here with me.

"Oh, Olivia!" My mother got up from the group of relatives she was sitting with and came over to give my frozen form a hug and a kiss on the cheek. "Goodness, I had forgotten how big you are!"

I'd inherited my biological father's height and bone density, and had always towered over the other women in the family. My mother and grandmother had never let an opportunity pass to tell me how unfeminine it was.

"Gary, come meet Olivia." My mother waved over her boyfriend, and my sister trailed along.

Gary grabbed my hand with a big smile and crushed it enthusiastically in his. "So this is the wayward daughter! It's great to finally meet ya!"

I smiled politely at him. "Hello, Gary. I have heard many good things about you."

When he released my hand, I turned to Warin, who had been watching the exchange in silence, a hand lightly against my lower back. "This is Warin," I said.

Gary grabbed his hand and gave him a hearty slap on the shoulder, and I shot Warin an apologetic sidelong glance when my mother pulled him into an awkward hug.

"Oh, it is so good to see that Olivia is finally socializing with people of class," my mom chirped, pulling him by the hand toward the group of relatives she had sat with before. "We have been so worried about her life choices these past years."

Warin let himself get led away, and I briefly greeted my sister before I nervously followed, only to get shanghaied by other aunts, uncles, and cousins for how-do-you-dos, including Kathy—with her fiancé (Brad, twenty-eight, successful local realtor, Audi)—who wanted to know how long I'd known Warin and what he did for a living.

"About a month." I looked around to locate him, and saw that he was sitting on the sofa in between Mom and Edna, a group of my relatives leaning in, unquestionably in order to ask him every detail of his life.

"And I honestly don't know what he works with— some form of business management. Excuse me, Kathy." I managed to duck past Uncle Rogan and find my way to Warin's side.

"...always had the urge to go against all rules and sensibility," I heard my mother say, which got a confirming laugh from Edna.

"Oh, do you remember when she just *had* to waste her money going to college—to study *art?* Of course, she never completed it."

I breathed deeply as I counted slowly to ten. Art school had been my big dream—the reward I'd clung on to to get me through the difficult years in middle and high school. I'd managed to get in on a scholarship, but during a big project that counted toward half of first year's grade, Mom had called to tell me my grandma was dying and I *had* to come home. I'd been too weak to tell her no, failed the project and thus my first year, lost my scholarship... and Grandma was still very much alive.

And that's the how the story of *"Liv can never complete anything"* came to be family legend, retold at every gathering.

When I opened my eyes again, Warin caught my gaze. He reached up and grabbed my hand in his so he could pull me down next to him, making Edna scoot to the side.

"I appreciate Liv's free spirit. And she is an amazing artist," he said.

Blessed be Warin. I pressed against him for a brief moment to let him know I appreciated it.

"But you can't live off being an *artist,*" my mom snorted, earning a nod from Gary. "It's alright for women who have the necessary qualities to find a man to support them, but Liv…" She laughed lightly. "Liv isn't exactly that type."

She was right about that, really. I didn't like the thought of depending on someone to take care of me, but I was pretty sure she wasn't talking about my independence.

"Oh, I absolutely disagree. If she wasn't so modest, her art could easily decorate some of Chicago's finest galleries," Warin said. "The life of an artist isn't for everyone—it requires talent and spirit beyond what most of us possess. But I'm sure you know your daughter's got both in excess."

My cousin Melba, who'd wedged in at the edge of our small cluster to not miss a word, half-succeeded in choking off a giggle at that comment. When Warin raised his eyebrows in question, she studiously avoided looking at him by pouring herself another glass of wine.

"So, Warin," Gary interrupted. "How did you meet our Olivia?"

'Our Olivia'? I had never met the man before today, but he apparently felt he was part of the family. Must be nice.

"I saw her through a window at a bar and knew I had to know her," Warin answered, not missing a beat.

Oh, suave. Even though I knew it was a lie, my cheeks still heated up.

My mom giggled, managing that perfect balance between surprised amusement and mild derision she'd perfected to an art form. "Oh, isn't that sweet? It's such a rare man who can appreciate a more, ah, difficult body type. I know it's been hard for Liv to find boyfriends with her build and that unfortunate jawline. A leftover from her father, I'm afraid. How wonderful you could look past it so easily."

I clenched Warin's hand. *Every time*—she always had to humiliate me. I knew this, expected it. So why did it still hurt so much?

"Difficult body type?" The barest hint of ice penetrated Warin's voice, though his tone was nothing but polite disbelief. "There's nothing *difficult* or *unfortunate* about Liv's appearance, and certainly nothing I need to look past. She's a beautiful woman."

"So, Mom, how did you and Gary meet?" I quickly intervened. I had heard the story multiple times, but making my mother talk about herself was always a good diversion.

It worked flawlessly. For the next half hour, until dinner was served, my mother talked about their relationship in minute detail, but at least it changed the focus from me. I leaned against Warin for the duration, thankful for his support. He kept his hand in mine the whole time, and for that, I was grateful. It was the first time I'd had to face my family without feeling alone.

Dinner passed in a blur of fly fishing talk from Uncle Rogan, a million and one questions about the Ferrari we'd arrived in, discussion of Kathy and Brad's upcoming nuptials, and the occasional insult to my lack of education and career. But during the entire meal, Warin was there, his hand on my knee under the table, lending me his strength. His presence steeled me enough that, for the first time in as long as I can remember, I didn't feel like crying at every dig that came my way.

And when my mother asked me to clear the table after dessert, I even found the strength to say, "Sorry, I was gonna show Warin the garden. We'll be in in a bit."

"It's dark," my mother protested from her seat. "And Edna could really use the help."

"You should help her, then," I said, a thin smile in place as I grabbed Warin's hand and pulled him toward the door.

It was such a small thing, telling my mother no... but my heart was hammering in my chest as I led Warin across the lawn to the old willow tree I'd always escaped to during family gatherings as a kid.

The swing still hung from one of its sturdy branches, and I patted the thick trunk affectionately. It was so blessedly quiet out here.

"Sit—I'll push you," I said to my silent companion as I nodded at the swing.

He shot me a hesitant glance, but did as I asked.

When I pushed him, the stiffness of his posture made it obvious he'd never been on a swing before.

"Just relax," I said. "And lift your feet, or I'm not moving you anywhere. Vamp strength and all."

Warin obeyed again, and made a small noise of surprise when I pushed him and he rocked slowly on the swing.

"Fun?" I asked.

"Interesting," he said as he looked up in the willow's branches.

"I used to come here as a kid. It's so peaceful," I said as I pushed against his wool-clad back again.

"I don't understand your family," he said, after a moment's silence. "They treat you so... poorly." The touch of anger in his voice warmed me.

"I'm not like them," I said softly. "Not everyone sees 'weird human' as a good trait. I've always been different—I even *look* different, thanks to my dad's apparently overpowering genetics."

"That doesn't explain the vehemence I sense in these people," he said. "Human society has been built around the very concept of family—of caring for your blood. And uniqueness... is celebrated. Or it should be."

The pain I always felt when I thought too much about my upbringing flared in my gut, tightening my throat. This time, when Warin swung back, I didn't push him.

The air swooshed between us, and then he was by my

side, his hand resting on my shoulder. "Liv, what did these people do to you?" His voice was very quiet, but it had an unmistakable core of steel.

I shook my head and leaned in so my forehead pressed against his shoulder. "I don't want to talk about it. Not now, when I have to face them again this evening."

His hand moved from my shoulder to circle my waist, and I relaxed in his embrace. "You don't have to go back. I'll take you anywhere you wish."

My mouth pulled up in a soft smile against his wool coat. "Thank you," I whispered.

Feather light lips brushed against my hair. "Shall I take you back to the hotel?"

I pulled myself back upright and looked at him, the thankful smile still on my lips. "Not yet. If we leave now, they'll just think they got to me."

"Does their conviction matter?"

Unfortunately, it did. I sighed and nodded. "I'm sorry. I know I'm weak."

Warin shook his head. "You're not weak. Blood... has power over everyone, even mortals."

"Isn't that a bitch?" I sighed.

He chuckled in response. "Indeed."

"Come on, let's get back inside. The sooner we get coffee over with, the sooner we can go home." I pulled back and offered him a teasing wink. "And if you're *really* lucky, Brad will have some more car questions for you."

. . .

THE FAMILY HAD SPREAD out over the house in small groups when we came back in. Brad, with Kathy in tow, made a beeline for Warin the second we stepped inside, and if I'd been the betting sort, I'd have won big when he immediately began talking engine size.

I, however, excused myself and went upstairs to find the bathroom.

I spent some time in front of the mirror giving myself a pep talk, not terribly concerned with having left Warin alone with my relatives. He could handle himself in a group of small-minded humans just fine—especially when they were all fawning all over him due to his obvious wealth.

"*Olivia?*" My mother's voice sounded from the other side of the bathroom door, followed by a rap of her knuckles. "*Open up.*"

I grimaced at my own reflection. "Just a minute, Mom."

She rapped her knuckles against the door again, and I allowed myself a deep breath before I unlocked it. "Hey, sorry, I'll get out of yo—"

"What do you think you're doing?" she hissed, grabbing onto my arm when I tried to walk past her.

"What do you mean?" I asked as calmly as I could,

even as my heart sped up to overdrive, my knees feeling oddly weak as adrenaline kicked in.

"How dare you speak to me like that in front of the family! I've never been more humiliated! If you think you'll endear yourself to that man by mouthing off to your own mother, you're in for a nasty surprise. He'll dump you the second he realizes what a trashy piece of shit you are." The contempt in my mother's eyes cut through my chest, making me tremble as I struggled to keep calm and breathe evenly.

"Is this about cleaning the stupid table?" I managed.

"It's about you and your big mouth, as it always is, Olivia! God, I don't understand what went wrong with you! I've given you everything—everyone has! You've had everything served to you on a silver platter, and what do you do? Throw it in my face the second you're asked for the tiniest favor!" She shook my shoulder, eyes wide with fury. "You ungrateful, spoiled *cun—*"

I gust of wind cut her short. An extremely pissed-looking Warin was inches from her face, and the hand she'd been holding onto me with was uselessly raised in the air, the vampire's fingers wrapped tightly around her wrist.

"*Be. Quiet,*" he hissed, and when he spoke I saw the length of his fangs gleaming menacingly.

My mother trembled in his grasp, eyes bulging with fear—but she was completely silent.

"If you *ever* speak to Liv like that again, you'll regret it. If you ever touch her, you'll regret it. If you ever mention another ill word about her to anyone in this family, you'll regret it. Have I made myself clear?" he asked, and though his voice was low, the deadly quality to it gave me goosebumps.

My mother nodded violently, though.

"You'll never be able to tell anyone, in any way, what I've told you tonight—or even that you fear me. But you *will* remember my words. And you will live the rest of your miserable life knowing that just *one* mistake will bring you pain like nothing you've ever experienced." Warin released his hold on her wrist and, after one final stare through narrowed eyes, turned to me. "Come, Liv. It's time to leave."

TWENTY-THREE

Neither one of us uttered a word on the drive back to the hotel. Warin was quietly seething by my side, knuckles tight around the steering-wheel. And I... I was too stunned to say anything, or even wipe away the steady streams of tears rolling down my cheeks.

At the hotel, Warin walked me to my room, a hand resting on the small of my back as a gentle but constant reminder that he'd kept his promise—he'd stuck by my side through a night I hadn't known how to get through.

And he'd stood up for me, like no one ever had. Not even me, truth be told. I'd never had the strength to. There'd always been that small voice at the back of mind telling me that I deserved what my family said to me. What they did.

It wasn't until tonight, until Warin had showed me

that I truly wasn't alone, that I realized that voice had been my mother's all along.

Once inside my suite, Warin walked over to the side of my bed and sat down, face still drawn with anger.

I sucked in a shuddering breath and wiped at my eyes, calm finally closing in around me now that there was a closed door between me and the rest of the world. "You don't have to stay. I'm okay, and Aleric must be expecting you."

"He can wait. Come here, little one. Please."

I bit my lip, hesitating. On one hand, I wanted nothing more than to be with him right now... because I knew no one else would ever take away the pain. But on the other hand, I knew if I sat on that bed, I'd not be able to hide my brokenness anymore. And there'd be no coming back from that.

"Liv," he said, so softly I knew if I closed my eyes his words would feel like a caress. "Tell me."

And so I sat on the bed, letting him intertwine his slender fingers with mine.

And I told him everything.

I told him about my dad leaving my mom and never contacting us again after I'd just turned three, about how she's always resented me for looking so much like him, reminding her of how he'd mistreated her. I told him about how that meant I'd grown up feeling ugly and unlovable. I told him about the man she met when I was four—my sister's dad, Bruce—about how he was so outgoing, successful, and well-loved by the entire family, especially my mom.

And while carefully avoiding Warin's gaze, I told him how I, when I was seven, had confessed to my Mom that Bruce was touching me.

Warin's thumb, which had been gently stroking over mine again and again while I talked, stopped. But I didn't. I couldn't.

So I kept talking. About how my mother had called me a liar, a sick and twisted liar trying to ruin a good man's reputation.

How she'd stayed with him.

And how he'd kept sneaking into my bedroom until the day he died several months later.

"He only touched," I whispered. "He never *hurt* me, or raped me. He'd tell me once I became a woman, that he'd be my first, but he... died long before I did. I think my mom blamed me for his death. I don't... I don't really remember what happened, but I was with him when he died. Anyway, because he died in my bedroom and the paramedics asked me why he was there... it became known in the neighborhood that he was a kiddy fiddler. My family never forgave me for ruining his reputation."

I wasn't aware of the fresh tears until Warin wiped them from my cheek with his free hand before wrapping his hand around my cheeks to lift my gaze to his. Soft sapphire eyes sought and held mine.

"He did hurt you, Liv. Do not ever minimize what he put you through. I know the damage he did to you. There is no excuse, no extenuating circumstances. He hurt you, and you survived it because you are strong beyond words. Not because what he did wasn't painful."

I shook my head, biting my quivering bottom lip. It hadn't been invasive or painful, and sometimes it had been... The shame from those times was the worst of it all. "It wasn't... You don't understand—"

"No, Liv. I understand." The softness of his gaze didn't change, but the intensity did. "I know the hurt you went through. *All* of it. The physical pain is the easiest damage to recover from."

I stared wide-eyed at him, recognized the age-old pain in the depths of his eyes. He did understand.

Warin moved his hand from my chin to clasp it behind the back of my neck, pulling my forehead in to rest against his. "As for your family's reaction..." His gentle tone had gained a sharp edge. "They were wrong. Are wrong. None of this was ever your fault, and there's nothing wrong with you, Liv. Nothing. *They* failed the most sacred obligation of any being on this Earth—they failed to protect their young. And they are *wrong*."

I sniffled in response, too overwhelmed by the intensity of his words to keep his gaze.

And then his arms wrapped around me, pulling me to his lap, holding me tightly. Gluing me together with the strength of his presence.

"My little one," he murmured in my ear, his steely tone stronger. "Your mother is a weak, wretched human, and she has no excuse for the abuse you have suffered at the hands of her and her family. I know you've been taught to accept it, but this time, you need to listen to *me*: They are wrong; *you* are wrong. You're the strongest, most precious thing in this world, and no one will *ever* tell you otherwise again. I will not allow it."

His words made me shake violently—from fear, from anger, from relief—from reasons I didn't understand. But he held me so tightly while he whispered soothing things in my hair that I finally, for the first time since Bruce's death, broke down and sobbed over the loss of my childhood. My family.

Sobs wracked my body, my hands desperately fisting in Warin's shirt, but when I finally—a long time later— had no more tears left, I felt... free.

I slowly lifted my red and puffy face from the vampire's shoulder and looked into ancient eyes that were completely focused on *me*.

"I'm sor..."

His finger against my lips made me silent. When he was sure I wasn't going to continue, he removed it.

"Do not apologize. Do not." His gaze was as serious as

I'd ever seen it. "Never, ever be sorry for sharing your pain with me. I am honored that you chose me."

The only thing I could do after that statement was to bury my head under his chin and clutch his shirt again.

We sat like that for a long time, doing nothing more than simply being. Together.

"My Sire was a sadist," Warin said after what must have been nearly an hour's silence. His voice was quiet, calm. Devoid of emotion. "He found me as a young man, and he thought me beautiful. For twenty-one nights he kept me alive, and for twenty-one nights I would beg him for death. He hurt me in every way, but before the sun rose after each of those nights, he would give me pleasure as he violated me. That was when I would plead with him to end my life.

"On the final night, I knew he'd gone too far—I felt my life slip away, and I knew there'd be no coming back this time. I felt such... relief.

"The next night, I arose as a vampire. Tied to him with a bond more suffocating than any chain he could ever shackle my flesh with. I could feel him, all the time, inside my blood. Could feel the pleasure he got from my torment. The bond between a Sire and Child is... There is no force like it. I have been told it is the greatest gift, but... for me, it was not. I was with him for decades. How many, I don't know. Something... broke in me during that time. I became... something else.

"One night, he brought home Aleric. They say the bond between a Sire and his Child is unbreakable. But I... I finally found a way to shatter his chains. I couldn't bear the pain in my blood when he hurt my new brother. So I killed him.

"Even now... Sometimes I feel the broken bond aching in my chest. I feel the echo of everything he did to me. But the only thing that still hurts... is the memory of the times there'd be no pain. When I allowed his touch to bring me pleasure... relief."

"Warin," I whispered, because there was nothing else to say. My own pained past was a flickering candle in comparison to the roar of agony in my chest as I pressed myself to him, wishing with every fiber of my being that I could take away the torment of his entry into the night. Fresh tears rolled down my cheeks, soaking his already ruined shirt.

Warin held me as tightly as I did him, his lips pressed against the top of my head. "Don't cry, Liv," he mumbled. "Those nights with my Sire brought me to you. If I were given a choice, I would not have picked a different path now that I know where it has led."

"What did I do to deserve you in my life?" I croaked against his collarbone.

He whispered something against the top of my head, but it was too quiet for me to make out.

Soon, I fell asleep. Safe in Warin's arms.

TWENTY-FOUR

I didn't see Warin for nearly a week after we returned to Chicago. He called me the night after I flew back to let me know that he had a lead on the potential backer of the skinwalkers, and would be too busy to visit for a few nights.

As much as I wanted to see him, I knew it was probably best to take some time apart to cool off after our emotional trip to Denver. There'd been such a massive shift in our relationship, and I needed time to sort through my feelings. I even went so far as to google "vampire + human relationships"—but all that brought up was some *really* creepy porn.

The relentless sex dreams thanks to our most recent blood exchange didn't help matters, *at all*, but I was still hesitant to cross that final line. And not just because of that porn clip, either.

As close as I'd felt to Warin in Denver, and as much as I knew he was already all the way in, behind every wall and every barrier I'd ever erected to protect myself, if we actually tried a... a *relationship*, and it went wrong...

I'd lose him.

And that was one thing I couldn't do.

In the end, I decided to confine my urges for more to the hazy mornings when I woke up covered in sweat and aching from debauched dreams. I spent my days focused on work, on finishing the painting of Warin I'd been working on for weeks now, on chatting with Raven about witchy stuff and Roy about blessedly normal stuff, like football (he was a die-hard Packers fan) and gardening (and had a surprising love for his begonias).

When Warin finally texted me to check if he could come over, I'd managed to get enough distance from our intense time in Denver that I could ignore the flutter of butterflies in my stomach, even if I was entirely unable to get the giant and involuntary smile off my face.

He buzzed my door phone some fifteen minutes later, and I practically skipped over to let him in. It wasn't until his face lit up in an unusually warm smile when I opened the door that I realized that I hadn't managed to get rid of my excited grin since he texted.

I coughed and stepped back behind the door to try

and school my features into at least a somewhat less insane expression, gesturing for him to come in.

"I have missed you," he said softly as I closed the door behind him.

The pesky butterflies returned with a vengeance. "I missed you too."

We stared at each other in silence for a too-long moment, until I managed to get a grip and turned my focus to the wrapped package I'd gotten ready on the coffee table. "I... got you a gift. An early Christmas present."

"Oh. That is... very kind, but I do not want you to spend your money on gifts for me," he said, surprise clear in his voice as he followed me to the couch.

"I didn't," I said as I plopped down on the couch in my usual spot and nudged the present toward him. "Open it. I'm dying to see what you think."

Warin eased down on the couch, plucking the present from the table to study the wrapping for a moment.

I was really quite excited to see if he would like it, as I had put a great deal of time and thought into it, but I did my best not to rush him.

Finally, Warin carefully unwrapped the paper, his fingers deftly undoing the tape and ribbon until the framed picture was finally between his hands.

It was the charcoal drawing of him I'd been working on while we got to know each other, set on the background of a sunrise similar to the one on my wall he'd admired so much.

Warin stared at with a completely blank expression for the longest time, and for a moment I worried he didn't like it. Then his eyes softened and he let his finger slide over the canvas in a featherlight caress.

"Do you like it?" I asked, incapable of holding back my anticipation any longer.

"It's... very beautiful." He finally lifted his gaze from the picture to my face and held my gaze until I began to fidget, heat rising in my cheeks. There was so much emotion in his blue eyes... which made me completely uncomfortable, so my brain decided to spit information at him to ease the awkwardness I felt under his intense focus.

"The sunrise is made mainly in pastel crayons, and as you can see, I did you mostly in charcoal, but I've just used that to highlight the colors of the sky, emphasizing the light. It was really hard to capture the glow of your skin without clashing with the sun, so I had to put in some blue and purple tones in as a contrast, but your features were just so *easy* to get right. Almost like what drawing one of the old Roman statues would be like—perfect balance and contouring," I rambled.

Warin leaned back in the couch, a half-smile on his face. "I appreciate your gift very much, little one. Thank you."

"You're welcome," I mumbled, clearing my throat in an attempt not to word-vomit all over him again.

"Does this mean you are done drawing me?" he asked.

"Oh... well..." I bit my lip and tried to find the courage to ask something I'd wanted to since the first time he fed me his blood. "I know you have... a couple tattoos. The one on your arm, and... on your collarbone?" I'd glanced at that one when he'd asked me to bite his shoulder.

"Yes?"

"Would you maybe be okay with me drawing them?"

His eyebrows rose. "You wish to draw my tattoos?"

"Yeah, from what I've seen of them, they look really cool, and it would be so insanely amazing to trace up real, centuries-old tattoos." I frowned. "Er, if... they're from your human years, of course. Can you get ink *after...?*"

"It's impossible to permanently mark vampire skin. They are from my human years." He sighed good-naturedly. "If it will please you to draw them, I don't mind."

I think I squealed a little bit, if Warin's chuckle was an indicator, but I was way too excited care. I jumped up and speed-walked to get my sketchbook and pencils (because running would be too undignified). When I returned, he was standing up, and just as I realized that wait, this had to be done shirtless, Warin would be *topless*, he easily un-tugged his crisp shirt, pulling it over his head in one, swift motion that made the muscles in his torso flex and contract in a most hypnotic way.

And then there he stood, right in front of me, bare from the waist up so I could see the entirety of his lean, muscled upper body.

It wasn't that I hadn't had my share of perverted fantasies of Warin naked, but... somehow, my imagination hadn't been sufficient.

His skin was smooth and wintry, rippling over the tightest six-pack I'd ever seen. His pants hung low enough on his hips that I could just make out the top of a distinct "V," and his chest broadened into well-defined pecs decorated with a gray-blue tattoo running along his collarbones. He wasn't bodybuilder big, but he'd obviously been at his absolute physical peak when he was Changed.

The arm tattoo traveled all the way up his bicep and joined with the collarbone tattoo by his shoulders.

Oh, good goddess!

It wasn't until I pulled my eyes up high enough to notice his sly smirk that I realized I'd not only been thoroughly ogling him, but at some point I'd also started... panting? *Oh, holy wow, Liv, way to be a fucking creepo!*

"Uh..." I quickly looked down at my sketchpad, all the while pretending like I wasn't blushing. "They're nice." Oh *goddess,* were they nice, stretched over hard muscle and smooth skin. *So. Much. Bare. Skin.*

"Hmm." That damned smirk was evident in his voice too. Yeah, I really hadn't been subtle.

I glanced up, willing myself into artist mode. With determination, I grabbed a pencil and walked over to him, careful to keep my eyes on his tattoos. They seemed reminiscent of tribal tattoos, but when I got closer, I could tell they'd not been made with modern needles. The edges weren't as crisp, and his skin was slightly raised over them. I let my gaze follow the curve of the design, until the heat between my legs reminded me that I was balancing on the edge of being a creepster again.

Clearing my throat, I quickly stepped around him to see if he had more on his back.

He did.

"Oh, wow," I mumbled at the intricate blue ink that ran the length and breadth of his spine. But instead of just geometric lines, it looked like it depicted a tree of some sort, intertwined with runes. Without thinking, I brushed my fingertips up along it, letting the raised skin tell me the story of every line that had gone into this piece of art. I'd never seen anything like it.

Too late, I sensed Warin tense, his strong back muscles locking up tight.

"Oh, sorry!" I quickly pulled my hand back. "I was just so amazed. I didn't think..."

Warin exhaled slowly. "No, it's okay. You can touch, if you wish."

Well, I did sort of see with my fingers... I let my pencil-free hand smooth back down his spine, noticing how the shape of his muscles gave depth to the design.

"Does it mean anything?"

"It's the symbol of my people's belief of the world. The runes are signs of a warrior's path through it."

"You were a warrior?" I asked. That explained his incredible shape.

"I was."

I let my fingers stroke up higher, across a particularly intricate set of lines. "Was it painful to have done?"

"Very," he said.

I smiled at his complete lack of masculine posturing. I guessed a thousand years calmed down a guy's need to pretend nothing ever hurt. I rubbed my hand gently against his spine, part of me wishing to soothe the pain that no longer lingered, before I moved back around, dragging a finger along to rest against his shoulder tattoo.

"And this? Does this mean anything?"

"A mark of my clan."

My hand found the neck tattoo, and I stroked across it with my palm.

"It's meant as a protective ward," he said before I could ask.

Something husky in his voice made me look up from his neck to his eyes.

They were dark, and that something down low in my stomach pulsed hotly in response.

And then his gaze flickered to my mouth.

I didn't pause to think—I just leaned in and pressed my lips against his.

Warin drew in a sharp breath the second before my mouth touched his, and then he just stood there, frozen... for about three seconds.

Strong hands landed on my hips, and for a moment, I thought he was going to push me away.

I was wrong.

Suddenly, I was flush against his hard body, his mouth opening under mine, and I had time to think *"oh, yes!"* before instinct took over and I was kissing him with all I had, enjoying his lips and tongue claiming mine, egging me on.

He pushed me back until I slammed hard against the wall, and I groaned on impact as he body pinned me there, pressing into my soft curves.

My hands slipped up over his naked chest and locked around his neck, trying to pull him closer still, until I had to turn my head from his forceful kiss so I could inhale a few gulps of air.

Warin didn't waste time, dipping his head to my now-exposed jawline and neck. He pressed his lips desperately against my skin, over and over, moaning in need, until I heard a *snick,* followed by a groan.

I couldn't help the small laugh that escaped me as he pulled his head back and forced his fangs to retract, running his tongue over his teeth as he did, as if to alleviate some pressure.

"Having trouble?" I breathed. My fingers snaked into the short hair at the back of his neck and I ground my hips into his, making it clear I knew his fangs were not the only parts of him wanting to break free.

He growled—actually growled—at me and attacked my mouth again, fingers digging painfully but deliciously into the swell of my hips so he could lift me.

Obediently, I wrapped my legs around his waist, only to gasp into his mouth when the pressure of his body was now focused right against my clit. He pulled his hips back a little, only to slam them back against me, rubbing me in just the right way. This time, I was the one to groan as moisture rushed from my core, readying me.

Warin inhaled deeply, only to growl again, one of his hands moving from my hips to fist in my hair, pulling my head back roughly. Exposing my throat to him.

His kisses to my neck were fevered, demanding my submission, and I whimpered in response, my brain and body happily giving in to him.

Pleased with my surrender, Warin pulled back a little, letting me slide to the floor as his hands grabbed my shirt and *ripped*, sending buttons flying. He snarled at the sight of my bra, ripping it off with one hand, carelessly throwing it to the floor.

Oh, wow, this was actually going to happen!

His demanding kisses continued down my chest, nibbling and licking at my heated skin. When he reached my left breast, his hand coming up to cup the right, I leaned forward and bit down on his shoulder, right where I'd taken his blood last.

Warin responded with a hoarse moan before he sucked my left nipple in between his soft lips.

I laughed as the tips of his fangs grazed my sensitive flesh—he was obviously struggling to keep them retracted.

"You don't have to hold them back for me," I whispered, my voice too thick with need for anything louder.

Warin pulled from my breast a little and let his fangs slide out, moaning in relief before he buried his mouth in my cleavage again. He sucked my nipples into aching points, teasing them with his sharp fangs until I was panting hard.

Only then did he sink to his knees in front of me.

"*Oh,*" I breathed as he looked up at me with desire thick in his lust-darkened eyes. "You want to...? You don't *have* to..."

"Liv, I've *ached* to taste you since you opened the door smelling like sex and blood," he said, a wicked smirk pulling at the corner of his mouth. And then he grabbed my pants and *ripped,* sending them to the floor in a shredded pile. My panties followed before my dazed brain caught on to what he was referring to.

He meant the time I'd been on my period.

I'd thought he wanted to eat me.

Not... well, *eat* me.

"I'm not... um, *on*," I said, not entirely sure if I was feeling awkward about any potential disappointment he was about to experience, or the fact that I'd entirely misunderstood his reaction back then.

Warin didn't respond—he leaned in to give my stomach a nip—and then lifted my left leg over his shoulder and stroked his thumbs up my slit, parting me.

I whimpered and clutched frantically at the wall when he buried his mouth against my already soaking pussy, groaning as his tongue brushed up along the center once before his cool lips closed tightly around my clit.

He wasn't gentle, and he didn't ease into it. My hips bucked fervently for his lashing tongue, and I groaned when he slipped two fingers into me with ease without ever letting up. When he curled them after *that* spot, pressing roughly, I flew over the edge with a wail, fingers grasping desperately at his hair.

"Oh, my goddess. Wow, Warin, that...*Oh!* Holy—!" My broken cry died on a long moan when he delved right back, giving my swollen clit no respite.

He licked, sucked, and finger-fucked me through three orgasms, until there was no shred of doubt left in my mind that he was definitely not disappointed. He wasn't as loud about his pleasure as I was, but the sexy noises he groaned against my pussy were unmistakable.

Finally, when my clit couldn't take any more and I feebly pushed at his head to give my screaming nerves a break, he relented and eased off.

But before I could slump back against the wall and try to collect myself again, a sharp sting in my inner thigh paired with sudden and rough pressure against my G-spot sent me over again so hard I saw stars.

Through a haze of spent pleasure I looked down at Warin still kneeling between my legs. His mouth was against my inner thigh, sucking a few more times before his tongue darted out, licking the skin and sending delicious shivers up my body.

"Hungry?" I teased.

Warin looked up from his crouched position with a dark smirk. "Oh, Liv, you have no idea."

Pleasant tingles spread through my body at his dark voice and equally dark eyes, centering between my thighs. I tugged at his hair, willing him to get up so we could continue.

In a blur of speed he was on his feet, picking me up and—apparently—getting out of his pants. His naked flesh chilled my thighs while he rested me against his own.

"There is no going back now, my love," he whispered, staring into my eyes with fire in his gaze.

I wrapped my arms around his neck, leaning my forehead against his. "I wouldn't dream of it." My voice was hoarse. Needy.

He lifted me up higher and pressed me hard against the wall again, and then, with no further warning, he entered me. Fully.

"Fuck!" I stiffened and grasped onto his shoulders as my body struggled to adapt to the sudden intrusion. I was plenty wet enough to take him, but he was *thick,* and the difference between our body temperatures made my pussy clamp tight around his hard flesh.

Warin hissed his pleasure out as he held me to his body, his muscles shaking with the iron control he was exercising in order to give me enough time to accept his presence within me.

We both felt the moment I was ready.

I threw my head against the wall as he pulled back, only to slam right back, filling me completely.

I had honestly imagined sex with Warin many, many times, courtesy of the blood exchanges, but even in the most desperate times, I had never imagined *this.*

His need was as intense as my own, and he drove into me mercilessly, my paintings plummeting from the wall we were fucking against. My back slammed against the surface, but he bracketed the impact with his arms as he kept fucking me harder and faster than any human could ever replicate.

I don't know how long he took me up against the wall —I was too lost in hazy pleasure of the delicious friction against every sensitive spot inside my clenching sex—but some time later, he decided it was time to change position.

He swung me around so swiftly my vision blurred, tossing me on the couch. I bounced once, and then he was between my legs again, anchoring me with the weight of his pelvis as he penetrated me all the way to the hilt once more. As if being parted from me was physically painful.

My only focus, the only thing I could even register, was the delicious, unrelenting, too-fast friction that was pushing me closer and closer to the brink of insanity for every smack of his hips against mine. When he reached in between us, rubbing my still-aching clit *just so* without ever stopping the brutal pace, I came again. And again. Bright lights burst behind my eyelids and I convulsed underneath him, keening my pleasure out as he took full control of my body.

At some point, the couch gave up underneath us. Warin braced me from the impact with his arms, easily rolling us off the ruined piece of furniture and tipping over the coffee table in the process.

We landed on the floor, still with me beneath him. I clung to him, desperately clawing at his skin, my hips slamming into the floor with enough strength for bursts of pain to seep through my lust-induced haze.

"Bed!" I managed to gasp.

He grunted and lifted me up, my legs still around his hips, only to slam me into the wall in the hallway, his arms taking the brunt of the impact.

I came again before we made it to the bedroom, just as Warin buried his fangs in my neck.

My pleasured scream turned into whimpers, not from pain, but from the intensity of the emotions burning through my body and mind as he drank from me.

Warin lifted his head from my neck at the sound of my whimper, my blood coloring his lips and teeth. The most intense look I'd ever seen burned in his dark eyes as he stared into mine. Into my soul. *"You. Are. Mine."*

"Always been yours," I gasped, feeling the truth of the words as I spoke them. He may have been claiming me with his body and words now, but I'd belonged to him from the moment I first saw him.

In a blur we were in bed, and soon my body was once again straining under his, fighting for release.

"Please," I begged as he tossed his head back, pinning my shoulders to the mattress, lost in our shared pleasure. "Please, Warin, I need you to... Oh, goddess, I need... with you!"

He heard me.

Letting go of my shoulders, he leaned back on his knees, pulling my lower body up by the hips while he increased the impossible speed he was driving into me with.

I was faintly aware of his growling shout of release as my entire body arched up, every muscle tensing in almost pained bliss. And then there was nothingness.

WHEN I CAME TO, it was to the feeling of Warin's slow licks along the side of my neck where he'd bitten me.

I cracked an eye open. "Still hungry?" My voice was hoarse, probably from screaming.

He looked up, his eyes softening. "No, my love. I'm not."

Love, huh? Someone certainly got in the sweet-talking mood after sex. Mind-blowing, out-of-this-world, fantastic-beyond-description sex.

I moved to scoot into his embrace, but winced when several of the muscles in my torso protested.

"Liv," he murmured. "I was too rough." His fangs *snicked* down and he lifted his wrist, without a doubt to bite into it.

I slapped a hand down on his arm. "Knock it off. I'm fine, just a bit sore." Okay, a bit more than a bit. But it was a comfortable, sultry ache that confirmed that I hadn't just passed out and had the best dream ever. I rolled over so I could cuddle into his armpit, nuzzling his chest.

"If you're sure," he sighed.

"I'm sure. Some of us don't get off on drinking blood, ya know."

He pulled me in closer and buried his face in my hair, muting his rumbling chuckle in my tangled locks.

We lay in comfortable silence for a while, and as far as I was concerned—basking in the best afterglow I'd ever experienced. Sex with Warin was *good*—so good I was pretty sure he'd ruined me for human men forevermore, but... there was so much more than the physical pleasure between us. In my bones, I knew everything was finally... *right*.

I knew then that I loved him.

Not as a friend. Not even as a bit of a crush.

No. I loved him with everything I was, and everything I'd ever be. I loved him like I'd been born with the sole purpose of loving this man. There was nothing else, and there would never *be* anything else.

"Your heart's beating faster again," Warin murmured into my hair. "And you smell of fear. What's troubling you, little one?"

"Nothing, I just... You never told me what you found out with the skinwalkers. Did you get an idea of who's helping them?"

Warin finally lifted his head, supporting it on one hand so he could look down at me. "You wish to speak about this now?"

"Well..." I couldn't really fault his surprised tone. It

probably wasn't the best post-sex subject, but it was infinitely safer than the frantic panic churning in my brain. "We didn't really get a chance to before."

Warin snorted, then sighed and rolled over onto his back, dragging me with him so I was resting against his chest. "It's not good news. They have vanished into thin air."

"What? The skinwalkers? Are you saying they're... they're *gone?*" The shock numbed my throbbing heart, and I raised up to stare down at him. "Can they just... how can they just *disappear?*"

"I was getting too close, and the vampire behind them must have decided to cover his tracks. Only by pulling them out so abruptly, I now have confirmation that it is another vampire behind their appearance in my city. And he's... very strong. And extraordinarily devious. Every path I went down came to a dead end. Missing people, but always with a reasonable explanation for their absence, cleverly disguised Compulsion that you'd have to know what to look for to spot."

"But if they're gone... does that mean he's given up?" I asked.

"Perhaps," Warin sighed. "There is a chance we spooked him when it became clear we were zeroing in on their hideouts. But... without knowing the motivations behind his plan, it's impossible to say. I do know he's deliberately sought out my domain, since no other Ancient has experienced similar issues in his territory."

"So what do we do now?" I worried my lip between my teeth, trying to shake the uncomfortable feeling that someone was out there, watching us. Waiting for another chance to pounce.

"*I* am going to monitor the situation, and if possible, make use of the witches' network so I can be prepared if and when any skinwalkers return to the area." Lifting both eyebrows in challenge, he put a hand between my legs and pressed up, sending a bolt of sensation through my much-abused clit. "Whereas *you*, my love... you are going to fuck me some more, since I clearly didn't exhaust you as much as I thought I did, if you have the energy to ask me about skinwalkers."

I laughed at his crudeness—it was such a change from his usually composed persona, and the glimmer in his eyes that accompanied it sent a wave of joy through me.

Clearly seeing it as permission, Warin rolled over and pinned me against the mattress. When his hips settled between my thighs, it was more than evident that he, at least, was ready for round two.

"Warin?" I asked softly, bracing my hands gently on his shoulders to stop his advances.

He brushed his mouth against mine, stilling. "Yes?"

"Why do you call me 'my love'? Is it an expression, or something you just...?"

"Liv," he whispered, one cool hand finding my cheek. "How can you not know...? How can you possibly think I am not in love with you?"

I blinked, swallowing thickly as the emotion in his gaze brushed over me like a near-physical caress.

He kept his gaze locked in mine as his thick cock parted my folds and slid home. And then he made love to me.

TWENTY-FIVE

Warin was, predictably, gone when I woke up, but his scent lingered in my bedding.

I rolled over with a happy sigh as my stiff limbs and sore abdomen reminded me of the night we'd spent together. With a satisfied hum, I buried my nose in the pillow he'd used, inhaling the wild, crisp, earthy aroma he'd left behind.

So this was what it felt like to have a vampire boyfriend.

I chuckled into the pillow as I remembered the blasted romance novel that'd caused our paths to cross. I'd have to gift Warin a copy—I was pretty sure he'd get a kick out of it. Especially since his part was played by an emo vampire king who spent his nights stalking the girl he'd become obsessed with.

I smiled softly at the reminder of how Warin had called me *his* multiple times, both during and after the sex. It was pretty impressive how swiftly he'd gone from calm and restrained to over-the-top possessive the second we'd given in to the attraction between us.

It was also pretty impressive how completely okay I was with it.

It took me a little while to get my ass out of bed thanks to that delicate *post-sex-with-vampire* ache between my legs and in my muscles, and when I finally did, I was greeted by an entirely different kind of destruction.

The hallway between my bedroom and the living room had a big chunk of plaster broken off. It lay in a crumbled heap on the floor next to a broken picture frame. The living room situation was even worse—it looked like a small tornado had blown through my apartment.

Well, there goes that security deposit.

I PUTTERED AROUND in the kitchen for a bit, getting coffee ready for Roy and sorting through my mail. I put all the junk aside, pulling out the depressingly large pile of bills... and paused when I got to a square envelope with my address handwritten across it.

Did I even know anyone well enough to get invited to a wedding?

Curious, I shoved the bills aside and ripped the hand-written envelope open.

It turned out to be a note written on cheap, blue-lined paper. It read,

---

I know you're a witch.

If you stay in Chicago, your vampire will know before next sunrise too. And even if he doesn't kill you himself, his kind will never tolerate your union. There are other Ancients who would only be too happy to execute him for betraying his race.

You have a choice to make today, Olivia, but only today. If you wait, I will make it for you.

Leave Illinois, leave the Night Lord and never come back...

Or follow your lover into the Final death.

Clock's ticking.

I STARED UNCOMPREHENDINGLY at the note for several long minutes, the cold tingle at the base of my spine making my hands tremble.

Who would send this?

Who even knew?

Joana? But there was no conceivable reason for her to want me out of Chicago. In fact, as long as I stayed, she had the curse as guarantee Warin would be kept in line.

And how on Earth would she have known Warin was my lover?

How would anyone know? It'd just happened, for crying out loud!

It didn't matter who'd send it. I couldn't leave Warin. Just the thought made my chest constrict and a knot of despair build in my gut. Life without Warin? No. Never again. I didn't know how, or why, but I belonged with him —I'd never felt this way before, this... complete. I wasn't giving that up, not today, not ever.

I stared blindly at the letter. But if I stayed...

I knew the sender was right. From both Warin's reaction to the mere mention of witches, and Aleric's threats should he ever find out *I* was one... I knew there would be dire consequences if anyone ever found out the Night Lord of Chicago was dating one. I didn't believe Warin would hurt me if he found out—not after last night. He couldn't. He'd be angry, but he'd protect me from others of his kind. Keep my secret.

Until they found out through other means.

Cold crept up my spine until my torso went numb. If I didn't leave, Warin would die.

I remembered the long procession of Ancient

vampires at his meeting. Most had been respectful, but some... I shuddered at the memory of Zeth's golden eyes. There was not a shred of doubt in my mind that some of them would grasp at this to get rid of him.

And that... that I could never let happen.

So what choice did I have? Wait until sundown, until the author of this damned letter took away my choices and spilled my secret?

But I knew Warin would never allow me to leave. He would rather risk his life than have us separate.

Which meant...

Which meant it was up to me to ensure that he was safe.

Without me.

With mechanical movements I stuffed the letter in my pocket and walked back to my bedroom. I pulled out an old weekend bag and packed the bare necessities—a change of clothes, toiletries, money, a few sentimental items—and then returned to the kitchen.

It took me twenty minutes to write the hardest note I'd ever had to write. I folded the white piece of paper in half and scribbled Warin's name across it, leaving it on the counter where I knew he'd find it.

Then I cast a last glance around the small living space, biting my bottom lip when my eyes fell on the painting of a sunset Warin loved so much. It lay on the floor where it had fallen the night before.

Agony tore at me from the inside, but I gritted my teeth against the tears stinging my eyes. Now was not the time to cry. I could do that later. And for the rest of my life.

Pulling on strength I didn't know I had, I walked to my bedroom and opened the window there as wide as it would go. There was a pretty good chance Roy would let me leave, if I told him I'd had a change of heart and I needed out of the vampire world, but I didn't want him to risk Warin's wrath. So instead, I climbed out my bedroom window at the back of the building, bringing only my weekend bag with me from the life I'd built in Chicago. I didn't stop to call a taxi until I was two blocks away.

***

"LIV?" Joana looked at me, eyebrows raised in surprise as she opened the derelict shop door wider. It was her coven's headquarters, Raven had told me when I'd texted her asking for her High Priestess' whereabouts.

"I need your help," I said. "Please."

Joana's eyebrows drew into a frown, but she nodded and opened the door wide enough for me to slip in.

The shop was as old and dusty as it'd looked like from the outside, the boards covering its windows only allowing a few cracks of light to reach its depths. From what little I could see, it looked like it'd been an antique store, once upon a time.

Joana led me out back and up a flight of rickety stairs. I could hear a faint murmur of voices from one of the rooms farther down the small hallway, but she opened the door into an empty space hosting only a few pillows on the floor, what looked like an incense burner, and a wooden bookshelf with piles of herbs and clusters of crystals.

"What can I do for you, Liv?" she asked as she knelt down on one of the floor cushions, motioning for me to take a seat in front of her.

I did, and took a moment to gather myself before I looked up at her again. Her expression was gentle, and it offered me the strength I needed to speak the words I needed.

"I have to disappear. And Warin can't know where I've gone to."

She nodded after a moment's silence. "I see."

I took another deep breath. "I have taken his blood—which means he will know where I am whenever he's awake. I was hoping... is there a way to remove this effect? Something you can do? A spell?"

Joana hesitated for a moment, but then she nodded again. "There is a spell. It won't sever your connection completely—only time can do this, and only if you have taken his blood less than three times. But, if we do this, he will no longer be able to tell where you are. Just that you are out there, somewhere. Alive."

At least it wouldn't be a complete severance. At least there would still be some small part of our connection lingering, even if I wouldn't feel it. Even if it would fade with time. "Will it hurt him?"

Joana smiled softly. "No, child. He will only know you're gone when he wakes and searches his bond for your location. You are not the first witch to need this spell, nor will you be the last. There have been instances through the centuries of powerful vampires capturing our brothers and sisters and forcing a blood bond on them, either through threats or Compulsion. This spell was crafted to give the vampire as little notice of their bond being broken as possible, to allow the witch time to flee."

I nodded. "Good. Can we... get started? I need to be out of the city before dusk."

"Of course." She reached out and grasped my hands in hers. "Close your eyes, Liv. And see with your inner eye the last time you took his blood."

The memory of Warin's party welled up. I remembered the look of adoration in Warin's eyes, his comforting presence as he held me to him so tightly as if we were the only people left in the world. The heat in my body and the zing on my tongue as his blood filled my mouth. His hardness pressing up against my legs and his moans of pleasure.

"Mother goddess, release your daughter from the bond of the Damned. Free her from his blood and protect her from his sight. Goddess of witches, goddess of life— protect my sister. Free her of her bonds." Joana spoke clearly, but as she said the words to the spell, a rushing from deep inside of me mixed with her voice, turning it woolen. That same power from within me that had tried to fight against the curse rose up, struggling against the gentle press of her magic. But it was no use.

I felt the moment my connection to Warin dampened, as if a cold, clammy fog wrapped around a part of me I hadn't even known existed. Cutting me off from the only source of warmth I'd ever known.

"Thy will be done," Joana whispered. She reached out and brushed her fingers against my cheeks, and only then did I notice the tears trickling down my face.

I opened my eyes and wiped at my face. I didn't have time to cry. Not yet. Not before I was out of the city and Warin was safe.

"I promised you that, when you were ready to leave the vampire, I would put you on the path to discover your magic," Joana said, voice gentle. "I have a friend in Kentucky. Maggie. She is the High Priestess of a coven there. If I ask, she will take you in and help you open up the connection to your powers. Do you want my help, little sister?"

I drew in a shuddering breath before I nodded. Maybe

if I hadn't been so weak, I could have fought against whoever it was who was so adamant to rip me away from the only man I'd ever loved. Maybe one day, if I was strong enough to protect us both, I could come back. "Please."

Warin,

I can't do this. I can't be yours.

I have left Chicago, and I will not be coming back. If you truly do love me, let me go. Please, Warin. Let me go.

Forgive me.

Liv

TWENTY-SIX
3 MONTHS LATER

"Again!"

I gritted my teeth and steadied my shaking hands as I tried to force a connection to the green light. The tiniest thread obeyed, and the air around my fingers crackled... and died with a fizz.

Breathing heavily, I let my arms fall to my sides, too exhausted to even wipe the sweat off my brow. "I can't."

"Yes, you can! Do you have any idea how many witches would give their left tit to have a connection to their magic like yours?" Maggie, my silver-haired High Priestess, hocked a loogie at the barn floor and wiped her face in her arm. "Stop being such a fucking wimp, grab your power by the fucking balls, and *do* something!"

Maggie wasn't your stereotypical High Priestess. Where Joana had given off sweet Earth Mother vibes,

Maggie... Maggie was more *"biker witch gone mad on power-trip."*

And she was no fan of mine. Apparently, my inability to connect with the green light within came from having been "pampered" all my life, and something about *"millennials expecting to have their magic handed to them on a silver platter."*

But, our instant and mutual dislike aside, she had taken me into her coven to help *"set me on my path"* as Joana had said, and she'd helped me land a waitressing job and set me up with a rental trailer of my very own. I was pretty sure it was only to keep in good standing with Joana, but still. I'd have been royally screwed without her help, so I tried to keep my temper in check, even when she screamed at me.

"I'm telling you, I *can't*," I said through gritted teeth. "I'm about to keel over, and I still have a shift at the diner to get through. Can we try again tomorrow?"

"Fine, whatever. Can't have the princess fainting, can we?" She shot me a dark look. "I expect you here tomorrow at nine a.m."

I glared after her as she strode out of the barn. For someone who *looked* like a sweet grandmother, she sure was a mean old witch.

MY EVENING SHIFT at the diner was an absolute nightmare. I wasn't too fond of waitressing on the best of days, but that evening I spilled an entire liter of soda all over myself, got yelled at by my boss for being clumsy, got yelled at again by a customer wanting extra pickles, and had my ass pinched so hard I was pretty sure it was gonna leave a bruise.

When I got back to my trailer, I only managed to strip out of my uniform before I slid to the floor for a good cry.

It was my new pastime these days—sobbing in a heap when I was finally alone. I hated my life. I hated my job. I hated Maggie and her stupid coven.

And I missed Warin.

Oh, goddess, I missed him so much it hurt to breathe when I allowed myself to even think his name. So I didn't. In the daytime, I would keep myself too busy to think, either with work or with training with Maggie, and at night, when I was alone and the memories came crawling back...

I got up from the floor, a hand pressed tightly to my ribs where the ache of loss radiated from whenever I thought of him. It was always there, always gnawing at me, but at night, there was only one thing that could dull the pain.

I scrambled to my little kitchenette and got a bottle of whiskey out of the cupboard.

And I proceeded to get hideously drunk. Sat alone in my trailer. High class 'til the end.

I don't know what was different about tonight—drinking alone to numb the pain had been my evening ritual for the past three months. But tonight...

It had been so long since I'd even heard his voice. I closed my eyes and thought back to our final night together—remembered every touch of his body against mine, the taste of his kiss and the softness of his voice as he'd told me he loved me.

I would never, ever get over the heartache of losing him. I'd known that even when I left. But even this pain was infinitely better than risking his life by my presence in it. I just wished... I wished I could hear his voice one more time.

Before I even realized what I was doing, I was stumbling around the trailer, looking for my old phone. I turned it on, after a bit of drunken trial and error. I hadn't had it turned on since I left Chicago, and a new voicemail flashed up on the display as soon as it flicked on.

It was from the day I left.

Breathing deeply, I pressed it.

"DON'T DO THIS, *Liv. Please, my love. Please don't do this. Come back to me.*"

· · ·

IT WAS like a punch to the gut. The agony in his voice as he spoke those few words radiated through me, tearing open the wound in my chest as I gasped for air.

I didn't think as I pawed at my phone, searching for his number. I needed to know... I *had* to know that he was better now, that he wasn't in pain anymore.

My heart thumped hard in my chest while I waited for the call to connect, every ring increasing my need to hear him. What if he wouldn't pick up when he saw my name flash on the screen? What if he hated me now? What if he'd gotten a new number?

"Liv?"

The smooth, soft voice floating into my ear sent a shudder of pain and pleasure through me, and I choked on a sob, pressing it down.

"Liv," he said again, and then there was a long silence while I breathed raggedly into the phone, wishing he would say my name again. Hearing him say it after so long felt like what I imagined a crack addict felt like after getting their first fix in a month—laced with heartache, of course.

"Please, just tell me you're safe."

The plea in his tone tore at me, making me gasp from the ache in my stomach. Oh, he was not okay. He was in pain too. Pain I'd caused him.

"Please."

"I'm safe," I whispered.

He exhaled into the phone, into my ear, and I couldn't hold it together anymore. Just as he spoke again, I hung up, disconnecting the call and turning off my phone. I sank down to the floor, curling up around my old phone and cried until I fell into a restless, drunken slumber.

I WAS PREDICTABLY *REALLY* HUNGOVER when I woke up the next day, but I had to meet Maggie at nine. So instead of curling up and pretending like the world had stopped existing, I crawled around my small living space, showering and drinking as much coffee as I could fit in my stomach while I studiously avoided looking at the phone that was still laying in the middle of the floor.

I'd heard his voice, and all it'd done was rip open every aching wound with the knowledge that he hurt too... and there was nothing I could do about it.

I couldn't return to Chicago. I knew, deep down, that even if I told Warin I was a witch, he wouldn't hurt me. He would be furious, no doubt, but the connection between us was too strong for even age-old hatred to stand between us.

But the one thing that *could*... the one thing that kept me away even as everything in me ached to just jump into my car and drive until I hit Chicago, was the risk to his life.

A world where Warin was still alive, even if I couldn't be with him, was infinitely better than a world without him.

But...

Without thinking about why, I bent to snatch up my old phone, shoving it to the deepest recesses of my overfilled handbag, before I rushed out the door to meet up with Maggie. For once, getting yelled at for being a failed witch would be a welcome distraction.

MY SHIFT at the diner ended at ten p.m. that evening, and since the small trailer park I lived in was just a mile down the road, I walked back to save on gas. It was a relatively balmy evening, and the sky was clear, letting the stars above shine like they never did in Chicago, and I very determinedly forced back thoughts of what sitting on Warin's skyscraper this time of year would be like.

A small *"thud"* sounded from the road behind me, startling me out of my morose thoughts. Before I even managed to tell myself that it was probably just some clumsy, nocturnal animal, I heard the very, *very* last thing I'd expected:

"Found you, Snack."

I spun around, automatically clutching my handbag in front of my chest—because of course this was a mugging situation—and saw a tall, eerily familiar figure looming in the middle of the road, hands casually thrust into the front pockets of his tight jeans.

"Aleric?" My voice broke in disbelief.

His eyes narrowed slightly, and I shivered at the cold expression in them. "Oh, good, so you aren't suffering from amnesia."

I gaped at him. "W-wha..?"

"That would be about the only excuse I'd accept from you. And since that isn't the case, I get to do this the fun way." He removed his hands from his pockets, a predatory edge to his posture.

Gulping, I slowly backed away. "Look, I don't know what you're doing here, but I'm sure Warin wouldn't want you to drain me, no matter how bad things ended!" Quite the cowardly move to throw Warin's name at him, but when faced with a lethal predator, you really just try anything.

He snorted and then started stalking me, copying each of my steps backwards with a cocky saunter, cold eyes never leaving mine. "My brother is rather dumb when it comes to you, you little cunt. So I will do what he failed at. No one denies a Waldlitch, especially not an insignifi-cant human like yourself."

I gasped at the insult, which was really not the thing to get upset over at this time, as I was fairly certain I only had moments left to live.

He smirked at my reaction. *"Ooh.* You don't like that name?"

"Please, Aleric," I said, changing tactics. "I'm sorry for what I did, leaving him, but I thought you'd be happy. You wanted me gone, didn't you?"

"Oh, I'm *ecstatic."* The smirk slipped off his face, leaving blankness and those icy blue eyes.

I swallowed hard as he hunched just a tad more, muscles contracting in that tell-tale way I'd seen on nature programs when a feline was seconds from jumping their prey.

My instincts took over and I spun around to run.

Which was, of course, borderline idiotic. He caught me before I took more than one step, pulling my back into his chest, lifting me off the ground.

"Now, now," he purred into my ear. "You don't wanna be doing that, little Snack. I'll forget why I'm here." He trailed his nose along my neck, inhaling deeply, and I shuddered and went rigid in his grasp.

"Please," I gasped. "You don't understand—"

"Oh, I *understand.* And in a moment, so will you," he hissed into my ear, and then everything blurred for a few seconds until we were off the road and in the middle of the small bit of woodland that lined the trailer park.

The tall vampire lowered us to the ground in a sitting position, still with my back pressed against his chest, easily immobilizing my attempts to kick at him and wriggle away by throwing a long leg over my thighs, crossing down over my knees. I might as well have tried to kick off a mountain range. He simply ignored my flailing arms, not even deeming them enough of an annoyance to pin them.

And then his bleeding wrist suddenly appeared in front of my face.

"Drink."

"No! Are you insan—*mmph!*"

He didn't wait for me to finish my protest, and pressed his wrist hard against my mouth—which I instantly clamped shut, lips tightly pressed together.

Sighing, he grabbed my nose with his free hand, pinching off my air supply. "Why must you be such a difficult pet?"

I tried to thrash my head to breathe, but he didn't release his grasp. Eventually, I had to gasp for air, and instantly, I had his bloody wrist in my mouth, thick liquid flooding my tastebuds.

I coughed and sputtered but he kept his arm in place, ensuring that I swallowed everything, until my struggle became more frantic as I was choking from the lack of air.

Aleric let me have a moment to cough and gasp before he bit into his wrist again, pressing it right back.

Not wanting to have my nose pinched shut again, like some child not wanting to take her medicine, I didn't close my lips this time, but I did bite him as hard as I could.

Unfortunately, that just got a pleasured groan from the asshole, so I quickly let go, allowing the blood to drip past my lips.

"There's a good girl," he purred, a husky note evident in his tone. "When I'm done with you, there will be no more running away, ever again."

I growled angrily against his arm, to absolutely no avail as gulp after gulp of his heady, dark life essence passed my throat. The fact that Aleric moaned during the entire process, his excitement hard and evident against my back, made the whole experience quite a bit more rapey than being force-fed blood really should have been.

Aleric bit into his wrist three more times, making me drink until the wound closed, and I was getting quite woozy.

When he finally released me, I felt pretty buzzed.

"You psychopathic asshole!" I gasped, spitting out what little of his blood remained in my mouth.

"Brave words, little Snack." He got up effortlessly, hard eyes staring me down. "You're lucky I'm here to fetch you. I'd *much* rather snap your neck."

I rolled over on my back, my legs too oddly energized to want to cooperate to get up. The night above me was alight in colors, and I could make out the energy sparkling within every single leaf on the bushes and trees above us. I vaguely remembered Warin mentioning that too much of his blood would "intoxicate" me, and boy had he been right. I was *so* high.

"Warin sent you for me?" I asked as I rubbed against the earth beneath me. It felt so good, like being embraced by the planet. "Did he ask you to fucking blood-rape me, too?" I looked up at Aleric. He seemed aglow with the source of life itself.

"Ooh!" I breathed. "You're pretty! A pretty sociopath!"

Aleric sighed. "No. He's been stubborn as a goddamn mule. Wouldn't look for you, wouldn't want *me* looking for you. Whatever you said to him must've been pretty fucking convincing, so well done you. Now *get up*. We've got a long trip. Who the hell runs away *to* Kentucky, anyway?"

"Oh." I frowned up at the glowing night sky. "But if he didn't... send you...? Why are you here?"

The vampire crouched down by my side in a smooth movement. Long, strong fingers grasped my throat—not tight enough to block off my air supply, but hard enough that a spark of worry made it through my drugged-out haze. Ice-blue eyes bored into mine, and in them I saw hate... and mind-numbing fear. "I am here because I don't have a choice. He won't live through losing you again. So you're gonna get your ass back to Chicago, you're gonna grovel at his feet and beg for forgiveness... and you're gonna *stay* with him. And if you don't, if you ever so much as *think* of running again, I'll find you. And I will murder every single person you have ever cared about in front of you, slowly and painfully. Got it?"

"What do you mean, *again?*" I asked, choosing to ignore the disturbing threats of violence. My buzz helped.

His full lips pinched into a narrow line. "Do not concern yourself with matters you are too dimwitted to grasp."

"You're such a dick," I said, smiling peacefully at him. "I can't go back. I'm a witch. If anyone finds out, and he tries to protect me, he'll be a target."

Aleric's eyes widened in shock, then narrowed into slits as his hand against my throat tightened a bit more than was comfortable.

Belatedly, I realized what I'd just done. But even through my dawning realization that I'd fucked up, my buzz kept me calm. "Well, shit."

"Why are you always such a fucking thorn in my side?" he hissed. "What *kind* of a witch?"

"The terrible kind." I shrugged awkwardly, his hand making the motion difficult. "I can't seem to get it right."

"I mean, *what* do you do? Potions, energy, necromancy...fucking tarot cards? What?" he growled.

I wheezed a laugh. "If I'd been a necromancer, your ass would be sooo screwed. I can do an energy-blast thingy. Well, I can *sometimes* do an energy thingy." I lifted my hands to mimic a blast.

Aleric finally released my throat with a low groan and scrubbed both hands over his face. "Fuck!"

"That's why I left," I said. "I got a letter saying someone knew what I was... and if I didn't disappear, they'd make sure Warin was targeted for shielding me. I didn't *want* to leave. I love him so, so much. He can't die for me, I won't let him. So... I came here. He's safe now."

"He's not *safe,* you stupid, ignorant bloodsack." Aleric lowered his hands so he could glare at me. "He needs you. I can feel him, *here.*" He pressed a closed fist to his chest. "He was hollow for eight *hundred* fucking years, he was numb—but he was safe. Until you waltzed back into his life. And now... now all I feel in our bond is *pain. You* did this to him. And *you* are going to fix it. There is no other way."

"But the letter." I blinked up at him in surprise at the agony crossing his features. I'd not seen Aleric this animated before. "My powers..."

"Suppress them," he said, his face sliding back into a cool mask. "Don't ever mention them again. Don't ever think about them. I will find the one who sent you that letter. Until then, don't mention them to Warin."

"But I—"

"No! He's too blind when it comes to you—he'll declare war on every fucking Ancient on the continent in a bid to keep you safe. He can't know until the threat is gone. If you want him safe, you'll do as I say."

I sighed, defeated. Whatever else I may have thought of Aleric, as I looked up at his glowing features, I knew that in this one thing, our goals aligned. We wanted Warin safe at all costs. "Okay. But... Aleric?"

He arched an eyebrow at me.

"How did you find me?"

"I traced your cell phone, you idiot. The moment you turned it on, the GPS in it alerted me."

"Oh. I'd imagined something... I dunno, a bit more mystical." I rolled around on my belly, sniffing the ground beneath me. It smelled amazing, so full of scents I didn't recognize.

"I won't need a GPS anymore. Remember that." Without warning, he hoisted me up by my jacket, and I squealed and laughed at the floating sensation.

"*Humans,*" Aleric sneered from somewhere above me.

"Aleric?"

"*What?*"

"Did you make Diva tell me all those awful things about vampires? About the stalking, and that you can't feel love?"

"Well, well. Not as stupid as you look," he mused, finally placing me down on my feet. I stumbled, but managed to keep upright.

"I just don't... why did you try to scare me away from him, when now you're saying he needs me?"

He sighed. "I hoped he didn't."

"Aleric?"

"Gods, you're a fucking nuisance!" he hissed.

"Who's Thea?"

The irritation on his face drained away, leaving blankness in its stead. "You heard."

"You and that dick... was it Zeth? Yes." I frowned, trying to focus through my high. "*'Eight-hundred years'* always comes up. And he said that name... did he think I was her? Who is she?"

Ice-blue eyes locked in mine. "She is no one. And you will never speak her name again. If you want Warin happy, if you want Warin safe... you will never mention her name, and you will never again speak of what you heard that night. Zeth is not someone to be trifled with, and if he hears of that name coming from your lips... You will die."

TWENTY-SEVEN

Aleric did not book me a first-class flight from Kentucky to Chicago.

Instead, I spent four hours shuddering in his grasp as he flew us, vampire-style, high above the ground at speeds that made my eyes water if I tried to peek out from his shoulder. It was the least comfortable road trip of my life, and by the end of it, I was so cold I wasn't sure I'd ever warm up again. My only consolation was that Aleric had had about as much fun as me, since I spent the whole trip bitching about how horrible the ordeal was.

But when we finally landed in Warin's back yard, my discomfort and irritation faded to white noise as butter-flies the size of bald eagles swarmed in my stomach.

"What if he doesn't want me back?" I whispered as I stared at the mansion.

Aleric rolled his eyes and put a hand on my shoulder, shoving me forward. "Then you'll beg until he does. Now move it. It's been a long fucking night, and I'm getting hungry. You took a lot of my blood, and your neck's been in my face for hours."

I'd give him that—the dude knew how to be motivating.

I scrambled forward, forcing my stiff and cramping legs to keep up with Aleric's much longer strides as he walked me around the front of the house and rang the doorbell.

A moment passed before the door opened, and Carina stared at us, eyebrows raised in question.

When her eyes landed on me, her blank mask fell.

"Thank the gods," she whispered—and then she did the least vampirey thing any vampire had ever done in my presence: she pulled me into a tight hug.

"Uh, hey," I croaked, awkwardly putting my hands on her shoulders to return the gesture. "Is Warin in?"

"The Lord is in his study," she said, finally putting me down inside the grand foyer. "Come—he will want to see you straight away."

I let her drag me through the foyer and down the hallway, casting a bewildered look at Aleric over my shoulder. But the tall vampire didn't pay me any more mind as he strode into the mansion and headed for the grand living room. Apparently, his job was done.

"Carina, how... how has he been?" I asked my blonde companion.

She glanced down at me. "He has been... like he was before."

"Oh." I felt terrible for the flicker of disappointment in my gut at that answer. It wasn't that I wanted him to suffer, far from it, but after what Aleric had said I'd expected... well, the same kind of heartache I'd been dealing with. "Well, that's good."

"No, Liv. It's not," she said.

I wanted to ask her what she meant, but before I could she stopped before a closed door and knocked lightly. "My lord?"

An affirmative murmur sounded from within, and she pushed the door open. "You have a visitor, my lord," she said, giving me a light nudge to push me over the threshold.

And there he sat in a hideous, white modern chair, staring at two vampires who were kneeling in front of him, heads bent. We were obviously interrupting something.

"Show them to the waiting area, Carina. This will take a while." Warin's voice was icy and detached and so... so different. It made my heart ache. I made to turn around and leave, but Carina's light grip on my arm stopped me.

"I don't think this can wait, my lord," she insisted.

He looked up then, pale face impassive and as perfectly sculpted as I remembered it, but there was something different there. It seemed like pain was straining behind that flawless mask, threatening to break through the cracks. I wondered if my face looked the same.

When his eyes locked on my form, they widened, but the rest of him was still as a statue. Until he, in a smooth but authoritarian tone, said, "Leave."

The shock that went through me nearly made my knees buckle. Tears stung my eyes as I tried to turn around, dazed, but again Carina's hand stopped me.

Warin had turned his head to the vampires on the floor. "I will summon you when I wish to resume this."

The two looked relieved. They got up and *swooshed* past me before I'd fully realized he hadn't spoken to me. A light squeeze on my arm notified me of Carina's departure.

And then it was just him and me in the big office.

Warin stood, slowly, but stayed by the chair, keeping distance between us.

"Hey," I croaked.

"Why are you here, Liv?" The velvet touch of his voice made me shiver.

"I..." I took in a deep breath. "I'm here because I...I know I made a mistake. I shouldn't have left, and I'm... hoping you..." I gritted my teeth, trying to force the words out. In the face of his detached agony, I hated myself like I'd never hated myself before. *I'd* caused this. *I'd* hurt him. He may have looked the regal, detached vampire to everyone else, but I recognized the wound of our separation in him, because it resonated in my own broken soul. I wanted to tell him so bad *why* I'd left, but Aleric was right —it wasn't safe.

"Please take me back, Warin," I whispered. "Please forgive my stupidity. I was scared, and I was stupid, and I... I am so, so sorry."

He shook his head, breathing deeply. "I sense Aleric here. I know he brought you. My brother... has an unfortunate tendency of ignoring my orders. I will ask Carina to arrange for your travels back—and I will ensure Aleric obeys me this time. Whatever he has threatened, you have my word I will not allow him to fulfill it."

I blinked, confused at that response. Sure, I hadn't expected him to just take me back, no questions asked, but trying to send me back? Then it hit me—he thought my apology was forced by his brother.

"No, Warin. No, no, no." I crossed the floor and, hesitating for a just a second, put my hands on his shoulders. He tensed under my touch, like he had the first few times, and I fought back the bloom of hurt. He had every right to build his walls back up.

"I am not here because Aleric *made* me. Yes, he brought me here, but I'm not asking for another chance because of your asshole brother force blood bonding me. I'm asking you—"

"*What?*" Warin interrupted me, a flare of anger taking

over his face. The change was feral and terrifying as fuck. "He did *what?*"

"Uh... blood bonded... me?" I squeaked.

"*Aleric!*" It was a roar, but the dark *power* welling up around my beloved was what made me take a startled step backward. His nostrils flared, his eyes nearly black with fury.

"W-what's happening?" I stuttered. "Warin—?"

The study door banged open and Aleric came stumbling in, a hand pressed tight against his ribs. "*Fuck,* calm down!" he groaned through gritted teeth.

"You forced a blood bond on my beloved?" Warin snarled. "Without my permission? *Against her will?*"

Aleric groaned again and dropped to his knees. "Had to. You were suffering, Warin, I—"

Warin's growl shut him up. "You went against my direct orders—you brought her here against her will, and *tied her with your blood!* You know what the punishment is!"

Aleric drew in a shuddering breath and finally lowered his hand from his ribs. "I do. Do what you must, Elder. I do not regret my actions."

"You will," Warin promised, his voice low and deadly.

"Warin," I interrupted as he made to step toward the other vampire. When he looked at me, I reached out for him again, placing a hand on his arm. "Stop it. Please."

He didn't respond, but at least he didn't advance on Aleric, either.

"Your brother's an ass, but he did what he did for you. I know that, even if I'm not happy about his methods. And he came to get me when I was too much of a coward to come on my own. Please, can we... can we just talk?"

Warin drew in a shuddering breath, and as quickly as the anger had arrived, it melted off his features until only weary regret remained. Slowly, he lifted a hand to touch my hair. "No, my love. You need to leave before it's too late. If we talk, it will be too late."

"W-what do you mean?" I whispered. Was he really... sending me away? I blinked my tears away, but they just kept coming.

"I mean that if you stay, Liv... if we talk... if you tell me you're sorry, I won't... I won't be able to let you leave again. Ever." He brushed his hand from my hair to my cheek, capturing the trickle of tears with the pad of his thumb. "Leave, my love. Now. If you ever wish to be free again, you have to leave."

I shook my head and clutched his hands, pressing my cheek into his cool palm. "No, Warin. I don't want to leave. I don't ever want to leave."

"Don't say that," he said, a sliver of the growl making its way back into his voice. "You don't know what you're saying."

"I'm saying I love you, and I want to be yours. Just

yours." I kissed his palm and looked up into his eyes, willing him to understand the depth of my devotion. And the sincerity of my regret. "There is no freedom away from you. There is just pain. I don't know why... I don't understand why I need you, but I do. I need you so much it hurts, Warin. Please. Don't send me away. Please. Forgive me."

He closed his eyes with a soft groan, tangling his hand in my hair and pulling me closer to his strong body as he buried his face against the side of my head. "Liv... you deserve so much more. I am... so tainted. So... wretched. I fear, if you stay... I will swallow your light and pull you into my darkness. When you left... I almost... I was going to *force* you back, I... I was going to hurt people, anyone I had to, to get you back. This darkness inside of me, the monster... it's still there. It will never go away. All I want, Liv, all I *ache* for, is to tie you to my side. I love you so deeply, I love you with everything I am, *everything*—and what I am, my love... It's dark and it's ugly. And if you don't run, I fear I will *take* you, and I'll *break* the light within you. It's what I did, before. When I escaped my Sire. I broke everything beautiful in my path. Please, don't let me break you, too. I beg you, Liv. I can't... I can't hurt you. I can't bear the thought of looking into your eyes and not see your light. Leave me. I beg you. Leave. Now."

"Warin," I whispered, pulling my head back so I could lock my gaze in his. "I'm not leaving. Not now, not ever."

"Liv—"

"No. I *know* you. You are here, *inside* me." I pressed a hand to my chest. "I can feel you—I can *see* you. You are not a monster. And you will never hurt me. I know your fears, I know why you're so scared of doing to me what your Sire did to you, but you won't. You can't. It's just me and you now, Warin. He's not here. He can't hurt you—he can't make you hurt *me*." I moved my hand from my chest to his, where he'd once told me he still felt the broken bond to the vampire who Changed him. "*He* was a monster. And for a long time, even after his death, you carried him with you. But he has no more power over you. And you will never, ever be alone again. I am here, Warin. And I'm not leaving you. Never again."

"My beautiful fool," he whispered, his hand coming up to press against mine. "It's too late. You're out of time. You belong to me now. Forever and always."

"I want to belong to you," I said, leaning in to rest my head against his shoulder.

"You've said that before."

"I meant it then too."

Warin pressed a kiss to my temple. "And yet you ran."

"I know," I murmured, leaning closer so he could kiss my jaw. "Will you forgive me?"

"Maybe one day," he whispered, his voice husky as his lips danced along my jaw up to my ear, making it hard to think. Heat curled in my abdomen, sparking with every kiss he placed against my skin.

I turned my head to capture his mouth with mine, and moaned at the burning need flaming between us as he kissed me deeply.

"I'm so, so sorry, Warin," I gasped when he pulled back to allow me to breathe.

"If you ever leave again, you'll be more than sorry," he said, and this time, the growl in his voice was more than a hint. Dark possessiveness flared in his eyes, making me gasp at the desire rushing through my veins in response.

"I won't," I promised, pressing closer to his strong body until my breasts, stomach, and hips were flush against him and I could wrap my arms around the back of his neck. When I went for another kiss, he growled and pushed me backward, never breaking our desperate kiss. My back hit the wall, his cool fingers tugging at my top, ripping the fabric in their haste.

"Warin," I moaned, and then whimpered when he tore my bra off my, the straps catching before they ripped, and he buried his mouth in my breasts. His tongue flicked against an already stiff nipple while his hands went for my pants, rending the zipper. They were off me in the blink of an eye, his fingers sliding through my curls and into my already dampening slit.

"Missed you so much," he groaned, his thumb finding my clit as he drove two fingers into my sheath.

I whined in response, my hips arching out for more even as my pussy twitched at the rough penetration. It didn't take long before his fingers' movements were accompanied by the slick sounds of my eagerness.

"Take me," I moaned, clutching at his hair as he sucked my nipples in rhythm with his thumb's circles on my clit. "Show me I'm yours!"

Warin growled in response, his fingers leaving my pussy. The next second he hoisted me up by the hips, unzipped his pants, and lined the throbbing head of his cock up against my dripping opening.

"Yes," I pleaded. "Do it. Please. Make it *hurt!*"

Warin thrust in, forcing me wide with enough force to make me cry out as delicious pain shivered up along my spine. His hips slapped against mine as he seated himself fully inside of me. Giving me no time to accept his thickness, he drew his hips back—and then he fucked me. *Hard.*

I screamed as my pussy convulsed around his big cock, trying to accept the brutal pounding, but not finding any respite. He fucked me like no human ever could, so hard and so fast it hurt as my G-spot took the brunt of his pent-up anger, his fear. His pain. Feral need burned in his eyes as he took me for everything I was worth, like a wounded beast finding release after centuries of agony. He had never been less human—and I had never loved him more.

I clung to his shoulders, crying out his name over and over and over again as he showed me everything he was and everything he'd been, lost and alone in the darkness.

When I came, it wasn't blissful and it wasn't sweet. Every inch of my pussy burned from the speed of his thrusts and the width of his cock, but he pounded my G-spot so hard I couldn't avoid the agonizing release that rose from my pelvis in a tsunami of endorphins. I cried out as I crested, digging my nails into his shoulders while my body twitched and cramped, my pussy milking his hard cock in fluttering pulses.

Warin's release followed mine, his soothingly cool essence flooding my battered depths as he shouted in ecstasy—and buried his fangs in my neck.

I whimpered at the sharp sting as he pierced my skin, and then moaned at the pleasurable pulse of my lifeblood sustaining my beloved.

We stayed like that for a long while, embracing as he drank from me, his softening cock still lodged deep inside of me while I whispered professions of my eternal love in his ear. It was such an intimate moment, filled with nothing but our relief from finally being united again.

That is, until Aleric's voice broke through our blissful bubble.

"I hope you're planning on offering a taste. I'm famished."

I squeaked, mortified.

Warin pulled back from my neck, giving it a few slow licks. He seemed undisturbed that we'd just fucked in front of his asshole of a brother—in fact, he ignored him as he let me slide to the floor, hand clasped around my shoulder to ensure I was okay to stand.

"Are you okay?" he murmured, and when our eyes locked, I saw they were light with happiness—and relief.

"Yeah. Peachy. Just, ya know, not thrilled about being naked in front of your perverted brother." I crossed my arms over my breasts and glared at Aleric. He was still sitting on the floor, but instead of kneeling, he'd sprawled out, leaning against Warin's desk as if to watch the show. Judging from the scary-looking bulge in his tight, black jeans, he'd certainly gotten his money's worth.

Warin finally looked at Aleric then. "Your penance will start tonight. You will not feed for five nights. Not a drop of blood shall pass your lips until the sixth evening. This is your punishment for forcing your blood on my companion."

Aleric's face fell. "Seriously? I'm starving. She had a lot of my blood, brother. I will be too weak—"

"Enough!" Warin snapped, some of the anger from before flaring in his eyes again. "Your weakness is your own doing. Be thankful I am not taking my penance from your flesh, as is my right for what you did!"

Aleric's sullen expression stiffened into a resigned

grimace, and he bowed his head. "Yes, Elder. May I retire for the night?"

"You may." Warin returned his focus to me, his expression softening again once the slam of the door announced Aleric's departure.

"I was so lost without you," he murmured, stroking a hand through my hair before he pulled me in to rest against his shoulder.

"As I was without you," I whispered against his neck. Fat tears formed at the corners of my eyes and trickled down my cheeks, and I clung to him as he held me so wonderfully tight, whispering soothing words in my ear.

I cried quite a bit more that night, but it was all right, because I did it in Warin's embrace.

TWENTY-EIGHT

The main downside to being force-fed Aleric's blood turned out not so much to be that he could now track me down wherever I went.

No, the worst part was waking up panting and so horny I wanted to crawl out of my own skin after a very dirty, very detailed dream involving Warin's infuriating brother and a sex dungeon.

It took me more than a few moments to compose myself enough to not roll over and try to straddle Warin's passed-out form next to me. For one, it seemed highly inappropriate to take my dreams of his brother out on him —and for another, the fact that he was literally still as a corpse while sleeping was pretty much the biggest turn-off ever.

Instead, I rolled over to look at him while the yearning in my abdomen slowly settled down.

It was the first time since we met that I watched Warin sleep.

He'd taken me to his secret sleeping area the night before, which turned out to be behind a trap door in his walk-in closet.

I spent some time tracing the lines of his face and silently thanking the goddess that he had taken me back. I was even thankful to Aleric, the massive prick, for forcing me to come back. The quiet hum in my chest as I looked at Warin's sleeping figure was such a contrast to the ache that'd haunted me during my stay in Kentucky. So long as Aleric found out who'd given me that note and put a stop to their plans of exposing me, everything would be all right.

EVENTUALLY, the urge for the bathroom became too overwhelming, so I fought my way out of Warin's surprisingly strong grasp and climbed into the walk-in.

After a good, long, *cold* shower and some breakfast, the delicate ache in my body from our reunion wasn't too bad, and I decided to take care of some errands while Warin slept. Mainly because I was pretty sure his *"you will stay by my side"* claims from last night meant it'd be a while before I'd get to go out on my own, once he'd had time to get Roy back on guard duty, and partly because I kind of had to. I'd disappeared from Kentucky without a trace, and if Maggie had informed Joana, I had to let her know I was all right. With everything she'd done for me, it wouldn't be right to let her think the worst.

I scrounged up a notepad and a pen in Warin's study and left him a note on the bed, explaining where I'd gone and that I'd be back soon, just in case I wasn't back before the sun set, and then I went to see Joana.

***

NO ONE ANSWERED when I knocked on the boarded-up storefront I knew housed the Coven of the Moon's headquarters, but I was persistent. It took ten full minutes of non-stop knocking before the door finally creaked open, and Kevin, Joana's First Disciple, peeked out the crack. He looked as sullen as the last time I saw him, but his grumpy expression fell for one of surprise when he saw me.

"*You?*" he said.

"Yeah, hi to you too." I gave him a tight smile—I hadn't particularly been a fan of Joana's sour right-hand man when I'd been drunk as a skunk, and to be honest, he didn't seem much more amenable when I was sober. "Is Joana here? I need to speak with her."

"Not here," he said—and then proceeded to close the door in my face.

I managed to wedge a foot in the gap and put my hand on the door before he succeeded. "Hey, rude much? I really need to see her—it's important. Any idea where I can find her?"

Kevin glowered at me, and from the way his jaw was working, I guessed he had more than a few choice words he wanted to sling at me. Seemed his dislike of the girl who got their peace treaty with the vampire Lord rolling hadn't eased in my absence. "Try *Dark Dreams*," he snapped. "Now leave—I'm busy." He reached out and gave my shoulder a shove, making me stumble two steps backward. Before I'd regained my balance, he'd shut the door again.

"Busy asking the wizard for manners, I hope!" I yelled at the closed door. Jesus fuck, that dude was an asshole!

DESPITE MY IRRITATION with Joana's First Disciple, I did as he'd suggested and went to see if Joana was at *Dark Dreams*. Even if she wasn't, Raven might be—and Skye and Dennis too. A small stab of guilt sliced through me at the thought of my former colleagues. I'd been so consumed with longing for Warin while I'd been gone, I hadn't really spared many thoughts for them. But they'd been my friends, too. Or at least, they could have been my friends, had I stayed in Chicago long enough. And I'd disappeared without a word.

Hopefully my reception wouldn't be as unpleasant as it'd been when I turned up at Joana's place. Kevin was an asshole, but my colleagues had actually cared about me, once upon a time. And I'd repaid them by leaving them high and dry, too wrapped up in my own drama to even feel bad about it.

THE STORE WAS quiet when I walked in, the merrily jingling bell above the door announcing my entry. There wasn't any customers, and no one behind the cash register either.

"Hey, welcome to *Dark Dreams!*"

I looked up just in time to see Skye come around the corner from the staff room, bright smile in place. She froze in place when our eyes met, trading in her smile for an open-mouthed gasp.

"Hey, Skye," I said.

"*Liv!*" she screeched, and before I knew it, she'd crossed the store and thrown herself around my neck. "Oh my goodness, we thought you were dead!"

"Not dead," I said, returning her hug. "I just... had to skip town for a little while."

She pulled back and looked at me, mouth pinched in

worry. "Was it because of that vampire? We tried to report you missing, but... no one ever came to take statements, or even look at your apartment. Are you okay?"

"I'm okay," I said. "I'm sorry I worried you. And no, it wasn't really because of Warin. It's... complicated."

She sighed, mouth still locked in an unhappy frown. "Complicated... everything's *complicated* around here these days." Then her face lit up in a half-smile. "But maybe it'll be better now that you're back. Dennis has been such a prick since you left—I think he was worried about you. You know how he's always had a bit of a thing for you."

I blinked. "Uh... no."

Skye rolled her eyes and grabbed me by the hand, leading me toward the back of the shop. "You're so oblivious, girl. Raven! Look who's back!" The last bit she called out as she dragged me through the beaded curtain to the back.

"What?" Raven's head popped out from the break room. When she saw me, her eyes went wide, and a wide grin stretched across her normally stern face. "Liv! Fucking hell, I thought the vamper had eaten you!"

"I just had to go away for a while. Hey, have you seen Joana? I need to speak with her, ideally today... before the sun sets."

"She should be at, uh... home." Raven glanced at Skye,

and for a moment, I pitied our blonde colleague, who had no idea her boss and two co-workers were actual witches. Even if one of them was a pretty shitty witch.

But then I thought back to how uncomplicated life had been before I fell down the supernatural rabbit-hole, and my pity turned to envy.

"I just came from there—Kevin answered the door, said she might be here."

Raven rolled her eyes. "Ugh, Kevin. He's been such an asshole lately. I'll shoot her a text and ask, tell her you're looking for her. She'll be happy you're back!"

"And speaking of being back," Skye interjected, "you're going to sit down with us and have a cup of tea, and tell us what you've been up to for the past three freaking months!"

"But I have to—"

"Yes, yes, you have to see this Joana girl, but it can wait until she texts back, right?" Skye looked at me with such a sad frown that my guilt flared hotly again.

"Yeah, I guess it can. I... I missed you two," I said, rubbing my neck awkwardly. It'd been easy enough to tell Warin how much I'd missed him. It was something else with the two girls I'd befriended without really realizing it.

"Aw, we missed you too, didn't we, Raven?" Skye beamed. "Now come, sit! We've gotten *the* best herbal blend in stock since you left."

. . .

WE SAT in the staff break room and gossiped for a few hours while waiting for Joana to text back.

It was a slow day, customer-wise, so we weren't disturbed by the jingling bell much. It was always nice when work didn't get in the way of socializing.

It was only when I happened to glance at the time on my phone that I realized how late it'd gotten.

"Yikes, it's gonna get dark soon! I need to get my ass back," I said, finishing off my final mug of tea. Skye had been right—it *was* the best blend in the store, and I'd had about five cups.

"Someone have a sunset curfew, huh?" Raven said, eyebrows arched. "I take it you're staying with Warin?"

"Oh, how very kind of your '*completely platonic, definitely not banging him, nuh-uh*' vampire friend," Skye said, a shit-eating grin on her lips.

"You guys are jerks." I couldn't hold back a laugh, even as my cheeks heated. "Okay, so maybe we're not *completely* platonic friends anymore."

"Ha, I knew it!" Skye lit up. "I have *so* many questions! Is it cold? Does he—"

I held up a hand, interrupting what was undoubtedly about to turn into a *way* too intimate Q&A on sex with the undead. "I *really* have to get back. And also, I *really* don't want to answer any of that."

"Prude." Skye sulked. "Fine, be that way. It's not like you just left us for three whole months, and we missed you and you should feel guilty enough to divulge every dirty detail of your sex life. I mean, jeez, Liv, what are girlfriends for?"

"You never did answer me about the friction thing," Raven joined in with a teasing smirk.

"Really, you too? I thought the mere thought of a nightwalker had your skin crawling," I huffed.

"It's just for *science,* of course," Raven said as she pulled out her phone. Her smirk became a frown. "I don't understand why Joana hasn't texted back—it's not like her."

"You think something's wrong?" I asked.

"Nah, probably not," she said, but the frown didn't leave her face. "But I think I'll head over to her house once we've closed up. Do you still have your old phone number? I'll text you once I've got a hold of her."

"Yeah, I do. Thanks, Raven." I turned to my blonde friend. "And thank you, Skye. I've really missed you both. It was great catching up."

"Will you be looking for a job? Dennis would probably hire you back," Skye said.

I grimaced. "Maybe. I, uh... need to work some things out with Warin, first. But I'll definitely stay in touch. I promise."

I left *Dark Dreams* out the back entrance this time,

thinking to cut across the alleyway and run-down staff parking to hail a taxi off the large road a few blocks away from the shop. It'd be much quicker than calling for a cab and having to wait for it to arrive, and the sky was darkening swiftly now.

A flutter of heavy wings made me look up just as the backdoor to *Dark Dreams* clicked shut. A large raven landed on one of the trash containers on the other side of the alley, its dark eyes gleaming as it cawed at me.

There were probably a bazillion ravens in the Chicago area, but there was just something... oddly familiar about this one. "Hello, you. Have we met before?"

The raven cawed again and flew to the floor, landing right in front of my feet.

"Oh, wow, you're a friendly fell—*oh my goddess!*" My cheerful greeting died on a shriek when the bird's wings cracked, fanning out in an unnatural angle. I quickly dropped to my knees, wanting to see if I could somehow help the poor creature even if I didn't know the first thing about bird anatomy. The raven fluttered awkwardly a few times, and then its chest bulged outward, fragile bones breaking with loud snaps in a flurry of feathers. Raw flesh expanded rapidly up and out, and I fell back on my ass with a squeak from the burst of energy. When I looked up again, mouth open in shock, Dennis stood in front of me. Stark naked.

"Oh, what the fuck?!" I gasped as my former boss

worked his shoulders with a grimace. "What the actual fuck?!"

"You shouldn't have come back, Liv," he said, voice grim. "It's not safe."

"I don't... *what?*" I struggled to get a hold of my scattered mental capabilities, because what I was seeing just couldn't be true. It couldn't be. "You do *not* get to explode out of a fucking raven right in front of me, and then that not be the first topic at hand! Tell me I'm fucking hallucinating—tell me you're not a goddamn skinwalker!"

"Of course I am," he growled. "Why do you think you weren't killed the second you stepped foot in the slaughterhouse? *I* kept you safe. *I* told them you weren't her. And now here you are, back in Chicago. Do you *want* to die, Liv? Do you want to sacrifice yourself for that... *thing?*"

"I'm not who?" As much as I tried to keep my eyes on his face, it was impossible not to notice that he'd changed while I'd been gone. He seemed thinner, and there were dark hollows under his eyes that hadn't been there before.

Dennis drew in a deep breath, trying to fight back his apparent anger at my presence. "Eight hundred years ago, my coven was tasked with watching over the vampire Lord you have spent so many nights with. Through generations, through countless rebirths, we have fulfilled our duty. I was beginning to think it was just another stupid legend. I thought him harmless. And yet…" His gaze swept over me, odd possessiveness flaming in its depths. "And yet there was *you*. Do you know who my coven thinks you are? Do you know what your little infatuation with the undead Ancient has caused?"

"Dennis, you're not making any sense," I told him. I wanted to get to my feet, so I wasn't in such a vulnerable position in front of him, but he seemed so unhinged, I didn't dare to make any sudden movements.

"They think you're *her*, Liv! His *soulmate*, reincarnated to finally heal his black soul! When he claimed you for everyone to see, as his little blood whore, they were so sure. But I proved them wrong… I got you to leave. You were safe—so why the *fuck* are you back?"

Eight hundred years ago. His soulmate. My mind fogged, and something… something *clawed* at my mind, as if there was something I was supposed to remember.

"Thea?" I whispered. "Thea was his… his soulmate?"

Dennis' eyes widened. "How do you know that name?"

I shook my head, trying to clear it. There were other, more pressing matters to focus on. "*You* sent me away? *You* sent me that letter? But… but why? And how did you know I… that I'm… a witch?"

"To *protect* you!" he snarled. "To prove that you are no threat! And then I get a fucking text from Kevin, saying you're back. Don't you get it, Liv? He knows you're back now! He knows you came back for your precious vamper!"

"Who, Kevin?" I asked, blinking at him. "Why the hell does it matter if Kevin knows I'm back?"

"My master," Dennis hissed, "will gut you like a fish before he will see the Night Lord bonded with his soulmate. Is that what you want, Liv? To die?"

"N-no," I croaked. Dennis looked absolutely deranged in his fury. He glowered down at me, and the shadows seemed to draw around him, blotting out the sky.

"Then I am your only hope," he hissed. And then he launched himself at me.

I tried to scramble backward and away, but I wasn't fast enough. Dennis landed on top of me, pinning me down, and though he was thin, he was freakishly strong.

"Get off me! What are you doing?!" I shrieked. "Help!"

"No one can hear you," he rasped. "It's just me and you, Liv. I'll save you from my master. I'll make you my mate. He'll see you don't belong to the vampire once you carry my mark!"

"Are you insane? I don't want to be your damn *mate!* Get your goddamn hands off me!" The last bit I screamed as he put a hand between my legs, feeling for the outline of my sex through my pants.

"You don't have to want it," Dennis gritted. His

questing hand pulled up higher, ripping at my zipper. "You just have to take it."

The snap of my jeans breaking sounded like a gunshot in my ears. Unwanted fingers reached inside my pants, touching me—and in a horrible, thick fog of panic, I was transported back into the body of a child. *My* body. My bed, when my stepdad came for me those late nights.

But I wasn't helpless. Not anymore.

"No!" I roared, and grabbed at the well of *power* flooding up from deep within. This time, I recognized the green light as I pulled on its strength and let it explode out of my body in a wave of energy.

Dennis flew off me with a shocked cry, his body flipping through the air until it smacked hard against the trash containers with a painful-sounding *crack*.

Gasping, I scrambled to my feet just as Dennis groaned and rolled over. His nose looked like it'd been broken, blood spurting from his wrecked face.

I remembered the wolves, and how little time it'd taken them to renew their attacks.

I ran.

I didn't pause to look back as I crossed the parking lot, instincts telling me to find a place with lots of people. He wouldn't be able to attack me again in public without attracting attention from the human population, and psychotic as he might be, I doubted he'd want that. But I couldn't get into a cab. One lone taxi driver would be too easy for him to dispose of. I glanced frantically at the sky and cussed. The sun hadn't set—Warin would still be asleep, trapped in his hiding place. Unable to help me.

But Roy wouldn't be.

I frantically rummaged through my purse until I managed to pull out my old phone. Thank the goddess I'd had the urge to put it in my bag the day after I'd called Warin from Kentucky.

I turned it on and scrolled through to find Roy's number as I power-walked down the crowded pavement, away from *Dark Dreams*.

The line rang five times, each buzz in my ear ramping up my anxiety. *Come on, Roy, pick up! Please, pick up!*

"Yeah?" The gruff voice in my ear might have well belonged to an angel. My heart skipped a beat form pure relief.

"Roy! Roy, it's me! Liv. Please, I need your help!"

"Liv? Calm down. What's goin' on?"

"I'm being chased by an asshole skinwalker and I need you to come pick me up. Please, can you come get me?" I ignored the look that sentence got me from the passersby. I guess I did look pretty insane, with my clothes in wild disarray while talking about skinwalkers.

"Shit. Yeah, just stay ahead of him, ya hear? Where are you?"

"Downtown," I said. "Southside."

"All right. Can you make it to the Union Stock Yard Gate? I'll be there in fifteen, tops."

"Yes, I'll be there."

He hung up without saying goodbye, but right then, I appreciated speed over manners. Doing my best to breathe evenly, I crossed the street and headed for the agreed upon pickup point.

That was when I saw the raven overhead, circling like a vulture.

"Fuck!" I muttered. Warm energy rose inside of me without my conscious thought, making me gasp. But when I didn't call for it, it just... hovered inside of me. Waiting.

"Nice time to start working," I mumbled, but even if my magic had chosen the absolute best possible time to finally function, I couldn't use it. Not when stuck in the middle of a crowded town center. Like Dennis couldn't change shape in public, I couldn't very well start slinging green light at birds, either.

He followed me in his raven form all the way to the square, and to my dread, I saw the crowd of people thinning as the sun slowly set. But before I could panic too much, Roy's big truck pulled up across the square.

I'd never been so relieved to see my former bodyguard. No longer caring if I drew any attention, I sprinted toward the car and—as he swung open the passenger side door—jumped in.

"Oh my goddess, thank you!" I gasped, flinging myself around his neck. "Thank you, thank you, thank you!"

"Hello, little lady," he said peering over my shoulder. "Where's the skinwalker?"

I pulled back and pointed upward, as I fastened my seatbelt with my other hand. "Flying around up there somewhere. He's a raven. I didn't know they could do birds!"

"Some can," he grumbled, trying to catch a glimpse of my stalker out the windscreen. "Let's get you out of here before he has the chance to meet up with more."

THE SUN finally disappeared below the horizon as Roy drove us along the deserted road to Warin's fancy neighborhood, and I breathed a sigh of relief. He was awake now. Soon, I'd be back safe in his arms, and I could—

My thoughts came to an abrupt halt when something heavy crashed into the the truck's roof.

I screamed and Roy swerved, swearing up a storm as he tried to get control of the car again, but before he could, claws smashed through the roof and ripped long, screeching lines in the metal.

"Sonuvabitch!" Roy growled, slamming on the brakes. He ripped the door open and jumped out, shouting, "I just paid the fucking thing off!"

The wolf that had landed on the roof launched itself

at him with a ferocious snarl. They both tumbled to the ground, outside of my view.

I fumbled with the seatbelt and rushed out the passenger side door, only to find Roy locked in a wrestling match with the huge wolf. He was doing pretty well for a man fighting with a beast with huge fangs and claws, but the bloody rips along his face and shredded leather jacket spoke in no uncertain terms of the danger this skinwalker posed, even to a man Roy's size.

"Dennis! Get off him, you fucking psycho!" I screeched.

Neither man paid me any mind.

Breathing in deeply, I closed my eyes and felt for the warmth of my magic. It was still there, just underneath the surface, waiting. It came flowing like a wild stream when I called to it.

"I said, *get off him!*" I shouted, aiming my hands at the wolf. Green light burst forward and into the two combatants—but whereas Dennis went flying several yards down the road, Roy just grunted.

"Jesus, woman, learn to aim," he moaned before he got to his feet to face off against the wolf again. But before he could get to it, its furry body collapsed inward on itself, bones snapping, until a large raven sat in its place.

"Oh, no you fucking don't," Roy snarled, lunging at the bird. It took off before he got there, cawing in triumph.

"Shit!" He growled, staring after the fleeing raven. It was headed back toward town.

"*Liv!*"

I jumped at the sound of my name, but the voice registered almost immediately. I only managed to see the air blur in front of my, before I was scooped into strong arms. By my lover's side, Aleric stopped, looking at the destroyed truck with an arched eyebrow.

"What happened here?" Warin's hands slid over my body, searching for injuries as he pressed his face to my neck, inhaling deeply. "Are you hurt?"

"No, I'm fine. But Roy's hurt. He's bleeding," I said, squirming like a trapped kitten to get put down so he could focus on my injured bodyguard. Warin didn't comply.

"I'm fine—just a few scratches," Roy rumbled. "A skinwalker was stalking her, Mr. Waldlitch. He got away —fucker can fly."

"A skinwalker?" Warin hissed, gaze moving from the giant to me. "You sneak out and attract the attention of a stray *skinwalker?* What did I say about staying by my side?!"

"He wasn't just some rando, Warin. He was my former boss—Dennis. He said... a lot of crazy stuff. I don't think they ever left. I think whoever's behind them has been plotting in the wings while they've been laying low."

"I'm taking you home. Then you're going to tell me—"

Warin's stern tone was interrupted by my phone's shrill ringtone. More on instinct than anything else, I pulled it out. Raven's name flashed on the display.

Shit, I needed to warn her about Dennis! Quickly, I swiped my thumb over the display, answering her call.

"Liv! Liv, they've got us, they've got the coven! Hel—!" Raven's frantic voice was cut off by a cracking sound, followed by an unmistakable cry of pain. Then something *crunched,* and the call cut off.

TWENTY-NINE

"They are our allies. We will help them in their time of need." Warin gave his brother a stern look. "Not to mention once the witches have been disposed of, no doubt the skinwalkers will come for us. And for Liv."

Aleric grimaced. "They're fucking witches, Warin! Let them annihilate each other—whoever's left standing will be weak enough to pick off with ease."

"You don't know these skinwalkers, brother. They have fed from Ancient blood," Warin said, his voice patient. "And if what Liv was told is correct, their master will not rest until he has overthrown me."

"Not to mention, Raven's my *friend!* Joana's my friend! They got into this mess because they aligned with us. We're helping them!" I snapped. I hadn't told Warin everything Dennis had said—I hadn't mentioned he'd left me a note, because that would mean I'd have to tell Warin about my powers. And I hadn't mentioned the ramblings about his soulmate, because now... now was so not the time to try to unpack what that could mean.

I glanced at Aleric. Or what it meant that he knew the name of this Thea, when Warin did not.

Later, once we'd saved my friends, there would be time to get to the bottom of it all. But not now.

"*We're* not helping anyone." To my surprise, it was Aleric, not Warin. "*You* need to stay out of this—far, *far* out."

"She has to come with us," Warin said. "We cannot leave her behind—it could easily be a ploy to pull us away so she's vulnerable."

"I'll watch over her," Roy said. He was standing at the other end of Warin's study, arms crossed over his massive chest as he kept an eye on the gathered vampires. Besides Aleric and Warin, Carina was also in attendance, as were five male vampires. I vaguely recognized a couple of them from the first time I visited Warin's home, and from his meeting with the other Ancients. They were his Guard— vampires he tasked with upholding the law of his territory and the security of his home.

"Thank you," Warin said. Then he turned to his Guard, face solemn. "We go to war tonight, against skin-walkers who have drank the blood of an Ancient. These beasts will not be easy to kill. We need the witches for this fight—and so we will all need to put away our prejudice for the time being. I know we have centuries of mistrust to feed our mutual hatred, but tonight... we need each other. Do not disappoint me."

The other vampires nodded in begrudging agreement. None looked happy, but they understood their place in this, and above all else, they trusted their Lord.

I too trusted Warin, though I was hardly thrilled about being left in the car. As Carina and the others turned to leave, Aleric cast a long, hard look my way before lifting his gaze to Warin.

"Be careful, brother," he said, to which Warin nodded so solemnly, it must have been some kind of vow.

Aleric retreated with the others and Warin turned to me, his face a grim mask. "I only wish to keep you safe, Liv," he said at my sour expression. Not that I wanted to be in the middle of this fight, anyway, but it still felt a lot like being sidelined. "I have only your best interests at heart."

"I know," I told him, taking a step forward to lay my hand over his chest. It was unnerving, his lack of pulse, but I knew that didn't matter in terms of what he felt for me. There was nothing but warmth, love, and desire in there, despite how cool he was to the touch. "And Aleric's right. Please—be careful."

Lifting my hand to his mouth, Warin folded my fingers down and kissed my knuckles. It was such a formal, yet intimate gesture that it spawned butterflies in my stomach and fire in my cheeks.

"After all we've done, I can still make you blush," he mused, his lips tipped at an amused slant. "You amaze me, little one."

"I'll amaze you even more if you come back to me," I promised, and Warin blew a laugh through his nose. But the moment couldn't last, and all tenderness melted from his face like candle wax in the face of a vengeful flame as he turned and headed out with the rest of his Guard.

"C'mon," Roy said from behind me, "the vampers'll be all right. Worry about yourself."

But that was just it. Where Warin was involved, I couldn't bring myself to care about my own safety—and that, I realized as Roy led me out to the car, had been the case from the very start.

BY THE TIME Roy pulled up our Lexus in front of the shop where I'd last confronted Kevin, the butterflies in my stomach had turned to pure bile. I curled up against the tinted window, cradling my midsection as if holding onto it would somehow stem the tide of nausea threatening to rise. There wasn't just tension inside our car—it spilled out over the world outside too, the air tight and charged like the moments before a storm.

In the rearview, Roy's eyes flicked to my face. "Won't be long now," he said.

I nodded mutely, afraid that if I said anything, I'd throw up.

"Didn't get a chance before, but I guess now's as good a time as any," he continued, eyes shifting to the coven's safehouse. "But thanks. For savin' my life back there. With your—"

"Warin can't know," I interrupted him, one worry traded for another. The last thing I needed, that *any* of us needed, was for Warin and the others to think I was in league with the witches somehow. Even if I kind of was. They were my friends, after all, and I'd summoned a small vampire army to defend them. I'd been brokering deals between the coven and the Night Lord of Chicago for a while now, and I'd even hidden the extent of those terms from Warin in favor of keeping my abilities a secret.

I chewed my lip until it stung. Couldn't I be loyal to both? Why did I have to choose a side in their stupid feud?

"I get it," Roy said, lifting his hands in a disarming gesture. "Heard 'em go on enough about witches to see why you'd wanna keep it under wraps. Your secret's safe with me."

"Thank you, Roy," I murmured, my attention still fixed on the safehouse.

He nodded in my periphery. "Least I can do, after you sent that skinwalker ass over teakettle."

"About that..." I turned to him finally, curiosity winning out over concern. "How'd you do it? Withstand my magic, I mean. It didn't affect you like it did Dennis."

When he chuckled, it made the whole car vibrate. "Ain't you been listenin'? I got giant's blood in me, girl. Literally. And giants are as close to immune to magic as most creatures get."

I blinked at him. "Really? So it just... doesn't work on you?"

"Pretty much," Roy said with a shrug. "'Course, it did sting some, and I think you singed my eyebrows a bit." He brushed a finger over the tail end of his brow demonstrably. "But then, I'm not a purebreed, am I?"

I smiled a little, then turned to the window again. "You know what they say about mutts, though."

He nodded knowingly. "Yeah. They make the best dogs. I'm sure your boyfriend would agree."

I went to tell him that wasn't what I meant to imply, but judging by Roy's smirk, he already knew that.

The door to the safehouse opened, and I sat up so hard and fast I bumped my head into the roof.

Carina was the first out, dusting off her clothes and adjusting the sleeves of her blazer with a look of vague disinterest. A few Guardsmen followed her, and then

Aleric, but my heart didn't resume its normal rhythm until Warin filled the doorframe, a scowl on his face.

He said something to the others, then headed straight for the Lexus. Roy rolled down the window on my side.

"They've been moved," Warin said. "But they definitely *were* there." He scrutinized me for a moment before adding, "There were signs of a struggle."

The bottom of my stomach dropped out. Joana could probably handle herself, but Raven? It was so easy to imagine her broken and bloodied, maybe worse. *Too* easy.

I sat back in my seat, trying to clear my head as Warin reached through the window and took one of my hands. "We'll find them, Liv. I promise."

"Yeah," I mumbled. But what state would they be in when we did?

His gaze softened, as it always did around me. "Do you have any idea where they might have gone? Where the skinwalkers might have taken them? I know you and your friends from the shop were close, and then... there is the matter of your boss..."

"He didn't say anything to me about his plans," I told him, looking up into his face. "I mean, he ranted about some things, but nothing that would hint at where he'd be stashing a collection of witches."

Warin sighed. "I will make inquiries. But you must understand, getting answers at this stage may take a while."

I closed my eyes. "And that's time they might not have."

Warin didn't answer me, but he covered our joined hands with his free one.

I sat, thinking. Mostly I thought of what Raven and Joana were going through. The pain they must be in, and the terror. I thought too of Dennis, of his betrayal, not just where I was concerned. He had betrayed all of us.

We'd trusted him. He'd spent months, if not years, cultivating that trust. All so he could take advantage of it in the end. Every kind word, every smile, every morning where he brought donuts and coffee to the shop—it was all a long-con. Our whole relationship had been based on nothing but deception.

Was this why Warin and his brethren hated witches? Was Dennis an outlier, or a symptom of a more systemic problem running throughout the witching world? It wasn't as if he was the first witch I'd run into who'd tried to harm me. There were the other skinwalkers, of course, and Kevin was an absolute dick, and then there was—

My train of thought came to a sudden halt, and I sat bolt upright again. Warin made a noise of concern, but he needn't have worried, because I'd had an epiphany. I knew *exactly* where my friends had been taken.

I turned to him, clutching his hands. "The slaughterhouse. Where everything started. Where I met that witch who tried to make me tell him about you. That's where they are, Warin. I'm sure of it."

Warin regarded me for several long moments, his eyes searching mine. The level of my certainty and determination must have been reflected there, because at length he nodded firmly, gripping my hands right back.

"Then that is where we will go, my love."

THE FIRST TIME I'd arrived at the slaughterhouse, I'd gotten a bad feeling. Some sixth sense had twanged like a guitar string pulled too tight, and all I'd wanted to do was run.

Now, that feeling was amplified a thousandfold. Roy pulled us up into the back lot at the same time Warin and his Guardsmen were slipping in through the back, as silent and dark as the shadows.

"There they go," Roy said, his eyes fixed on Carina heading up the back. As second-in-command, it was her job to both protect the other Guards and the Night Lord himself. "This is bound to get messy."

It was already a mess—the skinwalkers had made sure of that. Nothing they'd done had been clean. Whoever was pulling their strings might have intended to be more subtle than this, but if that was the case, they'd picked the wrong minions to do their bidding. They were sloppy. Forces of sheer destruction. Sure, Dennis had been calculating, to some degree, but in the end, it seemed they all went the same way: absolutely bat-shit crazy.

"How do you think they'll do it?" I asked Roy. "I mean... you've seen them do this before, right? How does it usually go?"

Roy shifted, leather seat creaking in protest. "It's usually a massacre. Occasionally, a vamp gets hit, maybe even taken out, but... for the most part, what you have to look forward to is a lot of blood. And it ain't usually theirs."

I was both disturbed and comforted by that fact. But the skinwalkers had left us no choice. If there'd been any other way, I would've been the first to champion it. It wasn't like I hadn't defied Warin before, and even Aleric, who at times was so much more terrifying than his brother was.

But they'd tried to kill me, over and over again, and now they had my friends—true innocents in this fight. It had to end here. Now. After what they'd done to me, I was almost sorry I couldn't be a part of it.

Or maybe I could. Not that I wanted to be in the middle of the actual fray, but...

I unbuckled my seatbelt and leaned forward. "A massacre sounds like a pretty effective distraction, doesn't it?"

Roy narrowed his eyes at me over his shoulder. "What are you on about?"

"I mean..." I nibbled my lip again. "I mean that if the Guard is busy fighting the skinwalkers, and the skinwalkers are busy fighting the Guard, then maybe we could sneak in and free the coven. Get them out of harm's way."

He stared. "Have you lost your mind? Do you know what Warin would do to me if you got hurt—if he came back to this car and so much as a hair on your pretty little head were out of place? No, Liv. It's a bad idea. Too much could go wrong. I can't promise I'd be able to protect you, and since that's my job..."

I opened my door before he could lock it, squirming out of reach as he lunged for me. Roy was big and strong, but I had agility on my side.

"Hey!" he barked at a stage whisper. "Get back here!"

"I'm going," I told him through the open car door. "One way or the other. Either you'll be there to protect me as best you can, or you won't."

I slammed the door shut before Roy could sputter a reply. Halfway up the back stairs, I heard gravel crunching behind me, as well as a low, furious grumbling about how maybe it was time for him to retire and settle down.

The door was already open. The Guard had seen to that. Carefully, I opened it, and was overwhelmed by the stench of decaying meat.

I gagged, hard, pressing a hand to my mouth and nose. Roy put his hands on my shoulders and said into my ear,

"If you're gonna do this, you're gonna have to be prepared to see and smell a lot worse."

I swallowed the next urge to retch and nodded weakly. Then I pressed through the door, puddles of standing water tinged with blood sloshing beneath my feet as Roy and I crept into the dark.

We began our journey in the chamber I'd visited before, the one where the slaughterhouse workers hung and bled the dead animals. Several carcasses were dangling from meathooks still, abandoned for other pursuits, it seemed. I pulled the collar of my shirt up over my nose, content to inhale the scent of my own fear, rather than the stench of old death around me. If Roy was bothered by it, he showed no signs except to pull his gun from the back of his pants and click the safety off.

A low, eerie hum echoed around us. So did every one of our footsteps. And, at least in my own ears, my heartbeat.

"Let me go first into the next room," Roy demanded as we approached the hall. I nodded to him. I'd let him take point. Even though I could feel my magic thrumming beneath my skin, you could never go wrong hiding behind a man with a gun.

We didn't have to go far, though. As Roy scanned the offices for signs of life, a weak, rhythmic thumping drew my attention to the boiler room.

I tugged on Roy's sleeve and pointed. He listened,

then pushed ahead of me, wrapped his hand around the knob, and tugged it free from the door as easily as I might pull a ticket for the deli counter.

The door swung out. Two familiar faces, and three unknown, stared up at us, eyes wide.

Raven stopped kicking the wall. Behind a silver swath of duct tape, she said something that might have been my name.

"We've got you," I promised at a whisper, eyes filling with tears of relief as I stooped to begin seeing to the witches' bondage. Their wrists were all cinched tight with two layers of zip-ties. Joanna's fingers were a deep purple at their tips. "Roy—do you have a knife?"

"Do I have a knife?" he snorted, as if the question were absurd. He plucked one from his jacket pocket, flicked it open, and—

The wall outside the boiler room exploded in a cloud of plaster. An inhuman howl went up from inside the new hole a skinwalker had made in it, followed by a wet gurgle.

My jaw hung slack. Roy shrugged and said, "One down, too goddamn many to go."

"I'm so sorry," I said to my friends as I tore the duct tape from their mouths. In the meantime, Roy set about freeing their hands, though he eyed them warily each time he did so.

Raven winced when the tape pulled, then wiggled her

nose. "Shit, it could be worse. I needed an upper lip wax, anyway."

Another crash, this one more distant, blew debris down the hall. An animal snarl rippled in reply. Roy abandoned Joana's hands to peek out past the door frame.

"They're takin' the fight out into the hall," he said grimly. "The skinwalkers are on the retreat."

"Good," Raven hissed, spitting on the ground for emphasis. "Bastards."

"We gotta hurry," Roy continued. "C'mon, let's—"

A hot lance of pain tore through my shoulder, and for a moment, I thought I'd been shot. I screamed, clutching at an invisible wound somewhere deep in my bones. My vision blurred as a second wave of agony rolled up my spine, and I doubled on myself, one arm hanging uselessly at my side.

"Liv!" Roy bellowed, trying to turn me toward him, but moving even an inch hurt. "Liv, what's wrong?"

My lower lip split, blood gushing down my chin from it and my nostrils. I was so small in Roy's massive hands, and I thought maybe I was safe too, but that illusion was quickly dispelled as my knees and elbows cracked like I'd just slammed face-first into the floor.

"I don't know!" I whimpered, pulse hammering, tears streaming down my face in cold trails. "What's happening to me?!"

Fingers curled around the door frame from the opposite side. Roy pulled his gun, aiming it at the bloodied face which appeared next.

Kevin. He was dragging himself along the floor, leaving a thick trail of blood behind him. One of his arms was clearly broken, tucked against his body on the same side as my own injured arm dangled.

Joana began kicking at the wall now, and she didn't stop until I braved my own pain enough to free her from the duct tape across her mouth. As soon as I did, she shouted, "Warin! No! You can't hurt him! Kevin's still part of the coven!"

And that was when I knew. When I understood why I felt like I was dying.

It was because *Kevin* was dying. And Joana's curse still linked me to the coven.

THIRTY

Roy looked back at Joana, arching a brow. "You got funny priorities, lady."

"Joana," I croaked, desperate for her not to tell. Even though my life was on the line, I really didn't want Warin to know what I'd done. Some part of me trusted he'd save me, and that part didn't want to deal with the fallout of what he and his court would surely see as a betrayal.

But while Joana's priorities weren't exactly what Roy assumed, they were vastly different from my own. She shot me a sympathetic look before continuing, "Olivia made a pact with our coven. If Warin hurts us, any of us, it's Olivia who will bear the pain."

Roy's brows both lifted this time. Disappointment flickered in his eyes, but it was swiftly subsumed by horror. "Oh, shit."

"You bitch," Kevin rasped from the floor, pulling himself up to his knees. I looked up at him, at the red coating the bottom half of his face. Just like mine. "You weak, simpering cunt."

"Go to hell, Kevin," Joana countered, lip curled in a sneer. "After what you've done here, it's the least you deserve."

"What I've done?" Kevin spat blood onto the floor. "You did this! You and your waiting, your wishful thinking about the vampires. I used to worship you and your wisdom. It took me far too long to see you'd always been soft. Incompetent. Unfit for your position as our High Priestess. Our blood is on your hands."

Cutting words, especially coming from one of the coven's own. But Joana only regarded him evenly, offering a slow blink. "You started a war, Kevin. Did you not think there would be casualties? Or were you just arrogant enough to believe one of them wouldn't be you?"

"I can shoot him," Roy offered, pulling the hammer back on his gun with a shrug. "I ain't Warin."

Kevin bared his teeth. But before anyone could do anything else, his eyes widened and he screamed as he was yanked back down the hallway by his broken arm.

I screamed too, the agony enough to make my stomach turn. The edges of my vision blurred, then blackened.

"C'mon," Roy said, forcing me to my feet. I tried to sit back down, but he pulled me in close and added, "Liv, we gotta tell him. He's gonna kill that guy. He's gonna kill you."

Roy was right. Warin was going to kill me. And he wouldn't even know. Not until it was too late.

Leaning against Roy for support, I let him guide me out into the hallway, now slippery with blood. Drywall dust choked the air, whole pieces of it crumbling beneath our feet as I staggered toward where Warin and the others were fighting.

Carina had a skinwalker on the ground, straddling his enormous wolf form with one hand on each of his jaws. He bucked and writhed beneath her as she pulled in opposite directions, the dark glint in her eyes telling me she could be breaking him apart faster, but that she preferred to do it slow. His eyes bulged as she snapped back his snout inch by inch, bringing his lower jaw all the way down to his chest. Blood rattled in his throat, spraying over her face as the skinwalker desperately tried to keep breathing—and then stopped.

Aleric was humming as he tore through bodies, his lithe body slipping easily between combatants to come up behind them and go in for the kill. Throats dislodged. Severed jugulars sprayed in wild arcs. And when Aleric did suffer a scratch, he gasped, looked offended, and then proceeded to give new meaning to the term "slaughterhouse."

But Warin—Warin was the most terrifying creature of them all.

He held Kevin by his broken arm, staring deep into the other man's eyes. Kevin must have felt he was gazing into the abyss, because I could *feel* his horror as if it were my own, could see even at a distance the nothingness reflected in Warin's eyes. That eerie blankness spread over his entire face as, with his other hand, he closed his fingers around Kevin's throat, lifting him up into the air as he helplessly kicked several feet above the ground.

I immediately gasped for breath, hands flying to my own throat as oxygen refused to come. Pressure pounded in my head, my face flushing with constricted blood flow as Roy called out.

"Boss!"

Warin stopped. He looked our way. And when he saw me...

He dropped Kevin to the ground. A new pain bloomed in my tailbone as he connected with the pile of bodies at Warin's feet, but at least I could breathe again, and I was so relieved about that, I too crumpled to the floor.

"Liv!" Warin roared, and as our eyes met again, I saw a spark of humanity return to his gaze.

Just before Dennis, half-shifted, leaped into the air, and landed upon Warin's back with his lupine jaws in his neck.

Despite the rawness of my throat, I screamed. "No!"

Warin stumbled forward, then twisted, trying to throw Dennis off, but Kevin surged forward at the same instant, tackling Warin around his knees with a roar. My knees threatened to buckle again as the pain of Kevin's exertion filled me, but I had to stand up. I had to do something, or Warin—

He went down hard, on his side, with a wolf tearing at his shoulder, and Kevin began his full shift.

No!

I saw those powerful jaws snap around Warin, and I didn't pause to think.

Tethering myself to Roy for strength, I got my feet beneath me, and with a cry summoned from the deepest well of my being, held my hands before me and called to my magic—to what had been inside me all along, the weapon and the miracle which had always had the power to save me.

Verdant energy crackled between my fingers, snapping and hissing, trying to strike a spark. I poured everything I had behind it, thinking of Warin's eyes when he smiled, his lips when he kissed me, the way he'd gazed so adoringly at my sunset painting... and later, at me.

Tears scalded my face and copper bit my tongue as all my love, all my rage, burst from my palms and across the hall, one torrent striking Dennis, the other Kevin. Dennis caught air in a spin as the green enveloped him, turning him in seconds to a whirlwind of ash that crashed over the other vampires like a tidal wave, while Kevin arched, howled, and disintegrated in a white-hot flash, atoms dividing so violently it painted the wall with a nuclear shadow.

Warin gaped at me, but I couldn't hold his gaze. He'd seen. They'd all seen.

The light flickered, then faded as I started to go down again, Roy's embrace the only thing that kept me from meeting the floor head-on. The pain from the curse linking me to Kevin no longer pulsed through my body, and even my split lip had stopped bleeding, but the energy expenditure had taken its toll.

I clung to Roy's arm as I stared at the carnage. Warin and his Guard were busy dispatching the rest of the skin-walkers with indiscriminate fury, but I saw the glances they threw in my direction. His court knew I was a witch. A witch who'd drank of Ancient blood.

As Warin stood over one of the skinwalkers, using his Compulsion to extract what he needed to know, Aleric met my eyes. There was a distant respect somewhere in his expression, far-off though it may have been, but mostly, what I saw there was disgust. Rage.

He had told me what would happen if anyone found out. He had warned me of my fate, and worse, of Warin's.

I couldn't let those awful things happen to him. I had

saved his life, and maybe that would be enough to spare him in the court's eyes—if I turned tail and ran, right now.

Again. Right after I'd promised that I wouldn't.

The skinwalker Warin had tried to Compel slumped, skull cracking against the floor, eyes rolling back as blood-flecked foam gathered at the corners of his mouth. Warin huffed, kicking his corpse.

"Fuck!"

Aleric came to his side, but Warin waved him off. "Nothing. We've got nothing. The damn thing couldn't talk."

"You pushed too hard," Aleric observed carefully.

Snarling, Warin rounded on him. "I'm tired of being in the dark on this! I am *done* reacting to the skinwalkers' and witches' attacks. We must get ahead of them. We cannot continue on like this."

Raising his hands, Aleric offered an emphatic nod. "I hear you, brother. But we need to regroup first. We have..." His gaze slid to focus on me. "...other matters to discuss."

Before Warin's eyes could find me too, I turned from them both, extracting myself from Roy's grip. I had to get out of there, before it was too late. Before my magic doomed the man I loved.

THIRTY-ONE

I made it to the car Roy had driven us in, Warin's silver Lexus, and hauled myself into the driver's seat. Thankfully, Roy had left the keys in the ignition, and I twisted it and slammed the car into reverse, pulling away from the slaughterhouse as fast as I could.

I didn't think as I barreled down the deserted road leading away from the industrial estate—all I knew was that I had to get away, had to keep Warin safe. They'd all seen me—his Guard, Carina... *Warin*. They knew what I was, and what I was was a danger to the man I loved.

I'd only made it maybe two hundred yards down the road when, out of nowhere, a figure dropped from the sky ahead of my car, landing in the middle of my path like an unmovable boulder.

I screamed and slammed on the brakes, my seat belt

cutting into my shoulder as I lurched forward from the sudden stop. The car skidded to a halt inches from the figure.

I wheezed as I caught my breath—and finally saw who had dropped from the sky.

He was covered in blood, dark eyes flaming with feral fury in the Lexus' headlights.

Warin.

He looked... wild. Like an animal, as he stared me down. Not moving. Not even blinking.

The hairs at my nape stood on end, an instinctive response to being faced with a primeval being. He was my lover, the only man I would ever trust—but right then, he was also the monster he'd warned me about so many times.

Slowly, so to not make any sudden movements or perturb my arm further, I undid my seatbelt and opened the door.

Warin's eyes followed me as I crawled out of the Lexus and held out my hands in a calming gesture.

"Warin," I whispered. "Warin, I have to go. I'm a danger to you, my love. You have to let me go."

"*No.*"

"Please, just listen—"

In the blink of an eye, he was in front of me, and then his hand snatched my jaw in a firm grip. He pushed me backward, making me stumble a few steps until the hood of the car pressed into my hamstrings. He kept pressing my head back, until my throat was exposed to him.

"Warin," I croaked.

"Submit." It was a low hiss that had goosebumps crawling down my arms, and a not entirely unpleasant shiver traveled up the length of my spine.

"Love—" I stopped speaking when his hand constricted ever so slightly around the top of my throat. A clear warning.

"Submit. *Now.*" His voice was dark and dangerous, and despite my panic to save him by fleeing, something stupidly primitive in the baser parts of my brain responded without my consent. My body went lax in his grip, and a thrill of sexual excitement coursed through my abdomen. I panted, not expecting the rush of need as I stared into this wild being's furious gaze.

Warin growled low in his throat at my submission, and equal amounts of adrenaline and arousal spiked in my blood in response. Which was fortunate, because the next second he buried his fangs in my neck, his grip shifting from my jaw to my hair.

I moaned brokenly, whimpering in surrender and my nipples hardening to points as Warin pierced my skin, his soft lips pressing against my throat. I sagged in his arms as he drank from me, abuzz with shock and sheer, unadulterated arousal. Some faraway part of my brain was outraged at my body's easy submission—this was *so* not the time to get all Fifty Shades of Vampire. But the longer I remained in Warin's embrace, his tongue lapping at my throat and his body dominating mine, the more muted the protesting part of my mind became.

When he pulled back from my neck, I saw dark possession in his gaze as my blood dripped from his lips. Then he spun me around and forced me over the hood of the car. I managed to break my impact with the Lexus with my hands, grunting from the force of it and the pain that radiated through my shoulder. Then again, when Warin ripped at my jeans, breaking them as if they were made of paper as he tore them and my panties down my hips .

His knees pressed against the insides of my thighs, parting them as much as my ruined jeans would allow. One hand slid up between my legs, opening me. Then, growling like a beast, he drove his cock into me. Fully.

I cried out, my voice echoing brokenly through the night as Warin seated his thick length inside me. I was aroused, but I hadn't been prepared for him, and it *hurt*. I reared up, instinctively trying to get away from the pain of penetration, but Warin pressed a strong hand to the back of my neck, forcing me down onto the hood again. His other hand clamped down over my mouth, silencing my screams.

"You tried to *leave*." Warin's voice was gruff and raw,

so unlike his usual silken tone. "You left me once—never again. *You. Are. Mine!*"

He began to move then, dragging his cock halfway out of my trembling pussy only to slam it back in. I whimpered against his palm, then screamed when he began to fuck me, hard and fast... so, so fast. He used his supernatural strength and speed to pummel my still unprepared pussy while I sobbed and clawed at the car.

I'd thought our first time together had been rough. I'd been wrong.

The ache in my too-tight sheath echoed through me for every brutal slap of his hips against my ass, but underneath the pain rose an unmistakable flood of mind-bending pleasure. The friction of his fat cock pulled deliciously at my now fully slick channel, every push inside of me pounding into my G-spot, and soon I was climbing toward a desperate release.

It hit me like a tidal wave, crashing over me and flooding my nervous system as my entire body convulsed underneath the vampire fucking me for all I was worth, my poor pussy clutching and milking his punishing girth until every muscle in my body relaxed with a shudder.

Warin stilled his hips and removed his hand from my mouth.

"Don't ever leave me again," he whispered, voice still rough but somewhat less aggressive now that I had given in to his dominance so completely. "I cannot bear this life without you."

"I'm a witch," I croaked. "And now everyone knows. I can't risk your life—*ungh!*"

He thrust back into me. Though he was still rough on my battered pussy, he set a more human pace this time, and his hands found the swell of my hips rather than the back of my neck and my mouth.

"I don't care! You are *mine!* You'll always be mine."

I grunted again, too lost in the sensation of his body moving against mine to object. And... I didn't want to. He was right. I was his, as he was mine. I belonged to him, *with* him. Everything inside of me sang as he merged his body with mine in hard, firm thrusts that brought me to the edge of ecstasy. I wasn't sure if he was trying to punish me, or if he was just working out the primal fury sparked by the fight and my attempt to flee—but if it was the former, he was failing miserably.

"Say you're mine," he growled into my ear, never slowing thrusts. "Say you'll never leave. Tell me I am all that matters to you, as you are for me."

His cool breath raised goosebumps along my neck, tightening my nipples ever harder and making my clit throb, but as much as I wanted to reassure him...

"Warin, please, I love you. I love you so, so much. That's why I can't—" I didn't get to finish my sentence, because Warin interrupted me with a furious snarl. He dug his fingertips deeper into my hips and slipped back into his brutal, inhuman pace.

I squealed and bucked, my hands slipping as I scrambled for purchase. He ravaged my pussy without mercy, taking me for every inch I had until I could no longer tell where he stopped and I began.

It finally sunk in, then.

I couldn't leave, because we *were* one. I couldn't save him by fleeing any more than I could live without my heart. There was no me without him. And there was no him without me.

If I left, I'd kill us both.

"I'll stay! I'll stay, my love. Always! I'm yours!" I cried out into the darkness.

Warin didn't slow down, but he pulled me up so he could hold my body tight against his, wrapping his strong arms around my ribcage.

I clutched onto his arms, drawing red lines in his skin as he pounded me brutally, perfectly, showing me how we belonged together. He drove me over the edge twice in quick succession before a deep groan finally escaped his lips, and his cool essence filled me.

We stilled together, me breathing heavily as the blood pumped in my veins, the delicious aftershocks of my orgasms making me shiver. Warin with his mouth pressed to my neck, brushing kisses to my still blood-tainted skin.

"What will we do?" I whispered after a few moments of quietness.

"I'll speak with the Guard. They are loyal. But if they are not... I will end them." Warin shifted his hips, pulling out of me much more gently than he entered. "Nothing else matters, little one. Nothing and no one. Only you."

I turned in his grasp, wincing from the ache between my legs. "You don't mean that," I said softly, placing my hand against his cheek.

"I can't live without you, Liv," he whispered. "How can anyone compare to you? I am nothing but animated flesh without you. I was... hollow."

I closed my eyes and raised up to press my lips to his. We kissed slowly, such a gentle contrast to the wild sex just moments before, sweet brushes of his lips and tongue against mine until he finally pulled back.

"Why didn't you just tell me?" he asked, blue eyes searching mine. "Why keep your powers a secret?"

"I thought, if you didn't know... I could protect you. And Aleric said—"

"Aleric?" Warin's eyes narrowed. "*Aleric* knows?"

"Yeah, I... When he blood bonded me, I was so high, and I... told him. I thought he was gonna kill me, but he just told me to keep it secret. He was scared you'd get yourself killed to protect me."

"I will speak with my brother later," Warin said, and from the tone in his voice I didn't expect it'd be a pleasant conversation. At least not for Aleric. "For now, I will ensure no one who survived the slaughterhouse will speak of this. I will Compel the witches, and have my Guard and Carina swear a blood oath. You will be safe, my love." He reached up to brush my tangled hair from my face, and in his eyes I saw devotion so deep it stole my breath away. "No one will know of your magic."

"Well, well, well!" A mocking voice made both Warin and I jolt. Warin spun around faster than my eyes could follow, his back to me and his arms spread out to protect me. A low snarl rumbled out of his chest as we both stared into the darkness where the voice had come from.

Slowly, as if he had all the time in the world, a male figure walked into my range of vision. He stopped a few yards from us, dark eyebrows raised in challenge. "The infamous Warin Waldlitch, promising his blood bonded witch he'll keep her magic secret? How *very* naughty of you, my lord."

Icy dread settled in my veins as I stared at the golden-eyed Ancient.

Zeth.

THIRTY-TWO

"What are you doing here?" Warin growled, not moving out of his defensive pose in front of me while I fumbled with my ruined pants to cover myself up.

"Let's just say a little bird told me Chicago's Night Lord was conspiring with *witches,* of all things." Zeth smiled pleasantly, but the deadly danger in his eyes was unmistakable. "As the oldest vampire currently on the continent, it's my duty to look into such *serious* allegations. And what do I come across? Warin Waldlitch, promising a dirty little witch he'll keep her secret. The same witch I saw him feed his own blood to not two weeks ago. How very, *very* unfortunate."

"*You're* the Ancient behind the skinwalkers," Warin said, dawning realization in his voice. "You came all the way from the Old World to orchestrate this. Why? Why do you care about my territory? Why risk involvement with skinwalkers?"

"Now, now, that's a very *serious* allegation to level at an Elder," Zeth purred. "One, you have no proof to support your hypothesis. Please, don't tarnish your dignity, my lord. It's all you have left. As an Ancient, you have the right to stand trial for your crimes." His eyes gleamed as he stared Warin down, silently challenging him.

Warin growled—but then his shoulders slumped and his back straightened. "I will come with you willingly," he said. "If you swear to leave Liv unharmed."

"Warin, no! No, this isn't his fault—please, he didn't know." I turned to Zeth. "Please, take me. Not him. He didn't know what I am."

Zeth laughed—a chilling sound that cut through the night. "Oh, how *adorable*. A witch trying to sacrifice herself for her master. I'm afraid I can grant neither of your wishes. The Lord learned of your *persuasion* and did not end your life. And your little witch, my lord... well, you and I both know what the only outcome is for a witch who's tasted vampire blood."

"*No!*" Warin's voice was a furious snarl. "You will not put your hands on her!" He launched himself at the other Ancient faster than my eyes could follow.

But Zeth simply raised his arm and backhanded

Warin, sending him to the ground with a sickening crunch of bones.

"Warin!" I cried.

My lover lay crumpled by Zeth's feet. The Elder looked down at him, eyes glowing dangerously. "That was very, very stupid," he whispered.

I didn't think—the sight of Warin at this vile creature's feet made me reach for the magic inside of me before I could reconsider. I hurled a ball of green energy at Zeth with a scream of rage. He'd *hurt* Warin—he was going to *pay*.

But my magic was as ineffective as Warin's strength. Zeth merely moved out of the way of the ball of energy hurtling toward him, and the next second, I had a cold hand wrapped around my throat.

"It takes a lot more than a baby witch to take down an Ancient, little girl," he sneered.

"Let her go!" Warin demanded from the ground. I saw him fight to get up and launch himself at Zeth again, but the black-haired vampire swept his arm out, knocking Warin to the ground with another crunch of bones.

"*Warin!*" I kicked at Zeth and clawed at his fingers around my neck to no effect. Growling like Warin had, I reached for my magic again, but Zeth shook me hard once, and the connection with my inner power slipped on a wave of pain.

"You son of a bitch!" I wheezed.

"Careful now," Zeth said softly. "As you are the Lord's pet, I am expected to extend you the courtesy of not killing you before his sentence has fallen. But, if you try that little magic trick one more time, I'm afraid I have no other choice than to end you now."

"Liv," Warin groaned. His voice was thick and hoarse, as if he were struggling to speak. "Don't fight him. Don't... He's too strong. I can't..."

The sound of defeat in my lover's voice was what finally made me stop struggling.

Through our time together, Warin had been an unquestionable strength—he'd been my shield against the world and its horrors, and I'd known from the day I met him that there was nothing he couldn't fight against.

Except this. Except a vampire many times his age.

Warin's surrender drained every last vestige of fight from my body as true despair finally sank in.

We were lost.

"Zeth!"

The shout carried through the night, and as I saw Aleric approaching with long strides, a shimmer of hope bloomed in my belly. Maybe there was a way... maybe Aleric had found a way out.

"Please. Whatever you think of the girl, it's not true. She's harmless. Barely a witch at all. Our Ancients are too few and far between as it is—don't let a pathetic human be the reason we lose another."

That hope withered and died at the desperate look on Aleric's face. He didn't have a plan—he hadn't found a weakness in the Ancient we could exploit.

"Aleric Waldlitch... I *know* you're not telling me you had any knowledge whatsoever of your brother's blood bonded companion being a witch—weak as she may be." Zeth leveled his disturbing eyes at Warin's brother. "Because *if* you did... I would have no choice but to bring you to trial as well."

"Zeth... please," Aleric whispered. "He's my brother. Please."

"Which is it, young Waldlitch?" the black-haired vampire asked, voice hard. "Do you have knowledge of this witch you wish to disclose? Or do you wish to live?"

Aleric stared at the Ancient for a long moment. Regret dimmed his blue eyes as he turned to Warin. "I'm sorry, brother," he whispered.

And then he turned and ran.

Leaving us at Zeth's mercy.

"IT'S TERRIFYING, ISN'T IT?" Zeth said as the heavy silver door swung shut behind us, lock clicking in place. "*Love.* Twelve hundred years, and *love* is what will finally end your existence, young Lord."

"I thought you were bringing us to a trial," Warin

sneered. He was chained in silver by his wrists and ankles inside the cage and still covered in the dried blood of his enemies. He looked like a trapped animal, and my heart ached for him.

Not that I was in a much better state. Zeth had brought us to a mortician's residence in Indiana, a territory left mostly unclaimed by the undead, Warin told me. His servants, I suspected skinwalkers, had trussed me up on the other end of the cage in much the same manner as Warin, and my shoulders and wrists already hurt from carrying my weight.

Zeth snorted. "Oh, I will. And I will be your judge, your jury, and your executioner. If you have some desperate hope that you will live through the end of your trial, I must strongly advise you against such foolish hopes. It would be much wiser if you spent your time saying goodbye to the witch you've thrown your immortal life away for. Once the sun sets tonight, you will not get another chance."

The Ancient vampire snapped his fingers at the men who'd brought us into the silver cage. He threw us one final, derisive look and then walked out of the basement, servants scurrying after him.

"Liv." Warin's voice, so soft and tender, made me turn my head to look at him. There was so much love in his eyes, it made my heart clench with longing. What torture, that the man I loved more than life itself was only a few yards away, yet I would never feel his arms around me again.

"I want you to know that I do not regret a single moment that led me to this place. Twelve hundred years of night I have lived, yet it wasn't until you that I finally understood why I was put on this Earth."

"Warin—" I tried, a clump of sorrow filling my throat. He was saying goodbye.

"We don't have much time, my love," he said. "Please, listen to me. Once the sun rises, I need you to break free. Call your power, do whatever you have to—but get out. His interest is with me. You are just a catalyst—he must have been plotting my demise for a long time. Once you are out of his reach, he will not pursue you until I am gone."

"Warin—"

"Let me finish—the sun is almost up." The desperation in Warin's voice cut through me like a knife, and I silenced, though nothing could stop the tears trickling down my cheeks.

"You have to leave me behind, my love. There is no way out for me, but there is for you. Please. Please, find it. I cannot bear the thought of your death. Please. Find Aleric. He will help you disappear."

"I can't leave you behind!" I sobbed. "I can't."

"You must. You have to live. You have to grow old, bring a family into the world. Have children and grandchildren you can one day tell the story of a beautiful witch who stole the heart of a vampire and saved his soul from the darkness." Tears were trickling down his face too, and it only made mine come that much harder and faster. "It was Fate that I found you, my Liv. Maybe if there truly is something more after this existence, Fate will bring us together again once you have lived a long and happy life. But even if there isn't... I am so grateful that I met you. Please. Please, do not let me meet my Final death regretting that I found you, because meeting me doomed you."

"I love you," I hiccuped. "I love you. I love you."

"Then I can die happy," he whispered, eyelids slowly closing. "The sun is here. Run, my love. Live."

"Warin?" I croaked. "Warin!"

He didn't respond, his body hanging immobile from the chains like one of those animal carcasses from the slaughterhouse.

I breathed in sharply through my nose—such comparisons were not going to do me any good, and right now... right now, I had to find some semblance of strength. Because he had asked it of me, his final wish, I had to find some way out. There had to be a way.

I clutched my hands uselessly above my head, trying to summon my magic. It responded, but I didn't know how to direct it when I couldn't aim with my hands. And if I just pushed it *up,* worst-case scenario, I'd break the ceiling on top of both of us. Warin might survive that, but me...? Much more dicey.

"What's with everyone and their fucking aunt having a silver cage in their basement these days? Come *on*." I squeezed my eyes shut and focused on the magic inside. It rose in a soft wave, awaiting direction, and I groaned. "Just... blast the *bars!*"

I'd only voiced my frustration—I didn't expect my magic to obey. But as I imagined my magic blasting a hole through the cage... the power inside me shuddered, swelled... and released.

I opened my eyes just in time to see my green magic blast against the bars, bending them outward.

"What the...?" I blinked and stared from the almost-big-enough gap in the bars to my still-tied hands above my head. Was that...? Was that how it worked? Maggie *had* mentioned something about visualizing hitting the targets she tried to get me to hit, but I'd never managed.

Deciding I could wonder at the temperamental nature of my magic later, I focused on my hands and tried to picture green flames licking up along the silver chain, melting it.

I gasped when my magic rolled through my body and *up,* encasing the chain.

It only took a few moments before I landed heavily on the bottom of the cage. It was almost easy now, and I freed my ankles before I returned my focus to the bars. It was a little harder bending a large enough gap in them that I wouldn't have trouble getting through.

Then, I turned to the sleeping vampire at the other side of the cage. He still hung as if dead, oblivious to my magic break-through.

Leave me, he'd said.

My heart wrenched in my chest at the echo of his voice. How could he expect me to leave him behind to die? I walked over to him and wrapped my arms around his still form. He was so solid... so real, even without the reassurance of a heartbeat. If I left him, he would be nothing more than an aching memory. No longer solid. No longer real.

"Fuck this," I growled, squeezing my eyes shut to stem the tears. Now was not the time to cry. "I'm not leaving you. I'm getting you out, you hear? I don't want fucking grandbabies to tell stories to! I want *you.* I want to live my life with you, not memories to cry over!"

I pulled away from my sleeping lover, and a new fire burned in my belly as I turned to take stock of the room we'd been trapped in. I needed to find a way out of here—and then I was going to save us both.

Fuck Zeth and his plans. He wasn't taking Warin from me.

THIRTY-THREE

The good thing about Zeth's secret base being a theme-appropriate funeral parlor was that the issue of transporting Warin during the day was at least partly solved. Caskets galore.

Only problem would be to locate them without being detected... and of course, get Warin into one. And get said casket into a hearse, which I was banking on being somewhere on the premises.

But one problem at a time.

They hadn't locked the basement door behind them, which meant I didn't have to blast it open. Once you've got people strung up like cattle for slaughter inside a cage, there's not much point in worrying about locking doors, I supposed.

I snuck out of the room we'd been locked in, and saw

that the basement stretched out with a wide hallway and several other rooms laying past closed doors. It seemed the only way forward was to go exploring...

I kept my magic close to the surface as I crept from room to room, searching for a casket. Only the last room—of course—had a casket in it, and judging from the tools and the metal table, it was intended for another inhabitant. I gagged at the smell of disinfectant and that unmistakable stench of death no cleaning agent could ever fully mask, then went to investigate the casket.

Thankfully, it was still empty when I lifted the lid to check. However, just the lid was heavy as fuck, and I mentally cursed my lack of ever stepping foot in a gym.

Biting my lip, I stared at my hands and wondered just how much I could use my magic for...

It took a bit of trial and error, but with the help of my magic, I managed to lift the full casket. It floated in the air next to me as I stared at it, trying to determine if it'd be stable enough to transport a sleeping vampire outside in the daylight. I gave it an experimental shove. It moved slightly to the side, but didn't so much as wobble.

Well, looked like it'd be my best bet.

GETTING Warin down from the silver chains and into the casket took a bit more effort, but I managed. I drew in a deep breath as I looked at his pale face.

"This is it, my love," I whispered, before I pressed a gentle kiss to his lips and dragged the lid on, ensuring it clicked shut. And then I pushed my magic out of my body once more to raise the coffin.

It was surprisingly harder to lift it now that Warin was inside—almost as if my power struggled with the extra weight. Only then did it dawn on me that my powers might not come from an unlimited source—and I didn't know how much more I to draw on before they ran out.

"*Shit!*" I grunted as I forced the casket up. But there wasn't any other option—so my magic *had* to last. I didn't care if it vanished for good as soon as we were safe, but it was going to last until then. No matter what.

The basement was quiet as I led the way out of the room we'd been trapped in, and I prayed whatever guards were awake wouldn't be too worried about the two prisoners tied up in a cage escaping. If luck was on our side, they wouldn't realize anything was wrong until we'd made it out.

No sooner had I thought the word "out" than the door to the stairs opened and a big, burly man stepped in. His eyes widened at the sight of me, one foot on the bottom step and coffin hovering behind me.

I didn't stop to think—I just reached out for him with my magic and *ripped*.

The man let out a strangled yelp as he tumbled down

the stairs, blood spraying from the gash in his side still oozing with green energy.

His own green power rose around him, but I slung a bolt of energy directly at his head before he could release it. His cranium cracked like a melon, blood and brain matter leaking out across the steps.

It took everything I had not to hurl at the gruesome sight.

Now's not the time to be a shrinking violet, Liv!

"Pete, you all right, man?"

I froze at the gruff voice sounding from somewhere upstairs, followed by steps nearing the still half-open door.

As quickly and quietly as I could, I sprinted up the steps, leaving Warin's coffin behind. I made it to the top just as another man came through the door. This time, I was prepared. I reached out with my power, let it wrap around his neck... and pulled. He only managed to make a gargling gasp before his head ripped off his shoulders and clonked down the stairs three steps at a time. I stepped to the side just in time to dodge his huge body slamming down the steps after his head, landing on top of Pete's corpse.

I didn't pause to contemplate what I'd done—there wasn't time to mourn, wasn't time to freak out. All that mattered was getting Warin out before it was too late.

I reached out with my magic to the coffin, and groaned at the strain it was to lift it this time. My powers were definitely depleting fast now. I gritted my teeth and sort of *yanked,* and the coffin came, one step at a time, bumping against the stairs. I dug deeper and forced it up a few extra inches so as to not call any more guards with the noise. By the time I was up the stairs, I was dripping with sweat and my hands were shaking.

Fuck.

"Just a little longer," I whispered, more to myself than the gently flowing energy inside me. "Come on, just a bit more."

I closed the door to the stairs and snuck into the main floor of the funeral home, coffin in tow, searching for a way out. It didn't take me long to find the door leading to the garage, and I sent a grateful thought to my goddess at the sight of the hearse parked inside.

Getting Warin's casket into the back was hard. It hurt to use my magic now—an odd, internal ache that ran the length of my veins, but I managed. Only when I jumped into the driver's seat, there were no keys.

"Of course. Of-fucking-course," I hissed as I wiped the sweat from my brow while frantically looking around for the keys. But why would escaping a psycho Ancient vampire and his skinwalker minions be fucking *easy?*

"Fuck!" I rested my head in my hands as I leaned on the steering wheel, trying desperately to come up with a solution.

It was simple, when it came down to it. There was

only one solution. I had no idea if it would work, if this was how it was supposed to work, but it had to... because it was my only option when it came to saving Warin. I breathed in deeply as I stared at my shaking hands, and tried to visualize a key of green magic twisting in the ignition.

Pain lanced up my arms, and I cried out as magic burned through my veins—but the engine switched on.

I could hardly stand when I stumbled out of the hearse to hit the garage door button, but the image of Warin's still face as I closed the casket over him pulled me through. He needed me. And so I had to be strong.

The driveway from the mortician's to the road looked clear. I staggered back into the hearse and forced my trembling arms and legs to obey as I set the car into reverse and backed out.

"We're going to make it, my love," I whispered at the quiet coffin in the back. "It'll be all rig—"

"*Hey!*"

My heart slammed into my throat at the sound of an angry voice. In the rearview mirror I saw a woman jump out on the driveway, a hand lifted as she stared at the hearse. Red energy crackled in her palm, and I knew I didn't have the strength left to kill her before she unleashed her magic.

"*Stop!*" she snarled, lip curling back.

"Never," I whispered between gritted teeth. And then I stomped on the accelerator as hard as I could.

The hearse screeched against the pavement as it roared backward. The woman jumped out of the way, her red energy missing the car but taking off a side mirror. But I knew that if she lived, she would take up pursuit... and I wouldn't get away a second time. So instead of barreling down the driveway and onto the road, I turned the steering-wheel and, at full speed, backed over the woman still on the ground.

There was a sickly crunch and a rough bump that made me hit my head on the steering wheel and Warin's coffin slide in the back, but when I looked up again, the woman was lying still on the path. From the angle of her neck, I knew she was dead.

I pulled us out onto the deserted road as fast as humanly possible and sped off without another look back. I knew they'd follow us, that it wouldn't take long before someone saw the open garage and the dead woman on the path, and our only shot was if I got us as far away as possible before that happened.

Zeth's hideout was in an isolated part of Indiana—not that those are few and far between, mind—and I hadn't been in a position to pay attention to where we were going when he brought us here. I glanced at the time on the hearse's dashboard and grimaced. Only noon, and the gas was pretty low. I wasn't going to be able to just keep driving until the sun set and Warin could fly us off some-where safe. I needed a plan.

It was only fifteen minutes later, when I passed what looked like a small, deserted path, that a plan started to take form. I turned down it, and after a few turns, came across a shack half-buried in junk—parts of rusted agricul-tural machines, oil cans, and moldy bales of hay.

I got out of the hearse and ran to the shed. It took me a couple of minutes to open the creaky old door and peer inside. It was filled with the same sort of junk as was leaning against its outsides, but... there was enough room for a coffin.

My veins burned as I dragged Warin from the hearse with my magic. It took everything I had to keep the casket even and hovering above the ground as I got it inside the shed and safely shoved into a corner. I didn't have enough energy to try and conceal it, but I prayed that this would be enough.

"Be safe, my love," I whispered as I touched a shaking hand to the lid. "Stay hidden."

Sunlight streamed in through cracks in the shed, glinting off the polished wood of his coffin, reflecting green in the specks of dust floating in the air. I wanted to curl up next to it so bad, wanted to just fall asleep and wake up when he could rise and take over. But I couldn't. It was up to me, and to me alone, to keep him safe. Which meant I had to leave him behind.

I dragged myself out of the shed and back into the hearse, wishing that for once, I could protect my lover without abandoning him. But the skinwalkers would be looking for a hearse, and there was no way to hide a vehicle this size in the shed. The best I could do was to keep driving, hopefully luring them far away from where Warin slept.

My plan was to drive until I hit a town, abandon the hearse, and somehow find another means of transportation out of there, to throw the skinwalkers off my trail for long enough that Warin could find me again.

Only, as I drove away from the shed and back out onto the road, it was so hard to keep my eyes open, and my vision kept blurring at the edges. I gritted my teeth and forced myself to focus on the road and my trembling hands to keep steady on the wheel.

I don't know how long I drove for. Maybe half an hour. One minute I was trying to ignore the sweat dripping from my forehead, because I knew if I took my hand off the wheel to wipe it away, I'd never straighten up the hearse again.

The next, everything went black, and then I was staring into the dashboard.

I blinked, trying to figure out why my shoulder and waist hurt so much, and why I had the oddest sensation of vertigo. It took me a little while to realize that the car was flipped on its side, and only the seatbelt kept me strapped in. I'd crashed the hearse, and I didn't remember doing it.

"Shit," I groaned, fumbling for the seatbelt's release button. I found it, and fell to the floor—which was now the passenger-side window—in a graceless heap. Everything hurt, and my vision doubled as I gasped for air. But I had to keep moving. If they found the car with me still in it, they'd know I'd left him somewhere. And they'd find him.

A *caw* sounded from outside, and a shudder of terror went through me. I fought to get up, to get out, but my hands slipped on the seats as I tried to climb up them, and the world spun. Groaning, I slipped back down, cutting myself on broken glass. The pain lanced through my already aching body, and I hunched over and threw up. I didn't have anything but bile in my stomach, and it hurt my throat.

A threatening snarl from right outside the hearse made me heave for breath, panic pulling on my brain to try to manage one last ditch effort to get out, but before I could, something *big* slammed into the side of the car, pushing it several several feet along the pavement with a screech of metal. I lurched to the side, falling over in my own sick and more broken glass. My vision darkened at the edges just as the car rocked again.

I fell into unconsciousness knowing I'd failed us both.

"...KNOW he might just kill her, anyway. Do you really want to risk that?"

"Dammit, Carl, Pete was my mentor! My brother! And he was yours too. We don't have enough time to find another witch, and she's right *there!* He'll be gone, *forever,* if we don't use her! Is that what you want?"

I blinked to try and clear the spots dancing before my eyes. Everything was still dark, but it slowly dawned on me that it was more due to low lighting in wherever I'd been taken than it was my inability to see. There was a flicker of light just at the edge of my vision, almost as if someone had started a campfire, but from the hardness against my back and the lack of wind, I knew we were inside somewhere.

Everything hurt—my veins, my throat, my arms and hands. And I felt weak as a newborn kitten. When I tried to lift my arms, I could barely move my fingers, and it quickly became apparent that my hands had been tied behind my back.

"Of course not!" The first voice I'd heard upon waking spoke again, and I tried to locate the sound. As far as I could tell, they were over by the flickering fire. "But if we do it, and he kills her, do you really want to live the rest of your miserable existence with a chunk of your soul gone?"

"He might let her live. We lost so many last night, he'll want to protect those of us who're left," the second guy said. He sounded desperate.

The first guy scoffed. "Yeah, I wouldn't count on it. We let her escape with the vamp, let her put a fucking protection spell over wherever the fuck she's hidden him. Once Zeth rises, heads are gonna roll. I doubt he'll give two flying fucks about our dwindling numbers."

"It's his own goddamn fault! He said she was weak! If we'd known and he'd given us a fucking heads up, we'd have strengthened the cell with magic. Fuck, the bitch killed *three* of us! And he made it sound as if she were just some fucking tarot reader!"

"She's completely drained, though. Must've used a lot of her life essence to keep the vamp safe. Crazy cunt. She must be new to it, so maybe he didn't know." The first guy sighed. "Look, even if we tried, she'd likely not survive long enough for Pete's soul to catch. I think she's tapped out in the bad way."

Pete's soul? With horror, it finally dawned on me what they were talking about. Raven had told me once what skinwalkers did with witches they caught. They raped them to reincarnate fallen brothers. And the first guy I'd killed on the stairs... his name was Pete.

So that's why they hadn't killed me. They were debating whether or not to knock me up with their friend's soul.

"I swear, if you try to rape me, I will end you." It came out as a hoarse whisper, but it caught their attention.

Heavy footsteps came nearer, until two shadowy figures loomed over me in the dark corner they'd tossed me in.

"She's awake," the first voice said. I couldn't see who it belonged to, and I didn't much care either.

"Barely." The other guy nudged me with a foot, and I groaned in pain. "If you really want to try, you better fucking hurry. The sun's down—and once Zeth finds us, he's not likely to let you get another shot in."

The first guy grunted something I didn't catch before he walked away. He came back moments later and knelt down. I tried to roll away from him, but my body was too heavy to respond. And then water dripped on my lips. I drank greedily, and he held my head up so I didn't choke. It was gone before my thirst had been sated, but it was better than nothing.

"Thank... you," I croaked.

"You sure you want to do this?" the first voice, Carl, said. "If she lasts through the mating but doesn't make it through the night—either because her essence is too low or Zeth throws a fit and drains her..."

"I know," the second guy said. It sounded like he was speaking through gritted teeth. "But I can't let him disappear."

And then hands touched my hips, pulling my ruined jeans over my hips and down my legs.

"No..." I moaned, trying to kick at him, but my legs might as well have been dead rolls of flesh. I couldn't move them, and I couldn't stop the skinwalker from spreading my thighs and pressing a hand to my exposed sex.

"Fuck, bitch is dry as a dessert. Do we have any grease or something? If I rip into her, she's gonna bleed."

I closed my eyes as the first guy walked away, presumably to look for what my would-be rapist requested. If I was going to die tonight, I didn't want it to be like this. I didn't want to meet the end with my final memory of being violated so gruesomely. And so, perhaps thanks to the mouthful of water giving me just enough to do so, I reached inside myself with the very last strength I could muster, and found the spindly residue of my power. I grabbed onto it and *pushed*.

"Sonuvabitch!" The guy between my legs fell backward as green fire flickered around his hand for the briefest moment. "You stupid cunt! What have you done?!"

I didn't answer him. I just smiled softly into the darkness as cold crept in around me. I knew I was dying—there was no maybe about it now. That last push of power had sealed my fate. But at least I'd die on my own terms.

And Warin was safe. My magic had protected him,

even when I'd thought I couldn't save him. That was enough. Maybe I'd reincarnate. I could find him again. One day.

A deafening *bang* echoed through the room. Snarls and roars followed, but I didn't care. Sighing, I closed my eyes and let go.

"Don't you fucking dare!" It was a furious growl. I vaguely sensed someone hoisting me up off the ground, and tried to open my eyes to see who was disturbing my peace.

Aleric, eyes wild and panicked, stared down at me. He bit into his wrist and pressed it to my lips. "You can't die. Not again. He won't live through it. *Drink!*"

I gasped, trying to obey more on instinct than any conscious thought. But my lips wouldn't respond, and I couldn't swallow.

"Dammit, Liv!" Aleric, realizing his blood wasn't working, pulled his wrist away and grasped me by the jaw. "You're his soulmate! You can't give up! Shit!"

And then his teeth sunk into my neck, piercing deep. I gasped again, not prepared for the sharp pain as he drank deep.

"Aleric!" It was a roar—of pain and fury. And it pulled on me, despite the darkness flickering at the edges of my conscience. Suddenly there was no more peace in my death.

Warin.

He needed me. I couldn't die. He needed... me.

Aleric lifted his head from my throat. "Please, there's no time," he said, voice urgent. "If she isn't Embraced *now*, it'll be too late. You can't let her die. She's... she's your soulmate. You met her before. In London—eight hundred years ago. She died. Zeth and I... I didn't know. I didn't know! And you *hurt*... when she was gone, you were... I couldn't lose you, Warin! I couldn't... I had Zeth's witch curse our bloodline. You forgot her. But it's her—I know it's her."

"Release. Her." The anger in Warin's voice was like nothing I'd ever heard before—cold and terrible, and so filled with sorrow I wanted to wrap my arms around him to comfort him. Tell him everything would be okay.

But it wouldn't. I felt myself slipping away, and knew in the depths of my soul that it was too late.

"Don't leave me. Please, my love, please. Stay. I can't... I can't go on without you."

Warin's voice followed me into the abyss. The very last thing I sensed was the echo of his despair as I disappeared into the nothingness.

Forgive me.

THIRTY-FOUR

I was safe in the darkness. So completely and utterly at peace. Energy seemed to spark around and inside me, vibrating with the rhythm of life itself. But best of all... best of all was the warm, golden bond that seemed to run from the deepest part of my being to *him*. I felt his presence in that bond before I even noticed the solid form behind me, holding me so wonderfully tight. It hummed quietly, contentedly as I carefully prodded at it with my mind.

Warin.

A sense of love so pure it made me quiver ran toward me through the bond when I thought his name, and the arms holding me constricted tighter for a moment.

"Where *are* we?" I asked—but the second I opened

my mouth, something gritty and unpleasant fell into my mouth. *Dirt.*

I hacked and spat, only to get more of it in my mouth. My hands hit more of it as I flailed to free myself from the unpleasant sensation of eating soil.

Warin chuckled behind me, sending a wave of amusement and fondness through the bond. Then he finally moved, reaching up above us to push at the darkness surrounding us. It broke apart and crumbled, and I shielded my eyes as dirt rained down over us.

"Come, my love. It's time to rise." Warin released his grip on me and jumped out of what turned out to be the hole we'd been laying in. He crouched down on the edge of it and reached a hand down toward me.

I blinked up at him, squinting through the soil that still clung to my eyelashes—and gasped in awe at the sight that met me. Behind Warin was a vast expanse of midnight blue night sky dotted with millions upon millions of stars. High above us, galaxies swirled in the distance.

A gust of wind hit my nostrils, setting my senses alive with the thousands of scents it carried. But strongest among them was Warin's. Crisp, earthy, and *powerful.* Goddess, the *power* radiating off him made me dizzy with longing. I looked up at him then, truly looked... and gaped in wonder. He was even more beautiful than before. His skin glowed in the starlight, and those blue eyes... they were so filled with love and light.

I didn't think—only reacted as *need* so urgent I couldn't control it washed over me.

Warin laughed, but it was cut short when I leapt out of the hole and into him, knocking him to the ground. I straddled his sprawled-out form and pressed my mouth to his, kissing him with everything I was worth. He wasn't cold to the touch anymore.

The golden bond inside me still hummed, but I was too focused on the velvety sensation of his lips and tongue against mine, and his arms around my body.

"Warin," I breathed into his mouth.

"Hmm?"

"I'm *hungry*."

"I know. I've brought you something to eat." He sat up, gently moving me from his body to the ground. I looked around us as he got up. We were surrounded by a thick coverage of brambles and bushes.

"Where are we?" I asked with a frown.

"Michigan," he said. He was reaching for something underneath a particularly thick cover of bushes.

Michigan?

"What... happened?"

Warin sighed softly. In the bond, I felt hesitance... and a wave of guilt. He returned to me and crouched down as he handed me a plastic bag filled with something dark and viscous. "How much do you remember?"

"I..." I forced my mind to go back. It was hazy... almost as if my memories were dulled in comparison to the present. Everything was so crisp and clear now, as if my senses had been fine-tuned after a lifetime of being too weak to properly grasp the full colors and contrasts of the world. "I remember Zeth bringing us to Indiana. Escaping the cage..."

"You were so clever, my love," he whispered, but I could sense his sadness in the bond.

"I killed someone," I said, rubbing at the place in my chest where the unhappy hum from the bond seemed to be tied. "I hid you—I didn't know my magic could do that. They said... Oh, goddess, the skinwalkers! The captured me again, they—"

"They're dead," Warin said. "Aleric killed them when he came for you."

Something in his voice... a hardness that hadn't been there before mixed with the pang of sorrow and fury in the bond made my memories finally click into place.

Aleric. Aleric had tried to Embrace me. I'd been dying, and it was the only way... And I'd been slipping away, but I remembered what he'd said.

"I'm Thea?" I whispered. "I'm... I was... We met before? Eight hundred years ago? I died?"

"Yes," he said. "You were my soulmate, and you died."

Then something else dawned on me. I stared at the bag Warin had offered me.

It was filled with blood. Donor blood.

"I *died*," I repeated, eyes wide in horror. "Oh my goddess, I'm a fucking vampire!"

"I am... so sorry." It was a soft whisper, but in the bond I felt tenderness and shame. "I couldn't... I couldn't lose you, Liv. I—"

I put a hand on his arm, silencing him. "Warin—please, don't. Don't apologize for saving my life."

He drew in a deep, shuddering breath. So unnecessary, yet I found myself mimicking it. "I passed my curse on to you. The one I wished to protect the most. I was too weak to let you go, and I doomed you to the eternal night by my side. How can I not apologi—"

This time, I clapped my hand over his mouth to stop him. "Oh, for fuck's sake, Warin. I *felt* you when I woke up. You were *happy*. And I... I am alive. Or... kind of alive, as it were. I'd be dead if you hadn't Embraced me. Truly dead. Do you know what I felt when I woke up? *Peace.* I knew you were with me, I knew we were together, and I felt nothing but peace. This... this was always going to happen." I moved my hand from his mouth and gave him a small smile. "You don't fall in love with an immortal and then just kick it after a good sixty or so years. That'd be pretty dickish."

"How are you so calm?" he asked, searching my eyes.

He reached out and touched his fingers to my cheek, as if in wonder. "I took your humanity."

I wrapped my hand around his, pressing my cheek to his palm. "You gave me so much more in return. This? This doesn't feel like a curse to me. I can feel you, *inside.*" I pressed my free hand to my chest where the bond hummed contentedly.

"I feel you too," he whispered.

I leaned in and kissed him again, and moaned when he parted his lips and took me in, clutching me to him.

"Liv," he moaned in between passionate kisses. "My Liv. My soulmate."

I pulled back at that word, eyes widening. "Warin, what... what *happened?* With Thea, I mean. Why did Aleric know about her when you didn't?"

His gaze hardened even as he stroked my back soothingly. "Around the year 1200, he and I were traveling on the British Isles. Raiding remote villages. He told me... we came across her—across *you*—in one of these villages. And I recognized you. I took you with me. But we didn't know *what* you were, so we sought out the nearest Ancient for guidance."

"Zeth," I whispered.

"Yes." Warin's eyes darkened for a moment. "*Zeth.* He knew what you were. And he and Aleric conspired to kill you."

I gasped. "That *prick!* Why?"

"Aleric didn't go into details for Zeth's motivations, but when I woke with you this evening, I understood why. It's the power... I have never felt stronger than this night, with you by my side. He must have known... and wanted to get rid of a potential rival before our bond solidified. As for Aleric..." Warin closed his eyes for a moment, and I felt sadness and fiery anger flare in our bond. "He thought you were twisting me... changing me. He was afraid he'd lose me because of you. But when you died, he realized his mistake. He felt my pain in our bond, and knew I wouldn't live long with a shattered soul... so he sought out a witch. Zeth's witch. She placed a curse on our bloodline, to make me forget. To ensure I, if you ever came back, wouldn't know you for what you are."

"I am going to *kill* him," I growled, running my tongue over my teeth when they ached in response to my anger.

"There's no need." Warin touched his finger to my lips, parting them to rub the pad of his thumb over my canines. It instantly eased the ache. "In playing Zeth's games, Aleric has created what he sought so desperately to avoid. He has lost me. He is alone now. And he will be alone forevermore."

Despite my anger, a small pang of pity bloomed in my gut. I'd seen how much Aleric loved his brother—how he would do anything to protect him. Losing Warin was the worst punishment the volatile vampire could endure.

But Aleric's pain wasn't my problem. He'd apparently *killed* me, after all.

I pushed the thread of pity away and focused on my lover. My Sire. "And Zeth? How do we stay safe from him?"

Warin snorted. "My love... Zeth isn't going to come *near* us. Feel your power."

I frowned in confusion, but did what he asked. The moment I focused inward, the energy inside of me rose like a tidal wave, sparking against my senses.

"Holy crap!"

"The completed soulmate connection," Warin said softly. "Two halves of a whole are far stronger together than apart. Zeth will not be able to harm us ever again."

"Especially not if *we* take the fight to *him*," I said, glee flooding my system as images of tearing into the haughty Ancient played before my mind's eye. My canines ached again, deeper this time, until something released in my gums. A soft *snick* startled me, but the flood of relief was so intense it took me a moment to realize the sound had come from my own mouth. Carefully, I prodded at my newly elongated fangs with the tip of my tongue. "Well, I'll be damned."

Warin rumbled a laugh. "You should feed, Liv. Some blood should quell any urges to run off and start a war with an Ancient on your first night."

I eyeballed the bag of blood. It didn't look super appetizing. "How about you take me hunting?"

He grasped my face lightly between his hands and pressed a kiss to my forehead before he peered into my eyes. "I will teach you everything there is to know about this life, my love. We have eternity together—and I want to show you every last corner of the world. But I'm not taking my newborn Daughter anywhere before you finish that blood bag—and the citizens of Michigan will thank me for it."

"Fine, *fine*," I huffed, reaching for the blood bag. "Making me eat damn donor blood for my first meal. You're lucky I love you so much."

"Yes," he said softly, kissing my nose. "Yes, I am."

EPILOGUE

Aleric

"Back to London so soon?" Aleric arched an eyebrow at the Egyptian as he leaned against the limousine's passenger door.

Zeth leveled him with a cold glare. "If you think this breaks our agreement, youngling, you are sorely mistaken."

"*Really?*" Aleric offered the Elder his most surprised expression. "Because I could have sworn your hold over me just vanished into thin air. Warin knows now."

"Yes. He does," Zeth said, tone as infuriatingly superior as always. As if he hadn't just lost—and lost so spectacularly he was running away with his tail tucked between his legs. Not something that happened often to the Ancient being. In the eight hundred cursed years Aleric had known him, it was a first, for sure.

"Yet you and I are still bound by our word... if you remember. He may have bonded with his *soulmate*," Zeth spat out the word as if it tasted foul on his tongue, "but *you* are still in my debt. Don't ever forget that, Aleric Waldlitch. You won't like it if I have to remind you. I promise you that."

Aleric suppressed a grimace. He knew all too well what happened to the wretched souls who didn't uphold their end of Zeth's twisted bargains.

"Besides..." Zeth pulled on the limousine door, slamming it shut so Aleric had to jump back, though the tinted window was still rolled halfway down. "I'm all you have left now. I wonder, would your brother even care if something unfortunate should happen to you? Would he coming looking for you? Mayhap he would simply feel... relieved?"

Aleric gritted his teeth under Zeth's defiant, golden gaze.

The black-haired vampire's lips curved in a small smile. "I shall be in touch, Waldlitch. Do make sure you pick up the phone when I call."

Aleric stared silently after the black limousine as it made its way down the driveway and out onto the road.

He didn't allow Zeth the satisfaction of seeing him press a hand to his chest where the torn bond with his brother jabbed painfully behind his ribs, saving the gesture for when the car had disappeared behind a hill.

Yes. He was alone now. All alone. The fury in Warin's face had echoed through their bond so violently that Aleric could still feel the agony as his brother cut him off.

Through his eleven hundred years, he had never been alone before. Not truly. Warin had been there, through the death of their Sire, through every moment of every night. He'd been muted, since Thea's death. Numb. But he'd been there.

Now there was nothing but pain. Pain, and a gaping hole threatening to swallow him up.

Aleric gritted his teeth and looked to the sky. Maybe... maybe if he could bring Zeth to his knees, Warin would find a way to forgive him.

One day.

It was only the faintest thread of hope, but it was all he needed. Zeth had to pay for what he'd done. The humiliation of running from a vampire several thousand years his junior, and a newborn witchling, was not enough. It had to be... something more permanent.

Something that would render the ancient being incapable of extracting the debt he had manipulated from Aleric.

Aleric let the cool night air fill his senses and wash

away the raw pain in his chest, suppressing it until it was only a dull, throbbing ache. *There. Better.*

And now... now it was time to locate a necromancer. Ideally one so clueless they could be easily manipulated into doing his bidding... yet strong enough to make life miserable for a vampire as old as time.

Before Liv, there was Thea

Want to read the story of how Warin's first meeting with his soulmate led to 800 years of treachery and betrayal?

Get to know Warin back when he was young and feral - and follow him as his world is turned upside down by a human female whose sea green eyes threaten to tame the beast inside.

Into the Darkness

Hidden in Darkness

Shades of Darkness

Fires in the Darkness

MADE & BROKEN

Dangerous

Monster

Trouble